SGT. HAWK AND THE LOST TEMPLE

SGT. HAWK BOOK SIX

PATRICK CLAY

ROUGH
EDGES
PRESS

Sgt. Hawk and the Lost Temple
Paperback Edition
Copyright © 2023 Patrick Clay

Rough Edges Press
An Imprint of Wolfpack Publishing
9850 S. Maryland Parkway, Suite A-5 #323
Las Vegas, Nevada 89183

roughedgespress.com

Paperback ISBN 978-1-68549-257-1
eBook ISBN 978-1-68549-256-4
LCCN 2023932570

To Marissa Suzanne Clay

SGT. HAWK AND THE LOST TEMPLE

1

OFF THE LINE

THEY BROUGHT THOSE KILLED OUT OF THE DRAW. THE front line moved toward the Japanese defenders at a brutally slow pace. Superior American technology and manpower had proven to be of little advantage in the grim struggle.

Sergeant James Hawk fell, as much as he climbed, out of the back of the truck. He muttered half-hearted instructions to his men falling beside him. Most of them were young and new, but a few of the older ones had made it this far. The truck engine idled impatiently, sounding like rocks revolving in a metal barrel. The clutch popped and the truck began sliding away before the last two men could hit the ground. The truck driver had other runs to make, and he could hear all that he wanted to hear of the conflict up on the line. Dead bodies lined both sides of the dirt road, their boots jutting from beneath the covering ponchos. The wind rippled the coverings. The truck left behind another layer of dust on them.

Hawk watched the lumbering cloud of smoke fleeing toward safety, leaving behind the world in which he lived. He smelled the burning air. The air itself had been set afire, like all remaining decency. The smell was familiar to him.

He glanced at the eyes of the men, studying the bodies all around them. It was a hell of a place to dump these new kids, he thought. Some of the dead were only partially covered, and a few even looked uninjured and unmarked. Healthy, young, muscular—dead—bodies, lined in rows. Hawk turned from the faces of the living. He didn't want to see anything that might make a man unique to him. It made it easier when they transitioned to a position beneath the ponchos. He rubbed his hard palm across his forehead. Behind the lined forehead lay the few cubic inches of hell that defined him.

His eyes glided with a threatening slowness. They were the pellucid and hooded eyes of a leopard. Blue and oddly detached from his surroundings, they recorded all of the unimaginable scene for his simmering brain. One look told observers that the eyes had seen too many horrible things. He seldom blinked, finally looking down and searching the rock beneath his faded boots. For something that wasn't there.

He sighed and tried to think. It wasn't the ability to think that he was losing, it was the ability to feel, both emotionally and physically. His face felt numb, as if he had too much alcohol, or had been hit with a shovel. He had no reason to think, because there were no answers. He was in a numb hell.

"Finally got there," he said to himself. The crystal eyes floated imperceptibly back and forth, missing nothing. Nature had designed James Hawk for war, however. The evolving mental state would only make him better at making war. He would be an unfeeling, unthinking actor. There was nothing about his slouching, menacing presence that aroused any sort of sympathy.

Joe Canlon stopped and stood beside him. "This looks like some shit, don't it. Just throw you out on the road like garbage." Canlon could see the shards of what had been an old castle in the distance, sharp and twisted against a yellow sky. Black, battle air clung to the remnants of the old structure, and rose into the sky above it. Between himself and there, Joe could see drab colored men moving across blasted drab ground. On the horizon, gray and black explosions occasionally sprouted, and closer in were the colorful red and orange bursts, topped by gaseous mushroom evaporations that quickly rose and disappeared. The men walked between them, as if the bursts were nothing but a rain storm. Joe lit a cigarette.

Hawk slid a block of chewing tobacco from his herringbone twill shirt pocket, stenciled with the anchor, globe and eagle of the Marine Corps. He tore off a piece with some method habitual to him and stuck it in his mouth.

"It does," Hawk agreed. A few years ago, he would have said, "It do." But now, he knew that wasn't right. It branded him as a person, from a certain place and time. He wasn't a person anymore. He was a U. S. Marine. The Marine Corps had taught him a lot of things and brought him into the twentieth century. Except, that is, for the vital part of him that the Corps wanted to remain in the brutal medieval past: his soul.

Joe looked around, and seeing a sturdy square rock

near the road, threw himself down and against it. It was strategically located between him and the front, and he chose it with his veteran instinct for staying alive. Hawk sat beside him. Behind them, the behemoths of war traded blows. It wasn't just noise to them. They had plenty of old visions to inform them as to what was going on out there. It was an artillery duel. Artillery, that did not care who you were, where you were, or anything about you. It only wanted to kill you, with no more thought than a termite eating the woodwork. The new men stood about idly, mostly avoiding the sight of the dead. The whooping bravado that had accompanied their getting into the truck had left them when they got out. Different leaders, with creased uniforms and shiny helmets, had put them into the truck with words of encouragement. Sergeant Hawk took them out of it. He was not shiny and new. He was part of...whatever this was. It wasn't the brass bands, medals, and hugs and kisses part of the war. It was the random, uncaring, mutilated, inevitable ass end of the war. Hawk saw their eyes flickering large and suspicious under their helmets, as they realized what they had gotten themselves into.

Joe stretched his legs. He was tired. He stayed tired. He could hardly stay awake. His nerves wanted to recover in rest what they had lost in the last months of vigilant terror. Rest. Sleep. Resurrection. His eyes closed halfway. Hawk was beside him: hulking, silent and watching. Hawk was always watching. Joe felt rather safe. Hawk was a ferocious killer of men, but he was cautious. They would never catch him unaware.

Joe closed it all off. His thoughts became disconnected and softer. The incredible sounds drifted away to a farther distance. He was asleep. He felt an intense, though unidentifiable anxiety in his sleep. His eyes twitched and it started to take shape. The fear in his sleep was not of the war. He was a small child again. Joe's father had left, and Joe sensed that it was forever. Joe's chin rested on his knees. The ball of grinding misery chewed at his mind. His eyes half opened, but he only murkily saw his Marine boots. He went to sleep with his mother that night. Crying. *It's a good thing nobody can hear this shit,* Joe told his dream.

His eyes opened quickly. In that instant, he felt the difference between boyhood and manhood, and he wasn't sure which of the two he was a part of. He was a boy again and his mother was beside him. Strong and loving. He was weak and small and dependent in many ways that he did not even understand. He did not understand all of the bad things out there. But she was there, and it was all right. She could make everything all right.

Joe batted his eyes and sat back. Now he was a man again, with strong arms, stronger than ever his mother would be, holding on tight to vicious weapons, and with knowledge of the world, and independence. Beside him was James Hawk, and behind him the deadly front line. And nothing could ever make that all right.

"Wake me up when we move out," Joe mumbled. Hawk spat. "Yeah. I was thinking on leaving your ass here." Joe smiled and shut his eyes. Almost immediately, two officers approached. Hawk nudged Joe.

"Lieutenant Klemer," Hawk said. A common shudder passed through the men at the sight of the platoon leader. Here it came: their future, brief as it might be. The smell of terror hung over Klemer. His slight European accent and dramatic bearing would only make it all worse. Hawk, and Joe, knew that the terror would be replaced again and again by greater terrors.

"First squad, and Sgt. Hawk," the Lieutenant looked at his clip board. "Return to the CP." He looked up at the others, and with a pause, added, "Everyone else go with Lieutenant Harold, here." He sounded apologetic, because Klemer was a nice guy.

"Hey, a break," Joe said, and stood quickly, the reprieve having restored his energy. It was a miracle. They were out of it. Had they met their limit of allowable combat hours? Did their points add up?

Hawk stood. He shrugged. "Yeah." He didn't sound as optimistic.

"You men hurry it up, too," Klemer said to Hawk. "I told you that you would probably get out of it, didn't I?" Hawk nodded and imitated a smile. It was a smile like that of a dog, exposing its teeth, and not really assuring you whether the animal liked you, or was going to bite you. It was a labored and unnatural smile. Hawk vaguely remembered Klemer telling him something, although he had not interpreted it as anything good at the time. Klemer turned and walked down the road to a waiting jeep. First squad gathered around Hawk, and their corporal, Joe Canlon. There were cautious smiles, real smiles. Hawk looked down the road for a passing truck. He didn't see any. He saw the other men following Lieutenant Harold, walking into the draw. "Hmmph," Hawk shook his head. They were walking into terror, that was for certain, but also into grinding boredom, filth, sickness, and other untold miseries.

Hawk wasn't sure how he felt. Was he relieved or guilty? Guilt was a heavy part of the painful burden out here. Being alive made one feel guilty. But then, Sgt. Hawk had forgotten how to feel. He also didn't know where he was going, or just how relieved he should be.

2

THE CLOUDS ARE ON FIRE

ADMIRAL ISHAKAWI DROPPED THE NEWSPAPER ON TOP OF his desk. He often studied the American papers. He paced uncomfortably. Headlines about the imminent German defeat and the steady Japanese losses screamed up at him. Ishakawi had resisted any mention of surrender for years. His passion for war had more to do with his career than with Japan's manifest destiny in the Pacific. Without the war, his career was over. It might end quickly now. Unwelcome surprises happened every day. There were whispers of the end, and the cowards were crawling out of their holes. There were people who could do other things with their lives, besides fight useless wars. Japan might fall as early as spring 1946. Ishakawi knew of his country's new weapons, Projects A and B. It would take Japan two years, at the very least, to develop these weapons. They needed time. He needed time. The Admiral checked his watch. Time fled. He had a decision to make.

Men close to Ishakawi had also conceded that Japan might fall. Allied forces were closing in on the home islands. All of the enemy's resources were trained on Japan. Without Germany, the whole world would train its sights on Japan, including the relentless Russians. But what if nothing were there when they arrived, and the Allies had already spent all of their energy fighting for it?

The bulk of the Empire remained untouched out there in the wide Pacific, and beyond. Some felt that the battle could be carried on, in Asia and in the far South Pacific, perhaps with the help of some of the Empire's indigenous populations, who had experienced a small taste of independence from the colonial power of the Allies. A new base of operations was needed to run the Empire. It was not Ishakawi's plan, this plan to move to a new base of operations, but the plan could not work without him. He had the gravitas. He checked his watch again, and only a minute had passed.

A general and two cabinet ministers waited outside. The plane was ready to take them to China, and from there to the Dutch East Indies. The Dutch East Indies were under pressure, but it was the best place to head-quarter a new order. A massive Japanese army was still in the field there, and largely untried. Many other far-flung units could congregate there with a minimum of effort, due to the enemy's preoccupation with the Japanese home islands. The huge armies in the Philip-pines could be transported there.

Time. If the admiral could gain time, this would be a different war. Ishakawi had not fought his way up to admiral just to be hanged or to commit *seppuku*. He was a success, not a failure. And, something else waited in the Dutch East Indies. There was this other, all-impor-tant, hidden thing. If Ishakawi could find it, in the name of the war effort, it wouldn't matter whether he won or lost this war. He snapped up his cap and walked out the door, to greet his high-ranking colleagues. The Dutch East Indies, he thought. Bugs. Snakes. Disease. Death. Jungles. And, something else.

* * *

THE FINAL DESTINATION of Hawk and Joe Canlon remained vague. Those with power over them felt that they had no particular need to know. Indeed, his orders had taken Joe off the line, and that's all he needed to know. He didn't worry about the future, that was his way of staying out of a padded cell. Hawk didn't worry either, as there were too many possibilities. Unlike Joe, however, his instinct told him that wherever they were going had to be worse than where they had been. That was just his history.

They were soon separated from the others, which was odd. Near the Philippines, they were placed on a hospital ship headed south. They were to report to a General McCoy. They had never heard of him. There were a lot of new generals now. There was a lot new everything. The war had unleashed all sorts of technology. Civilization had gone from the horses and candles of forty years ago, to the planes and submarines of modernity by the beginning of the war. The last four short years had added almost as many new developments as the previous forty. It was a new world, but no braver, and even more brutal.

In many ways, it was the same world for James Hawk. He knew when the war ended, there would only be manual labor for him, as it had been for his ancestors for thousands of years. At this point, none of that seemed so bad. He would be alive. The war had taught him the value of that. Maybe he wouldn't be going back to a job chopping cotton for a dollar a day. Maybe he could get a job on a railroad section crew. He had been talking to people. He knew things now, that he didn't know before the war. There was more to life than being head down and ass up from daylight to dark. He had gone from a young Mississippi peon to a mature man of the world.

They never saw General McCoy. Too damned busy. Evidently, the general had rubber-stamped his approval to whatever role he constituted in the travels of the two Marines and moved them along. A lieutenant in McCoy's headquarters informed them that they were to board a C-54 Skymaster immediately, with a destination of Kawe, an important island to Allied command, located off the northwestern coast of New Guinea. It had long been a hub of Naval operations.

Joe Canlon had a permanent smile on his face throughout all of these maneuvers, feeling rather special with all of the individual attention given him. He had never been more than a small cog in the wheel of the war machine.

"I know we're going to Australia now," Joe said. He said it more than once, and with growing enthusiasm. "Why would they separate us from the others? I just know it. Australia. Women walking around on the streets, just like they're regular people." He nudged Hawk. "Them Aussie women liked me, you know? On account of my accent."

"Your accent? A goddam New York accent?"

"Shit, yeah. They see all the American movies there.

All the big stars got New York accents, you know, like me."

"I ain't never heard no big star with no accent like that shit," said Hawk. "Unless it was maybe Jimmy Durante."

"Australia," Joe repeated, with a knowing shove.

The nudgings usually received little more than a grunt in reply. Hawk wouldn't speculate. It looked good, however, for a trip to Australia. The fighting was in the north, and they continued speeding south. The possibilities were quickly dwindling to Australia, or the South Pole. Rabaul crossed Hawk's mind. It was the bypassed Japanese stronghold to the south, east of New Guinea. Someone may have decided to un-bypass it. It would be a rough show to take that place. He might also be transported to Australia, only to train for the ghastly invasion of Japan itself. He was pretty sure he wasn't being sent to escort the star struck ladies of Australia down their unsafe streets, to watch Jimmy Durante movies. There was a lot to think about.

Hawk soon had a lot more to think about. His flight aboard the C-54 was not going to be a pleasant one. It was a hospital plane, and not the ordinary kind, carrying horribly mangled men for expedited medical treatment. Instead, the craft was filled to capacity and beyond, with psychiatric patients, considered suitable for Section 8 discharges. To make it even more unusual, most of the patients were WACs, who evidently had been exposed to rather harsh combat conditions in the course of their supportive duties. It had been a while since the two Marines had seen this many women gathered in one place. They felt pretty safe among the cargo. A few male soldiers were aboard, as well, also with emotional issues. All were Army personnel. The Marine mental cases were elsewhere, probably back up north, somewhere on the line.

His traveling companions made the ordinarily unflappable Sergeant Hawk a bit uneasy. He didn't like seeing people who had lost their minds. He didn't want to be reminded of the stages of possibilities along that slippery slope.

He and Joe were directed to the rear of the plane, and filed past the rows of already seated women. Some were strapped to the seats by their wrists. One or two howled. Several were confined in white straightjackets. The afflicted male soldiers sat doubly strapped down. But, some among the passengers were unrestrained, and staring straight ahead in silence. Hawk recognized the eerie looks on their faces. It was like looking into a mirror. He heard snatches of peculiar conversations, most of which the patients conducted with themselves, in low voices, as if conversing with friends.

"Shit. Let's get outta here. This can't be right," Hawk mumbled.

"Nah, nah. This is right," Joe answered, putting a hand in the middle of Hawk's back and shoving him down the aisle. "It's fine. This'll be great."

"I wonder if they're trying to tell us something," said Hawk, stepping around an orderly.

"Yeah. That we're nuts? Huh, huh, huh." Joe laughed without restraint. His laugh sounded like the cry of a donkey.

"Something like that."

They reached the last row of seats and stepped over and through bulging cotton mattress covers, serving as body bags for more Marines killed in action, haphazardly stacked and jutting into the aisle.

A flight sergeant came down the aisle toward them. He finally stopped, and shouted at the two Marines over the chaos. "There ain't no more seats. You gotta sit on the floor behind the stiffs. Hold onto those poles when we take off," said the airman. Some of the women turned contorted faces at the flight sergeant, occasionally screaming incoherent things at him. He screamed back, in a heartless manner, and returned back down the aisle.

"Stiffs?" Hawk growled. "Them's Marines, to you, buddy," he said, wrapping a hand around the designated pole.

"Yeah. I didn't like that. I might punch that guy," said Joe. Joe was a fairly sociable person, but he had been known to throw some pretty good punches.

Hawk looked up at the bolts in the cabin's overhead. He didn't especially like planes. He knew he belonged elsewhere, with the fighting men on the line. "I'm starting to miss the outfit," he said.

"Not me," said Joe. "They can have all that shit they want."

The crew eventually sealed the doors. The big Skymaster vibrated into life. Joe and Hawk looked at one another. They didn't say anything. If the Army Air Force could do it, so could they. The plane moved. Hawk tightened his lips, ducked a bit, and looked out the nearest window. The scenery blurred as they picked up speed on the runway.

Joe leaned over to see out the window. They were over the ocean. It did not take long to leave the tiny island. The end of the island was the end of the runway.

Joe's stomach sank. That was the deepest water in the world out there. He would rather fly over land. You knew you were good and dead when you crashed into the ground.

Hawk stared at the piles of corpses, appearing to shiver on the trembling deck. He began to sweat as the plane bucked. Wind whipped through the cabin from somewhere and the engines roared. *What's with the draft? Ain't this thing put together in one piece?* The Sergeant's helmet bumped against the pipe he held, and he unconsciously put both hands around the pole.

"Sit down!" The flight sergeant screamed at them from the front of the plane, with an accompanying instructive gesture. Hawk didn't like the man's looks or his tone. The two Marines continued to stand, and Joe braced his back against a partition. Of course, they had been warned. The flying train suddenly dropped a few feet and Hawk's helmet leapt playfully on his head.

"Just like a carnival," Hawk commented.

"Never liked carnivals," Joe replied.

The turbulence worsened. The sea below grew stormy. The pilot plowed steadily onward. The particular seas below them were storm tossed more often than they were calm. A few patients strained under the added stress of the trembling plane. They began shouting and pulling at their bonds. Joe sympathized with them. He would not like to be tied down in this.

The proper fastening of the seatbelt of woman in a straightjacket had been overlooked, and after a violent shake, she flew across the aisle. She smashed her face on the seat supports there, and her front teeth fell out with a globule of blood. The blood spilled down the white jacket. Joe cringed as if it had happened to him.

"Damn," he said.

The flight sergeant ran to her, and she wobbled to her feet, just in time to kick him in the leg. Two orderlies joined the fray, finally ending the struggle by sitting on her.

"We ought to give her a hand. Them ain't gentlemen," said Joe above the noise.

"Yeah," Hawk answered. He felt queasy. His equilibrium was not adjusting well to all of this conflicting motion. He took out his block of chewing tobacco, but it was only bitter and uncomfortable, the way old habits can be. The deck jumped angrily beneath him. The walls twisted to one side and the other. The floor stopped at a forty-five-degree angle. Joe looked at Hawk. He reached in his pocket and pulled out a can of snuff.

"You want this stuff? A guy gave it to me. Makes me puke." Hawk took it.

"Shit, yeah. Better than betel nut." His jaw already filled with tobacco, he stuffed snuff into his lower lip. It was hot and singed his gums. The snuff had a much better kick, but it did not last as long as the tobacco. The interior of his brain expanded as the nicotine hit his system. It was kind of like eating a package of cigarettes. "Yeah, that's damn good," he told Joe. He spat on the floor and half closed his eyes. The plane shimmied roughly, trying to shake off its wings. "Hell with this," he said dreamily, and spat again.

"Hey! Hey! Are you spitting on my deck?" The flight sergeant screamed.

"No," Hawk bellowed back. He was in an excellent mood for a confrontation: partially disoriented, partially sick, and totally Marine Corps nuts. He spat.

Rain began to splatter the windows as the flight

sergeant made his way down the aisle to the rear. A stitch of lightning sewed its luminous way through the hard and dark clouds outside. The stocky airman stopped and looked up at Hawk. The clear, deep-set eyes of the Marine, and the wide cruel mouth made him pause and think. But, he was here now.

"What's your name, soldier?" The airman demanded. There was no answer. Joe felt a little nervous. He had seen Hawk in similar circumstances, and it never ended well, for anyone.

"That's Bob Hope," said Joe. "Don't you know nothing?" The airman looked at Joe.

"You a comedian, corporal?" Joe had suddenly turned the conflict into his own. He kind of wished he hadn't.

No one said anything for a few seconds, and then Hawk spat. "You better get on back up front where you belong," he said in his low Delta accented voice.

The airman did not quite know what to do next. He knew that he was clearly in the right. People do not spit on floors. Marines were not exactly people, but they were still on his plane. He was relieved of having to worry about it, when the plane rolled to the left, turning almost onto its side. The flight sergeant flew into a row of seats filled with patients. Joe and Hawk hung onto the poles, which bowed significantly under their weight.

"I gotta get a look at who's driving this thing," Joe said, hugging the pole with one arm and his helmet with the other. The floor slowly righted itself.

A patient bit the flight sergeant before he could untangle himself from the crowd. He looked back briefly at Hawk, most of his scolding ferocity spent in the unexpected jostling, and then swung down the aisle toward the front of the plane like an ape, using the corners of the seats for handholds.

"I hope he don't put us in the brig," Joe said.

Hawk snorted, unsure if this was Joe's idea of sarcasm or a sincere fear. Brig time would be a vacation from this sort of fare. Combat Marines only went to the brig between invasions, never during. But then, he recalled, he didn't know where the hell he was going, or even where he was. The motors droned fitfully against the weather. Nature's omnipotent fury remained uninterested in the turmoil of the people inside the little bouncing tin can. One thing he was sure of, that never changed: he managed to stir up shit wherever he went.

"Let me loose!" one of the women screamed, louder than either the storm or the other unfortunates. The cry of the female, like the cry of a baby, was designed by nature to unnerve a man. It did.

"Man," Joe choked. "We better be going to Australia, that's all I gotta say."

"Let me loose!"

"We ain't," Hawk told him.

"Why not?"

"Just the way it is."

"Let me loose!"

The flight sergeant screamed an obscenity at the howling woman. Hawk looked out the window. The wings flapped like that of a bird. Slowly, the weather began to clear. The pilot had tried to go under the storm, failed, and now had gone over it. It grew colder. The clouds looked level enough to walk on. The sun crouched at the end of the cloud-top plains. The scene was serene, a view of heaven, compared to the inside of the Skymaster. To Hawk, it was an alien scene that he did not like. He was a rural creature of humble origins. He did not like modern things, like flying, or looking down on clouds instead of up at them.

"This looks a little better," Hawk mumbled.

"Let me loose!" The excruciating pitch of the scream settled into his consciousness.

An officer came out of the cockpit. Joe saw him coming down the aisle first. He and Hawk saluted suspiciously when the captain got within range. He didn't look like the kind of guy you could mess with. He was kind of older and pasty, with one of those thin mustaches that Hollywood had made the fashion.

"You men hang around after we land," the officer said. "We will need help with a few of these people, getting them off, and I don't know what the situation will be at the airfield. They've a had a little trouble there in the last few days."

"Aye, aye, sir," Hawk said, emphasizing the fact that he was a Marine.

"And don't spit on the floor. Get a can or something."

"Aye, aye, sir," Hawk repeated, swallowing half a burning lump. The officer went back down the aisle. Hawk tried unsuccessfully to spit what was left in his mouth on the floor.

"Trouble at the airfield?" Joe turned to Hawk. That didn't strike an especially positive note.

Hawk shrugged. "Maybe the sewer's backed up."

The motors drilled into Hawk's brain. They sounded like hell, even to his untrained ear. He became acutely aware of the few inches of decking between him and outer space. He thought of Mississippi, something that he rarely did. His anxiety over the doomed atmosphere proved prophetic. Mississippi was a long way off that day.

As they flew over Halmahera, Joe glanced out the window. He choked on an obscenity. Then he gasped. "Uh, oh. *Shit!*"

Hawk leaned over and looked into the shining glare outside, trying to see what Joe was looking at. Two Japanese Betty bombers skidded shark-like along the surface of the clouds. Obviously patched and limping, they were probably the last of their kind in a 500-mile radius. Hawk stared at them for a moment, not knowing how to take them in this unfamiliar environment. On the ground, he would be jumping in a hole. Maybe they were headed to Kawe on a bombing run. Or maybe, they were going to do something else, a little more immediate. They were bristling with machine guns, and were probably not bashful about using them. He elbowed Joe.

"Better go tell the Captain."

Joe quickly advanced hand over hand down the aisle, the patients clutching madly at him as he went. "Hey, shit!" Hawk could hear Joe's stupid sounding voice reprimanding them.

The Bettys followed at a polite distance. Hawk lowered his brows and let his eyes settle on them. He worked the gritty snuff between his teeth. The bird of prey shadows slid ahead of the Japanese craft. The glare on the satin cloud tops cast a strange glow on the undersides of the bombers. It all looked weird, like the kind of a place you just might die in.

Joe must have reached the cockpit by now. The front of the plane pitched forward. Its nose chopped through the layer of clouds in a dive. The window went blind.

Smoky wisps were all that could be seen as the Skymaster dropped through the ocean of whiteness. Hawk clung tighter to the pole, having nothing else to hang onto, and wondered why radar and radios had not given an earlier warning of this obvious threat. So much for modern technology. It's very impressive, until you needed it.

The C-54's engines shrieked in terror as it dropped. Joe crawled back down the aisle. The passengers reached a new level of vocal panic. By the look in his eyes, Joe was about to join them. The spartan panels of the cabin shook beneath the noise. The patients flailed and scratched, some of them injuring their seatmates.

Joe grabbed the pipe at Hawk's feet. He could not say anything. There was not much to say, it was a madman's nightmare come true. They were locked in a falling pile of metal with two furious monsters in close pursuit.

Joe then heard the rattling of machine guns over the screaming bedlam. He knew that C-54's didn't have machine guns.

"How come we got no escort?" Joe screamed.

"I don't know. What did the Captain say?"

"Not too goddam much."

"You got no control. That's the bad thing about this," Hawk commented. Joe could think of a lot worse things than that at the moment. For instance, where were those bullets landing?

"He's trying to shake them!" Joe shrieked, as the plane struggled. Joe sounded much like the other patients. "The tail is the best place to be!" He might have been asking a question. "The tail is the best place to be!"

"Yeah!" Hawk bellowed. The tail of an unarmed bus did not seem particularly safe to him. Hawk listened to the nervous, quick rattle of the machine guns. It was the same sound as some land variety of weapon that he had heard. It occurred to him as important to identify it. He settled on a 7.7 mm. His handhold shook. The nose lowered further, until it was pointed almost straight down. The scream of the engines finally drowned out all of the voices.

"Are we hit! Are we hit?" Joe looked up.

"How the shit would I know?" Hawk screamed down at him. The engines sounded the same as before —hysterical.

A panel fell from the overhead amidst a shower of bolts. A seat near the front of the plane tore free from the deck. People were thrown forward against the hatch leading to the cockpit. Hawk glanced at the bound and swinging creatures writhing about in horror. He noticed that several of them were not moving at all. They had fainted, or possibly died of fright. Dying was not a bad option at the moment. He did not care to relish every moment of this unusual phenomenon. His luck being what it was, however, he knew that he would. He supposed that his heart had withstood worse.

No more plane trips for me, he thought. *One way or the other, this is it, baby.* He thought that he felt the nose jerk. It shuddered again. Yes, the pilot was trying to pull it up. He had gone into a power dive, and Hawk decided that the pilot just might be having a little trouble getting out of it. The fuselage shuddered.

Get out of it, Hawk mentally commanded the plane.

"Mother of God!" Joe shouted.

"We ain't hit!" Hawk yelled back at him. He didn't

think the enemy could hit anything plunging down through the air like this.

The nose bumped as if it had struck something solid. Hawk was swung around to the front of the pole. He managed to hold on with the last joints of his fingers. He slid down to one knee, desperately clinging to the pipe.

"Are we hit?" Joe cried to Hawk's knee. His eyes were screwed shut, back into the middle of his skull.

"No." Hawk clenched his teeth. The nose jerked again. The damned plane was going to break in two. *The bastard can't pull out of it,* Hawk realized. The pilot was tugging at thirty tons of falling junk and could not get it airborne again.

Amidst the bone-jarring thumps of the nose, Hawk heard determined, stitching hammer blows on the tail. *Now*, Hawk thought, *now we're hit.* Joe's hand clawed into his calf.

"Hyneah! Son of a... Let go of me!" Hawk shouted at him. Joe had stopped breathing. A fist squeezed his heart into his forehead. His heart did not beat as it resided there, it only expanded.

"Will we crash? Are we over water? Will we go deep?"

"Cut it out! You're rippin' my leg off, you stupid bastard."

"Will we burn? Will we drown? It's a tomb! We're in a tomb!"

Hawk clawed back at the hand clawing his leg. "Knock—it—off!"

The C-54 did a barrel roll. The nose jumped harder than ever and the floor tried to level. The speed of the fall mercifully lessened a bit.

"He got out of it," Hawk reported matter-of-factly. Cold sweat was frozen into his body. He was a block of ice.

Joe stuck his turtle head up from beneath his helmet shell, that lay low over his eyes. "We're landing," he said, smiling ludicrously.

"That's some shit," Hawk answered. If they were, it was in 3000 fathoms of hellish sea.

The chugging Japanese machine gun fire spat close to their window. No one could do much about that. It was a shooting gallery and they were the unarmed target. Joe was wishing he was on the ground, swearing he would tie a knot in the gun, if he had land underfoot.

A moment later, he was forced into a more realistic assessment of the matter. The glass of the nearest window disintegrated, blowing inside the cabin like finally shredded confetti. Hawk felt the tiny flecks of glass pepper his face. Wind blasted across the cabin, lifting his heavy helmet from his head and tossing it to the deck. Tiny droplets of blood on the side of his face failed to run, as they dried in place. The harmless wounds itched.

Hawk tried to think. The Japanese had to be riding right beside the American plane. He thought he heard something extra in the indecipherable din. The Skymaster was flirting with its stalling speed. Hawk reasoned that they must have lost an engine or two already. *They are on us like flies on shit. We are dead sons of bitches now.*

He accepted death, as he had many times before. He only wished it would end, if nothing could be done about it. But there was the other part of him, the dark part that promised it would never be captured, and never commit suicide. The part that always fought back. That part accepted none of this entire bizarre predicament. He didn't want to wait until he was on the ground to tie a knot in the machine gun.

The fuselage banged under the force of a stream of huge pellets. One of the enemy bombers must have trained its larger machine cannon on them, as well as the smaller machine guns. Funnels of smoke leapt in and out of the shattered window, filling the cabin. Where before, the cabin had smelled like a filling station restroom, it now smelled like a burning oil drum. Huge black holes, framed by shards of steel appeared on the opposite wall of the cabin as the bullets freely entered the plane and stitched the bulkhead. The burst had sliced just above Hawk's head, though he had not heard it. The floor finally leveled out. This was no consolation by now.

Hawk let go of the pole. He grabbed onto the back of the last seat, and walking on the dead with his knees, pulled himself to the open window. As he got closer, the air ceased to be a torrent disgorged from the outside. Now, it pulled at him. Startled by this, he pulled back against it, less he be suctioned out. He found that he could easily withstand the pressure. He latched a hand onto the glass-fringed window. It was getting dark outside. One source of light was immediately apparent. A tattered orange banner of flame flapped behind one of the C-54's engines. Its cowl dangled from the wing. Oil spurted straight up.

The shadows of the flames played across the greenish outer hulls of the two pursuers. The round rising sun emblem, painted on the side of the closest plane, shined a vivid red. One Betty hung high over the

Skymaster's tail, while the other cruised up beside the American plane. The one behind was in a perfect killing position, had it been a fighter plane, and had it not been for the other plane blocking its shot. The closer Japanese plane was hungry for the kill, and did not seem to want the other's help, as it put itself in harm's way. The two enemy attackers had set up an unhealthy competition. Team spirit had been abandoned.

This was an easy one, and they both wanted her.

Hawk could see into the blister turret on the side of the nearest bomber. The Japanese gunner had the breech open on his machine gun as he jammed a belt of ammunition into the chamber. He slammed it shut and pulled on the bolt, his head, elbows and shoulders moving wildly with anxious movement. Hawk slapped an arm behind his back, pulling his Thompson off with one hand. He had been forced to become adroit at the quick draw with the submachine gun. The Thompson, however, had not been designed with air-to-air combat in mind. Hawk knew that the chances of doing any damage were slim. He only wanted to have some say in this contest, rather than being a target, or a mere part of a target. The enemy gunner maneuvered awkwardly behind the glass of the blister. His target was getting too close for accuracy, the barrel of the gun having been forced to one extreme side. As the enemy's weapon spilled a shower of smoking lead across the C-54's tail, Hawk retaliated. The Thompson leapt in his one-armed grip. The muzzle flash crackled through the awesome wind like lightning. The windage made his fire about as effective as throwing tacks. Hawk held the trigger back steering the heavy blunt slugs toward the glass cage that held his enemy. The altitudes of the two planes see-sawed back and forth. The jolting stock pounded at the American's ribs and elbow.

Behind the blinding muzzle flashes coming toward himself, Hawk could see the turret gunner's bobbing leather headgear, with fur, goggles and ear flaps. It was an accident, but the Thompson shells finally struck the turret's glass as the clip emptied. A couple of holes appeared at first. Then the entire cage blew asunder as the glass gave way. The .45s pulled the throat from the gunner, though it was actually the rough fall on the sharp glass, as the wind pulled him downward, that chopped his head off. A syrupy red streak flowed from the shattered blister turret.

Hawk immediately ducked beneath the window and the vacuum of pulling air. He knew the net effect of his extraordinary luck would be zero. He heard rattling fire in the distance, as the other plane joined in the duel once again. The fire inaccurately struck the night air, either above or below the American plane.

The chaos prevented Hawk from any mental cele-brating of the damage inflicted. It was merely a factual accomplishment. Both of the Japanese bombers dropped behind their oversized prey for a better view through their gunsights. Hawk struggled back to the pole he had been clinging to. The jittery speed of the C-54 was suddenly cut. We *are* landing, Hawk thought.

The plane tilted to one side as if it were going into a slow downward spiral. The descent was deliberate this time, and with none of the panicky attributes of the earlier maneuvers. Hawk no longer felt the dark wind blowing through the window. It now lashed toward the back of the cabin.

Hawk saw the white face of the flight sergeant at the front of the craft. The crewman had really liked to fly... before this. All aboard, who survived, would remember this experience for the remainder of their lives, and few would fly again.

Hawk swung halfway up the aisle. "Where are we going down?" he shouted to the sergeant.

"Kawe!" Came the reply. *We made it*, Hawk thought. Or...we *will* make it.

The disrupted electrical system caused the lights to blink on and off. It was all dark and horrible outside, and enough of the horror came inside with each flicker to make the passengers despair. Hawk turned around and swung back toward Joe. The wind sounded much louder in the middle of the plane than it did in the back. A WAC grabbed his arm.

"Let me go! In the name of God, turn me loose," she begged.

Hawk considered it. She had a leather strap on each wrist. He had a knife in his belt. Her arms bled where she had pulled on the straps. "I...can't," he said, looking into her unfocused eyes. He did not want her being slung all over the cabin like the woman who had lost her teeth. He would not forget the terrified mask of her face.

"If I were your sister, you'd let me loose!"

Hawk fought his way up the incline to the rear of the plane. He did not look or listen to any of the other pleading unfortunates.

"We made it," he told Joe. "We're landing at Kawe."

"Where's the Japs!" Joe low ranged voice raised almost to a squeal.

Hawk looked out the broken window. He thought

that he could see a red muzzle stuttering in the blackness. "Shit. They're going in with us." Joe hugged the base of the pipe, near the floor. "You gotta get up, Joe. We gotta get the hell off here."

"I can't move. Leave me."

"You got to." Hawk pried at Joe's fingers. Joe was not kidding. He could not let go. Hawk got an index finger free and pushed it back. Joe ignored the pain and kept his grip. "Let go!" Hawk pounded his back with hollow thumps.

"I can't!" Joe sobbed.

"We *got* to get out of here! The goddam bastards are followin' us in!"

The plane leveled over the jagged coast of Kawe, sliding above the strait known as Selat Bapen. Hawk removed one of Joe's frozen fingers at a time from the pole, wondering what kind of shape Joe would be in, even if he succeeded in freeing him.

The pilot could easily see the southern coast of the island hulking in the gray, early night sea. "There she is. Home," the pilot told the copilot.

"Sea Bird 109 to Kawe," the copilot stuttered into the microphone, "approaching you...with two bogeys... Bettys...maybe more...in pursuit. Make appropriate preparations. We are coming down."

"Roger, Sea bird," a calm voice crackled in the headsets. "Field lights are coming on."

"No!" the copilot cried into the microphone. But it was too late. The parallel beads of light blazed along the ground under him. "Douse the lights!"

No one did. The heavy plane dropped to the different cushioning levels of the atmosphere.

"They'll nail us on the runway!" the copilot shouted at the pilot.

The pilot shrugged. He had a strong urge to put his wheels on some kind of earth, regardless of the cost or complications. The copilot read this in the position of his hands.

"Douse those lights!" the copilot screamed into the microphone. Kawe remained lit like Broadway in the damp Pacific night. The airfield would be a target. Only tiny and muted electric and kerosene dots of illumination could be seen in the dark hinterlands. The people on Kawe took it for granted at this point that America ruled the skies. They had already forgotten the terror of 1942, when Japan was in control.

Some of the C-54's passengers were unconscious or dead. Some, however, were quite alive, wailing and waving as best they could with fettered arms. The landing gear went down with a groan and locked into place with a thump. Seconds later the tires bounced roughly on solid ground. Strength surged through Hawk's body when he felt that it was once again connected to the earth. All consideration of defeat drained away. He pulled Joe to his feet. Joe may have experienced a surge of his own. The front hatch had already been thrown open. It fell to the steel runway with a rocking, clanking splatter.

Pulling Joe down the aisle, Hawk stopped in front of the flight sergeant. He thought that he could hear the steady whine of the bombers above the unsteady warbling of the people. The passengers remained strapped in place.

"What about these people?" Hawk asked the airman. Brilliant electric lighting flooded into the gloomy interior of the plane. It turned faces phosphorescent white.

"That's not your business. Here, get these women out," the flight sergeant said, pointing to three women whom an orderly had led forward. They seemed more in control of themselves than the others. Given the situation, it was difficult to tell whether that was a good or bad sign.

Hawk looked out the hatch. He saw the interwoven steel panels of the runway below him, under the shiny glare of the light. It was a good ankle twisting jump to the ground for the average person. It was not as daunting for a young Marine.

"Stay up here and help me get them women off," Hawk told Joe, and proceeded to jump out. But Joe hit the runway before Hawk. Joe had his own opinion of the circumstances. He fled down the field. *Good initiative*, Hawk thought.

"Tell them to knock out those lights!" Hawk shouted after him.

A girl, presumably in her twenties, sat on the floor of the C-54, with her legs hanging out of the hatch. It was a little high to get a grip on her. Hawk grabbed her ankle and pulled her. She resisted.

"Jump, lady!" he ordered, but she did not move. "Jump! I got you."

It caught him by surprise when she did jump. His back buckled under the weight. He managed to let her down easily. The next woman flew at him without warning, and he let her down a little less easily. The next one was older, overweight, uncoordinated, and flying like a bat out of hell. They fell on the strip together. He prevented her from breaking her leg, nearly breaking his own with the effort. He stood. The women were standing paralyzed around him. He looked up. The door was empty. No one else was coming out. The hatch yawned like the open grave that it was. Hawk studied it for a moment and looked back at the women on the ground. He wasn't entirely sure what to do.

"Get the hell out of here!" Hawk waved his arm at the dazed women. "Run for the dark! Get out of the light!"

They did nothing. The air raid siren was a ranting banshee.

"Damnation, woman," Hawk took the hand of one of them. "Here, y'all go. Hold hands." He ran with them for a few feet. "Keep going," he told the leader. "Don't stop until somebody stops you." They pulled each other into the darkness behind the lights.

The air cracked. The ground shook. A bright red ball of fire leapt from the earth on either side of the Skymaster. Hawk knew that he was in the middle of the bombardment now. In it or out of it: that was all that his brain could tell him about the jerking, blurred, flashing, and deafening cauldron surrounding him. Other planes may have joined in the attack. He felt all sorts of unpleasant things, feelings that he would remember, and yet not remember where they came from. To the left, another blaze shot up from hell and opened the armor of the runway. Bits of steel were fired against the side of the plane at high velocity. He could distinguish the cracking sounds as the razor-edged pieces hit. Hawk jumped for the hatch and tried to pull himself up. He had to start cutting straps off the passengers. He knew that he might not get very far.

An escaping foot kicked him in the shoulder, and he

landed on his back, in the midst of the shattered and stabbing pieces of the runway.

He looked up to see the huge white star on the back of the fuselage. It had bullet holes in it. Two or three pairs of nylon covered legs passed over him. He got up slowly. Another explosion collided with the ground, sounding like the sky had turned into a solid object and slapped the earth. Hawk estimated that he was dead center on the enemy's target, which had to be the plane. The stocky flight sergeant suddenly jumped from the opening to the ground beside Hawk.

"Come on, get out of here," the airman told him. Hawk picked himself up slowly yet again. It was becoming increasingly difficult. The flight sergeant looked for a direction in which to run. Nothing looked inviting.

"We ain't going nowhere without them people inside," Hawk told him.

"Suit yourself," the other answered. He turned to run. The field lights remained brutally bright.

Flames added pulsation to the hellish glow. The belated sirens screamed. Had American planes been ordered to the defense of the airfield? Hawk turned toward the stricken plane as the airman turned the other way, and they managed to collide with one another. Hawk's boot tangled with the other man's leg and tripped him. The flight sergeant slid across the runway on his chest. Hawk turned back for the hatch and jumped for it once more. He hung there, struggling to pull himself up.

A bomb killed the airman. His stumbling into Hawk had likely been the ultimate cause of his death. The explosion might have caught him anyway.

Unfortunately, Hawk was rather close to the massive event. The shockwave jolted his hands from the slick hatch entrance, as if they had never been there, moving himself and the plane into two different directions, and again he slammed viciously onto the ground. Under normal circumstances, the blow would have winded him. The human body is capable of the super human, however, when confronted with such a supernatural crescendo of noise and vibration. The blast had actually knocked him unconscious. And yet, unconscious as he was, his nervous system was apparently having none of that, and he got up and ran.

He had no idea of how, but when he regained consciousness, he found himself fifty yards from the plane. He was on his knees and digging at the steel runway with his fingers, and doing a damned good job of it. As he knocked more and more flesh off his finger-tips, a better approach came to mind. The earth jumped about him, looking like a dropped movie camera that continued to operate without human direction. A crater lay nearby, rimmed by misty and frayed steel.

He crawled toward it, ending the effort by rolling into the deep hole. The interior was hot. Bombs fell outside, coming from low altitude without warning. There was no whoosh or whistle, just the colliding thunderclap of the universe opening up, with rock and steel raining down after each concussion. In spite of the overwhelming bedlam, he clearly heard the C-54 explode, taking a direct hit. There would be no more going back to it.

Spears of shimmering white-orange stabbed the black sky over his sheltering crater. The spears of light retreated and wilted like murdered snakes, only to return seconds later after a secondary explosion. The after-image of the flash stayed in Hawk's retinas. It seemed as bright as daylight, even when he closed his eyes. He was left only able to see the outlines of things. He jerked his hand suddenly off the scalding ground. His palm had been resting, for some time, on burning shrapnel.

American anti-aircraft fire eventually responded to the attackers. For the first time, Hawk recognized the welcome rattling of the hardware of his own forces. The guns sounded random and panic-stricken. A bomb fell a few hundred yards away, which sounded like a major improvement compared to the location of the last few. Taking this as a good sign, and an opportunity not to be wasted, Hawk pulled a leg under himself, and dove over the top of the hole.

Timing is everything in the art of staying alive. He ran through the smothering smoke for the deepest darkness that he could find. A one hundred twenty-five pounder shattered the C-54 behind him, dwarfing his scrambling silhouette with a bright pillar of scarlet set against the black velvet sky.

3

THE NIGHT BEAST

FIFTEEN HUNDRED MILES TO THE EAST, IN THE smoldering jungle night of Basah, one of the larger islands of the Dutch East Indies, the world lay much more quiet and serene. And yet, while the terrifying noise on Kawe threatened certain death, the quiet of the night here equally threatened the same. A religious and medical mission, staffed by French and Americans, lay sleeping deep in the equatorial rain forest. Long a part of the Japanese Empire, the isolated compound had been little affected by the Japanese occupation. The occupiers tolerated their remote guests, for the time being at least, as harmless humanitarians.

Supplies still arrived on schedule from the coast. The indigenous people interested in medical care, and disinterested in religious instruction, still came and went as they always had. Tending to their needs lent a bit of stability and civilization to the area, stability that was lacking elsewhere in the wild country.

Even here, however, change was in the wind, as news of Australian landings on the northern coast filtered into the steaming bush country. There were those men at the compound who knew what was coming; for even harmless humanitarians sometimes play double roles. A radio can be a dangerous thing. They knew that the Japanese would soon be moving into even this remote area, and would not easily let it fall to a foreign flag. The residents of the area had been undisturbed thus far, only because the rule of the Empire had been unchallenged. The undercover personnel at the mission had been waiting for an opportunity to launch that challenge for years. Their altruistic interest in the Iban, Murut, and Penan people was about to wane, and be exposed for the ruse that it had been. The question remained as to how much of a cover it had been, as the Japanese were not easily fooled. They had seized radio communication devices everywhere else, and yet, not here. Which side knew the most about the other? Whose plans had been compromised, to the greatest degree?

But on this night, the night James Hawk barely escaped with his life on the airfield at Kawe, the staff at Sacred Blood Mission slept. The half-moon rose high in the purple sky, as night sounds reverberated through the jungle. For not all of God's creatures slept.

One such creature, if indeed God made all creatures, padded silently through the foliage near the compound's palisades. It walked rapidly in an awkward manner on two legs, similar to the way that man, the most dangerous of creatures, walked. Although, as a man's legs are straight, this creature's joints were bent backwards, like the legs of a four-footed animal. The knees of the creature folded in the direction opposite to that of a man. Its back was stooped, its face hairy. One of its arms, or forelegs, dangled thin and idle. The other arm hung almost to the ground. The creature was only slightly smaller than a man, and probably would have been the same size, had it stood upright. The large feet were triangular, though solid and without webbing. The creature paused as it heard the approach of happy voices.

Two Iban tribesmen walked in the shadows of the moon beside the compound's rickety palisade. They left the gray obscurity, laughing at each other's conversation. They planned an evening of clamming in the nearby swamp, and had both had a cheering portion of rice beer. They disappeared into the heavy undergrowth, unafraid of the night. Basah was their world, and they little feared it. A lone bird clucked intermittently at them from above.

The unwelcoming night creature raised his head to watch them. Two horns stood black against the moon. Two tiny red specks glowed like embers where eyes should be. The creature began to move. He followed the path of the Ibans. It seemed awkward for him to walk. He strutted purposefully, like a rooster, thrusting his head out in front of himself with every step and swaying wide, side to side, with each motion of his grotesque body. The hair-covered face was invisible in the night, except for the red eyes. A wide, heavily boned forehead bulged beneath the horns.

The hunter entered the jungle and slowed his pace, holding his longer arm with his short arm. A snarl, or perhaps a smile, exposed the rows of tiny white teeth in the hair draped mouth.

The night remained silent, and when this devil returned to whatever hell that had borne it, the two

Ibans lay dead and sinking into the quicksand near their favorite clamming spot. Enormous footprints trailed off into the tangled emptiness nearby.

* * *

KAWE HAD RETURNED to its calm, industrious state of normality. They hauled the bodies out of the twisted and burned remains of the C-54 all night. Joe Canlon and Sergeant Hawk sat at a table in the flight crew's club, not far from all of this. The club consisted of a grass roofed hut with an open front. It afforded an excellent view of the landing strip, and of the shattered Skymaster. One had but to look out at the shell pocked earth to relive the past twenty-four hours. Navy firemen had stopped the flames, but smoke continued to rise into the early morning darkness. Searchlights shined and slid about in the upper reaches of the fumes, making them white at the top, and dark down below. The quiet process of attending to the dead contrasted sharply with their violent struggle for life only hours earlier. Occasionally, a raised voice of instruction would pierce the night, but for the most part, the crew of responders worked silently.

Joe sat at the table, still suffering from occasional fits of shaking. His shoulders bunched tautly around his neck. His hands pressed against his legs from the inside of his pockets. He looked from the table top to Hawk and back. He didn't know what to say about any of it. It had been rather intense. He thought of things and then dismissed them.

He faced away from the wreckage outside. Hawk faced it. Joe saw no expression on Hawk's face. The tragedy haunted eyes reflected the dead plane. *What was he thinking? Did he ever—think?* Considering all of the things that had happened to him, he had a lot to think about.

Hawk thought of faces and screams. He decided that he should have started cutting them free before the ship landed. He found it difficult to re-create the sequence of events. But that's what he should have done. What had he done instead? He couldn't quite piece that together. What had he actually been doing at this point, or that point? *You would help me, if I were your sister.* He clearly remembered that. He should have cut them loose. Yes, that's what he should have done. *Why in the hell didn't he do that?*

A sea breeze blew the smoke in a direction away from the hut. But it would return. The sultry, salty night air was not refreshing.

The corporal tending the bar watched the two Marines. The bartender leaned toward a pilot who was slumped over his drink. The pilot was an officer, and the bartender knew the man well.

"Those two came off that C-54," the bartender told the pilot.

The pilot pivoted on his wooden stool and glanced at Joe and Hawk. "Psychos," he mumbled with the superior and disinterested air that alcohol can give a person. "They were all psychos."

The bartender nodded. "Better get the MPs. Quick. Those were all bad cases. Those two are Marines and that one is carrying a Tommy gun. I don't know where he got that. I don't think he had it when he came in here."

The pilot set his drink down, eyeing Hawk. The

Marine looked like a certified maniac. The pilot was right of course, except for the certification.

The Thompson was not a reassuring sight for those in the rear echelons. The pilot slid off his stool and walked out the front of the hut, quickly donning his cap upon reaching the outside, and sprinting off to add his contribution to the war effort.

Hawk sat motionless. The landing gear had been knocked from beneath the Skymaster. Two shirtless men were lowering a stretcher from the cabin.

"Hey, watch it!" A distant voice floated high and thin through the night air, and lingered in the damp hut. High columns of smoke remained trapped overhead, trying desperately to leave the earth for their eternal voyage. The body was well strapped and covered. All night this continued. "Damn! My fingers!"

A young Army lieutenant came and stood by the table. He looked from Hawk to Joe. They did not look up. Joe had an untouched drink in front of him. Hawk's hand rested against a tall beer bottle.

"I tried to go out there. They wouldn't let me go. They held me," the lieutenant told them.

Hawk didn't look directly at him. He didn't want to see another face right now. "You couldn't do nothing, sir. I was out there. I couldn't do nothin'."

"I wanted to get them out. They wouldn't let me."

"Couldn't do nothin'." Now that he had been drawn from his own thoughts, Hawk noticed the beer, lifted it, but set it down suddenly. "I think I should have got them loose before we landed. I think that was it. I don't know. Should've done...something." He looked up to meet this new face, because this was someone actually interested in what was preoccupying him. "There just wasn't anything you could do, by then. You couldn't get back inside the damn thing. No fault of yours, Lieutenant."

The lieutenant looked away from Hawk's eyes. He didn't know what he wanted to say. He just wanted to repeat what he had already said, but that would sound absurd. He thought of sitting down with them. He didn't.

"It..." Hawk shrugged and looked at Joe. Joe offered no assistance; he wasn't saying anything. "It all happened so fast." Hawk hated that expression. Yet, here he was saying it like a dumb ass. How many times had he heard that phrase? It was his job to act faster than things happened. It happened and it was over, and so what? People were ridiculous. They acted inefficiently, they thought inefficiently, at a speed slower than the things happening around them. And so, they died inefficiently. Or someone else died.

Thinking was designed to be done rapidly for a reason. You can think fast a hundred times; then, a hundred and one things happen.

The lieutenant walked to the front of the bar. The air crew of a B-29 were shouting and laughing outside. They came through the open front of the building in a merry melee of joking grabass. No one looked at them, except the bartender. He was glad to have them around. They could at least absorb a few Thompson rounds, if worse came to worse. The crew ordered beer, and went jostling over to one of the larger tables. One of them was shouting about a Zero he had almost seen. He had big teeth that pushed the front of his face way out. It seemed a smile was the only expression to which he was accustomed.

After a few minutes, the happy man noticed the two somber Marines. He nudged one of his buddies, got up and walked over to the quiet table.

"Hey, Marines!" he shouted and slapped Hawk hard on the back. The back did not move, remaining perched like a tombstone. Actually, the happy man's hand got the worst of it. "Don't see too many Marines around here! Hear you guys been winning the war!" He turned his teeth to his buddies and roared with laughter. They, too, roared, but from a safer distance. Joe frowned a little, dimly returning to his surroundings. He thought perhaps he had missed a punch line somewhere.

"Hey! Want a cigar?" he asked Hawk, leaning down toward his face and shouting, as if to an invalid.

"Yeah...thanks." Hawk liked cigars. It was difficult for Marines to get cigars.

The flier unwrapped it and handed it to him. Hawk took the cigar and held it in his large hand, steady as ever. He wondered how fliers could get cigars so easily. Probably the same reason they laughed so much. What was so goddam funny? He lost himself for a moment, as he tried to recall anything that was funny. When had he last laughed, and what could it possibly have been about?

"I hear you Marines are tough sons of bitches!" the pilot shouted. The recurring noise made Hawk wonder if the man was deaf, and what the hell he was talking about. He had just had his ears blown out by 125 pounders, and yet this man's voice still struck him as loud. It also struck him as being a little...rude. "You must be pretty tough, carrying a Tommy gun around here on Kawe!" He howled with laughter. His buddies joined in. It seemed sort of funny, to them.

"We weren't here yesterday," Joe said quickly. Was that yesterday? What difference did it make? Joe was only trying to save the man's magnificent teeth.

Hawk had a grim temper. Death was commonplace to him. He had been routinely killing men who had done nothing to him, for months. His social restraints were stretched a little thin at the moment.

"No kidding? You sure get around! Fighting machines!"

"Yep," said Hawk. He couldn't argue with that. "Got a light, there, sport?"

"For a Marine? Damn right," he said, reaching into his jacket pocket. "Not for no sailors, now. But for you, you bet." He opened his lighter. "Hell, you're winning the war, while the rest of us are here relaxing."

It occurred to Joe that maybe the guy didn't think he was getting his due credit for his war efforts. He supposed things were tough all over. What did he want the Marine Corps to do? Send him an apology?

"Feels like it," Hawk said quietly.

The men form the Seabee maintenance unit lowered another woman's body from the carcass of the plane. The pilot held a lighter a foot from Hawk's face. He didn't seem to notice what was happening on the runway, where the cold blue eyes of the Marine were focused. Hawk put the cigar into his mouth. The pilot snapped the lighter shut on the cigar, shredding the tip of it. He convulsed with laughter. His buddies rolled with pleasure.

"Here, I'm sorry," the happy man said. Then he snapped the lighter on the cigar again and laughed even louder. The bartender shook his head. He had a strong urge to go to the latrine.

Joe considered hitting the troublemaker. That would stop Hawk from doing anything to him. Hitting the guy would be much better than the "anything" that Hawk might do. Killers instinctively use weapons, whether needed or not. But then if Joe started something, a free-for-all would break out, and Hawk would still probably kill someone else. Better that it should be this guy. He was asking for it.

Joe considered laughing along so that maybe Hawk would take the cue, defusing the situation—because there was another complicating factor: pilots were officers. The guy wouldn't be pulling this shit if he wasn't an officer. He wouldn't have the nerve.

In ordinary life, Joe would try to talk his way out of the scuffle. But he had been in combat for a long time. The situation held little intimidation for him. It was merely civilized society operating the way it ordinarily operated, and he was numb to that. Joe knew, however, that the people here would probably not take a stomped in skull lightly. They were probably touchy about violence. That's what the Marine Corps was for, after all, to keep that stuff away from them.

Hawk took the torn cigar out of his mouth. Something was about to happen. Even the happy man could tell that, by the way his heart stopped beating. About that time, twelve members of the Shore Patrol appeared breathlessly at the front of the bar. They had shiny, newly painted helmets and shiny new M1s with fixed bayonets. They carried clubs, and a large dragging net, that met Navy specifications for fielding errant lunatics. Their black clubs glistened in the weak light. The men were young and bright-eyed. A bar confrontation was pure excitement for them. This was their World War II.

"Where are the escapees?" the officer in charge asked. He looked at Hawk. Any untrained eye could identify at least one escapee.

"That must be us," Hawk said solemnly. He stood. He took the lighter quickly out of the hand of the officer, as if from a child, and lit his cigar. The frayed end of it flamed high and close to the face of the pilot. Hawk's heavy arm pushed him out of the way like a broomstick as he rounded the table. Hawk had a certain deliberate, though casual style. He felt the soft unused muscle under the pilot's jacket. Or was it just padded flesh? What the hell kind of man was that? Probably a normal one. Hawk knew that he had become hard and brutal, unfit to coexist with humans. He felt all sorts of horrible strengths coursing through his body.

"Come on, Joe," he said, "looks like we got an appointment with these folks." He dropped the lighter on the floor.

Hawk swaggered in his usual shrugging gait toward the policemen. Joe followed, looking over his shoulder as he left.

"The joker will pick up the tab," Joe told the bartender. The Shore Patrol took away the Thompson.

The bartender blew out his breath in relief, unaware that the Thompson was the least dangerous thing in the bar.

4

DEEP IN THE HEART OF THE DUTCH EAST INDIES

It took a while for Joe and Hawk to make their way through the hospital bureaucracy, and to get anyone worthwhile to look at their orders. At one point, they were actually placed in a padded cell.

An impatient Major Wimberley, the man that had ordered them to report to Kawe in the first place, eventually had to have them tracked down. He was concerned that they may have been killed. Without the good offices of the major, they might have never gotten out.

A quiet captain and his quiet driver escorted the two Marines to the north side of the island to meet the Major. Amidst this stoic company, Joe had only the colorless sights of the base, flying past the jeep, to occupy him. It had been constructed by Seabees early in the war, and by now had all of the modern conveniences.

They soon found themselves brought into Major Wimberly's office. Wimberly stood, and instead of saluting, shook their hands. A little surprised at this, they took two seats in front of his desk.

The officer told them that they could smoke. Of course, they didn't, because they knew he didn't really mean it. But Joe already liked Wimberly. What a regular guy! Being treated like a human being was all that Joe asked of anyone.

Hawk sat suspiciously watching the officer's face and listening to the tone of his voice. He asked for a little more, before he would lower his guard. When someone who has the ax on you treats you like a human being, there must be a pretty good reason for it.

"Nice weather here, sir," Joe said, getting into the friendly spirit.

"Yes," the Major agreed. "Really mild. It rained yesterday." He looked at Joe. Joe didn't strike him as being very bright. He looked as if his features might have been rearranged in a boxing ring. The officer supposed that intelligence was not paramount for the mission. "How was General McCoy doing up north?"

"Oh, he was too busy to see us, sir. Probably out fighting the Japs barehanded, like them generals do, you know," Joe laughed stupidly, and looked at his feet. Interviews made Joe giddy, and the Major obviously wanted to be friendly. Hawk decided to step in and salvage whatever rapport was left.

"We didn't see him, sir. We don't know why we're here. No time to fill us in, I guess."

Major Wimberly then began a lengthy monologue. Hawk, unused to listening, lost most of the meaning of it in the boredom. This was not going to be the short version. Hawk hoped for a summation at the end, because not much was registering. The Major was the liaison for such and such under General such and such. Hawk heard the acronym "OSS" once. But when he heard the history of the organization that followed, he again became lost and looked for an open window with any type of scenery: perhaps a bird on a roof, or something.

Hawk had learned from earlier missions that the OSS was not popular in the Pacific theater, due to the hostility of General MacArthur towards it. He missed the part of the briefing, however, stating that he would be leaving the Pacific Theater. He heard the Dutch East Indies mentioned, and he knew about where that was. He had been close to it a few times. He always thought that it was just another part of the Pacific. He didn't know that he was sitting in it at the moment.

Joe started talking and this caught Hawk's attention, causing him to focus on the conversation. Joe always produced a sort of a moaning grunt before he said anything, giving you plenty of warning that some stupid comment was on the way. What the hell was the dumb bastard going to say now?

"Uhhh...yeah, we hear of all kind of outfits that go by letters," said Joe. "They always got to use letters instead of words. You know what A-R-M-Y stands for, don't you, sir?"

The Major paused suddenly in his discourse, trying to be polite, and trying not to look irritated. The educated and willing participation of these men, and many others, was necessary for the success of the operation. "Oh...why no, I don't believe so. What is that, Corporal?"

"Ain't Ready for the Marines Yet!" Joe laughed with enthusiasm. The Major stared at him.

"Sorry, sir," Hawk said quickly. "He's real ignorant. They gave him something over at the hospital. It made it worse. They thought we were patients."

"Yes. Bad situation." The Major resumed at his former pace. He was evidently determined to give them a certain prepared amount of information, whether they absorbed it or not. "So, you see," he said, having arrived at a key turning point, "Basah is going to be pretty important in the closing days of this war." Hawk nodded in agreement. The Major took the Sergeant's tense and fierce features to represent interest.

"High level Japanese officers and political officials have been discovered to be traveling down there. We have it on good authority that they are relocating their government in the region." Neither Hawk, nor even the Major, knew that the Americans had virtually every move the Japanese made on "good authority," as the United States had completely broken their code. "They are assembling a government in exile, in preparation for the fall of Japan. The Australians have already begun to invade the island at Hazelton, and the Japanese have retreated inland. I don't have to tell you they don't retreat without a pretty good reason. The interior of Basah is rough, unexplored country. We will have a tough time getting them out of there, once they settle in."

"Yes, sir," Hawk said. That much had to be true.

"And, I'm sure you are well aware that there are political troubles down there. The Dutch and the British have had difficulty with the native population. If the Japanese can get these islanders stirred up, and turn them even partially against us, we will have problems. We have concerns about Basah leaving the Dutch East

Indies as an independent nation, either allied with, or controlled by Japan."

Hawk listened, but he wasn't sure he agreed. He couldn't imagine anyone allying themselves with the Japanese. The Imperial forces didn't go out of their way to make many friends. He knew little of the Asia for the Asians campaign launched by Japan.

"And so it is," the Major continued, "that we are bringing together a force of experienced men from all over the Pacific Theater of Operations to go into this region and work with the natives. We want, in particular, to harass the Japanese and keep them off balance as we are doing in the China-Burma-India Theater." The Major stopped and looked at them. "Men, what do you think?"

Hawk stared back at him. He had gotten stuck on the "working with the natives" part. He was not really much of a missionary. Someone may have given someone a little misinformation about him. And there was all the rest of it. He was not a politician of any sort. What *was* all this crap? He did not belong here.

"Yes. Well," Hawk tried to sound diplomatic. But there was no other way to put it. "Is this voluntary, sir?"

Wimberly continued staring at him without answering for a moment. Then he raised a hand. "Let me show you something." The major opened a file lying on the desk, turned it around and pointed firmly to a signature at the bottom of the top page: *Henry L. Stimson.*

Hawk studied the signature. Joe stretched his neck to see it. Neither of them commented. For good reason.

"Yessir," said Hawk. "That's really something. The thing is, though, me...and Joe, too...are just rank and file type infantry. We don't know anything about passing out food bags and teaching folks to brush their teeth and that stuff. They don't teach riflemen how to cook or any of that."

The Major's pleasant expression darkened a bit. His tone became a little less friendly.

"I may have misled you. That would not be your mission. You will be in action against the Japanese. Perhaps, irregular action at times, but for the most part, intense action involving fully equipped large troop movements of the type with which you are familiar. I can make a notation to excuse you from any training exercises, in case those arise. There are several reasons why this operation is of such strategic importance. One of them is time. We cannot spend two years taking Japan, two years taking China, and two years taking the Dutch East Indies. We cannot simply react every time they move their headquarters. For practical reasons we need this war to end quickly, and simply, without it turning into some endless colonial revolution, with the Japanese benefiting from local unrest. We are developing new weapons every day. But, so are they. We have the edge on them now, but we certainly don't want to give them any more time to play with than we absolutely have to. Any questions?"

Joe leaned forward. "So, what you're saying then…it ain't voluntary, sir?" Joe did not have the slightest idea what was going on here, and he wanted at least that part cleared up, if nothing else.

Wimberly folded his hands and growled at Joe. "Yes, Canlon. It *is* voluntary."

Wimberly had been led to believe that he was interviewing two gung ho, patriotic Marines. He was not pleased with this reaction. "It is dangerous. You are going into an area where you will be vastly outnumbered, an area occupied for years by an enormous Japanese Army and Navy presence. We are not *ordering* anyone into this. Are you in or out?"

Hawk and Joe both knew by the Major's angry tone of voice that they were *in*. Joe looked at Hawk, and Hawk did not look back. Neither of them said anything. Wimberly nodded.

"Very well. You will deploy for Sacred Blood Mission, Basah, Dutch East Indies, tonight. Our personnel are engaged there now with civilian operatives. Through considerable forethought, we have an outpost inside the target area." Joe nodded. "Deploy" sounded like both the friendly and the voluntary parts of the Major's discussion were over.

"Any chance we can be discharged, if we get back, sir?" Joe asked. "We been in a long time. I mean a *long* time."

"How long did you sign up for?"

"The duration," said Hawk.

Wimberly sighed. "I can't tell you anything about that. They have the point system. I'm in the Army and you're in the Marine Corps."

Then why are we here? Joe thought. Since the Major was a nice guy, Joe decided to push it. "Can you find out, sir?"

"I'll try."

He didn't. After they left the office, Joe said, "What do you think of all that bullshit he was shoveling on us?"

"I didn't catch all of it. It can't be no worse than

where we were. You didn't like that, either. It's better than going into Japan."

"Yeah," Joe agreed. "But it sure as hell ain't as good as going to Australia. Or New York. Sounds like we're gonna be way the hell out in some crazy ass place with no kind of shit or nothing."

"That's awright," said Hawk. "Nobody gives a damn about that."

"Or us."

Joe Canlon and Hawk reunited with several members of their old first squad in Hazelton. Located on Basah's northeastern coast, Hazelton had been liberated by the Australians only a few days before. Locations on the northern and eastern coasts were rumored to be the next targets for Australian landings, though they were still considered to be enemy strongholds. The Marines were not going to be a part of these coastal operations.

Hawk found that his mission led into the interior, geographically behind enemy lines. The mouth of the Pageas River met the South China Sea at Hazelton. The allies controlled this lifeline into the interior, or at least the part of it near Hazelton. No one really knew much about the interior, or the untracked wilderness between here and Sacred Blood Mission. Although no one could control it, anything could be in it.

An old launch left the seaport, headed south, the day after Hawk's arrival in Hazelton. It had been requisitioned for Marine Corps use. Hawk and Joe were among those assigned to it. The destination was Sacred Blood Mission, several days downriver, through the forest and the Abu Hama mountain range. Sacred Blood was located in territory that few of even the local residents cared to visit. Technically, it was still designated as occupied by the Japanese. No one knew where the enemy were regrouping, however, with any certainty.

The outskirts of primitive Hazelton looked wild enough for Joe Canlon, and he became skeptical as to how any place as remote as this could be strategic. The isolation alone was oppressive.

A company of Marines under the command of a Captain Franklin boarded the riverboat. First platoon consisted of many of the men taken off the front line with Joe and Hawk. First squad was almost identical to the one Hawk had been in charge of when leaving the draw up north. Several of the older men had been in the First Marine Division. The company was heavily armed. Clearly, these troops were not on a humanitarian mission, of the sort to pass out food bags.

As their travels settled into a boring pattern, Hawk did not find the experience pleasant. He had a lot of time to think, and that was not especially good. The darkening forest was not conducive to happy thoughts. Forests of this type conjured up a lot of memories best forgotten for the Marines. These were the thick, nasty environs they had to contend with in the early years of the war, on Guadalcanal and New Britain.

The Captain of the riverboat, an elderly Australian man by the name of Givens, spent most of his time in the wheelhouse. His primary occupation seemed to be the filling and smoking of an ornate pipe. The only crewman that the Marines saw much of was Clancy. Clancy seemed to have a lot of spare time. He was a thin, ravaged Irishman, although native-born to Basah. Clancy served as river guide and mechanic, being equally expert at both tasks. It was common knowledge that he had once been a captain himself, for the Pageas River Cargo Line Enterprises, LTD. But Clancy drank a little. No one ever saw him drink, no liquor had ever been found on him. It was his aroma and frequent spills into the river had given him away too many times. He either drank, or he was an exceptionally clumsy man with a whisky smelling aftershave. He could tell a lot of stories, covering a lot of years, about this eventful route into nothingness.

The boat left the slight civilization of the coast and proceeded south beyond a heavy concentration of Iban villages. The people lived in stilted structures designated as longhouses. The stilts protected them from headhunters. The observers on the banks expressed no interest in Givens' boat. Clancy informed the Marines that this was unusual. The excursions were usually confronted with local vendors clinging to the sides of the boat, sometimes for miles. The Japanese had moved to the interior and the river dwellers knew why the American Marines were there. They kept their distance from the combatants, as well as they could. The distance they kept aroused envy in the Americans. This looked like a poor place to die. It further dampened enthusiasm to know that one could easily die of some horrible disease here, long before ever being shot at.

The terrain grew worse. The low palm trees descended right to the muddy river banks. They sprouted taller, and grew closer together, the farther the boat traveled. Swampy jungle overtook the coffee-colored highway of water. The ramin and jelutong trees crowded closer, peeping through the ethereal mist for a sly and disapproving look at the invading human beings. The fetid air pressed close, making the simple act of breathing feel unhealthy. Lieutenant Klemer had already come down with some tropical malady. It appeared to have befallen him about the time he stepped onto the boat. His symptoms did not seem critical at this point, and all were assured that there was a functioning hospital at Sacred Blood Mission. Everything would improve, once their destination had been reached.

The ancient craft chugged on cautiously. The sky hid behind the thickening skein of foliage, but gave every indication of being a gray one. Joe Canlon looked up through the intricate patterns of the leaves as he leaned on the railing. Clouds of birds rolled from one dark forest giant's canopy to the next, following the boat like a tumbleweed. Grim-faced monkeys screamed angrily at the barge, protesting its incursion into their hallowed purgatory. Always, the darkness deepened.

Joe's first day on the river was drawing to a close. The day had felt like a week—a week of plunging into an absolute nothingness. Joe rubbed his large, warped nose. He pushed away from the railing, and walked down the deck to find Hawk, or any type of human society.

Hawk sat in the stern with Captain Franklin, USMC, at a folding table. Men with legs outstretched lined the railings nearby. Franklin was a young man, in his early twenties. He seemed older, and was often accepted and respected as being older than his years. The Captain struggled over a report. A wisp of hair hung on his forehead. He cracked his knuckles.

"I don't know why they need this stuff. Honest to God, I don't," Franklin said suddenly. His companion, the Sergeant, a rather morose creature given to minding his own business, looked over at the clipboard.

"What's wrong, Captain?" Hawk asked.

"They want the area of that triangular perimeter we set up in Hazelton. Why? There is no reason on earth anyone would ever want or need to know that." He shook his head and looked up. He was sweating more than normal. His color was bad. "I'm tired, I guess. I can't think straight today." He looked back down. There was frustration in his voice. This was quite unlike Captain Franklin.

Hawk looked blankly at the deck, a little embarrassed. He never liked being around when people fell apart. It happened in combat, but otherwise, almost never. Young men were usually too deeply invested in pretending to be tough and brave to fall apart over nothing. They would have plenty of real opportunities for that later.

"The area of a triangle," Franklin went on, the tip of his pen circling, "there is a formula for that. Simple high school geometry. Damn, I can't remember it. No geometry books out here, Sergeant." He shook his head.

Hawk, a man with a solid second grade education, said, "Well, sir, if you make that triangle into a square and divide by two, you'll get your area."

"Hmm. Yeah." He smiled. The yellow in his eyes turned white again. "You know, that's right."

"Old roofer's trick."

"By God." Franklin looked up. "We're stopping. I better see what's going on. It looks like this might be it for the night. I'd better finish this later." Hawk nodded silently and Franklin stood. The Captain stumbled ever so slightly as he walked away. Hawk knew that Franklin might be in trouble. In the tropics, if you did not feel well, you were going to feel a lot worse tomorrow.

Joe Canlon, who had been hovering nearby, sat in the rickety chair vacated by Franklin. "How you like this place?" Joe asked.

"I think I could do without it."

"That ain't no shit. Are we ever gonna stop? There's no end to this."

Hawk shrugged. They sat there in some sort of stubborn defiance of the alien night with its onslaught of mosquitoes.

Clancy lit a fire in a rusting brazier teetering on the deck. The nights in this dank catacomb of nature were cool, in spite of the torrid days. The two Marines watched Clancy's unsteady hands, busily at work. Joe nudged Hawk as if Clancy were a joke that they were both in on.

"Hey, old timer, you been in this country long?" Joe asked. Joe would strike up a conversation with a horse trough. He expected to get a laugh or two out of the old goat. It was obvious that Clancy was no tourist, or newcomer. "Seen a lot of changes, I bet," Joe said. He smiled at Hawk. As a cosmopolitan New Yorker, it was Joe's opinion that Basah could not have changed much since the last Ice Age.

Hawk observed that Clancy had recognized Joe's attitude, and likely did not appreciate it.

"He means with the Japs and all," Hawk said. Hawk always found himself dragged into conversations when Joe was around.

"Aye. Somewhat," Clancy said. "Changed since I was your age, that's for damn sure. One man owned this country then. Owned it, he did. Only a few owned the whole island. The white rajahs, they call them. She's changed, for sure." Clancy walked toward them.

Hawk bit off a plug of tobacco and chewed solemnly. He feared Clancy was about to launch into some sort of reminiscing. As the mosquitoes worsened, this was not particularly welcome. This was the kind of thing Joe Canlon was good at instigating.

"Muree," Clancy call to a deckhand, "stoke that fire for us, lad."

Clancy sat against the gunwale with a groan. The grime of the boiler on his light clothing was darker than even the filth on the side of the boat. The fire in the brazier lit the stubble in his hollow old cheeks. He glanced wildly at Hawk and Joe, looking just a little on the crazy side. They distinctly smelled the liquor from Clancy's mythical bottle. Hawk sensed the winding up of a drunken windbag.

"You're asking about old times, now," he began. *Oh, shit!* Hawk thought. *No, I wasn't.* "I remember young Mr. Winthrop," his voice grated out with an old and odd bitterness. "It was his day then, lads." Clancy rubbed the back of his hand across his forehead, in an effort to keep from smudging himself with the oil and grease on the front of his hand. The purpose of this gesture had been lost in his lost youth, back when some part of him might have been cleaner than another, for the back of his hand was just as dirty and stained as the front. "I was a boy, then," he continued, "though I wouldn't have fancied you calling me one. I was a fiery lad. I remember him bedight in his white finery with the red sashes and plumes." Clancy made a short clicking sound. "He was a spectacle. Now them was the days when I judged a man by his finery, before

I learned the shift of a man's eye and the sprawl of his limbs."

Joe shifted uneasily. He painfully squinted a bit, and stared at Clancy with stupid fascination. Hawk lolled there, as if dead. Clancy swallowed hard, perhaps longing for his invisible bottle. After a moment, he steeled himself to go on, without it.

"He had the 'grab,' did he. It's something that neither you nor I will have. A bloke such as that sees the till lying on the table and picks it up for his own, and to be sure, from then on, it is his. While the others is too bashful, thinking themselves having no right to it, a man with the 'grab' walks in and takes it all, with the rest of them standing there. That's what your rich man is made of. That's the difference between you and me, Mr. Hawk."

Hawk raised his head, upon hearing his name, and spat to the side. *That ain't the only difference,* he thought.

Clancy swallowed hard again. "Hidebound and convinced are we from the cradle, if we even had one, to the grave, which we will have, that we were meant for work, and that work will make our fortune." Clancy shook his head. "Work makes only men like us to spawn other men to pick up the yoke. It does!" The old drunk raised a brow and pointed an eye at Joe, who sat there with his mouth open. The light of the fire caught the white of the ravaged old eye, and Joe closed his mouth and sat back.

"Well, mate, there is justice to being a poor man. The world's your coffer and the world is an uncommon place to a rich man. They have the horror of it, the fear of having to wallow in it. They fear it so much, they don't learn the heart of it, seeing as how it don't reflect on them none." Clancy looked up at the blind sky and smiled a ferocious smile.

It smelled smoky on the deck, and the mosquitoes had fled.

"Mr. Winthrop was killed by a worthless lay-about, right in the streets of Hazelton. Shot down like a stray cur. It was a fair fight...I'll swear to it...but, phoo, my word is no good. It's true, Mr. Winthrop was fleeing the scene and his heels took the brunt of it. But he was just as dead, lads. And they hung the lay-about. They had to do that much. That's all they could do to him though. Jenkins was his name. But Mr. Winthrop was just as dead, all the same.

"Having means don't make you one of the Lord's own immortals. No, it was Jenkins that did that much for him. You two are young men, men that still got arms and legs that do what you will them to do. You could stumble onto a stash yourselves before the end of it. Remember, it won't make you an immortal. There is an end to it after all. You can't walk on the water or still the winds, or spit in the face of a lay-about."

Clancy aimed his accusing white eye at Hawk. Hawk stared back at him, having no idea as to what he was being accused of. He knew as much about the fragility of mortality as any man. He didn't need any lengthy parables from the edge of civilization. Or, so he thought at the time, on that smoky night. He still had things to learn about riches and lay-abouts—and the loss of one's soul.

He spat on the deck and Clancy's accusing eyes slid over to Joe Canlon. Joe cleared his throat.

Clancy's tone softened a bit at the unspoken hostility. He sensed these two had been through quite a bit and perhaps would not be as impressed as your average callow young man. "You're only a man, no more than that gentle animal stoking the fire there," Clancy nodded at Muree, half hidden in a bluish white cloud around the brazier. "There's the justice of being a poor man. A blanket is a blanket, a woman is a woman, and a drink—" Clancy nodded warmly, "—is still a drink. Mr. Winthrop and his finery has long since rotted, and I've seen the sunset many a day since. No, lads, the 'grab'—a pirate has that. It's baseness and nothing more."

Hawk coughed and leaned forward. "I reckon so, sir."

Clancy looked at the deck. The quick madness had left his eye. "If I could be a lad again, I'd want an education. Something inside me to please me when my head was alone. Ach. To be a lad again!" He shook his head.

Hawk looked over at the now flaming brazier. He spat out his tobacco and took a drink from a canteen. After a minute, he yawned. Joe stretched. Clancy saw that the evening's entertainment had ended. It was his last chance to interject the moral of this convoluted story.

"Don't believe that it's an accident to no purpose that you're here. Have they not told you why you're going out to this, of all forgotten places, lads?" Clancy asked suddenly. He watched the eyes of both Hawk and Joe, looking for some clue as to the truth.

Night birds moaned long and eerie cries behind them, cries of the dead, perhaps, who had been asked this same question time and again over the centuries.

"Why, sure," said Hawk, in his heavy Mississippi accent.

* * *

LUKA LED his patrol out of Sacred Blood. He had been involved in several ambushes of the Japanese over the course of the past two years. He knew the backcountry as well as any man. The American in charge of the Mission had placed Luka over the other civilian guerrillas, with a rank of corporal. He noticed that the white men did not like to venture into the bush. Luka had heard that this would change when the American Marines arrived. He hoped so. He hoped that the Americans were here to fight the Japanese. He suspected their motives. White men had come into this area before. They came to look, but they never found anything.

Luka had plans for his future. Once the Japanese were driven out, as he fully expected the Americans to triumph, this land would likely become independent. The weakened Dutch hold on it would be even weaker still. Luka could rise in importance then, as a former freedom fighter and ally of the Americans. He could, in fact, become a ruler in the new order.

Luka halted his patrol about three miles northeast of the mission. The Japanese had been reliably spotted here a few days earlier. Luka picked three point men and sent them ahead while he rested the others. The corporal caressed his Browning Automatic Rifle, the symbol of his authority, as he waited. He could be forgiven for this, as even the Americans coveted the position of being a BAR man. He liked playing soldier. The point men disappeared into the undergrowth, where the light of the bright moon could not reach.

A thing resembling a medieval Satan, or perhaps, resembling a great goat walking upright, depending on one's imagination and beliefs, followed the point men. The thing did not stumble as the men did, for its red eyes could see clearly in the night. It walked slowly, but its pace was steady and sure, as it wound unencumbered through the vines that tripped them. The creature was deliberate and quiet. The men met with this unusual creature only five minutes out into the darkness. Luka never found his point men. They did not return. What they might have thought, when they suddenly encountered their attacker, would only be conjecture. Their folklore was filled with jungle devils.

5

RIVERBOAT ATTACK

THE NEXT DAY ON THE PAGEAS GAVE EVERY INDICATION OF being a repetition of the first. Hawk felt a difference, however, as if they had crossed some unwelcoming imaginary line. The density of the jungle increased, possessively gripping the slow-moving river. The jungle squeezed subtly, but with unmistakable strength. The cramped quarters, the narrow banks, the low hanging trees, were ideal for a trap. Intelligence had indicated an absence of enemy presence, and even without that reassurance, one could become complacent due to the remoteness of the surroundings. The six thousand Japanese that had fled the coast, however, had to be somewhere. And after all, when one goes farther into something, he must be getting closer to something else.

The boat stopped.

The hull scraped a shallow sandbar, the engine straining without result. The operators did not consider the interruption a crisis, merely standard navigating procedure. The crew managed to pull the boat free.

Captain Givens tried to avoid the permanent and

the obvious obstacles that the waterway had to offer. Some of the shallows had appeared between his scheduled trips, and caught him by surprise, causing a lot of wear and tear on the bottom of the craft. But that is how it was done.

During the first day, where the river was deep, there had been no abrupt halts. Hawk was therefore unprepared when the boat stopped again, only a half hour after the first stop.

"What'd we hit?" Hawk asked Clancy, seeing nothing.

"Rock. Tree. Sand," Clancy offered choices. He was busy telling his native crew to put their backs into the poling. Their backs were strong, though they proved unable to free the boat. Whatever lay just under the opaque and unfriendly water persisted in its concealment.

"What now?" Hawk asked, curiously observing the primitive operation from close range. For all of the crew's experience, he saw no evidence of any brain power at work in solving these frequent problems. It was as if the workers were confronting the wilderness for the first time. The Marine watched the motionless walls of vegetation with even more curiosity. He was starting to dislike the entire set up.

"We'll pull her loose," Clancy assured him.

Let me loose. Hawk thought that he actually heard a voice come from the leaves around him, pleading with him. Probably just too good a memory, he consoled himself. The exact tone and pitch of the woman on the plane had sliced a groove in that portion of his brain where such grooves are sliced.

He walked around to the other side of the deck,

looking intensely at different conglomerations of leaves, and finding Joe Canlon along the way.

"Good way to get bushwhacked," he told Joe. Joe looked at the monstrous greenery jealously guarding the brown river, raising his eyebrows in agreement. "Be ready for damn near anything," Hawk said, and repeated the warning to Captain Franklin.

Franklin took Hawk's advice a good deal more seriously than had Joe. He arranged the men along the gunwales, their weapons locked and loaded. Clancy watched the precautions with some anxiety. He had made this run many times. It was just his job. The commonplace was taking on a different complexion today. Nevertheless, he went on unhurriedly with his work. The tourists were probably just a little restless. The Pageas always left strangers nervous. It took a while to get used to the peace and quiet.

A winch had been fastened onto the prow of the riverboat for just such emergencies. Clancy and Muree played the grinding cable out. Another crewman went over the side with the hooked end of the cable in hand. He waded to the riverbank far ahead of the boat, braving the many poisonous water snakes, and lashed the chain at the end of the line around a sturdy tree. Clancy ordered the cable reeled in, and the boat pulled herself off the obstruction with a throaty, grating complaint. The old girl shimmied to freedom.

"Have to check her ass on that one," Clancy laughed heartily. He instructed the crewmen to look for holes in the underside. He sent Muree below to check for leaks.

Hawk knew that all of this was not unusual. He had been around a lot of half-assed operations before. He also knew that such interruptions were dangerous in the light of current events. He wished for a more streamlined approach to the stalls, but had no suggestions.

The launch vibrated into motion again. It was just another day on the job for the old boat. It knew that it had to work. It could give the men a little vengeful trouble now and then, but eventually they would triumph, and the boat would have to plow through the muddy water again.

Joe looked over the side at the passing stream. He was in deep thought. He considered the universality of water. It was all over the world, even here. The same water had been at Guadalcanal, it was in the Hudson River, and it all connected to here. This was about as profound as Joe could get.

An hour passed, with similar disconnected observations. It was a little boring. Although, Joe well knew what could come out of all of those leaves out there.

The bottom scraped something again. It was a long, warning scrape, the kind that a man could think about while it was happening. It sounded like the hull might clear it, if it survived a puncture. The crewmen pushed dutifully with their poles to help the beleaguered craft. The keel rubbed and wallowed in the sand. Progress slowed to a tedious slide. Then the prow struck something solid and the contest ended.

Clancy screamed obscenities. "She's hung good this time. It's the damn water level. Never been this low." Muree released the clutch, letting out the winch, and a weathered brown crewmen waded to the far, right bank with the cable.

Hawk paced the deck. He glared at the rain forest. His limited authority over the situation prompted him to call for some sort of action, some sort of protest over this business-as-usual approach. His business was not usual.

He finally advised Givens to take greater pains to sail a smooth course, and to try to avoid these barriers. If they had to go slower, then they would go slower.

The punishment for their complacency started mercifully enough. Sharp cracks came from everywhere and nowhere, holes torn into the deck and wheelhouse roof. The crewmen ran for the cover of the tin-roofed shed. The Marines ducked along the gunwales. Their backs were protected by the wheelhouse and by another little shed, that stood over a ladder leading below the deck. Hawk stood inside the smaller shed, his legs on the iron stairway descending into the hold. Joe, Clancy, and Franklin clung to the ladder under him. Muree stood in the darkness below all of them. The attack had been sudden, but slowly executed. Almost everyone had chosen a place of safety, and arrived there intact.

The sharp-sounding shots continued to land heavily on the deck. They cracked and snapped into the wood, slapping up splinters, and ringing echoes and wisps of steam from the metal. The Americans hid and gathered their wits.

"I didn't hear anybody call for a corpsman," Joe said. Hawk glanced down below at all of the eyes glowing in the dark beneath him. Clancy had put out the kerosene lantern. Given that the enemy had made the first move, it was remarkable that no one had been hit.

Or so they thought at the time.

"No. Not yet," Hawk replied, shaking his head. He tried to pick out likely sources of the shots from the blind sameness of the thicket surrounding him. He knew that anything could happen. That's what combat was all about. The harmless shots may have had a purpose. The enemy could be herding everyone into neat little clumps, in preparation for a follow up mortar barrage. That would be logical in a fight between troops with standard armament on the front lines.

Here, nothing was logical.

"I've heard them Japs ain't the best marksmen," Clancy commented, his voice shaking with a certain hopefulness.

"Good enough," said Joe. "Lot of 'em got scopes. I ain't going for no strolls out there."

"Somebody's gonna have to," Hawk growled. "Unless we plan on homesteading this hump of shit."

Captain Franklin climbed past Joe and up to Hawk. "I've got to get some return fire trained on those woods," the Captain told Hawk.

An M1 boomed from nearby.

"There you go, Captain," said Hawk, putting a restraining hand on the officer's shoulder. Others began to fire into the jungle. The American fire was louder than the light cracks of the Japanese rifles, and soon reached parity in volume. "These boys know what to do. No sense running around out there just yet."

The adrenaline was flowing, as was the ammunition. Hawk saw no need to conserve it at this point. Somebody might even hit one of the hidden bastards. Franklin still wasn't quite satisfied with his position in the hold.

The Captain stared intently at the light on the deck above him. He knew that he had to do something. He didn't intend to say it, but the words, "What are we going to do?" slipped out.

Hawk had to think of a solution—the right solution —before the Captain came up with something dangerous, just to be doing something.

The Sergeant sighed as the firing continued. A number of crises were brewing at once. A mortar crew could be setting up to finish the boat off. The enemy bullets were playing hell with the old boat's seaworthiness. Any number of the men on the deck could be tagged by all of that flying lead.

"How were you planning on getting this pile of shit out of here, Clancy?" Hawk asked the boatman.

"Well, sir. We could give her some steam, but I don't think she'll be clearin' this one, Mr. Hawk. Without some help."

"That winch is the only way out of here?" Hawk snapped, above the increasing roar out on the deck.

"Yes, indeed. But under the circumstances, I don't see that working."

"What the hell do y'all do when the winch don't work?" Hawk asked.

"Make it work," came the answer. "Some fellers will sit here and wait for a work crew from Hazelton to come along and free 'em up. We always been able to fend for ourselves."

Hawk nodded. "This is one the work crew might not appreciate."

The sniper fire stopped. Joe remained silent and waited hopefully. Maybe the Japanese would just go away. Maybe the return fire had discouraged them.

Hawk, however, waited for an explosion. He had been waiting for the feared mortars since the attack began, and had not been sure what to do when that unwelcome escalation occurred.

The quiet outside lasted for a full two minutes. A single shot snapped from the drooping trees and hit the wheelhouse roof. A volley from the MI's replied. So, that was it, Hawk decided. There would only be rifle fire. We're going to shoot it out. As discouraging as that seemed, it was some relief to think that a shelling would not sink the boat and leave the Americans stranded in the wreckage, here in the middle of an unexplored river.

"Okay." Hawk took a deep breath. "Who's going out there with me?"

No one answered. Joe knew that it was his place to speak up. The others had no idea as to what Hawk was suggesting.

"Who's gonna do what? The winch?" Joe asked. "Are you crazy? How are you getting a line on one of them trees and running that winch under fire?"

"I ain't, without help."

"You ain't, period. You ain't bulletproof."

"That line might already be on the tree," Clancy interjected. "Wasn't that line done put on the tree, Muree?" Muree shrugged. He had an angry expression. He had news for them, if they thought he was going out there.

"Damn, that would be a break. I think you're right," said Hawk. In the excitement, he had forgotten what was happening before the attack. "I'll have to take a look." He stuck his helmeted head out of the hold. He could not see over the prow. He stepped higher on the ladder, going from a crouch to standing up straight on a rung. A crackle of fire pounded from the jungle. Hawk dropped, like a weight, putting a boot in Franklin's face. Bullets seared through the shed wall and spewed off the iron ladder, ricocheting bright blue, and viciously, about the dark hold like random, supersonic fireflies.

"Shit!" Hawk said, ducking. Sparks of red, white, orange, and blue climbed up and down the iron stairway. The fire subsided at last. Clancy had been nipped on the cheek by the shattered pieces of metal, and Joe had a cut across the back of one hand.

"I saw the damn thing," said Hawk. "It's hooked, awright, but I didn't see no sign of the fella that hooked it. I think they got him. I guess that's what all the shooting was about at the beginning."

"So, it's hooked. Now what?" Franklin asked. Joe looked at him and shook his head. Hawk needed no encouragement.

"Hell, all we got to do is pull the boat off, now. And get the hell out of here," said Hawk. He glanced along the deck, at his eye level. Beyond several clusters of bullet holes, he could see the winch, bolted into the nose of the boat. He saw the lever that would throw the winch into gear. "Where's the clutch on that son of a bitch?"

"In the wheelhouse," Clancy answered. Hawk snarled an obligatory obscenity. Nothing like modern technology. "But we can hail Captain Givens to let out the clutch," Clancy added, pointing to a call hose in a rack on the bulkhead.

"Ah. Okay." Hawk nodded. "Then all I really have to do is throw the bastard in gear, and we're out of this?"

Clancy nodded with a dubious look on his terrified face. "I suppose, Mr. Hawk. That could be enough in itself to end your days. That's a good ways out there."

Hawk looked at Joe. "That ain't too bad," he said, ignoring Clancy's admonition.

Joe shook his head. He tended more toward the wait and see option. "I don't know," he said. "I'd let this play out a little. Maybe try something like that at night."

"Aw, shit. Night, my ass. Sit here all goddam day getting shot at? Wait for every Jap in the Pacific Ocean to toot on down here from hell and half of Georgia?"

"That's what I think," said Joe.

"What do you think, Captain?" Hawk asked Franklin.

"It's your call, Sergeant," Franklin answered. He wanted out of the deadly trap as soon as possible. "If, you're going to be the one doing it." But Franklin didn't want to order anyone to kill themselves.

Hawk craned his neck around Joe to look at Clancy. "Tell him to push in the goddam clutch."

Clancy snatched the hose from the clamp on the wall and barked an unrecognizable order into it. Joe raised an eyebrow.

"All you're gonna do is get your stupid head shot off," said Joe.

"I don't know, maybe not." Hawk climbed up again.

All things considered, the Sergeant felt that he was not confronted by an army. There had been no machine guns, no barrage, and not even a hand grenade. The fire did not seem concentrated. He was facing a handful of snipers with light, bolt action rifles. The Japanese were likely far outnumbered. If one were going to consider all of the factors, however, one had to also realize that the Japanese had some sort of elevation in their favor. They were shooting down onto the deck, whether from tree-tops, or the natural lay of the land.

Hawk eased up onto the deck. It was like easing into a shark's mouth. He had the full length of his body on the planking before the shooting erupted. A shot exploded an inch in front of his nose. It broke the board in the decking, leaving a splintered V-shape of wood in front of his eyes. That was not your standard Japanese 6.5 mm rifle round. So much for the light, bolt action rifle theory. There would be no trips to the sick bay for the person hit with one of those babies, just a shovel full of dirt in the face. He pulled his body over the splintered hole. The sharp wood stabbed at his chest. The discomfort did not even register as another ripping blast split the wood on the right: another of the larger rounds. Someone out there was directing a heavy degree of stopping power Hawk's way. He was likely the most visible target, and getting the most serious attention from the enemy, although he heard more firing and ricochets, landing elsewhere, throughout the boat. The two large caliber misses were the only shots that he encountered before he reached the winch. His arm reached up and his fingers closed on the lever.

He pulled it out and back toward himself. A bullet struck the tip of the spool, spitting flecks of metal into his eyes and across his upturned face. He pivoted on his belly and crawled back for the companionway in the hold. Three shells perforated the corrugated wall of the shed covering the hold. He dove headfirst down the ladder. A tangle of arms caught him.

Hawk dug at the metal in his eyes, blinked, and spat more pulverized metal from his mouth. His chest heaved. "Aw'ight," he gasped, "tell him to let the clutch out."

Joe and Captain Franklin pulled Hawk to his feet. Clancy yelled the command into the funnel on the end of the hose. They heard the sound of the winch, and everyone sat down. The heavy boat began sliding again, though it strained greatly. The winch continued grinding louder, until it screeched, and they were no longer moving.

The unusual sound made Clancy jump to his feet. "Hold her!" he screamed into the funnel. Captain Givens pushed the clutch in, disengaging the motor of the winch.

"What's wrong?" Hawk asked.

"Check it," Clancy said, "I think the winch's breaking loose from the bow."

"*Check it?*" Hawk repeated. Checking things wasn't easy, but he did it. He thrust his head up into the now familiar meat grinder and pulled it back quickly. The base of the winch had rocked forward and two of the four bolts that held its frame to the deck had become unfastened. They dangled in the noon day sun.

"It's come unglued," Hawk told them.

"Aye, I seen the bolts needed tightening at the last sandbar. Good news, though, the threads ain't stripped, lad. They just unscrews themselves pretty often with the vibration and all. They've just got to be tightened some," Clancy said.

"Is that right?" Hawk asked angrily. "That's all?" *Good news.* The ratio of problems, danger, and chances of success were getting thinner. Maybe it was just those big holes in the deck that were getting to him. The damned things looked like .45 calibers. Hawk held his breath. "Awright..." He exhaled violently. He knew this was not going to be easy. "What kind of wrench do I need?"

"It's American-made. Five-eighths inch open end," Clancy responded immediately. He had tightened the bolts approximately a thousand times over the course of his employment here.

"Okay. We got one down here?" Clancy took a five-eighths open end wrench out of his back pocket. "Always carry that one with me." He handed it to Hawk. It was old, worn, thin, and greasy, just like Clancy.

"We gotta slack up some on the cable to get that bastard sitting level again," Hawk said, taking the wrench. "I'm gonna try and throw it in reverse, and then you're gonna give the word for Givens to give me some slack. The machinery's gotta ease back down level on the deck to bolt it. Somebody's gotta be watching all this, so there won't be any slip ups."

Joe knew that his number had come up. "Okay," he said.

Hawk crawled out. A slug whirred over his helmet with a spiraling whine. He smashed his face onto the filthy deck. One of the big holes lay smoking beside his head. "Goddam Jap son of a bitch!" he whispered. But it was encouraging. He had not been hit, yet again. He must be in a difficult to sight defilade. He inched forward. He heard at least three blasts striking the decking behind him. Hawk gauged his supply of luck, and it seemed to be running increasingly lower. He could safely cross this shooting gallery only so many times. Someone out there was likely enjoying the challenge he offered them. He inched forward again. The deck under his chin belched splinters. He moved faster on his elbows. He threw the lever forward, his hand high and exposed on the top of it. "Awright!" he screamed. "There it is!"

Joe got off easy. He didn't have to stick his head out. He didn't have to do anything. Clancy could hear

Hawk's excited shout and passed it along. The winch ground a bit, and as the cable slackened, the frame with its loose bolts settled back comfortably onto the deck.

"Okay, okay," Hawk called. He crawled into the extreme bow of the riverboat, seeking any kind of shelter from the piercing lead. He had a low gunwale to protect him there, and the tops of a couple of old tires that served as bumpers, or fenders.

The quickly fired enemy slugs bit at the wood in front of him like razors. He could see a half dozen of their blunted noses poking through the inside of the thick planks. With a little closer range, they might burrow through the bow.

A round hit the cable that was wound around the spool. The steel wire suffered little damage. Another round struck it with a hollow thunk. Hawk jabbed one of the bolts into its hole after a few shaky tries. He slipped the wrench around the bolt. It slid off. A shot skimmed his helmet. He felt the steel pot jump and shift on his head. Another round hit near the bolt he had been working on. He jerked his hand back and counted his fingers.

"Goddam!" he screamed in frustration. After bidding farewell to his fingers, he reached out again. The wrench merely slipped off again. He realized this time that it was not slipping off the head of the bolt, it was slipping off the bolt itself. It would not fit over the head.

He pulled his hand back and eyed the head of the bolt. "That bastard ain't no five-eighths," he whispered. Three rapid shots increased into an indeterminate number. Explosions smacked the bow, rang off the spool, and jumped across the lines of cable. A line of holes splashed across the deck.

"God Almighty!" Hawk dropped the wrench. Time to go. He ran mostly on his knees and dove for the shed over the hold. Bullets followed him closely, and showered the shed for a full two minutes after he disappeared inside.

The men lay inside with their faces on the bottom of the boat. The firing relaxed into its usual desultory pattern. The Americans were returning the fire in earnest now. Amidst all of this fury, no one had been hit, and no cries had been heard from the forest.

The five men sat up in the hold, staring at one another. "It wasn't no five-eighths, Clancy," Hawk informed him, fixing his deadly eyes on the little mechanic.

Clancy looked dumbfounded for a moment. "Ah," he said, "I recall I told Muree to change it out this trip. The bigger bolts fit tighter. I thought it might help. Forgot about that. Did you do it, lad? Did you change them out?"

Muree nodded solemnly, but said nothing. Hawk didn't like that.

Hawk slid roughly toward Muree. The casualness of this riverboat operation was finally getting to him, now that it included his crawling across the simmering deck every five minutes. The procedure was a little too loose for one routinely held to Marine Corps standards. Trial and error was fine and dandy for undershirted idlers sucking on a bottle in the noon day sun. Today, it was not appreciated.

"Hey, sport, can you talk?" he demanded. Muree slid quickly away from him and said nothing. Hawk was not going to let it go at that. "You got any more surprises, you little shitbag?"

"Better answer him, lad," Clancy advised.

"No, sir."

Hawk continued breathing heavily and glaring at Muree. Those present generally feared that there was not going to be any tolerance for language barriers, shyness, or selective mutism. Had Captain Franklin not been present, things might have become a little more heated. Hawk finally stood, turned away, and leaned against the ladder. The firing outside echoed inside the hollow darkness below the deck. Hawk hoped for an enemy assault. He wanted to get his hands on someone. This one-way flow of lead was not his style.

"I don't know," Hawk sighed at last, ready to move forward. "Time to try something else."

"Maybe it's a left-handed thread?" said Joe.

"Nah. That'll be the next goddam thing. I guess a three-quarter would fit it. You got one?" He turned to Clancy.

"We use something different for that," said the old man.

"Then get it."

Muree disappeared into a darker corner and came back with a wrench. Hawk inspected it. The number had been worn off. It was probably stamped in millimeters anyway, or some crazy foreign shit. It looked to Hawk like a three-quarter. He had to bet his life on it.

The men noticed a lull in the firing outside. A moment's rest would have been welcome, but Hawk knew that this was his opportunity. Whatever the Japanese were doing out there, they probably wouldn't do it again.

Hawk ran across the deck during the brief cease fire. He shrank into the protection of the bow, not expecting the peace to last. As if in response to his concern, the shooting started again, although a little late to have any effect on him. Ignoring the noise as something irrelevant, he went to work. Lying on this side of the winch provided him a good deal more cover than what he had during his other efforts. The wrench bit again and again into the head of the bolt until it was tight. He gave it another twist. Deftly, he moved the wrench to the other bolt. He had a better view and more room to work with this one. He switched to the box end of the wrench, tightening it down more quickly than the first.

Hawk reached up and slapped the lever down, activating the winch. He got up and ran. All of these were simple moves to make, but any one of them could have been his last. He thought only of the obstacles, and how to remove them, without considering his own sudden removal from the sequence of events.

The men in the darkness of the hold again waited for some sort of positive result. Hawk jumped down the ladder, pointing to the funnel of the call hose, before finishing his descent. Clancy gave the order. The boat pulled itself slowly forward.

Joe slapped Hawk on the back. That was about all the glory anyone would get out of that day. It wasn't over, but things had improved.

Joe came up with the next suggestion for dealing with the attackers. "Rifle grenades might do something to them, Captain," he said. "You know, spray them woods with them, and you're bound to get somebody."

"Yes, if we aren't going to lose this one, we might as well try to win," said Franklin.

As the boat moved slightly away from the point of attack, it became increasingly safer to move about the deck.

Franklin ascended the ladder. He had been impressed with Hawk's initiative, and even more so with his ability to put an idea into action. He realized that he could count heavily upon him. He resolved to confide in Hawk as to the importance of this mission. The enlisted men had not received the same briefing as the officers. The Captain had been advised not to divulge any of the higher level secrets, unless it became absolutely necessary. But a sighted man can do more than a blind man, and Franklin wanted Hawk to see what the Captain saw when they got out into that jungle.

"Better be careful on that deck, Captain," Joe Canlon advised. "They got us sighted in."

Franklin was not a novice when it came to combat. He would not have been in charge of the operation had he been. He knew how to move about under fire. He knew that the situation was still dangerous.

He ordered several men to attach their rifle grenades to the slotted M1 muzzles. Hawk, still catching his breath, heard the rifle grenades spew through the leafy foliage beside the river. The shock of the strikes vibrated on either bank as the cigar-shaped missiles ultimately connected with any sort of solid object.

Hawk stepped leisurely up to the top rung of the ladder. Smoke lingered over the water like a creeping, swirling ground fog. He decided to squeeze a few rounds aimlessly into the trees. He figured he might just hit one of the no-good bastards. He watched a rifle grenade speed straight and low, like a torpedo, into the green verdure along the bank, until it struck something.

Leaves fluttered down through the smoke following the blast. Still, there was no outcry from the enemy. Had all of that firepower totally missed?

The riverboat glided freely now, having cleared the offending shallows. The winch continued pulling it, and the bow veered ominously toward the bank where the cable had been lashed. The tree around which the cable had been chained seemed to be pulling the boat toward it, like a green monster.

"Watch that brush!" Franklin ordered, as the boat approached the bank. "There could be a boarding party over there, or grenades!"

The tow line slackened as the boat angled nearer to the anchoring tree. Standing on the deck by now, but within the shadow of the wheelhouse, Hawk noticed that they were floating rapidly toward one side of the river. He shouted to Clancy.

"Stop the winch!" Clancy gave the order, but the boat continued to glide. "Steer away from that bank! The woods are full of Japs!"

"But we're tethered, Mr. Hawk. We have to go over there and untie her!" Clancy replied. "We have to get close enough!"

"Ain't you got no cable cutter? What the hell? Have you lost your goddam mind?"

Franklin directed men to the side of the boat nearing the bank, to prevent any possible boarding. A Marine ran across the deck in front of Hawk, and was toppled by a single cracking shot from the forest. He fell solidly without a twitch, his face aimed up at Hawk. His eyes were open and his tightly strapped helmet had a hole in it. A curtain of blood descended from beneath the helmet. He was a young man, but he looked gaunt and older. He had probably been through the entire war, and it ended here. He looked small and dead.

Bent double, his limbs moving exceptionally fast, Clancy carried the cable cutter in one hand and a sledge hammer in the other, stopping between Hawk and the corpse. His errand complete, he dashed back to the hold. Joe Canlon ran to Hawk and took the cutter, a wedge-like guillotine. He wanted to be free of the deadly cable, and out of here.

"Get up behind the bulkhead there," Hawk waved Joe forward. "Put that thing on the cable and I'll hammer it." The cutter looked dull, and at least a hundred years old. Joe managed to get fairly good cover as he fitted the device over the cable. Hawk stood with one leg on the gunwale and swung the hammer high overhead. He brought the heavy hammerhead down on the wedge with a vengeance, but it was too dull. It didn't matter, Hawk was not stopping. He pounded it again, and again.

Finally, the cable surrendered to the unrelenting blows. It parted into two silvery edged portions, and the boat veered toward the center of the river again. The severed line hung defeated from the tree and down into the water. Hawk breathlessly threw the heavy sledge hammer into the middle of the deck.

Upon Franklin's orders, rifle grenades again lashed out from both the port and starboard sides. Smoke and noise obliterated the sight and sounds of the jungle. If the Japanese were out there, they were likely blinded by it all. Only one last shot issued from the clouded, anonymous surroundings, and as the gods of war would have it, it claimed a victim.

Captain Givens turned over the old engine. In minutes, they had sailed to safety.

It was a minor engagement by any standard of the war. Three had been killed, and only two were Marines. It was discovered that the crewman who had initially tied the cable to the tree had been shot before returning to the boat. They placed Franklin next to the other American who had been killed. Hawk shook his head. He had liked the Captain.

"Shame. Kid like that," the Sergeant said. "Gawdamighty." He was well aware of the arbitrariness of war, and this proved it once again. Hawk had crawled through at least two dozen well aimed bullets on the deck, without a scratch. Franklin went on the deck once and was dead, felled by a single shot. How many times had he heard of men killed their first time in combat, and yet others seemed to survive indefinitely?

Was someone deciding these things somewhere? And what was the message? There was probably something in the Bible about it, and he had probably heard it. But hell if he could put it all together. To assign it all to luck would have been a disservice to the recognition due the skills of Sergeant Hawk, however, for he had been trying to avoid being shot, whereas Franklin had not been.

"I told him not to go on the deck," said Joe. "He had them bars on, they probably picked him out. That thing on his helmet."

"Guess he felt like he had to," said Hawk. He knew a little bit about that feeling. "A kid like that. Shit."

Clancy took off his cap and looked down at the dead. "It's a poor man's justice," he said. "A poor man's going nowhere, but he always gets there, Mr. Hawk."

"Yeah," Hawk spat. Whatever in the hell that meant. He didn't know how rich or poor Franklin had been. He knew that the young fellow didn't know how to figure the area of a triangle. "I guess he does."

That was one of the most irritating things about being dead: people standing over you and saying stupid shit. He squinted at the sparse shafts of light able to cut through the trees, and reflect upon the water. He felt the loss, physically, as a vacuum inside his diaphragm. Perhaps he would have grown to think less of Franklin as time went on, or even hate him. But all that, whatever the future had held, was just over.

6

THE FORBIDDEN VOLCANO

THE VOYAGE GOT UNDERWAY AGAIN EARLY THE NEXT morning. Dull hours passed. The waterway was narrowing. An attack like the one on the previous day would have been much more deadly along this stretch.

"I ain't never seen anything like this," said Joe Canlon, as a clump of leaves and vines brushed his face. "Why in the name of God would anybody want to come into something like this?"

"You'd have to have a pretty good reason," Hawk answered. He had just been making conversation, but after he said it, it occurred to him, that it was the truth. And yet, here they were, for no reason.

A small dugout craft bounced against the riverbank ahead of them. It was an unusual apparition. There had been no traffic of any sort on the river, nor any sign of life. A person, native to the locale apparently, waved a greeting to them from the dugout. He wore a bowl haircut and little else. The encounter was evidently so unusual that Captain Givens cut his engine. Lieutenant Biedeker, now in charge, in the absence of Franklin, leaned over the rail to speak with the man. Givens came over as well.

Hawk watched it all silently from a distance. He didn't know much about Biedeker. He didn't really want to know much, but he supposed that he soon would. Biedeker had seemed content to let Franklin and Hawk run things up until this point. The dynamics had changed.

Several more dugouts lay hidden in the leaves along the side of the bank. A nipa swamp languished along the shore, like a dismal and diseased extension of the river itself.

Word spread that Sacred Blood Mission was located a few hundred yards through this same swamp. They had finally arrived—somewhere—although that somewhere did not appear to boast of any grandeur. Givens probably would not have found the hidden entrance to the Mission without the aid of the lone sentinel waiting there for them. It looked like any other stretch of wilderness along the Pageas. The swamp, indistinguishable from hundreds of others they had passed, concealed the little establishment, which had been built on an island in its center.

"Prepare for debarkation!" Biedeker called.

"Say! We're getting our asses debarked!" said Joe. "Things are looking...up?"

Hawk boarded a dugout, as did the others. They were powered in part by the same type of tribesmen who had first greeted the boat. The swamp did not look very navigable, but evidently that was the plan.

The marsh looked no better from within its dark confines. The palm trunks grew close together, and instead of paddling, the men propelled themselves along by pushing and pulling at the tree trunks, winding tightly through the natural maze. The trunks felt like wet paper. The lighting was several shades darker than even that on the gloomy river. Clouds of white insects, moth-like creatures, swirled from tree to tree. Leaves slapped across the faces of the men. At their passing, unhealthy pools of mist broke apart, as might disturbed old ghosts, chatting about their ancient regrets. The voyage became a sodden effort, like boring through a humid fabric. The water fell shallow in places, with the dugouts gliding over slick mud. The mud stank like death.

"You know," Joe called to Hawk over his shoulder, "This makes that damn river boat look good. This is about as deep into nothing as you can get." He looked over the side. "This is some scary shit. No telling what's in this water."

"Yeah." Hawk latched onto a tree, pulling his canoe along. "This must be one hell of a place we're going to. I mean, I wasn't expecting San Diego, but...shit."

After a relatively short while, they reached the more than welcome sight of the island. A little civilization can look like a lot under such circumstances. Because the island was large, it did not resemble an island to them upon their landing. The men climbed out of the ferrying boats and onto a small rotting pier fashioned from sticks. The pier looked as if it might have gotten lost in all of the surrounding nature a long, long time ago.

The file of men, burdened with equipment piled on their backs and shoulders, snaked through well-tended sago fields, and untended, rampant tropical foliage, by means of a dry and narrow path.

A log palisade surrounded the mission. Inside the big gates, the first thing to draw their attention was a large church building, plain in construction with an ironwood shingle roof. Two other even larger buildings stood on either side of it, though not arranged in such a way as to leave a straight avenue in front of the three of them. One of the buildings served as a commissary, galley, and general soup kitchen for both the residents and their visitors from the nearby forest. The other building served as a hospital. A few well-constructed, medium sized buildings made up the barracks and living quarters. Some of the occupants, presumably those with status, had their own one room structures. Other and more primitive sheds were scattered about haphazardly, serving as work and store rooms. An occasional hut of lesser craftsmanship also leaned here and there.

The curing of sago appeared to be the primary industry of the little establishment. Most of the shed-like structures were open walled and grass roofed. The grounds, overall, appeared neat, clean and well maintained, as might a place with an adequate and convenient unskilled labor source.

The forest around the palisades had been cleared to varying extents for a distance of two hundred yards at the most. Beyond this were fields of other agricultural endeavors, arranged in no discernible pattern. The mission did not have the appearance of a military installation, and from its history, this might well have been intentional.

Captain Givens informed Lieutenant Biedeker that the riverboat had to make the return trip to Hazelton immediately. He had a schedule to keep. Traveling back down the river would be easier, on the boat's engines at least, but the captain requested a few men for protection, in light of the deadly encounter on the way into Sacred Blood. Biedeker, not liking this at all, but realizing the danger that the boat would face, consented to letting five men return with the old barge to Hazelton. The Lieutenant took into consideration that he could be blamed if anything happened to the boat. He could also be stranded here—in this bird cage lining at the bottom of the universe—without the lifeline of the river. He had no orders regarding the escort, and had never heard Captain Franklin mention anything about having a duty to protect the returning boat.

The five men chosen to return did not appreciate the task, having to repeat their journey in the dugouts back to the boat, once more carrying all of the accoutrements they had just taken off. While Sacred Blood did not look like much, it looked better than the swamp, or the river.

The others watched with envy as the helmets of those returning disappeared along the leafy path back to the pier. The last to leave had a large orchid attached to his helmet. Those departing at least knew where they were going, and what was in store for them. For the others, the prospect of setting up housekeeping at Sacred Blood Mission for an indeterminate time, was a little daunting.

Clancy strolled out of the commissary dragging a dolly with a keg of rice beer rocking back and forth on it. The beer was a necessary prerequisite for the native crewmen. Hawk noticed the old boatman, and wondered why his employer had carried the barrel here on the boat at some point, just to carry it back later. A lot of duplicated effort seemed to go on in this place.

Hawk fell in with Clancy along the path to the pier, pulling the load for him. The Sergeant lifted the heavy barrel into the dugout. Clancy winked when he saw the ease with which Hawk handled it.

"Thankee, lad. As time goes by, a man needs a helping hand now and then." Hawk looked down at him from the pier.

"Good luck, podnuh. You might need it. Remember to stay in that hold when the shit hits the fan, off the deck."

"Aye, you're right. And you remember all I told you. Being rich don't mean you ain't ignorant. Get yourself an education."

Hawk waved as the canoe shoved off. "Yeah, I'll remember that," he said. *Crazy bastard. What the hell is he talking about?* Why was the old coot harping on that subject? Hawk had about as much chance of getting rich, especially getting rich *here*, as a turtle. He had to admit, however that the odds of getting rich were still much better than his getting an education, anywhere.

Clancy's canoe threaded its way through the trees. Hawk waved again.

"And don't forget your old friends when you get back!" Clancy called to him. *Right*, Hawk thought, *back from this place?* The old guy might have let a little too much river water soak into his thinking gear. Or a little too much fire water.

It took the rest of the day for the Marines to get accustomed to their new combat outpost. Biedeker set up a thin perimeter around the island, using native personnel to fill in the wider gaps. Watching this reinforced Hawk's fear of ending up in some sort of training detail. He saw the tribesmen enthusiastically carrying around their shiny, new weapons. This caused uneasiness among the new arrivals on several different levels, the first being the obvious possibility of getting accidentally, or intentionally, shot by one of the inexperienced locals. There was also the implication that the enemy out there existed in numbers too strong for the regular troops assigned here to handle.

The eastern shore of the Mission island was considered the most vulnerable, as the surrounding swamp was narrowest in breadth on that side. In all of these preparations, Hawk made an effort to avoid the executive decision-making end of things, steering himself toward the labor details, doing things like filling sand bags. This gave him the opportunity to make a few observations. Getting the lay of the land often saved your life. Granting a home field advantage might be accepted practice in sports, but there was nothing sporting about this, and nothing was granted.

Mr. Vincent Arnold occupied the largest of the one-room residences. Officially, he was a lay missionary in charge of Sacred Blood. He did not wear a uniform, and yet Biedeker acted especially subservient to him, and gradually, everyone else followed suit. No one explained the why or the wherefore of this, apparently one was supposed to learn things by example, and not ask questions. The air of secrecy was not exactly Marine Corps procedure. Hawk took it that Arnold was in charge of all of them, and that this was the way the OSS operated. He probably should have paid more attention when Major Wimberly briefed him on the pecking order here. He had not been interested at the time, assuming someone would tell him what to do when the time came. He had also assumed, however, that he would know who that person was. Were there other Mr. Arnolds, or only one? And how would you know the ranking Mr. Arnold, if there were more?

Biedeker called a meeting of the platoon leaders, during which he said little of note, other than restating the problem of the Japanese designs on Basah. The enemy effort consisted of the unprecedented reinforcing of the garrison already here on Basah, which was a major threat to the Allied effort. Another company of Marines was on the way. More would follow. Hawk listened patiently. The Japanese were always a threat to something. More men were always supposed to be coming. No real news here. Likely, nothing would change.

After the meeting Biedeker called Hawk aside. "Mr. Arnold wants a patrol to the east. We have to get a line on a primary base of operations the Japs are working out of. I told him you would be good for it. He has a map. You go as far as you can get in one day. Destroy every enemy constituent that can be safely eliminated. Disrupt their build-up in any way we can. Learn all you can. They've been sniping the natives at the mission. The Japs do anything to demoralize them, to discourage them from peacefully interacting with us. Two were shot last night and it caused an uproar. You know how natives are. Arnold thinks there is a big Jap outpost within a twenty-mile radius of here, and it is probably toward the east. I believe you have been briefed on what a big outpost means?"

"Yes, sir. They are bringing in their big shots. Maybe

relocating their government, or setting up something in exile," said Hawk.

"That's the general idea. We just have to do what we can with what we have, right now. Major Bearn is supposed to be on the way. This whole operation is going to...expand. I am hoping *we* expand in numbers before *it* does. We could be on the ground floor of an entirely new theater of operations here."

"Major Bearn was in the Raiders. He'll be good," said Hawk, finally able to have some confidence in somebody, or something, involved in the task at hand.

"Yes. The sooner he gets here the better," said the Lieutenant. They were both thinking the same thing: not just Bearn, Bearn *and* two companies of men. "I've already got two more fever cases and we just got here. We're going to need a steady supply of replacements, it looks like. They better keep that river open. We need some Marine transportation instead of that old garbage scow crawling back and forth."

"Yessir. If the Japs get hold of a fifty-caliber machine gun or a knee mortar, that's gonna be the end of that route." Hawk clearly recalled the holes in the deck of the old boat.

"Exactly. And probably, it wouldn't even take that much. Anyway, your patrol is set for tomorrow morning." He sighed. "We'll work out some of the details tonight."

"Yes, sir."

Hawk later checked on the sick men at the hospital, a habit he had gotten into elsewhere. It was always odd to see fighting men in such surroundings. It was a good reminder of how close you were to this forced helplessness, when you were out there dancing around in front of bullets. He needed a few reminders. Lieutenant Klemer was better. Klemer seemed like a hell of a nice guy, or maybe he was just glad to have a visitor, any visitor. He had been born in Lithuania and spoke with a slight accent. He had been through several of the recent campaigns. He assured Hawk that he would be back in action soon. After a short trading of information with the officer, the Sergeant went out the front doors of the hospital for a smoke in the entranceway there.

A French doctor from Saigon had been treating the fever victims. Hawk had been drinking unauthorized rice beer off and on all day, between sessions of carrying sandbags, and was feeling pretty sociable. He encountered the doctor near the open space in front of the door of the hospital and struck up a conversation.

"What kind of a thing you figure they got, Doc?" Hawk asked.

Dr. Lepreaux seemed too delicate for this rugged and remote outpost. He shrugged and dabbed his handkerchief to his thin-boned forehead. He looked uncomfortable in the fathoms of swimming heat. It resisted every motion of the body, including breathing.

The doctor spoke confidentially, as he might with another physician. "I don't know yet. We are studying the slides. It is an unusual malady, but the older cases look better. We will have to watch all of them, but I have recommended evacuation for the newest cases. They are all slightly built fellows, like birds. If they lose the will, they may become critical. It is very dangerous for one's health to be here in this place."

"Yeah. For more than one reason. Reckon it's the malaria or mumu?"

"I don't think so. I don't think I got your name?"

"I'm Sergeant James Hawk, sir."

"But, of course. A pleasure to meet you. I am Dr. Lepreaux. No, it resembles a severe dysentery. Dehydration is a problem. This is not the place for them. It might be a minor illness anywhere else, but..." He smiled at the Sergeant. "We do not know, do we? We are not anywhere else."

"Yeah? Well...that' sounds like there is some hope. They're pretty tough fellas... Is it catching, this stuff they got?"

"I am fairly certain about that. It is probably not transmitted from one man to another. Probably not. The literature suggests insect borne. I am thinking water borne." He shook his head and waved his hand. "All of this filthy water here. Either way, it is not transmissible."

"Well...they were all in first platoon."

Lepreaux shrugged. "A good observation, thank you. I'm not sure I realized that, or in any case, that I took notice. A coincidence, I would guess. We shall see. Something will present itself to us, and the mystery will be solved." He snapped his fingers. "That is how these matters are."

"I hope so. If you don't mind, I'd like to know what you turn up. The Lieutenant's kind of worried about it. The whole outfit might come down with that sh...crud."

"Certainly, Sergeant. It is so hot here, is it not?" Lepreaux smiled, and returned to the even more oppressive interior of the hospital.

* * *

HAWK MET the mysterious Mr. Arnold that night. Biedeker was there. Arnold was always referred to as

"Mister" Arnold, but Hawk figured the man was probably drawing a colonel's pay. He would watch closely when Major Bearn arrived, to see how they reacted to one another. He supposed all the secrecy was so no one could tell the enemy anything about Arnold, if captured. It was a little pretentious, and irritating, and Hawk saw why General MacArthur didn't like the OSS. If, this was even the OSS.

The meeting took place in Arnold's spacious hut, where a large map had been spread out on a table. The generators had shut down for the evening, and so the room's single light bulb hung dead, next to a supplementary kerosene lamp. The smell of the burning fumes created a confidential atmosphere. It just would not have been as mysterious with a light bulb, and a generator blasting in the distance. The mission was designated in the center of the map, and a healthy amount of blank space surrounded it on all sides. Arnold pointed to the southeast, indicating that Hawk was to patrol that area.

"Obviously, we're looking for Japs," Arnold said. He was a man in his late forties or early fifties. One eye veered slightly off course, so that you could not tell when he was looking at you. His face sagged a little, on heavy bone, in such a way that it still looked solid as rock. "Any Japs. What we would really like to find is a permanent installation. We have a lot of information about what they are supposed to be doing here, but no facts to confirm any of it. It's all speculation. They've been in the general area long before we arrived."

"Yes, sir," Hawk said. He basically had heard nothing of interest. He would be walking in the weeds, looking for Japanese. This was not exactly anything new. He spied a handful of cigars on Arnold's desk. It was kind of hard to pass up. He probably would have passed them up, if he had known for sure that Arnold was a colonel. "Mind if I have a smoke, sir?"

Arnold inhaled impatiently. "No, not at all, go ahead, Sergeant. Now, I am sending another patrol this way," he said, pointing to the northeast, "at the same time. One of you is likely to turn up something. I have a Sergeant Clifford Curry working with the natives. An excellent man, good with languages and the bush, and very experienced. They will be going here." He pointed to the northeast again.

Hawk lit his cigar without showing any sign of emotion. He knew Clifford Curry well. He was *not* an excellent man from Hawk's perspective. He was a conniving, crooked bastard. It had been almost two years since he had heard of Curry, and Hawk thought that he must be dead, or in the brig. A highly important secret mission would be the last place he would expect to hear Curry's name touted.

Hawk flicked the burnt match out the open window. "Yessir?" He squinted at the map through the cigar smoke.

"Yes," said Arnold. "Now, Sergeant Hawk, I want you to be on your guard, on the lookout, for anything unusual. Anything especially, let's say, that's not part of the natural terrain. Understand?"

Hawk was quiet for a moment, unsure as to how to answer, since he would quite obviously be both on his guard and on the lookout for damn near any and everything. He blew smoke toward the ceiling.

Arnold sized him up as a cocky, stupid brute. The

thick Delta accent added to this impression. And then, the cigar didn't help. Arnold's cigar.

At the same time, Hawk, too, was sizing Arnold up. There was something shifty about him. He had already discovered something "unusual" about the operation: Clifford Curry. "What exactly do you mean by unusual, sir? So's I have a reference point?" Hawk asked.

Arnold responded without hesitating. "Anything. Activity, people, places. Anything out there in that jungle that doesn't look like it's part of it. Understand?"

The kerosene lantern rocked back and forth above the map for some reason, sending gentle shadows gliding across the room.

"Yessir. I got it, sir." Hawk was not one to ask questions, unless there were going to be answers. Arnold wanted him to find something, but he wasn't going to tell him what it was. Just like he wasn't going to tell him *who* he was. The whole thing might have been a little tiresome in its opacity, except for the Clifford Curry angle. Hawk knew exactly who that gentleman was. He didn't believe that Curry would be wasting his time out there in that mess looking for pine cones and duck droppings. He was working an angle of some kind.

"Now," said Arnold. "Let me tell you a little bit about what you can expect to run into out there." Arnold started drawing little scratches on the blank spaces on the map. He described elevations, types of flora, and the thicknesses of vegetation. Hawk fought it valiantly, but he had to close his eyes as he listened.

Finally, the session ended. The Sergeant had the impression that Arnold did not care for him very much, as everyone bid their good evenings. He didn't worry about it, since he cared even less for Arnold. If the roles were reversed, Hawk would not pick Arnold to go on any patrols for him, or to do anything else. But Arnold was picking Hawk.

The Sergeant was tired when he reached his temporary quarters in an open-air laundry hut. He fell asleep immediately.

The next morning Hawk was up early preparing the patrol. Biedeker picked the men that were to go with the Sergeant, without any consultation, leaving Joe Canlon off the roster. Biedeker informed Hawk that the Mission was still in a defensive posture and that it would be a while before it could have the personnel necessary for any offensive action. Hawk supposed that this was a nice way of being told that if he ran into anything big, he could expect nothing more than the resultant collision. This left a lot of sharp edges on the orders that he had already received; which included, the mandate to attack the enemy.

As the Sergeant awaited the order to move out, he stacked his gear on a table the workers used to fold laundry. It was the same table he had slept under the night before.

Joe Canlon passed by with several men on a work detail. They all carried entrenching tools.

"Where y'all going?" Hawk asked.

"Dig some shit holes." Joe held up his shovel, pumping it proudly up and down.

"Good work if you can get it."

"Gotta know people. Where are you going?"

"Top-secret. You might be in with the Japs. Don't make me lie."

Joe rocked his head back and frowned. "No, seriously? Where you going? Looks like wild country out there." He stopped for a moment. "Wonder why I'm not going with you. Where you going?"

Hawk waved his hand across the panorama of the jungle around them. "Shit. Out there. Where is there *to* go?"

"Don't make sense. Well, I better get going before somebody shits their pants. You know what you need? You need a purpose, like me. That's how a man succeeds."

"Yeah. Dig 'em deep."

As dawn brightened, they turned the lights out in the hospital. Hawk unfolded his map, spread it on the table and studied it. It had been traced with carbon paper from the larger one. It was good for little other than giving one a relative idea of how far it might be from the coast or the river to here. There was a volcano about 20 miles to the east. That was about it. He supposed that a volcano would be kind of interesting. It had a name, but it was long and indecipherable on his version of the map. With a little study, he could also tell a little bit about the elevation and how that might affect the hike. He was basically going to have to cut his own trail. He looked forward to a little exploring.

A walk in the woods sounded good after being cooped up in one form of confining transportation after another for months. The farther he got from civilization, the better he felt. He was a self-sufficient unit that did not work well in civilization. He was a part of untamed and independent nature.

He sipped on a morning cup of rice beer, which helped to enhance his sunny outlook. As he folded the map, he was surprised to see Lieutenant Klemer up and about, carrying a bundle of canteens in one hand and a plate in the other. He stopped in front of Hawk.

"Filled your canteens," he said. "I brought you something, too. A hot breakfast." Klemer handed Hawk a plate of chicken and rice.

"Well, thank you, sir. Mighty nice of you." Hawk took it. That Klemer was all right. Though the sergeant had already had a can of C-rations, he quickly finished off the chicken and rice without any difficulty. You had to take your meals when you could get them.

"Going out today, is that right?" Klemer asked.

"Yeah," Hawk drawled, as if he did not want to go.

"I'll be glad when I can get up and around a little better. It makes you appreciate your health," he said.

"Sure enough."

"Just think of the people that spend their lives in the hospitals." Klemer turned his head sideways, as if he were ordering Hawk to actually think of it.

"Mm hmm," Hawk grunted, without thinking of too much of anything.

"You have to his feel sorry for sick people. The wounded and the maimed and the disfigured. They live in a different world, don't they?"

"Sure enough." Hawk nodded his way through the strange conversation. He supposed that Klemer was more of a foreigner than he had realized. They talked about crazy shit.

A woman in her early twenties walked past them. She had long and straight blonde hair. Hawk swallowed his beer a little too quickly. "Morning, miss," he managed to say. She smiled quickly.

"Good morning," the Lieutenant said, with a slight bow of the head. The woman didn't say anything. She swayed into the hospital. Hawk was relieved that Klemer had spoken to her as well, since he was not sure she was real. He saw no angel wings on her.

"Goddam." Hawk pushed his plate away. "Who the hell was that?"

"She is one of the bona fide civilians here," Klemer smiled fondly. "She is a nun, I think."

"Oh, shit."

"Yes."

"She ain't got no nun suit on," Hawk observed. The young lady had been wearing a blue jumper, with a hemline just below her knees. She may have had the face of a nun, or an angel, but the rest didn't fit.

"No. Not a Catholic, I suppose. I'm not certain. British or something." Klemer was still smiling and staring at the door she had passed through. His large eyes were misty, and easy to see beneath his balding scalp and large forehead. The officer sighed. "As I was saying, isn't it amazing the pain that people can live with?"

Hawk did not have to answer, as they both saw Biedeker coming out of the commissary. The party was about to start.

"Do I take this plate somewhere, sir?" Hawk asked Klemer.

"I'll take it. It's looks like you had better get going."

"Yessir. Probably see you in the morning, or so."

"Yes. Take care out there, Sergeant. Drink your canteen of water first and be sure to purify any after that."

Hawk was assigned an Iban scout named Luka. Luka had been on several patrols with Clifford Curry, and he had even led a few himself. He knew the immediate area surrounding the mission compound fairly well. No one knew the area farther out, with the possible exception of a few Japanese. No one was sure what the Japanese knew, but they had been here for years, and so it was believed that they knew quite a bit more than the Americans. And they were definitely out there. The prevailing questions were where and how many?

Luka appeared suited to the task of finding out. He had a bowl haircut, was short, powerfully built and heavily tattooed.

Hawk was given to understand that the rural native population were either lukewarm in their support of the Allied invaders, or apathetic. There was even some Japanese support in the urban areas of Basah, and the Dutch East Indies in general. Anti-Dutch and anti-British rebels could be found in the hinterlands. The Japanese had not done well at organizing these individuals to their advantage, and had not been very hospitable over all. The belief was that as the Japanese relocated to this area, that mindset would change. As the world crumbled around them, the Japanese had decided that maybe they needed a few more friends.

Luka led them out of the dense jungle surrounding Sacred Blood's island and onto a grassy plain of the mainland. Both the jungle and the plains were hilly, there being very little flatland. Well-traveled paths could be seen, though who was doing all of this traveling was a matter for speculation. Hawk was in charge of the patrol, and was instructed not to restrict himself to Luka's choice in either a route or a destination. This was easier said than done, having been set down in the middle of nowhere. The isolation was a tangible thing, and being in a group here felt like being on a small boat in a large ocean. Hawk began talking to Luka, with the hope of understanding the geography of the blind greenery he trudged through. Luka liked to talk, and few of the warring foreigners had ever talked to him at length. They only wanted to show him things, order him around, and hear him say how much he hated the Japanese.

Hawk asked about the absence of villages. He suspected that the Japanese would prefer to live off the industry of the local villagers. Luka replied that there were no villages this far from the river. The only indigenous people were the Penans, and most had migrated elsewhere because of the war. Even the Penans had never had permanent villages in the area. They moved around, hunting with blowguns and poison darts. When asked if they were dangerous, Luka gave a vague response that seemed to be negative.

They entered an area where the jungle thickened. It was still not as dense as that along the river. The trees were big and old and they shaded the ground more, discouraging the thicker undergrowth.

Luka shot a monkey for his lunch, drinking the blood from the bullet hole. When asked about the danger from any animals, he readily admitted there were many varieties of poisonous snakes, and it would be better to assume any snake was poisonous. And there were a lot of them. There were leopards, but they were small here, more like a wildcat, and they were relatively shy, but still not to be messed with. There were sun bears, who were fairly large and of a bad disposition. They were not as shy, and might just decide to visit you, regardless of your wishes. The people of the deep forest said there were tigers, but no one had ever really seen one. It was thought that maybe years ago, before the white rajahs, there had been tigers, but no longer.

The forest came to an end and they walked onto a rocky highland. A gray mountain could be seen in the distance, much higher than the surrounding hills. Hawk and Corporal Baker opened out their map. Baker had been with the squad for over a year. He and Hawk were not great friends, but they managed to get along because Baker was slightly insane and Hawk was entirely violent. They made good partners in dangerous situations, both quite willing to do the unthinkable. The mountain, one of the few things on their map, was the volcano, Delivalung. It was much closer to the mission than the chart indicated.

Luka looked at the mountain and shook his head. A cloud of volcanic steam obscured the gray marker's summit. "This is as far as men go," Luka said, gesturing at the mountain. "Pantung."

"Pantung?" Baker repeated with a laugh. He smiled crazily, with his eyes wobbling in their sockets. "Pantung," he nudged Hawk with his elbow.

"Uh...yeah," Hawk looked at him and then back to the scout. "So...like, what?"

"Cannot go there. In English, they say forbidden, and taboo."

"Oh. Why?"

"Angry spirits live there. English say ghosts, but spirits are so bad that there is no English word." Luka pointed and gestured at the rising smoke circling the invisible mountaintop.

"I'll be damned," Hawk commented amiably. "But... uh...has anybody checked this place out lately?"

"Nobody could ever go there, and come back. You see, yes?" Luka pointed to the west. "We go this way maybe. Yes?"

Hawk nodded thoughtfully. Delivalung was probably a full day's hike to the east. He sighted it with his compass and recorded the bearings. He was supposed to return to Sacred Blood by morning, and he suspected that he might have found what he was looking for. It was a nice quiet place with forbidden access, and closer than expected; an ideal place to nurture a Japanese army. Since no one had seen any Japanese bases of operation, if his guess was correct, they must have access to the staging area, this volcano, from another direction. He had not pinpointed anything, but with a larger and longer patrol, he felt that he could. Delivalung would have to be well scouted. Volcanoes meant caves, and to him, caves meant Japanese.

"Does that thing always smoke like that?" Hawk asked.

"Every time I see it."

"Does the damn thing ever blow?" Hawk slipped the map and his readings into a pocket on his belt.

"Many times. Not big. Always the fire rock flows from it, but never fast. Sometimes men can hear it at the mission. The ground shakes like thunder. Hurts only the bad spirits. Makes them very angry."

"I'll be damned," Hawk said again. "That would do it, I reckon." He slapped Luka on the back and turned to Baker. "This is it for today. Let's dig some holes. We'll probably rest up some and get going before daylight."

Luka nodded his approval.

"Scared of a little pantung, Sergeant?" Baker asked with his looney grin.

"Yeah. For now." Hawk took out a cigar and lit it. "We'll have to check that son of a bitch out good. I expect that's where they are. What do you think?"

Baker squinted at the gray phantom looming in the distance, silhouetted against a darkening turquoise sky. "Yeah. Could be. Spooky looking place. But, shit, they could be anywhere."

Another man walked up. His name was Carlson. "That is some sight, isn't it?" He asked the other two. They nodded enthusiastically. "Eye has not seen and ear has not heard what God has ready," he said.

Hawk nervously rubbed his nose. "Well, I'm thinking somebody's got something ready out there. Might not be God."

* * *

HAWK AWAKENED THEM EARLY, after the second watch, to get ready for the return. They lit a fire and made coffee. The night had been quiet. Luka sat with Hawk, watching the fire. Mosquitoes buzzed on the outskirts of the smoke.

Hawk sighed. "How'd y'all get along with the Japs?" he asked the scout.

"Hokay. They live in big village. Not bother you in country much. Never sure. Sometimes Jap share rice, sometimes chop your head off. Better to just stay away from Jap."

"I hear that they have been doing some sniping back at the Mission?"

"Not sure," Luka shook his head slowly. "People have been shot. Maybe Japs not shooting. Maybe Iban helping Japs. My people at the mission are afraid of the Gohoron more than Jap. Many are afraid. If you see him, you will die. Many have seen the Jap and lived. No one sees Gohoron and lives. Maybe this sniping is Gohoron."

"Oh, yeah? What the hell is that?" Hawk prepared himself for some local myth. Japanese were too mundane for the locals, he figured, they had to make up a good story to go with the atrocities.

"The English have no word for him. Gohoron means bad animal night spirit."

"Is that right? That covers about everything, don't it?" Hawk said, sipping his drink. He tightened his lips and looked out at the red glow of Delivalung's summit. It lit the underside of the wispy mist in the dark sky, with a swimming orange and pink shimmer. Above the unique coloring stretched the black sky with millions of brilliant stars. The sky seemed vast and higher here. It was too bad cameras could not take pictures of this kind of stuff, he thought. Not many people would ever get to see a thing like this.

He didn't figure he needed to hear any more about the Gohoron. It was strictly funny business. If there was one thing he was sure that he would never have to face in this deadly country, it was a Gohoron. But Luka elaborated without being asked.

"Gohoron kills at night. He has the head of the buffalo and eyes of fire. Some say he is a man who turns into a buffalo and only walks on two legs. The English say this is a werewolf in their forests. You have these in America?"

"Hunh? Oh, yeah. Shit, yeah. By the jillions." Hawk yawned. "Well, I guess we better saddle up and get out there. Them bugs in the jungle are waiting on their breakfast."

"There are those who have seen Gohoron. You must talk to them. He always kills. They will tell you many things of the werewolf."

Hawk stood and stretched. "I imagine they would. Ain't them the things with the teeth that sucks out your blood?"

Luka thought about the teeth. He had not heard that part, but it was consistent with the other terrible aspects of the monster. He did not know that his questioner had confused Bela Lugosi with Lon Chaney. Luka stood and put a hand on Hawk's arm.

"I will tell you, because you will listen," Luka said in a low voice. Hawk leaned an ear down. "Gohoron is no part man. He is all spirit. The English word is 'devil.' I have seen the picture in the English holy books." An eerie cry from a night bird could be heard in the distance. "Bad things happen in this place. Better that we leave."

"Yeah, I know what you're sayin'. I appreciate the information. I'm gonna keep a lookout for that damn fella."

Luka nodded. He liked Hawk. Hawk had taken the Gohoron report seriously. He was an intelligent man who could be trusted. None of the other foreigners at the Mission would heed the warnings.

Luka wondered if the Gohoron had killed any of the Japanese. He did not think that they would pay any attention either.

"But, you know what?" Hawk turned to Luka with a serious expression. "I think the Japs are out near that Delivalung thing."

"Bad luck is Delivalung."

"Good luck for us. If we find them there." Hawk winked.

Luka frowned. He was not sure what to say. "Bad luck for Japs. Americans kill them."

"Sure as shit. And you? Are you in on the fight at the mountain? Or, is it too scary?"

Luka was still frowning. "We fight. It is good to respect the spirits. A man can never understand these things. Respect is good. But..." Luka reasoned aloud, "the Jap will not be there, because of the spirits. If the Jap *is* there, there will be no spirits, and so then we fight."

"Yeah. Makes a lotta sense," Hawk agreed. He was thinking he should have slept one more hour.

* * *

SERGEANT CLIFFORD CURRY had been around a while. He was no sucker. He figured he had to make something of himself out of this war. The damned thing was going to last forever. He was already thirty, and he had no trade other than soldiering. He had been in the Navy, then the Army, and now the Marines. It was only over the last three years or so that he had made any money out of this racket, and that was because of the war. He had done a little black marketing of alcohol, souvenirs, and purloined supplies. Mostly, chickenfeed, with a good hit here and there. He was not a starry-eyed patriot when it came to the war. He had been on Guadalcanal, and remembered that as soon as the killing was over, the salvagers came in to collect the scrap iron. They would go back to America as millionaires, while the men who drove and fired that scrap iron got an all-expenses paid trip to the cemetery, if they were lucky. Curry had learned more than one lesson in that hell hole.

Perhaps he had achieved his biggest score there with the blackmailing of an old sergeant major, who had made the mistake of becoming involved with Curry. Curry came out on top of a lot of his enterprises on the Canal mainly by being one of only ten survivors from his original company. The cheated, the cheaters and the witnesses were all gone. When word of the assault on Tarawa came out, he had the foresight to see that it was not going to be good. He signed up for special operations, and ultimately wound up in Burma with the OSS. He didn't do much there, and that included turning a profit. He did acquire a unique entry on his resume. He was one of the few Marines with OSS experience. Thus, he landed here, working for Mr. Arnold. Curry was not sure what Arnold's angle was, but he could smell something less than legitimate like a rat smells burnt cheese.

Curry had taught some of the tribesmen which end of a rifle to hold, and had taken them on patrols. He kept the patrols short and safe. The Japanese had picked off a few of the locals in the area around the mission, and Curry wanted none of that. When Arnold told him to search for something "unusual," however, he developed a renewed interest in the longer patrols. When he was told that James Hawk would be patrolling to the south, his interest doubled. Now he had a little competition. He knew that son of a bitch, Hawk, would not be bashful about beating the bushes around here. Hawk might be stupid, but the guy wasn't bashful. He could possibly turn something up. Curry was uncertain about the objective of his competition, but he had heard a few rumors from the natives as to what was out there.

Curry knew Hawk well, and knew that Hawk hated him. He had no hatred for Hawk, as amoral men don't waste their time with hate. Unless, you include their hatred for the whole human race. But generally, the amoral seek to turn a profit, and hatred just interferes with that. Those who devote their lives to hatred are usually destitute idealists.

Curry had involved Hawk in one of his schemes a couple of years back. The outcome had tarnished Hawk's reputation, but no one could pin anything on either of them. Curry turned a profit. Hawk turned up nothing but a hatred for Curry. Since Hawk had never intended to make a profit, he forgot the incident for the most part. He didn't care much about his reputation. His honor was untouched as far as he was concerned. He never cared much what anyone else thought of him. Curry misunderstood this. He took Hawk for a criminal, for which Curry could be excused, as others had made the same assessment. There are different types of criminals, however. Hawk would have been more of the violent type of criminal, were he a criminal, rather than a mere sneak thief. Curry had never been to prison to learn the subtle difference between the two avocations. Lessons were coming his way.

The night that Hawk sat enchanted by the view of Delivalung, Curry led a patrol to the northeast, in a less scenic portion of Basah. The jungle was much heavier here, and Luka had spotted two Japanese soldiers there recently. Summoning all of his courage, for he was no coward when it came to his own self-interest, Sergeant Curry was determined to legitimately conduct the patrol after it was assigned to him. Ordinarily, he would have just walked out of sight, waited a respectable time, and returned to the Mission. On this occasion, he went deep into the woods, deep enough to justify an overnight stay. He had a sense that this time, he was really looking for something worthwhile.

"Sergeant." His Iban scout returned through the darkness with an excited expression. "Sergeant Curry, see Jap ahead. Many Jap."

A smile crossed Curry's narrow face. He was tall and slender, but far from frail. He could survive the jungle, or anything else, as well as any man.

Two red eyes watched him from the darkness. They studied his height. His skin was as dark as that of the tribesmen, due to his years of exposure to the sun. It was the height that gave him away. The beast with the red eyes cocked its head like a curious dog. Its small teeth became visible in its hairy face. The presence of an American interested the beast.

Curry crept through the jungle, and six of his Iban underlings accompanied him. Behind them, silent in the darkness, walked the horned creature with the legs of an animal. Moonlit gray moss swayed over him in the trees, like accompanying spectral dancers.

Curry brushed aside a fern. In a clearing, he could see a fire and battery powered lights. A dozen or so of the Japanese meandered about, conducting some sort of elaborate work project. Curry saw metal detectors. The sweepers looked like captured American equipment, likely designed to discover land mines. The enemy swept the discs over the ground and listened for signals on headsets. The discs connected to long broom handles. He could see three of the detectors, but there more men, wandering in and out of sight in an area over to the right of the clearing. Swirls of mist collided with insects, wavering in the electric lights, as if angered by the exposure of their nocturnal wandering.

"What they do, Sergeant?" asked Curry's scout in a whisper. It looked incredibly strange to him, like something a being from another planet might be doing during an earthly visit.

"Well, they ain't mopping the deck, Junior. I'm afraid we gotta send these gents on the way back to their ancestors."

7

THE TREASURE OF THE CHINESE EMPERORS

HAWK REPORTED TO MR. ARNOLD. HE HAD ALREADY TOLD Biedeker what he thought about the volcano. Arnold met Hawk in the mess hall that evening. Lieutenant Klemer and Hawk were sitting on one side of the table eating, and Arnold sat opposite them with a clear colored drink. It smelled alcoholic.

"I could've found out just as much by staying here and talking to Luka," Hawk admitted. He forgot that he was talking to the superior who had given him the order to go out there. Marine officers would not be sharing small talk over a meal, and Hawk was caught a little off guard. Superiors can always justify their orders and point out your short sightedness.

"On the contrary," said Mr. Arnold, "we now know that there was not a strong presence of the enemy between here and Delivalung. It was a very informative patrol. I agree with you, too, the mountain is a prime suspect, as far as I am concerned. I thought it much farther. Now we have a more exact reading. I only had the old Dutch map to go by. I doubt anyone has ever been there. Aerial reconnaissance has been poor in the area because of the jungle and the unnatural cloud cover."

Hawk stabbed a piece of chicken and thrust it into his mouth, all the while searching for another one on his plate. "Yeah. The mountain smokes all the time, according to Luka. That's the cloud cover. It may be too dangerous for the Japs. It sounds like it goes off sometimes, but not too bad. Maybe a little lava is always seeping out. Probably keeps the pressure down or something."

"Well, congratulations. You did fine. I hope Sergeant Curry did as well toward the north." Arnold stared into his drink with a preoccupied expression. This prevented him from noticing Hawk's sneer at the sound of the name.

Arnold was trying to decide between Hawk and Curry. Which of the two could he trust with this sensitive quest? They both seemed capable. Curry struck him as a little more intelligent, a little more polished; possibly even officer material. Unlike Hawk. And yet, something about Curry indicated a lack of motivation.

The girl, who Hawk and Klemer had greeted earlier at the hospital, came into the hall. She eventually found her way to their table. After greetings all around, she sat on the side of the table next to Arnold, across from Hawk and Klemer.

"I hate to be the bearer of bad news," she said in a small voice, "but Lieutenant Biedeker has brought in another sick patient."

Hawk looked up slowly at her anxious little face. He stopped chewing with his mouth open, even though it was a lot of trouble. Her voice barely carried across the table, as if it took great effort for her to speak. Hawk stared at her. What on earth was she doing here?

"Who was it?" Klemer asked, with genuine concern. She said a name, Carlson, and Klemer shook his head. "Well, maybe he is better off in the hospital," Klemer said. "At least you know you are safe for a few days. Oh, Miss Pearson, this is Sergeant Hawk. James Hawk, Jessica Pearson."

"How do you do?" she said, in her elfin, wood creature voice. It was loud enough this time for Hawk to detect an accent of some sort. She smiled politely at him for a moment. Then she let her eyes fall to the tabletop.

"That fella, Carlson, was in my patrol," Hawk said quietly. Carlson had never mentioned feeling ill.

"Was he?" She looked up again. "I hope you don't get sick. Oh, I shouldn't have said that. What a terrible thing to say." Her face reddened.

Hawk smiled. "That don't matter, Miss."

Klemer smiled and leaned across the table toward Miss Pearson, as if she had injured herself. "Sergeant Hawk is not that sensitive," he told her. "He would be better off in bed than where he has been, isn't that right, Sergeant?"

"Uh...yessir," Hawk replied, taking a bite. He wasn't quite sure how to answer such an off the wall question. There was an odd silence afterwards. "Lieutenant Klemer tells me that you're a nun, Miss," Hawk said.

It was Klemer's turn to blush. Arnold smiled.

"You know, you are the third man today who has told me that," she said. She looked at Klemer. "You must have told the whole world that I am a nun." She furrowed her smooth brow. "Why did you do that?"

Klemer's color deepened. He was wearing only his

T-shirt and pants since his hospitalization, and it seemed his entire neck and shoulders turned red. "Well," he explained, "I told them that I thought that you had been. It is so unusual to see a young lady here. It was only logical..." His voice trailed off, failing to ever fully explain himself.

"I was a novice once," she said, "but I dropped out, Sergeant Hawk. Vows are intimidating for me. I don't like commitment." She shook her head. Her long hair flowed rhythmically with the motion. "He knew that." Klemer shrugged, as if maybe he didn't know it. "I'm not a nun. I'm not a nurse,." She smiled and raised her shoulders. "I'm not anything." A server brought her a plate. "I'm here, but I'm nothing."

Hawk leaned back in his chair and winked at Arnold. "Well, you're the best looking nothing in a thousand miles then," he said. He was not much of a flirt, but everyone there had been thinking it, and he intended to lessen the obvious tension that had developed between her and Klemer with a joke. Hawk failed to notice, amidst the strained words and her beautiful face, that she had just admitted that there was no reason for her to be here.

He had been walking all morning, beginning long before daylight, and keeping a wary eye on the underbrush. He was tired. He would have liked to have heard more about Miss Pearson, and run interference for the Lieutenant, but being more practical than either romantic or sociable, he made his apologies.

"That was a good meal," he said. "I reckon I better get started on a siesta before something else comes up. It was nice meeting you, Miss Pearson." Hawk stood. "Lieutenant? Mr. Arnold?"

"Yes, of course, go ahead, Sergeant," said Klemer. The Lieutenant looked a little sheepish.

Arnold raised his hand in assent, in the manner of a superior, without saying anything. The move reinforced Hawk's opinion that Arnold had rank. He did not want anyone to know it. That was logical with the Japanese build up in full force, and only a company of half sick men to protect him. Perhaps when the odds improved, he would sprout a few oak leaves, or better.

"Good night, everybody," Hawk said. He picked up his helmet and walked for the door. He had a craving for chewing tobacco, which had helped in his decision to leave. They all waited for him to go through the door before speaking again.

"I believe that he may be the best man we've got here, to find what we're after," Arnold said. "More impressive than Curry. That man may have been a mistake." Arnold sipped his drink. "Maybe I'm wrong. Curry is not back yet. Anything can happen around here." He set his drink down, feeling a little lightheaded.

"He has sad eyes," Miss Pearson said.

Klemer cleared his throat. "Yes, but he is a dangerous man," Klemer said. "You must be careful around these men, Jessica," he warned. "I understand your concern for people, because I share it. But you should use your common sense, too." Klemer raised an admonishing finger, and his accent thickened. Perhaps he was quoting his mother.

"Lieutenant Klemer," she said, "I get the feeling you're trying to keep people away from me."

"I can try, can't I?"

* * *

REINFORCEMENTS ARRIVED THE NEXT MORNING. They consisted of another stripped-down company. And yet another company was reportedly on the way. Major Bearn did not arrive with the unit, reportedly coming down with some sort of fever in Hazelton. That left the men at Sacred Blood under the ranking officer of the newest contingent. His name was Captain Terhune, and there were no particularly good or bad rumors about him. The men in his own company did not even know him. They hardly knew one another.

With the landing of the riverboat, old Clancy sought out Hawk. He only had a few minutes before the boat would leave on its return trip to Hazelton. Hawk was eating breakfast under one of the unwalled, thatched-roof structures near the commissary. He sat on a woven mat. The natives felt that chairs were for old people and cripples. Seldom having the benefit of a chair, Hawk adapted easily.

A few dozen of the locals were nearby, taking advantage of the Mission's gratis benefits. Mad birds shrieked at one another in the distant jungle, frantically preparing for the struggles of their new day.

"Hello, mate!" Clancy greeted Hawk.

"Hi ya doin'? Pull up a seat. How was the trip?" Hawk asked.

"Smooth as glass, she was. Smooth as glass." Clancy laughed, folding his old legs under him. He had been forced to stay limber in his life as a laborer. "They tell me you been out there, lad. Is it true?" Clancy pointed his chin at Hawk.

"Yep. Not much to it."

"Haw! You're wrong, mate. No white man has ever been out there. Probably no living native of the island, either. Virgin country, it is. Not many places left like that on the face of the earth any more. No, sir. You've shared in the experiences of the old timers, Dr. Livingstone and the like. Had that feeling myself, as a boy. Many's been to the places I scouted since, of course. I refer to my youthful adventures along the coast. And many will be a-going to the places you've scouted some day. Now. For certain. Don't think they won't."

Hawk shrugged modestly. The patrol had been little more than idle entertainment. He enjoyed seeing what was over the next hill. Some people liked to visit stores and see the new stock, or visit lands that had been well traveled. Hawk liked to see a new lay of the land. It was always surprising and never quite as expected.

"Well..." Hawk said. "I'll be going back. Farther next time, according to Mr. Arnold and Lieutenant Biedeker. I won't be so proud when I find out that a couple thousand Japs been there first."

Clancy laughed and slapped his thigh. "Aye! Aye!" The river man quickly sobered and pointed his chin toward Hawk accusingly. He looked over his shoulder. "Tell me truthful, lad—did you find it?"

"It? The Jap army? Nah... Got some damn good leads, though."

"Nahr. Nahr," Clancy interrupted him angrily. "You knows to what I am referring. I know why you're here, mate. No time for being coy here. I'm on borrowed time. Listen...and not just with your ears. I know you're a boy that's down and out. A poor man can tell another poor man. But remember, old Clancy was down and out the day you were born. And long before and long after. Now, enough! Tell me, lad—*did you find it*?"

"What the hell *is* it?"

Clancy smiled impatiently. He said in a businesslike tone, "The treasure, mate, the treasure. Now as all our cards is lyin' face up, did you?" He moved his hands about as if he were turning over imaginary cards on their imaginary table.

"Uh...I guess not." Hawk looked down disinterestedly. Jessica Pearson walked by on her way to the commissary. Hawk half stood, with his interlocked legs. "Good morning, ma'am." She looked over and smiled. "That's a beautiful girl," Hawk said to his plate.

"Aye, aye." Clancy glanced over at her without interest. "Damned, if she ain't. The treasure is why you're here, Mr. Hawk. Now, you can't tell me that they didn't tell you that much?"

"Nah. They must've forgot. What with the war and all. The sons of bitches." Hawk smiled and took a drink of rice beer. He wasn't really sure why he was here yet. He was pretty sure that he wasn't on a treasure hunt, however. He had been used by his handlers exclusively for one thing: killing.

"Mm, if what you say is true, then they don't *want* you to know, lad. They'll let you find it for them and take it away."

"Oh...yeah...probably." Hawk gulped his beer. He noticed that the more beer that he drank, the better he felt. He decided that after demobilization, he would take a nip now and then, until he fit in smoothly with civilian life. It seemed like a good plan. He didn't realize that veterans from the First World War had already hatched that plan, and were living under bridges and in gutters all over America. He looked around. He had to find Biedeker and get the order on the next patrol.

"No one has been able to find it, not in 700 years. It would take an army to get in there and get it. And *you* are the first army to ever try, laddie. Don't let them take it all from you, boy. You'll be the one to see it first, as they's too scared to do it themselves. They needs a rough sort of fella to do their dirty work." Clancy winked. "You'll be the first. You got pockets, don't you? Don't be bashful. Don't end up a broken old ignorant fool like me. You know, you ain't no bright fellow, that's ever gonna have an education or do much of nothing with y'self. When you look at me, you are looking at y'self in a few years. When your back is brittle, lad, they don't send you on treasure hunts no more. It's up to you, now, and your empty head to get by. This is your only chance, boy." Clancy grew extremely agitated, obviously believing all that he was relating. He made Hawk's nerves tingle. It was a little early in the morning for uninvited madness at your elbow.

Hawk sat back. He sighed and took out his chewing tobacco. He took a heavy dose of water from his canteen to prepare his mouth. For the lack of anything else to do in the next five minutes, he decided to listen further. "What the goddam hell are you talking about?" he asked quietly. He wondered if there was any sense to this at all.

"The Emperors' treasure horde! The emperors of China! They sent a ship full of treasure here every year since 1200 or so. Right up to the turn-of-the-century. It was their insurance against uprising and revolt, though they never cashed in on it. And it's out there! Don't believe that it ain't. Don't believe them. Don't let them use you until the yoke breaks." Clancy leaned toward Hawk and his voice lowered. "I seen the ship myself in '87. I did! I was a boy, playing by the River Pageas. It was like a dream, at first, when that barge came gliding into view. Just a child, was I, and had never seen such a thing. Nor ever would again. The crewmen even was dressed like kings, they was. That dream turned into a vision, with all them colors set against the green forest. Solomon in all his glory! Full, that ship was—gold, silver, jewels, art-ee-facts. To Delivalung! That's what the Penans say. That's where she is—taboo to all. Exceptin' to *you!* Don't be fooled. Listen to a poor man!"

Hawk spat. He tried not to, but he laughed rather loudly. Something about Clancy's stretching of his neck reminded him of a chicken.

Jessica Pearson walked by again and Hawk stopped laughing. Clancy watched her with Hawk this time.

"Pretty lass, all right," Clancy admitted. "Women like the finer things, lad. Especially women like that. They look all meek and mild, but ain't nothing greedier than a pretty woman. And you ain't one of the finer things, mate. With gold in your pocket—that's another matter. Reflect upon it!" Clancy shook his finger. "A woman like that will spend everything you got, and ask where's the rest. You'll look around for what she squandered it on, and won't be a thing sittin' there. She don't work for it, and she don't care that you do. That's the way it is. You'll need that swag. More swag than any amount of working can ever give you."

"Well," Hawk stood, "if I find it, I'll let you know. It'd be hard to hide that much loot. You'd probably be dropping off pieces of it all the way from China to here. And seeing as how you're the one that clued me in on it, I'll cut you in." Hawk smiled wryly.

Clancy's eyes opened wider. "You should! It would be just! It would be justice, now! You was the babe in the woods till I tuned you in. A bloomin' eyewitness to it, am I! And how many of those are they still alive? You know that it ain't just the gibberish you're hearing, when you got an eyewitness, maybe the only eyewitness on earth!"

"That's for sure."

"Had I been a man in '87...why, you'd be feasting your eyes on a rich man right now. I'd have secured my interest then, would I. Of course, I would not be here for you to see, as I would be in one of them places like Paree."

Hawk started to say that if Clancy had been a man in 1887, he would be dead by now, but he did not want to provoke another onslaught of nonsense. Instead, he waved and began to walk away. Clancy followed him.

"Ten percent?" Clancy whined in an embarrassed tone. He ran along beside Hawk, almost bent double. "That would be fair, now wouldn't it, lad? You be the impartial judge of it, right now! You're taking all the risks of it. I know that." By risks, Clancy was referring not only to the jungle and the Japanese, he was well aware that the U. S. government was involved in this; or if it was not, someone powerful in the U. S. military was involved at his own behest. Hawk was aware only that it was hot and he had an irritating old coot attached to his fleeing heels. "Ten percent, now that's a fair one, ain't it?"

"Nah." Hawk shook his head contemptuously. "Thirty would be more like it."

"Thirty..." Clancy stopped walking. Hawk did not drive a particularly hard bargain. Of course, he did not believe in the treasure. He probably would not have bargained any better with the treasure sitting before them. "You mean it, don't you, lad?" Clancy frowned. "Would ye put that in writing?" He closed one eye.

Hawk stopped. Instead of bursting out laughing, he said with indignation, "Ain't a man's word worth nothing, anymore? A handshake's enough among gentlemen, ain't it?" Hawk stuck his thick hand out and spat to the side.

"Why, sure it is!" Clancy felt his hand engulfed by Hawk's grip. "Did you not see no signs already, lad?"

"*Hell* no. I saw every snake God ever created, and his brother-in-law. I got ten or fifteen miles from the volcano, turned around and come back. Didn't see shit. Just said, 'yep, that's a volcano,' and stomped on back. Nice volcano. I figure the Japs are out there. So—we'll be going back. Pay 'em a visit." Hawk winked. He liked paying back the Japanese.

Captain Givens of the riverboat shouted for Clancy. He was standing at the pier by the dugouts and looked angry. Clancy looked at him with a frightened expression.

"There's justice for you, too, mate," he muttered under his breath at Givens. "Got to go! Remember our deal, Mr. Hawk, and be careful with our loot. I can provide the transportation and financial arrangements, as it were, once you've accomplished your part."

"Yeah. Don't worry. Stay in that hold when y'all go to crossing all those sandbars," Hawk warned him. "I don't want any silent partners. I'm thinkin' you're gonna be havin' more and more company along the way, from here on out."

"To be sure! To be sure! The sons of bitches!" Clancy ran spryly away. Hawk figured he had made the old man's day. He had given him something to hope for in life, besides skinned knuckles and greasy hands.

Payday was coming up. Hawk hadn't seen a check in years. They must be piling up. He decided maybe he would give Clancy something. He had more money than he had any use for anyway. He was breaking twenty-five bucks a week now. No one was waiting for it, or him, back home. Then he had another thought, which was not quite as good natured.

Hawk spat. He had just told Clancy everything that had happened and everything that was going to happen here. At least, everything that he knew anything about. Hawk had never worried about divulging information. He had never talked much, nor had anyone around to spill any information to. Hawk was a Marine, not a spy. Such matters never came up.

He looked over at Clancy getting into a dugout. Yes, he had just emptied his guts about what was supposed to be a highly classified mission. Clancy could have made a few friends during the time when the Japanese occupied Hazelton. While the boatman was full of all sorts of funny stories, Hawk had never heard a single word about Clancy's experiences of the last three years among the Japanese. That seemed to be a sore subject.

"Damn!" Hawk whispered. Clancy waved at him. He waved back and spat at the ground. "That was stupid of me."

Because of the intense feelings Americans held against the Japanese, and vice versa, cooperation between the two had never been a realistic problem. It was considered something of a joke, or something you might see in a cheap movie, if it were ever referred to at all. This was a little different. Mistakes usually are. Clancy was not an American, or anything else, as far as Hawk could determine. He decided not to mention the indiscretion to anyone. Maybe it would go away. The guy was just an old drunk. The incident didn't help Hawk's uneasy composure. Maybe he would get another drink. "Treasure...why, that old bastard."

* * *

SERGEANT CLIFFORD CURRY crawled under the dark overhang of leaves, keeping well out of range of the bright Japanese lights. The enemy continued to work the ground diligently with their mine detectors. The ground was warm and damp under Curry's spidery limbs. He took a deep breath of the thick air. It was up to him now.

His plan was to catch the enemy in a crossfire. He would start a distraction from where he lay, and then the half dozen Ibans would mow the Japanese down from their rear.

Curry's eyes surveyed the positions of each enemy trooper. He calculated how quickly each man would be able to cover the distance to the stack of Arisaka rifles. He would have only a few seconds to half a minute before the return fire started. He licked his lips and pulled his MI carbine up beside him. Curry did not like this sort of thing, but he knew how to do it. One could get killed engaging in these affairs.

He sighted in on the man nearest the rifles. This was

the most active man among the Japanese. He may have been the *hancho*. He stepped out of Curry's sights and past the sight protectors on the end of the carbine's muzzle. The American moved his elbow and tracked the Japanese with the short rifle barrel. Curry had never trusted submachine guns. He once had a bad experience with a Reising. He wished he had a BAR. The Browning Automatic Rifle was one of the finest automatic weapons ever made. But it was heavy as hell, and Curry was lazy. He did not have a layer of fat on his frame to protect him from a bouncing chunk of metal that weighed that much. One didn't think seriously of such matters, until lying under a leafy bough, preparing to initiate a first strike, that had better work.

Curry once again framed his man in the peep sight. The lighting was superb. The foresight waved across him. Good enough. *Are you going to do it, or not?* The sniper was afraid that if he thought about it anymore, he might lose his nerve. Or what would be worse: the Ibans would lose their nerve, and he would be all alone over here. He did not especially trust them. It would have been much more reassuring to have Marines out there backing him up. He was willing to stick his neck out this time, however, as he wanted to find out everything he could about this little operation. Once the Japanese were dispatched, he would give the area a thorough examination.

He jerked the trigger three times. His target, the *hancho,* kicked a leg up like a punter and dropped backwards. The rest of the alarmed Japanese scattered in several directions. He aimed for another man who was reaching for a rifle. Curry's jerky shooting put two blunt thirty caliber rounds in his leg.

Curry eased up, lowered the rifle, and checked his results. He had created the diversion that he wanted. According to the plan, his job was completed. He did not want to be lying here with an empty clip. The Japanese had not located him.

With shaking hands, he pulled another clip out of his bandolier. He tried to bang it into the bottom of the clip already in the carbine. With panicky gestures, he realized what he had done and ejected the first clip. It took two hands for him to get the new clip inserted. When he looked up again, things were not going as well as when he had first taken his eyes off the action. He heard only one or two disinterested shots from the Ibans. A half dozen Japanese were pouring fire into their position, working the bolts of their one-shot Arisakas. But the most disconcerting part, was that twice as many Japanese were moving and firing toward him. He noticed the loud thumps in the moist ground around him. The enemy did not know exactly where he was, but they were peppering the general area, and would soon find out.

Had Curry continued firing, he might have discouraged several of the blind attackers. They were quite exposed, and lit up, as if by footlights on a stage. But discouraging several of them was not his prime concern at this point. He was quite suddenly more interested in seeing tomorrow's sunrise.

The Ibans had failed him. Had they lost their nerve? Had they run? What the hell had happened? They had plenty of time. One of them had a Sten gun, and could have done the job all by himself. All of the Japanese should have been easily eliminated with their automatic fire by now.

Curry's head wagged back and forth as he saw men entering the jungle, his jungle, in a line toward him. He pulled a leg under himself and fired at the man in front. Without waiting to see if the shot was a hit or miss, he got up and ran, never once turning around. He heard them firing through the leaves in his wake for a long time. He ran all the way back to Sacred Blood Mission, long after the firing had stopped, feeling no exhaustion at all. In fact, he could have done another few miles. With a little help from the Japanese, he might have qualified for the Olympics.

But he would not have won the games, for two of his Iban companions beat him home. He met them at the front gate to the palisade, and started kicking one of them. He still had enough energy for that task.

While he was ramming his thin fist into the cowering Iban, the other one stood nearby hopping about and screaming.

It was almost dawn and people came out to see what this uproar was all about. They found Curry standing over a bloodied and unconscious scout. The other continued to scream the one word that explained the reason for the failure of the attack: "Gohoron!"

An anxious and timid follow-up patrol found no Japanese operating in the designated area, dead or alive. Nor did it find Curry's four dead Ibans. It did find some huge footprints. They were similar to nothing that was human, nor for that matter, anything that an animal could make. There was an enormous amount of spilled blood on the greenery, even after the hungry insect population had done its duty.

Recruitment of the native population became troublesome from that point on.

8

THE QUEEN OF THE JUNGLE

PREOCCUPIED WITH HIS CONVERSATION WITH CLANCY, Hawk went out to the perimeter and found Joe Canlon. He decided to discuss the matter with Joe. Joe was his confidant, of a sort. This was in spite of their having differing backgrounds, one being an urban New Yorker, and the other being a rural Mississippian.

Joe was deep in a slit trench with two Marines named Dupuy and Lynwood. They had just finished widening the hole. Dupuy cursed perfunctorily when Hawk spat down onto the floor of the trench, but owing to the pecking order, he could do little else about it. Hawk jumped down. The four men sat in the moist dirt, staring at one another, in less than a friendly manner. Joe and Dupuy started talking. Hawk had tuned them out. He came here to talk to Joe, and these other two ass holes were mere irritations. He had *nothing* to say to them. He could have told them to go, but that would have meant admitting to himself that something was wrong. His nerves were bristling. He fought the urge to walk off, and resolved to sit there. He finally gave in and tried to follow their conversation.

"I tell you what," said Dupuy, "those native women are starting to look mighty good. They been giving me the eye. Know what I mean? I might do something about that today." He frowned and stared into the sky over the hole.

"You can probably catch all kind of shit out here in this place. Or get your throat cut," said Joe, cautious about such matters. He was cautious in New York as well.

"I've had it all," said Dupuy, scratching his broad hairy chest. "A few more barnacles on my hull ain't gonna be noticed." He felt the heat drilling into his skull, and put his helmet on.

"Them native men look like a grouchy bunch," said Joe.

Dupuy leaned over and blew his nose with his thumb. Evidently this was acceptable behavior, whereas spitting chewing tobacco on the earthen floor was not. "Canlon, that's your problem. All you can think about is men," said Dupuy. Joe and Dupuy laughed. Lynwood listened quietly. They all looked over at the newcomer, seeming to notice Hawk's searing eyes looking through them.

Joe rightly suspected the Sergeant was pissed off about something. Maybe it was the conversation. Joe decided to make the topic more official, in his official capacity as a corporal.

"The lieutenant says no fraternizing with civilians," said Joe, shifting his eyes meaningfully at Hawk. Hawk noticed it, and still said nothing. Everyone stirred uneasily. "What's new with you, Hawk?" Joe said finally. The Sergeant looked rather strange.

Joe was starting to get a little nervous. Men were known to go berserk. Some referred to it as "Asiatic." You didn't really want to be around when a guy with a Tommy Gun went berserk. Joe had always been a little afraid of some of the guys, like Baker, since Baker really was nuts, all of the time. But Hawk had always been his friend. Baker actually liked the killing, and truth be told, it did not seem to bother Hawk all that much. Usually, it was just a business—the exterminating business. But sometimes a person could put a little something extra into it.

"Nothin'," Hawk said. He spat. "Have you assholes ever heard any stories about treasure around here?"

"Treasure?" Joe echoed.

"That's right." It was a difficult word to misunderstand.

"No," said Joe.

"Nah," said Dupuy.

"Nothing like that," said Lynwood. "What about it?"

"I don't know," Hawk shrugged.

"Why did you ask?" Lynwood persisted.

"I don't know."

The other three looked at each other. No one seemed interested in the odd topic, and if they were, they had gotten all they were getting out of the Sergeant.

"Yep, today, I'm gonna do something about it," said Dupuy. "Ah, the *ladies*!"

For some reason that no one could quite remember, this launched Lynwood into a lecture on discipline and how a person must exhibit moderation in all things. It was something about how success in life depended on a person's discipline. He castigated Dupuy's plan as a clear lack of moderation and discipline. There was a vague religious tone to it, while remaining more academic rather than preachy. The others would recall this little speech and often refer to it when discussing Lynwood. It was his legacy.

Hawk heard little to nothing of it.

"And the lieutenant said no fraternizing," Joe added, in case philosophy had not been persuasive.

Hawk stood. "Well, I can see you bastards are full of shit." He stepped out of the hole. "Stay away from them goddam natives," he told Dupuy as he walked away. He went toward the hospital.

"That's a dangerous son of a bitch," Dupuy growled after Hawk was out of earshot.

Joe didn't say anything. It might just be that Dupuy was right. What was that deal about treasure? Joe suddenly realized that he should've asked. "Did he say *treasure*?"

Hawk asked Dr. Lepreaux if he had learned anything about the cause of the sickness afflicting the Marines. He received a long incomprehensible answer that seemed to indicate that it was caused by bacteria.

"Germs, huh? Yeah, plenty of those. I guess we gotta keep an eye on the sanitation around here," Hawk commented absently.

"Absolutely," the doctor agreed. "But, it's not typhus. I don't know. You preach and preach to people about watching the dirt. A little cleanliness is so important, and can do so much."

"Yeah." Hawk spat a black stream of tobacco. The

doctor cringed. "You can't tell these dirty bastards nothing."

Hawk noticed Jessica Pearson carrying a tray out of the hospital. She took it over to a table that had been placed beside a pump that was connected to a rain barrel next to the building. She was busily washing dishes, or something.

"Ever hear any stories about treasure around here?" Hawk suddenly asked the doctor.

Lepreaux looked up and smiled. The subject appeared to lighten his mood. "You mean the legend of the Chinese emperors? That is an old, old myth. It has made it to you, has it? Wherever you have an inaccessible region, people will make up such stories. You need a treasure to make these awful places more attractive. People don't want to believe that there are places without some sort of value. This place, definitely needs a treasure to make it worthwhile." The doctor took out his handkerchief and dabbed his forehead. "I have been accused of seeking it myself. I never denied the rumors. It makes me appear to be a sane man, to be here after gold. I would not want anyone to know that I really enjoy my profession and this misery."

"I know what you mean," Hawk agreed. "I like these woods here and stuff. It's kind of peaceful way out here. Except for the goddam Japs. See you around, Doc." He walked over to Jessica Pearson, whom he had been watching. She looked occupied.

"Can I help?" he asked.

"Oh, Sergeant Hawk. Hello. No, thank you. I'm almost finished," she said happily. He finally identified the accent as some sort of British. She always looked happy. She always had at least half of a smile on her face; like, doing this washing was somehow amusing. Today she wore a blouse and skirt and her hair was pinned atop her head. "I see more Americans here now," she said, when he neither said anything, nor went away.

"Yeah, another boatload hit." He changed his guess. She was not English; it was an Australian accent. *Good people, the Australians*, he thought. "Sure you don't need a hand? I got nothing else to do."

"Well, if you are going to insist," she laughed. He began to help. He looked down and noticed that he was washing bedpans. It did not appeal to him very much, but he was into it now.

"At least I know your name. So many names. I don't know how you keep up with them all. So many strangers," she said. "I used to be uneasy with strangers. Now, that is all that I know. It's good that I like everyone. Everyone is interesting in their own way, aren't they?"

"Yeah." He was not interested in anyone, with the possible exception of her. "You like it here, huh?" He was getting the impression that she might not be very bright. She was too damn pleasant. Of course, that might have been because men and women are always pleasant to each other, at first. Only later did things change. He was aware of that.

He thought of Lynwood and his philosophy of moderation and discipline. He supposed talking to Jessica Pearson was contrary to Lynwood's code. If you put a beer in front of Lynwood, of course, he would act just as stupid as any other man. He would be here washing bedpans, and talking even louder and longer about his code.

"Oh, yes, I like it here." She smiled broader. "It's like

Lieutenant Klemer said, I guess, I like helping people. My father thinks that I'm crazy, wasting my life here." She shrugged. "You could waste your life anywhere. I guess, it is a little dangerous. But really, it's less dangerous now than it has been. With your forces here, now, I mean."

"Klemer and your father have two different opinions. Yours is what matters. But, to tell you the truth, it still is a little dangerous. We might be more likely to attract trouble than keep it away. I don't know why you would want to be here. If I was you, I would probably take the next boat out." As soon as he said it, Hawk wished that he had not. It was a little preachy, and he did not want her to go anywhere.

"My father was born wealthy, you see. He's used to being given things. I don't want to be that way. It's an unhappy way of life. He has a sort of arrogance. An arrogance for no particular reason. I think we are happiest when we are giving, don't you?"

"Yes, ma'am," Hawk responded, with only vague conviction. He didn't do much giving...or taking. What the hell was she even talking about? Christmas presents?

"I really believe that. He says that will all change when I grow up. I don't know how much older I would have to be. I would hate to leave here, honestly. But any day now, I'm told, I will. I suppose there are safer places. We all got along with the Japanese authorities before. I know that they did wrong, with the war and all, but I don't believe that they are the monsters that people say they are. People can be different from their leaders, and be misled, you know?"

Hawk hung his head. He was more in the monster

camp. No common ground here. Where was she coming from? Not where he came from.

She paused as though she felt him seething. "I might have a different outlook were I back in Australia, waiting for an invasion of my homeland. Or, if I had lost someone. Everyone has their own perspective. Well, things will be different with your forces here, now."

"A lot different."

"Yes. I've heard the stories about the fighting. I can't even imagine that sort of thing. It's sounds like some great fiction being made up. I can't understand such hatred and meanness. It seems to me that things could be worked out in other ways, with everyone better off. I mean, way out here? What is there to fight over?" She stacked the bed pans neatly, the way things were, in her neat little world. Hawk handed her another one. "I don't know. There is such nobility in human nature, and it takes just a little effort to use it, and still things like this war happen."

Hawk did not say anything. She was on a different wavelength from his world. He was thinking that maybe he had made a mistake when he walked over here. Women were made to be looked at, and not listened to. That was one weakness he had yet to master. Lynwood might have been right about discipline and control. The Corps tried to teach you that. If she did not know that the world was full of bastards, and that those bastards would not leave you alone until you killed them, she did not know much. People who didn't believe that probably never would. They were the kind of people that wound up in slave camps. It was the required result, to be true to their moral code. He didn't really want to hear much more about the nobility of the human race, or such crap. From her, or anyone. It almost angered him.

Hawk tried to think of a way to make a graceful exit. He could barely think at all. His hands kept moving. They looked detached from the rest of him. He knew better than to argue with her. He had no interest in that. Hawk did his arguing with supersonic metal.

She noticed his silence. What on earth was he thinking of all of the time? She decided to make him talk. She didn't know that she would be much better off not knowing the thoughts of James Hawk. She knew that there was something that he wanted to say. Something was bothering him. She was curious as to what it was.

She was interested in him. His face was attractive and sensitive looking, but the voice was a paradox. It was rough and uncompromising. Which of the two represented his soul? He carried himself in a casual, yet ready way, that she thought was extremely masculine. Yes, he would have been masculine without the helmet or the Thompson on his back.

She sensed that she had somehow offended him, and couldn't imagine how. She supposed that she had somehow denigrated the war effort, something that was a big part of his life.

"You must feel that way too, Sergeant?" she said, looking over at him. Hawk looked from beneath his brooding brows, though not at her.

"How do you mean?" he asked, knowing that he disagreed with absolutely everything she had said, and was still determined not to argue.

"About helping. Giving. It solves everything. You must love your country a great deal to come this far and risk your life for it. It must be gratifying to be in the service and to know what a good thing you're doing. I mean, we here give only a little of our time, but you men are giving your health and your lives. Don't you find the sacrifice rewarding? You must."

"I like my country, yeah. I guess that's how I ended up here. I was mad about Pearl Harbor. What I do don't always give me a warm feeling, though. It's kind of a funny thing. It can get you to thinking." Hawk noticed that she had changed tactics on him. Now she was on his side. She had hit upon it, too. The war was indeed supposed to be a decent thing. He was supposed to be doing his duty for his country. He had forgotten about that. That's how he got into this.

He had come to think of himself as alone, a tiger in the wilderness, trapped on an island in a bloody hunt. He wanted to keep his men alive, he fought for them, to be sure. But for the most part, he was alone with the reality of the killing. She reminded him that he was not alone, that this was really none of his affair at all, he was part of something that involved the entire world. After all, he had been sitting in Issaquena County, mostly minding his own business, when this started. He had lost the ideals somewhere in the blood and cruelty. There are ideals, though. You can't dismiss that. Even James Hawk had ideals. Didn't he? Well. It was the war, he supposed. There actually was nothing good or decent about it. Or him.

"Do you feel all right?" she asked. His silent pauses disturbed her. "You look to me like you need cheering up." She laughed. Hawk smiled and looked at her. The heat had flushed her ivory complexion into pink.

Neither the heat nor the conversation had changed his metallic bronze skin. "Do you like music?"

"Well...not particularly," he admitted. Music was pretty much for women. Stupid noise. He had enough of noise.

"Very well. How about stamps? How can anyone not like stamps?"

"Stamps? Like on letters? Oh, we get our mail free." Not that he had any.

"Silly." She shook her head. "I have a Victrola and a stamp collection. I can show you either. That's about all I own. I can see that you're a difficult person to amuse."

Hawk laughed. He tried to shake his somber mood. Had that become his permanent condition? "That's all you got, huh?" He turned his head sideways with a smile that was somehow irresistible, and somehow frightening.

"We could weave baskets, that perks the children up."

"I'm probably too dumb for that. How about going for a walk? Walking is the only thing I'm good at. I get lots of practice, you know."

"That sounds interesting." She imitated his Mississippi accent, though he did not recognize himself in the imitation. He presumed that she was just being funny, doing an Al Jolson impression or something. Young people often tried to be funny. He had not been around much silliness, other than the Baker or Dupuy kind, which was as likely as not to end in a fist fight. Their idea of humor was sticking cigarettes on each other.

He nodded, not knowing what to say.

"You don't like to talk much, do you?"

"Sure." Hawk shrugged. "I didn't learn how until I

was about five years old. Or six. Takes me a while to get in gear."

"Five or six? Why on earth?"

Hawk shook his head. "Oh, I don't know. When you're three- or four-foot-tall, I reckon it's best to keep your comments to yourself, depending on the situation."

They looked at each other for a few moments, some type of understanding passing between them.

He finally looked down. "It paid off when I got into the Marines. They don't like a lot of back talk. I probably would have give them some. If I had any."

She smiled. "I'll see you this evening then," she said. "Unless you'd like to help me fill these up again?" she said, holding up a bedpan.

Hawk folded in his lips. "I imagine I can wait till tonight."

She laughed. He smiled and she touched his arm. She gathered the equipment and stepped around him. "Good day, then," she said.

"Yeah." He rocked back his helmet and sighed. The heat dropped like tonnage on his helmet. The cloth cover smelled like it was burning. He looked up at the mirror blaze of a torrid sky. It was a beautiful day. The jungle was all around, waving and smelling fresh. A hot breeze was blowing. A man could live in a place like this. After the war, of course.

He didn't realize that he had too readily accepted her misperception of him. A hand grenade can be carried into several battles and get battered and beaten, looking sad compared to the other new hand grenades in the crate. But it is still just a hand grenade that does what hand grenades do, and is not something that you can change, or should have anything to do with.

* * *

MR. ARNOLD STUDIED the weasel face of Sergeant Curry. Curry's eyes shifted and his mouth often leered into a nervous grin. Curry's utilities were torn and his skin scratched. Life at the Mission outside, visible through Arnold's open door, went on as usual.

"With all of this, you didn't see any excavation then?" Arnold persisted. Curry had finished his version of the failed patrol inside the northeastern forest.

"No, sir. We saw mine detectors. We did not see any digging yet."

Arnold nodded and put his chin in his hand. Then he shifted positions, putting the same hand at the back of his head and leaning back. "Damn, I wish you had taken them, Clifford," he said.

Curry looked at the desktop, blinked a few times, and took a deep breath. "Yes, sir. I just wasn't expecting the superstition of the natives to be that strong. We were in one of their forbidden areas, I guess, and they were a little spooked. They nearly got me killed, sir," Curry reminded him. "With all of that Gohoron business. I don't know if that is something new, or if they have always had that local devil. They sure get worked up about it. Enough to let themselves get killed by a Jap detail."

"That area has to be kept under surveillance. And now they know we're watching them it will be much more difficult." Arnold shook his head, as if he were wrestling with the problem. "As you know, Sergeant

Hawk is watching the area to the south and checking Delivalung proper. He seems to think something may be going on there. But your area is the one we're worried about. I mean, we know they are searching there for something. I'm going to level with you Curry, and you're not even to remotely refer to this to anyone..."

Sergeant Curry put on his most serious expression and leaned over the desk. "Yes, sir?" There was a pause and Curry's crooked grin accidentally slipped out.

"It's not just the buildup that we're worried about, Sergeant. In fact, we have little evidence so far of a strong build up here. We are still waiting on Hawk for word of that. We know that certain high-ranking Japanese officials intended to come here. That's all we have on the subject for now. As far as troop movements, it is undetermined. You would think that the two would be related, but we can't be sure yet. The other thing is..." Arnold hesitated. He felt odd confiding in Curry. The man just had an oily look about him. Arnold well knew this could be a mistake. "While in Burma we intercepted a German airplane containing scientific information of a military nature. The captured parties told us that it was destined for the interior of Basah. To put it simply, Curry, the Japanese are looking for something out there in the bush. Raw material possibly related to a weapons development program, and I don't want them to find it."

Curry had to smile. He knew that they would both be dancing around the truth here. But perhaps he would learn something from Arnold.

Arnold might have the information about what to be looking for, but he would never go out into that jungle to make any use of it. That took a little nerve. He would have to get Curry to do that part, but without Curry's knowing the full story. Or, of course, he also had the idiot, Hawk. That was the bad part. Curry was not indispensable, because there was someone else out there. Hawk was the wild card in all of this. He could stumble and bumble onto something and mess up everything. If it had been anyone else, Curry could negotiate with him, reason with him, or trick him. But, that bastard...

"Ah, huh." Curry caught himself. "I see, sir."

"What you saw may be connected to that, you understand?"

Yes, indeed, Curry thought. He understood all right. Metal detectors detected metal, not raw materials.

"I'm hoping we can get some troop strength in here before this blows up. You keep an eye on these Japanese operations. We've got another company coming tomorrow. In two more days, we should have still another one. I want to get the men here faster than they can get sick and evacuated out. That seems to be a problem. It's nothing new, we faced the same thing in Burma."

"Yes, sir. I'll keep an eye on it." Curry gave no consideration to getting sick. That was for suckers.

* * *

THAT NIGHT, Hawk met Jessica Pearson in front of the commissary. He had received the order earlier, concerning his next patrol. Biedeker would lead the patrol out in the morning, the destination Delivalung, and Hawk would be a part of it. Anything could happen.

It was way out there, and should anything happen, walking was the only way out of it.

It was already very dark, and people had stopped moving around. A large moon hung over the hospital roof, peering through the palm fronds. The air had cooled. Jessica wore a long sleeve shirt over her blouse. Hawk's fatigues were cleaned to a washed-out beige color.

"Night finally came," he said, looking down at her soft little face.

"Did you think that it wouldn't?"

"You never know." And he never did.

"Where shall we walk? There aren't many places left, with all of these soldiers."

"Any place. I guess we could see where we end up."

They walked off the crushed rock that lay between the hospital and the commissary. Although the night coolness was coming on, one could still feel the heat evaporating from the earth. An Iban laborer had just sprayed for mosquitoes, and they could smell the not unpleasant aroma of the insecticide. A kerosene lamp lit the interior of Mr. Arnold's hut, and the door stood half open. He was bent over his desk, studying a map, no doubt. It appeared that he was alone.

"He's a secretive man," she said, as they passed by.

"Yeah. That's his job," Hawk said.

"Have you noticed that you can describe anyone with a single word?" she laughed. "Secretive, that's Mr. Arnold."

Hawk disagreed with the general premise, but he immediately had a mental image of Joe Canlon. Stupid. That was his word. Hawk smiled.

"What's my word?" he asked.

"What's mine?" she asked in return.

"Oh, couldn't do it in one word."

"Very diplomatic. I'll be thinking of your word. I'll tell you later."

"Okay. That's a deal."

Hawk noticed that they were walking toward the perimeter the Marines had set up. He preferred the prying eyes of the Mission personnel to those of the Marines. He took her hand and said, "Let's go this way." The hand was relaxed, unresponsive. His hard hand swallowed it.

"When will you go back? Have you heard?" he asked. They walked under the sagging roof of an abandoned longhouse.

"On the next boat, they say. I'll bet Hazelton is a shambles after the Australian invasion. We are a warlike people, you know." She laughed.

"Oh." Hawk shook his head. "It didn't look too bad when I saw it. I guess the Japs ran for it. You'll probably like it there. It's a little nicer than here. You have the Navy protecting it and all. I don't see how you could like this. You don't fit in here much. I nearly dropped dead the first time I saw you out here, in a place like this." He shook his head. "I mean, this joint is about as far from anything as you can get."

"Oh? Too frail? Don't judge a book by its cover. Remember that, when you choose your word. I didn't just fall out of the sky, you know. I've been around a bit, and maybe that's how I ended up here."

"Yeah. Don't judge a book by its cover. That's a good one. You remember that, too." Hawk knew what his book cover looked like. Of course, he also knew that it resembled the rest of the book.

"I never do."

Hawk faced her. The moonlight slipped just under the torn and bent old roof. "No, it's not that you're too frail. Just too nice for this. Too pretty," he said, feeling rather stupid. She laughed, looking even more beautiful. It was the innocent laugh of a little girl.

"I thought we were ruling out book covers. Pretty? Is that my word?" She looked down. "Not sure I like it."

"No. Not good enough."

"Good. I had hoped for more." She took his other hand. "Anyone can be pretty. No one looks pretty for long. You would get tired of that. I had a cousin who worked in a movie theater. He loved Katherine Hepburn, until they showed one of her movies for two months straight. Now he hates her." She tilted her head. He smiled. "I like you better this way. You're always so business-like with the Lieutenant. You're worried about this place, aren't you? You have seen too much of the war, haven't you?"

"Worried? No, not especially," he answered truthfully. He hadn't seen anything here that even approached some of his earlier experiences. The only bad thing here was the utter isolation. If something went wrong, you were on your own.

"You always walk around in a trance, then?"

"No, not always. Just when there's nothing to do, I guess. Maybe I just don't know how to talk to you. We speak a different language in the Corps. Are you always happy?"

She stopped smiling, as if caught doing something wrong. "Not always. But I think that I'm getting close to it. Life is really wonderful, you know. I think I'd like for you to remember that, after I go. It's all in how you look at it. I think...I could teach you if we had the time. You may have gotten off the track. Understandably, but, off the track."

"Yeah." He had no answer for that. He couldn't teach her how to be miserable. That would take a twenty-month cruise from the Solomon Islands, north. "Maybe you could."

They stood close together. Hawk looked around self-consciously. He could see about a dozen people on all sides. It seemed like they were all looking at him and Jessica. There wasn't much else to look at.

"This country is lovely," she looked aside, also noticing the audience. "To think of it any other way is wrong. Bad things happen everywhere. So do the good." Her hand strengthened, and she pulled at him. They started walking again.

Hawk didn't say anything. Sacred Blood Mission was okay, maybe, but lovely? Probably not.

"Can you tell me what's wrong," she said. "Do you miss someone? Were you horribly frightened? Are you frightened?"

"Do I look like something's wrong?"

"Yes. You think more than you talk. You think before you speak, you think after you speak. You think while you're speaking. It's...unusual."

Hawk did feel an unusual sensation, like he had to hide something from her. Not hide, so much as protect. His dark soul tried to open to her. He wasn't about to let a thing like that happen. The things that he had seen, the things that he had done, were not for sharing.

"I don't know," he said. "Just tired mostly. Not sleeping right and all. Gets on your nerves. Scrambles your brain." He looked down.

She saw an expression of embarrassment. He didn't like talking about it, she thought. Actually, he didn't like making up stories.

"That's all," he added.

"I worry about people like you. The ones that go through it all and don't talk about it, keep it all inside."

Hawk sighed. "I wouldn't waste no time worrying about me. I just hit a low spot every now and then. I could do it all again, if I had to. People like me ain't too...sensitive...and all. That's why they got us doing this. Nothing bothers us, as long as we're in one piece."

"I see."

She became quiet after that. Hawk felt a little smaller. Telling people your problems was something that he did not believe in. Nobody wanted to hear that shit. Unless they wanted you to feel small, and make themselves feel large. That's the way he thought of life. Life was an adversarial situation and you never surrendered any ground. Not even to her. She had almost cracked him open. He sank deep into his hard shell as they stood in the doorway of the commissary. And it was hard.

"It's dark in there," she said. Hawk looked inside the canteen. They had come full circle.

"Yeah."

"Come here."

They walked inside, between the black rows of tables and into the galley. A stilted veranda opened off the galley. Bamboo screens shut out the moonlight. She opened one, and silver shadows blossomed across the room.

"I was getting tired of everyone looking at us," she

said. "Out there." Her lips tightened and she squinted up at the moon.

"I noticed that, too."

He put his arms around her narrow waist. That was always the difficult part, bridging the physical gap between two people. At least, she didn't scream or drop over in horror. Her leaning against him passed through him like an electrical shock. He put a hand beside her soft cheek and tilted her head back. They kissed for a minute and then she pulled away. Moonlight flashed across her hair and neck.

She smiled. "That was nice. Wasn't it?"

"Yeah." The emotion weakened him. She put her arms around his neck and pulled him to her gently. He sensed a command in the gentleness. They kissed for another minute. Her lips were soft and the breath easing from her was sweet. She pulled back again. He sat on a chair and she sat in one beside him. He held her hand and put an arm around her, resting their hands in her lap. He touched his lips to hers again and again, until she was breathless.

That was as far as things went.

They heard only a few voices outside now.

"It's getting rather late, isn't it?" she said.

"Yeah, I guess it is."

"Maybe we should go."

"Maybe so. Long day tomorrow." He kissed her again. He felt no resistance in her relaxed body.

She smiled and brushed the hair above his ear. "Let's go," she whispered.

What the hell, he thought, it will be a long day tomorrow. Might as well get going. "Okay."

They walked back to her hut and stopped at the

door. She took both his hands, smiled and looked down. "Well, what's my word?" she asked.

"Angel."

She laughed. "Do you want to know yours?"

"Yeah. What?"

"A man."

Hawk raised an eyebrow. "That could be good or bad."

"It depends on whether you're a woman or not."

9

THE REPTILES

THE HOT NIGHT DEEPENED AND THE MOON FELL CLOSER TO the horizon. Most of the Ibans and the other various tribesmen had abandoned the perimeter. Most were daylight to dark soldiers. After that: do not disturb. A thin, but capable Marine guard remained to protect the compound. Out in the forest roamed one of the biggest reasons for the abandonment of the paramilitary posts.

Within sight of the Mission, Gohoron, shuffled slowly from side to side, exhaling a barely audible groan with each laborious animal step. He stopped at a point where he could see a line of slit trenches in profile. At the end of the line, the palisade of stumpy logs rose from the flat ground. The heights of the logs did not precisely match one another. Gohoron stopped and faced the troops, concealed by festooned piles of leaves. He revealed only his head through an opening in the foliage. The head resembled a heap of stiff hair. Two blood red eyes shined from within the hair. Little teeth slithered from beneath invisible lips. He immediately noticed that there were less men protecting the Mission tonight. But even monsters respect the United States Marine Corps. Gohoron wheezed in disgust, pulled his horned head back through the leaves, and walked on, holding his long arm with the short one. Vines, creepers, and ghostly moss fell into the opening that he had peered through.

* * *

BIEDEKER TOOK his patrol out the front gate before dawn. The precise destination had not been shared with his men. The Lieutenant would likely have to go farther than Delivalung itself. His objective was to find a Japanese base of operations. Hawk, Joe Canlon, Baker, Dupuy, and Lynwood, all members of the old first squad, were part of the ambitious patrol.

Mr. Arnold fully expected them to come up with something. He sent Curry to the north again. It was necessary for Curry to take Americans with him this time. Not only did the local recruits refuse to go into the region with Curry, they appeared to be growing reluctant to do much of anything for the Americans. For some reason, Sergeant Curry could not seem to locate his earlier position, the area where the Japanese had been searching with metal detectors. After all, it was a big jungle. This was taken as a good sign by Arnold, however, because if there had been any large excavations under way, Curry would have easily discovered them.

Mr. Arnold visited Jessica Pearson after the patrols left. He told her that it would be best for her to leave the Mission immediately. More Americans would be arriving soon. Amphibious DUKW's, and other armored transports, would be replacing Givens' antique riverboat, if they could survive the trip. The Japanese presence was expected to dramatically increase. Jessica resisted the recommendation, saying that she was concerned about the safety of travel on Givens' boat. She preferred waiting for one of the armed military crafts. Arnold had to agree with the wisdom of the request, and did not press the matter.

Oddly enough, she thought, Arnold also asked her about James Hawk. Specifically, he asked if the Sergeant had mentioned the patrol toward Delivalung. Jessica shrugged and said that she did not recall. This part of the conversation made her a little uncomfortable. Why would Arnold ask her any of that?

Jessica returned to her duties at the hospital. The morning brought in four new patients. She was needed. She felt good about that, and about triumphing over Arnold. She was not really afraid of the riverboat. She was not afraid of very much. She had never been exposed to open combat, or a lot of other things. The sickness that she dealt with here was a detached thing, unrelated to herself, or anyone that she cared about. It was her job. She felt immune to any injury from it. She had never been one to contract illnesses.

She didn't admit to herself that she stayed because of James Hawk. It was too soon for that. Too soon for life changing decisions, based on a walk in the dark. She didn't worry about their relationship. She simply was not ready to leave Sacred Blood yet. She liked it here. She was too pleased with herself and the world to worry. The best expression of her feeling toward Hawk, was to admit that she wanted to see him again. And she did what she wanted. There was no room for frustration in her life.

* * *

BIEDEKER REACHED the point of greatest penetration of Hawk's first patrol. Hawk's former perimeter remained visible, the only sign of human passage for miles. The few holes that had been left there were eroding, and already under the threat of concealment by reaching creepers. A dead boar lay in one of the holes. They filled that one in, and reused the others. It was almost nightfall. The lieutenant did not allow campfires, being more cautious, and probably a little wiser, than Hawk had been. He did allow the men to smoke.

Biedeker surveyed Delivalung through his binoculars. The pale mountain jutted up against a granite sky tonight. The sky hovered two dimensionally over a kelly green tree line. The sky was striped with thin clouds, the color of the volcano. That same strange mist, the breath of the inner earth, encircled the summit in broken loops. The obscuring of the clouds, created by rocky steam, made it fruitless to look for distant enemy cook fires. Biedeker knew only that Delivalung floated out there on a sea of nothingness, at the end of perhaps another day's trek. If, that is, Delivalung were not a mirage, for there was something unreal about it."

Hawk sat alone and quiet in the hole he had gouged from the earth only a couple of nights before. The clean strokes of the entrenching tool had melted into the wet ground. The foxhole looked like a molding natural formation there on the edge of the plain. Hawk straightened out his legs. The night chill engulfed the air. He pulled his collar up until it hit the back of his helmet, and he buttoned his shirt. The lonely time for thinking had arrived.

Time passed slowly, heavily, through the night, like the unwelcoming steam over Delivalung. Hawk did not feel as much a part of it, a part of this "war time", as he usually did. It was probably Jessica. She was interfering with his way of life tonight. She should not be here, in his thoughts. None of this should have happened. Why had she come here? She seemed a bit of an adventurer, for she had no qualms about going on a walk with him. Not too many young ladies had, or would, take that risk.

His hands moved slowly as they reached for his tobacco. His cold blue eyes slid back and forth, hoping for a target in the boring, dark landscape. He saw only the mysterious scenery. There was only the waiting, and time itself. Time, followed by violence, that was the rhythm of it. You had to get into the rhythm. The alien wind, with unidentifiable smells, blew at his face.

He was a crude fellow, although he did not think of himself that way. He thought such things were superficial, since he was among a lot of other crude fellows. In ten years, they would own their own businesses, be professionals, have families, and be pillars of the community. No one would label them as crude then. All of this sort of life would be forgotten, never spoken of. It was too unpleasant to speak of. He had some hope of changing. He was not such an optimist as Jessica Pearson, of course. The war could quite easily be the end of him. But he expected something out of life, if he were to survive. There would be no more cotton picking. He had led men, and done so with some success. He had some talents, besides filling a pick sack.

He thought of her, and how he wanted to see her again. Would that take the fighting edge off him? Not likely. The enemy would find the same ignorant, vicious brute tonight that they would have found a week ago. After all, he hadn't changed yet.

A monkey screeched in the jungle beside him. He reflexively clicked the safety off. The thing fell quiet again. A single cry. Why did the stupid thing do that? A mournful bird ululated a strangely human sound. Had he been back in America, he would have thought that it was a screech owl, the type that his neighbors called a ghost owl. Here, God only knew what the unearthly noise was. Sometimes the Japanese attempted animal calls as they signaled to each other before surprise night attacks. They were not very good at it, being generally an urban people. It didn't stop them from trying, or doing a lot of other things. But even they were better than this bird. The bird sounded so human, so haunting, that it had to be real.

Hawk put the safety back on. The other men nearby sat with their own private thoughts, and in terror of the night. They were afraid to breathe. They knew that the enemy was probably out there. Or, they wouldn't have been brought here. Hawk spat. He knew nothing would happen tonight. Somehow, he knew those things. There was some sort of mood to it, or a pattern, or something. Maybe something on another plane of existence told him such things.

The others thought that he had the same expectations of an attack that they had, and that he was merely a nerveless, thickheaded brute. While that may have been true to a certain extent, it was not the reason for his calmness.

Hawk tried to doze. The others were paired two to a hole, in order to share their watchfulness. In theory, as the odd and alone man, he should stay awake all night.

His eyes closed. Somewhere between asleep and awake, he saw the flaming C-54. *Let me loose!* He remembered a dead priest on Guadalcanal. A dead child here, a dead mother there. A man hit by a flamethrower.

His eyes finally opened. He felt his heart pounding. "Shit," he whispered. He spat. His brain was churning again and there was a sad longing for—something. No need to worry about falling asleep with memories like those.

His hand ran along the chipped cooling ribs of his Thompson. He laughed bitterly to himself, and at himself. His bloodshot eyes took in the plains. He had that fullness in his throat, the need to shoot someone. He was not a gentle, or a very civilized man. His very decency had been in question time enough. Tonight, he questioned it himself. He knew what he was.

The night darkened now, when the clouds covered the moon. Time crawled slower with a passive malevolence. The black wind carried distant and forbidding volcanic odors: fire and brimstone. In all of the rush of unwelcome feelings that he had tonight, there was no regret. He tired of being awake, but dreaded sleep. Other night birds cried insults at him. He waited for the warning of the ghost owl, but never heard it again. He watched Delivalung glowing pink in the night. The enemy was out there, under that gravestone crater, and they were waiting for him. He would get there, and them, eventually.

He inevitably thought of Jessica again—the things she had said, and what she had meant. What she believed. The mountain began to look restful, and even a little pretty. The jungle beside him grew protective and friendly. The night became a little warmer and his eyes closed. He slept well, until disturbed by an unwelcome visitor.

Clifford Curry sat beside him. "Wake up, shit-for-brains."

Hawk opened his eyes deliberately, as if he had only been pretending to be asleep. The Thompson's muzzle was pointed at Curry's chest, perhaps by coincidence. "Curry."

"The one and only. Your old buddy. How you doing, Hawk?"

"Damn good, until just now. I been waitin' on you to turn up. How did you get here?"

"Walked. Just like you. See, I'm a privileged character, just like you. I go where the action is. Me and you are in the same club. We're where things happen." Curry flipped his crackle lighter open and lit a cigarette. His thin chest absorbed the smoke. "Let's not shit each other. Have you found anything?"

"Yeah. A nit-shit son of a bitch in my fighting hole."

"Still pissed off about those requisition papers that you signed for me?"

"Naw, *me*? What do you think? If I didn't have no better buddies than you, I'd be in Portsmouth bustin' rocks by now."

"Well, hell, I didn't know the deal wasn't on the level."

"Shee-it. The only thing that you didn't know about that crooked set up was that you would get caught. And that's the *only* thing. Since, you *did* know that *I* would get caught."

Curry shrugged. "That's over. Water under the duck's back. Time to move on. We could shoot the shit about old times all night. You think it's easy for me to come to you like this? A high-class guy like me? I wouldn't, if I didn't have to. I'm talking about something important right now. It's you and me again. We got no choice but to get along. Cooperation. Semper Fi. All that shit. I'll make you a deal. We're the only two with a chance to find this thing. The deal is fifty-fifty. Whoever finds it splits it with the other guy. One of us is bound to find it. Why should the other one be risking his neck for nothing? Winner take all is for suckers. You gotta cover your bets."

Hawk smiled. "I got no idea what you're talking about. Good to see you're covering something besides your ass."

"Gonna play it that way? The gold. Arnold told me some story about looking for scientific information, or raw materials or some shit. Something that the Japs got from the Germans. He's playing us both for saps. That bastard ain't supposed to be out on no gold hunt out here, no more than we are. But he is. He can't pin a thing on us, because he would expose himself to liability. I say, we find it, keep quiet, and come out all right. Hell, Hawk, even the *Japs* are looking for it. I've seen them with my own eyes, with mine detectors. That's the truth."

Hawk was quiet for a moment. A lot of people were telling him about things that they had seen with their own eyes. "Yeah? And Arnold told you that? Sounds like horse shit."

"That's exactly what I'm saying. He's keeping us apart. He tells you things, and he tells me different things. So as we don't figure it all out. He is taking us for a couple of rubes. You can't blame him...you act so goddam stupid. I mean, you *are* a rube, right? I think that damn Biedeker is in on the deal with him. It's not good that he's out here. What the hell is he doing here? He didn't come out here before, when you came. He's watching you. Something is up. I wouldn't say much to him, if I was you." Curry stood. "You think about it. You think about what I said. Show some common sense."

"Ain't got nothing to think about. Except maybe slapping the shit out of you. Fifty percent of nothing is nothing. Fifty percent of whatever you decided to share is less than nothing, unless it's jail time. If you think you got away with anything with me, you're in for few surprises. I ain't done with you, shithead."

"Okay, country Jake. Go back to your pea pickin'." Curry held up a hand in resignation. "You think about it." Curry slipped away.

Hawk lit a cigar. He thought about it.

* * *

THEY WERE on the march by 0600. Hawk walked beside Biedeker for a while. Biedeker was not a bad fellow. He had the usual arrogance of a young lieutenant, but that was to be expected. Hawk didn't hold that against him. You have to start somewhere. Biedeker's ears stuck straight out from his head. He had a small nose and lips that didn't exactly close. He looked like a tall elf.

On a whim, Hawk decided to find out what Biedeker knew about any of this. While Hawk distrusted Curry, and found Arnold hard to trust, Biedeker didn't seem to fit in with either of them. A young officer would not get mixed up with a couple of crooked old bastards, and they would probably be afraid to enter into a scheme with someone who might still be saturated with schoolboy ethics, and proud of his commission. Hawk was not sure which category he himself fell into. He had failed to notice that it was only the crooks who were approaching him, and that there might have been a reason for that. He was obviously no schoolboy.

"Might get there today, sir," Hawk said casually.

"Yes. I wonder if they are out there."

"I think so. If they're anywhere. Yes, sir."

"Yeah." Biedeker looked at Delivalung. His helmet was large for his head. "Man, I would like to catch old Tojo himself out there," said the Lieutenant. "We would be famous."

"I'm holding out for the Emperor." Hawk smiled. He thought that he had heard that Tojo was in disgrace. Or, in something. America would need a new villain. Biedeker probably didn't know anything about underhanded treasure hunting. He was just a kid with a little college that got swept up in the patriotic fervor. Curry was full of shit about this kid.

Hawk fell behind. He hadn't found a way to broach the subject with Biedeker. Once you mentioned something like that, the die was cast. It had occurred to Hawk, that for someone who didn't believe in the treasure, and had no interest in it, he spent a lot of time asking everyone about it. People might start noticing.

Eventually, Joe Canlon came up beside Hawk, breathing heavily. "What did the Lieutenant say?" Joe asked. He was always curious as to matters concerning his own immediate future.

"He said he thinks that were going to find Tojo and the Emperor out there at that volcano."

"No, shit? He believes all that shit?"

"Well, he ain't the only one. Hey, guess who I seen last night?"

"Groucho Marx?"

"Clifford Curry. Now, he says that we're after Germans, too."

"No, shit? They said a bunch of those Nazis are getting out of Berlin, you know. If the Jap big shots are here, maybe they are, too. Hey, you know?" Joe's eyes got big. "That's it! I bet we're after Hitler." Hawk said nothing. Enough seeds of nonsense had been sown. Joe became quiet as well. Finally, he said, "That Curry guy is bad news."

Hawk abruptly laughed at the understatement.

At midday, dark forms began crossing their path on the distant plains. Leading the patrol, and the first to see, Hawk raised his arm ordering a halt, and then gestured for everyone to hit the deck. The Sergeant had never done any close work, and he could see sharply for miles. He recognized the Japanese column for what it was. The enemy wore caps with havelocks.

Biedeker entered into a discussion with him, over whether to attack them or let them pass. Biedeker's mission, as he saw it, was to destroy every Japanese encountered. Twenty disembodied silhouettes were stretched out across the plain in front of him, with more coming out of the jungle.

"I wouldn't do that, sir," Hawk said. "We'll probably see a hell of a lot more of them before this is over." The count reached thirty, with no suggestion of an end.

"But that is the order," Biedeker insisted.

"Well, I'd at least let them all get out into the open, so that we can see what we're up against. Then we could hit the middle of the column. But then, I don't think we have any orders saying that we should attack a division. You gotta kinda evaluate the situation on the ground, in a deal like this."

"Yes, we don't know if any have already reached the jungle on the other side. You're right. They're could be more."

"Could be a lot," Hawk said, hoping to delay this inadvisable attack long enough to come up with a still better argument. When the count reached a definite forty, Biedeker decided to wait. When it got to the sixty mark, the Japanese reached the far jungle and their lead man disappeared into it. The column ended at a count of approximately a hundred men, give or take a few miscalculations. It was too many for Biedeker to take on. Everyone breathed a sigh of relief. They were skeptical of young lieutenants, still high on adolescent stories of the Alamo and the three hundred Spartans.

"Well, Lieutenant. It's better this way, anyhow," said Hawk. "We were supposed to be scouting the mountain and finding out total troop estimates. We would never find out anything if we got into a scrape here. That was a lot of Japs."

After a prudent wait, Biedeker led the patrol forward. The open country ended and the jungle returned. It was thick, and the trees grew to an enormous height and girth. Unlike most rain forests where the larger trees grow, thick vegetation grew under the cover of the canopy. Plants that did not require much light sprouted and overlapped, clutching and clawing at each other for the light that remained. Huge ferns dwarfed the men, as if they had entered a land of giants. The ancient trees extended upward forever, and the width of their trunks sprawled in knotted massiveness. Fuzzy toadstools grew in profusion on the ground. Shelf-like mushrooms stair-stepped up the bark of the trees. Monkeys rioted overhead, often falling to the earth in what seemed to be a suicidal pursuit of excitement.

Progress slowed. The point men used machetes. Vines protected themselves against the invaders with barbs. The pace would increase when the patrol struck upon a patch of hollow, water-filled tubers, only to slow again when they stumbled into more of the briars.

"Goddam shit is what this is," Joe cursed. He used to like to go up to the woods in Canada. The forest was clean and fresh, without all this crap growing between the trees. The vegetation here stank, and the leaves were dirty. Joe decided that he would never go into the woods again. They seemed a little scary now. It was not the threat of the Japanese so much as it was the choking, claustrophobic isolation.

"Spotted Hitler yet?" Hawk asked him.

"Kiss my ass, Hawk." Joe pulled a vine off his shoulder. "Like we're going to see anything in this shit. They told me to look for something, didn't they?"

"See it?"

"Kiss my ass."

Things got a little worse, as they sometimes do. They thought for a while that they had gone off course. Biedeker could not see the flat stump of Delivalung from beneath the encroaching forest roof. Map reading had never agreed with him. He could not even find his way out of the swamps in North Carolina during training. Fortunately, the heavy ground cover stopped at length, and they could again see the mountain, their primary point of reference. Unfortunately, the jungle ended in a gruesome swamp. Biedeker called for a rest. Everyone eyed the swamp with trepidation, and smoked cigarettes.

"Hope we don't go off into that shit," Joe said. He felt alone out here, in spite of having a dozen comrades.

Biedeker decided that the marshland must be crossed, or they risked losing sight of the objective again.

Fifteen minutes later, after taking a few readings on the location, they had unhappily plunged into the swamp. The vivid green water slithered at waist depth, with unseen muck languishing at about knee depth. Joe gasped and forced his legs through the slime. He held his rifle high overhead. The very real threat of perishing in this horror was uppermost in the minds of everyone there. Anything could be under that hostile, threatening surface.

Hawk did not like the looks of it. It was too much like New Britain. But he wanted to get to the mountain, with its answers to most of the questions on everyone's minds. Including, the minds of the Japanese.

They meandered through a network of grasping dead trees. A porous maroon fungus grew on the dead, white tree branches. It became a little clearer why this area had been declared taboo. Instead of superstitious nonsense, it appeared to be a completely logical assessment of the area. The men watched carefully for snakes, and the snakes generously accommodated their efforts, performing in animated troupes. But no one saw the thing that finally attacked them. An enormous, long-snouted crocodile, the same color as the mud, submarined under the bubble-topped, floating scum, snapping its toothed vise onto the leg of McLean, the BAR man. He had time to cry out before being slammed onto the water's surface and dragged under. It happened that Hawk was closest to the incident and reacted first. He saw the ugly ribbed tail of the creature gliding along the surface, curving in a serpentine effort to submerge back into the mud. Hawk quickly slung his Thompson with resignation, and instinctively grabbed at the tail with both hands. The others watched in surprise, with a natural reaction to avoid the horrid reptile.

Latching onto the animal was like trying to hold onto a moving car. In shallower water, Hawk might have stalled it. Here, the unperturbed crocodile jerked him off his feet, completely ignoring the added weight. The tail began moving in a slow and irritated way at first, and then the motion escalated into a deadly slashing back and forth. Hawk grabbed higher up on the appendage. His head went under several times, as the animal bobbed up and down. He saw black bubbles before his eyes and felt himself being carried into the endless marsh silt, to a destination known only within the tiny brain of the crocodile. He heard the BAR man scream once, and he knew that the victim was still alive. The crocodile finally stopped.

The creature bit spasmodically at the leg, seeking to strengthen its grip. The human prey tried to pull free, as his attacker choked on him. Hawk could see the man standing on one leg with the other stretched across and through the razor-toothed jaws. The boot on the bitten leg was turned backwards.

Hawk reached for the crocodile's hind legs. The

claws pointed away from him, and he was being pounded only by the back of the creature's rounded foot. Holding the tail under one arm, and a hind foot with the other hand, he decided that his grip was firm. The great muddy body wagged back and forth madly.

The crocodile had stopped because McLean was fouled in a dead tree. It was stuck between the tree and Hawk, with Hawk trying to increase its difficulties. The animal tried to go forward, and Hawk aided in the effort, pushing him in the same direction. The crocodile would not release McLean, and Hawk would not release the crocodile. It was a battle to see which of them had the smallest brain.

Hawk caught a glimpse of the men standing behind him. Biedeker did not want to fire at the animal for fear of alerting the Japanese. From Hawk's viewpoint, something had to give. He let go of the foot and wrestled his knife from its scabbard. He swung over the released hind leg, let go of the tail, and climbed up the metal hard, glass slick body. He reasoned that the animal was never going to let go of McLean's leg. Its instinct told it to pull the victim under the water, drown, and devour him. There was no room in its prehistoric mind for strategy, regrets or reconsiderations.

Joe Canlon watched, not having any idea as to what to do. He could not imagine what Hawk was trying to do. He had nothing in his history of human experience to compare the scene to. Joe found his hands attaching his bayonet to his rifle. His Marine Corps trained hands had a plan, even if his brain did not.

At the heart of the maelstrom, things could get no worse. Mercifully, the huge jaws were clamped shut, and determinedly so. No power on earth could open them.

The killer tail was behind Hawk. The short, barbed legs were swimming again, and not clawing at him. The snout was tilted upward, uncomfortably clinging to its prey. Hawk looked into the mindless, hooded eye of the beast. The protective underwater membrane flicked rapidly open and shut over the demonic orb.

Hawk quickly studied the shredded human leg, thrust through both sides of the rending eating machine. He would have to get to the other side, next to McLean, in order to cut the leg free, one way or the other. This would require somehow vaulting out of the water, onto the slick back, and climbing over the animal. He had experienced adolescent adventures with similar reptilian monsters, breeding a familiarity with the unfamiliar. This may have been one reason why there were less little boys in Mississippi than elsewhere. It may also have been why Hawk had grabbed the tail in the first place, while everyone else had stood watching.

As Hawk lifted himself over the crocodile, it lost some of its buoyancy under his weight. He madly rammed the point of the knife into the top of the crocodile's skull. It glanced harmlessly off, chipping some of the thick hide away. The head was like a slab of concrete. A branch as tough as iron stabbed Hawk in the face as he found himself now interwoven into the myriad of clawing tree limbs. The crocodile finally processed a slow-moving thought of its own, and threw his powerful engine into reverse. A branch impaling McLean's shoulder slid out a bit during the withdrawal. In that instant, Hawk saw that the battle would soon be over. Once free, beast and prey would disappear into the grotesque mire, and probably with a fatal clubbing to Hawk from the vengeful tail for good measure.

The rescuer held his knife in a blade over position. He was next to a pouch at the corner of the great lizard's mouth. This protuberance lay between the mouth and neck. The knife came up and into the pouch in a furious explosion of anger. McLean slipped free of the branch. Blood spurt from his unplugged shoulder. Hawk brought the knife up under the water. A surge of super charged adrenaline augmented his powerful upper body strength. The point passed all the way through the soft bottom of the snout, through the tongue and partly into the roof of the animal's mouth.

The crocodile would not let go. It probably hardly felt the knife, having little or no part of a brain to sense such matters. It continued to throw itself about wildly. Hawk could not pull the knife out and his hand was knocked free of the handle. The beast turned and twisted onto its back. McLean's leg was torn off. The root of the tail hit Hawk, pushing him through the water for several feet. The push was forceful, but without any whip-like snapping, or injurious blow at the end of it. When Hawk managed to stand again, the crocodile was rolling over and over in death throes. McLean was free, only his head above the vile liquid.

Hawk snatched the Thompson off his back and leveled it at the crocodile.

"Don't shoot!" Biedeker shouted. "The Japs!"

Hawk slung the weapon. Seeing that only advice was being offered, without any aid, he pulled McLean safely away from the endless rotating of the reptile. Finally, hands reached out to help with the injured man. With everyone gathered together again, that should have been the end of the remarkable incident. Instead, Hawk took the rifle and bayonet from Joe

Canlon and speared the flailing animal in a raging fit, until its undying reptilian nerves ceased to function. He sat in the water up to his neck, beside the carcass, breathing heavily. No one approached him, or the repulsive dragon he had slain.

Biedeker had to get McLean out of there. He told the men to make a stretcher out of lashed together rifles, and shirts. The leg was tied off, and a compress put on the shoulder. Everyone contributed their sulfa pouches, in the hope of staving off infection. McLean had gone into shock. He appeared to be close to death. Biedeker frequently checked his pulse, at the neck and the wrist, to see if it still thumped. With disappointment, and with the accompanying guilt at the disappointment, he found each time that McLean still lived. Biedeker was worried about abandoning the mission. This would be the end of it. It would mean a setback of several days, with the whole procedure having to be repeated. The Japanese build up would be even larger by then, for the world does not stand still, and perhaps no American would ever be able to get into the region again.

The Lieutenant resigned himself to failure, however, deciding to end the patrol and return to Sacred Blood. The men assembled on the edge of the swamp. Hawk sat apart from them, still dazed, watching none of the arrangements. His entire body ached and his heart still pounded. Biedeker considered him as ineffective as McLean. It would probably be days before Hawk recovered from the encounter. No one had approached Hawk to check for any physical injuries. Presumably, he was using this time to recover from the emotional trauma.

They eased McLean onto the stretcher. Baker grinned and said, "He's gonna die."

Biedeker told them to move out. Hawk at last stood, as if awakening.

"What the hell are y'all doing?" he asked, in a deep and knifing voice that seemed to come from the lungs of an animal. There were few human aspects about Hawk as he lurched up out of the mud with a violent and accusing attitude. Everyone froze like children caught scribbling on the living room wall, including Biedeker.

"We're going back, Sergeant. Come on," said the Lieutenant.

"That's some shit," Hawk said. "Send six men back with the stretcher. We can go on. There's no way in hell we can just go back. They're counting on us."

Biedeker's face reddened. His rank preserved him from some of the fear of Hawk shared by the others, but not entirely. They were a long way from anything that respected such intangible matters as rank.

Hawk rubbed his lacerated forehead and looked for his helmet floating in the water. The others watched him curiously. Some glanced at Biedeker. As Biedeker wasn't talking, it seemed the next move would come from the Sergeant.

Hawk's eye caught the stretcher. "What the hell are them rifles doin' tied to that stretcher?" he snarled. "Do you know what a goddam rifle is for? You got a swamp full of sticks out there. Go get the sons of bitches!" The men jumped as if they had been shot, everyone stopping what they were doing and dropping what they were holding. Four of them began ripping feverishly at the rifle lashings. Biedeker looked down in amazement and saw that he was one of those with his fingers tangled in the lashings.

Hawk muttered obscenities under his breath as he

tried to look into the distance of the swamp stretching all around them.

Biedeker walked slowly over to Hawk. "Sergeant, I'd like a word with you," he said meekly.

Hawk sensed that Biedeker was scared of him. He had not intended that. Perhaps his anger had gotten the best of him. In the heat of the moment, he had given the order that had to be given, and had forgotten to make it look like it was Biedeker's order.

"Yessir," Hawk said quietly.

Biedeker felt a little relieved, and back in control. He led the Sergeant away from the others. Hawk turned his profile to the officer as he listened. "I've got to get that man back," Biedeker explained. "He might live."

"No argument there, sir. He might. Get him back, Sir."

"Can you go on with three men, and Luka? You think you are up to it?"

"I can carry three men and Luka on my back. I can go on by myself, if I have to." *And be better off*, Hawk said to himself.

"So, you're all right?" The Lieutenant asked the question of, what to him, resembled an escaped mental patient; a role Hawk had recently played in fact.

"Fine. Just fine."

"Okay, then. I'll tell you what. You take Canlon, Dupuy, and Lynwood. And, I guess, Luka. Peep at the mountain and come back. They want to know what's there. Engagement is out of the question now. We just need surveillance. Report anything unusual between here and there and avoid contact."

"Got it." Hawk took a deep breath. His fists were clenched. He felt like hitting someone. Biedeker? Why

Biedeker? Why anyone? A rational thought crossed his mind. *What the hell are you mad at? A goddam dead alligator?*

He grew calm.

"The stretcher was my idea. I wasn't thinking. Be a little more discreet in your criticism, huh?"

"Yessir. Sorry, gotta little rude there."

Biedeker nodded solemnly. He motioned for the men to pick up McLean. Hawk noticed that Baker was on one of the makeshift handles. He didn't like that.

Long range patrols were still a tough business. Being a part of one was akin to being an old style, nineteenth century explorer, in the sense that with no ready access to air transport, when a man got out there, way out there, his feet were the only way back. The only other option was another kind hearted soul willing to carry him out. It was worse than being an explorer, of course, in that the distance was not the only problem. There were certain additional obstacles that explorers did not have to confront, and most of those obstacles were raised by Japanese combatants intent on destroying all opposition. Such war time obstacles could make any spot on earth seem as isolated as the dark side of the moon. But when one was already on the dark side of the moon, things looked even more grimly overwhelming.

The men doing this sort of thing sometimes had a rough set of morals. They were a self-sufficient breed, and expected their companions to be the same. Nevertheless, most were incredibly brave and willing to sacrifice a great deal to save a companion sharing their hardship. The Corps demanded as much. There were a few others, however, who were of less noble disposition, and had only the rough set of morals.

Sergeant Hawk knew all about this. He had been "way out there" many times, and knew the lifestyle. He had seen a lot of things happen. He had no mistaken notions about the basic goodness of humanity, or adherence to high ideals. He had seen the human psyche under stress.

Along with this knowledge, Hawk also had a certain familiarity specific to Corporal Baker. Baker was a good man in a fight, and could be counted upon. The upcoming return to Sacred Blood, however, was not a fight. It was a journey. To Baker, McLean was a heavy object, a problem impeding that journey. When a group was way out there, with no way back, problems could sometimes be solved with bullets. Then everybody survived, and lived happily ever after, except the one receiving the bullet. Biedeker did not understand this. It may have been one of those things you had to see to believe; which is probably good, because, do you really want to believe that about your fellow man? Hawk didn't have a lot of beliefs, but he had a lot of experience.

He didn't explain any of this, he just made a simple statement. His intuitive simplicity is why most people did not care for Sergeant Hawk. "I'll take Baker," Hawk said. "You keep Dupuy."

Biedeker was looking down, tying a canteen onto the stretcher. "Well, all right," said the Lieutenant. "See you in Sacred Blood."

"Yes, sir." Neither noticed that the person saying 'yes, sir,' was the one giving the order.

10

THE HEAD OF ISHAKAWI

BAKER WAS NOT HAPPY ABOUT THE CHANGE IN PLANS, BUT accepted them. Happiness was in short supply all around. He and Luka prepared to be a part of the less attractive half of the expedition. Baker had been with Hawk a long time and accepted him as part of his life. Baker, Canlon, and Lynwood followed him back into the swamp. Him. That's how they all three thought of Hawk. They were in his power. It was much different than being under the power of someone like Biedeker. Biedeker had human reason that adhered to such things as order, norms, regulations, common sense, and decency. You had a right to expect that.

They were now following a man with reasoning little different from that of the crocodile he had recently slain. He did not know how to let go. They absorbed the fear from the cold dirty water he led them through. Their teeth chattered. They were afraid of the reptile-infested swamp, the haunted volcano, the Japanese, and of *him*. They were afraid of God, who had arranged all of these things around them. They did not have the luxury of a college professor sipping his tea back at home, to doubt or complain to God, or to deny his existence in a fit of ego. They did not try to argue with God, and tell him that a nice God would not put people in such circumstances; circumstances that even they, with all of their flaws, would not inflict on someone. They knew full well that God was out there, and evidently not too thrilled with them, and they prayed for mercy. What had they done to deserve this? They had a lot of time to think about all of it. Between every deadly step.

Hawk's mood cooled. He could feel the quietness of the others. *What's wrong with those sons of bitches?* he thought. Like the crocodile, he had no conception of fear. He had attached his willpower to the lone concept of finding out what was at Delivalung as a crocodile latches onto a leg. Lives could be saved if he did his job right. The fear felt by the others was not a part of him. Sometimes this is the case with leaders, because they plan on the glory they will receive at the expense of the fear of their underlings. Hawk was a more dangerous type of leader. He had no interest in glory. He was just a dirty crocodile in a dirty swamp, doing what crocodiles do.

But the swamp was wide, and they all had a lot of time to think.

Eventually, a thought even crossed the mind of James Hawk. He was human, after all, or at least the unproven theory was that he had been spawned by human parents, of some sort. The thought that rose within him was of Jessica Pearson. Hawk was all business, and he did not like this thought. But there it was. He could see her green eyes. And then he saw himself, here: with his shirt open, his hairy, filthy, muscle knotted body wading through ass deep scum, clutching ten pounds of loaded steel, ready and willing to blow anything he saw into oblivion. And son of a bitching blood still leaking unchecked from his forehead. *A woman likes the finer things, mate. And you ain't one of the finer things.*

Hawk's cold blue eyes scanned the swamp. He spat, pushing his boots harder against the soft restraining mud. He was not afraid of her, either. You can't lose something you don't have. He had lost before. Not this time. He saw this one coming. Nothing sneaked up on James Hawk twice.

They crossed the swamp and came to dry land before midafternoon. According to the map, such as it was, it should have been easy going after this. Luka could not confirm the fact. He had never been here before. He didn't like being here now. He had wanted to go back with the others, with McLean. This place was forbidden to his people. If he failed to return, his tribal memory would consist of a big fat "I told you so" around the breakfast fire. After this patrol, he decided that he was retiring from military service. Pearl Harbor didn't mean a whole lot to Luka. James Hawk, however, was beginning to have some meaning.

The swamp stretched on endlessly, but now they were able to skirt it and head toward the jungle highlands beneath the crater of Delivalung. With the swamp and its concealed vipers behind him, Joe Canlon relaxed. He was not a timid soul. If things eased up a little, he was a resilient fellow. He felt no army in its right mind would be in this dense undergrowth. They were just messing around now. He could mess around with the best of them.

Hawk felt the same way. Only he wasn't pleased about it. If he didn't find the Japanese, this was all a waste of time. It had been his conviction that the enemy would be here. McLean might die because of it. And this thing wasn't over. There were more crocodiles out there.

The treetops grew shorter. Delivalung lunged out of the green canopy and glared ferociously down on them like the universe itself. It almost had a voice, or a soundtrack. They glanced silently up at it. Just a few kilometers to go, and still no enemy, only one more magnificently remote natural formation. The dead looking summit bubbled somewhat actively. Roiling steam wafted in flexing claws, blocking most of the aquamarine sky. It was easy to see why it had the reputation of an angry and evil spirit. Luka's eyes opened wide. His regrets evolved into a terror. Baker grinned. Hawk squinted distractedly up at the ancient and routine performances of the mountain. It meant nothing to him.

Joe and Lynwood squinted at Hawk. Would this ever end?

"We'll follow the edge of the swamp here for a look-see," Hawk said in a low voice. "Then I expect we'll go into this damn thing." Hawk unslung his Thompson and straightened a cotter pin on a grenade. "Y'all stay here. Joe, come with me."

Joe staggered reluctantly forward and followed him. Joe felt tired, as if his brain was in a vacuum. He wasn't ready for any life and death contests. *This is something a guy should do when he first wakes up*, he thought. He knew this was a dangerous feeling; this exhaustion. This was when things happen. His boot hit a lump of sedge roots and he caught himself with a hand on the uneven ground.

"Cut that shit out," Hawk snapped. Clumsiness irritated him. He didn't think that Joe paid enough attention to what he was doing. He worried too much about getting killed, and not enough about how to keep from getting killed. Hawk knew how to step on a dry stick, test it, and step over it, all in the fraction of an instant, to prevent it from snapping. Life was made up of instants, and you had to take advantage of them, before you went that one instant too far, and it was over. Things weren't divided into hours, minutes, or seconds. It was all in the instants. The present was an instant. He could slither free of detaining vines and creepers without effort, and had little patience for those who blundered into them. He slid through mud like a skater on ice. If you couldn't learn these things, you would probably get what you deserved.

Joe decided that this was a good time to broach a subject he had been thinking about. Perhaps, alone he could reason with Hawk, or in some manner, understand his motives.

"You didn't think Biedeker was right about going back? Giving this up?"

"No, shit, no. He was a pain in the ass. Dumb bastard."

That was probably the end of that subject. Argument over.

They wound through a stretch of half jungle and half marsh. Hawk stopped suddenly. Joe froze. His hands tingled and a balloon expanded at the back of skull, until it felt like it would break. Being on a patrol placed one under indescribable tension. When something finally happened, the build-up of stress was more of a hindrance than a help. Joe's nerves were overworked. They were twentieth century nerves operating at the cave man level over a long period of time. He stood very still, until he saw Hawk take another slow and deliberate step.

"Look at this," Hawk said in a low voice, waving his head. He was looking at the saturated earth at the edge of the marsh. Joe stepped forward gingerly. He didn't see much of anything.

"What? That log?" Joe whispered. That was about the only thing around, besides a few wet leaves, and their own boot prints.

"That ain't no log."

"Yeah, it is. It's like a big cedar, ain't it?"

"Look closer."

"Is it wired?"

"No. Look at it. Look at the grooves in it."

"Yeah. Like a cedar."

"No, *shithead*. A goddam cedar ain't got no grooves in it. That's rock."

Joe looked closer. He was clearly missing something here. The log did not appear to him to be that fascinating. What was this all about?

"I think you're right," Joe said. "I guess it's that petrified wood stuff. Probably something to do with the volcano, or the swamp. I don't know a lot about rocks. Had some petrified wood when I was a kid." Joe looked up again, and around at the strangely still foliage all around them. There was no sound, not even a breeze.

Then, perhaps it was only his imagination, but he could faintly hear something dragging—like a phantom, breathing heavily, and...walking slowly...way off. "So what?"

Hawk went to one knee. He was too engrossed in what he had found to pay attention to any unusual whisper in the distance. "Take a look at it now."

Joe craned his neck. He didn't see that the rock, or log, or petrified wood, had taken any action since the last time he had looked at it. "Mm," said Joe.

But Hawk saw a half-buried stone with a sort of abacus carved into it: the flat part of the top of a column. "This here is a post off'n a building."

Joe looked at the large-pored, gray stone. "Hmm, yeah. I see what you mean. Like on a courthouse or a post office or something."

"That's right." Hawk nodded. They looked at each other. Joe thought: *something unusual.* Hawk thought: *treasure.*

"What's it doing here?" Joe asked.

"Just layin' there," said Hawk. "Doing nothing."

"No, I mean, why would there be a post office out here?"

Hawk looked around the sloping bank of the swamp. He saw no other potential examples of architecture, until he turned almost all the way around and looked out into the marsh itself. Some thirty yards out, an algae-covered object, that could be the corner of an upturned pagoda roof, barely broke the surface. Or, it could be a tree stump. The water may have until recently covered the building, if that it is what it was. Recently, in archaeological terms, could be defined as within the last hundred years.

"Under that swamp. Under that shit," Hawk whispered.

Joe followed his line of sight. He saw nothing of interest. "What?" he asked.

"I don't know." Hawk's eyes flicked across the eerie morass. He thought he saw something that might be solid ground in the foggy water, past the sunken roof, maybe seventy-five yards out. The large living trees, blanketed with vines, leaned with an evil sway. "Then again, maybe it *ain't* under the water. There's dry ground out there." Joe looked out into the swamp. Fog swirled through the fungus encased tree claws.

"If I ever seen a son of a bitch that looked haunted, that's it," said Joe.

"Yeah," Hawk agreed, with a wicked smile. "Look over there." He pointed to a hump of mud in the distance. A score of crocodiles climbed languidly over one another, their short legs constantly peddling. Their island was surrounded by the litharge-colored liquid. "Wonder how hungry them old boys is?"

Joe shook his head as he watched one of the long snouts open. A noise that was something between a bellow and a hiss leaked out of the foul cavern. "I imagine they always got room for a snack." Joe looked around for closer dangers. He still heard that odd whispering sound.

Hawk's ears were full of water and swamp scum.

"You hear something? Sounds like breathing. Or something sliding," Joe asked. Hawk shook his head negatively. "Step over here. You can hear it better over here." Joe went to step aside, and half tripped over his feet.

"Nah, I don't hear nothing. You goddam oaf. Come on," Hawk said, turning away from the swamp. "Don't tell nobody about this here rock."

"Why not?"

"What for?"

Joe nodded his assent and reserved judgment for the time being. Petrified wood was not that interesting. Or unusual. Well, maybe a little, for a kid or something. But, hell. *Don't tell anybody?* Nobody would give a shit. What would you tell? It would be a short story.

Hawk moved toward the volcano. They reached a break in the tree line and saw the whole of the breathtaking spectacle. Delivalung's massive base crouched broad and angry in the black-floored jungle.

"Another kilometer or so. We'll see what's what, then we can go back," Hawk rumbled.

"Yeah. Looks quiet to me." Joe looked at Hawk's smoldering eyes. "Don't it?"

"Yeah. So far. Come on."

They walked for a while under the concealment of some trees growing along a sandy rift. A refreshingly clean breeze swung under the shadowy branches. Grains of sand scintillated in the sun below them in the narrow formation. Joe was positive that he heard voices this time. The sound drifted vaguely on the wind, like a poor radio signal. *It's what a ghost would sound like*, Joe thought, or a hallucination.

"You hear something now?" Joe stuttered.

"Yeah."

"What the hell is that?"

"Japs. It's a couple of Japs talking."

Joe looked around. Sometimes it can be difficult to tell which direction a sound is coming from. In this setting, it was even more difficult. But it was also more important. "Where? Where are they?"

"Just up ahead. Come on, and don't make any of your stupid noises."

The rift became shallower. Hawk paused. He and Joe heard stone crunching underfoot. Hawk brushed aside a fern. They could see the burnt-orange layer of sediment in the little canyon below. Two men walked beneath them. One wore a white Naval uniform, heavily decorated. The other wore nothing. The one with the uniform had his arm around the other one.

"Get a load of this," said Hawk. Joe strained his eyes through the leaves, and was speechless. A bird, not far above their heads, whooped loudly. Hawk quickly let the screening foliage drop back into place, and crouched. The bird flew away, and neither of the Japanese turned around.

"Son of a bitch!" Hawk whispered, watching the bird soar over the jungle on the other side of the rift. "Goddam stupid ass bird!" He continued peering through the green needles of the leaves. "You know what?"

"Yeah, I got to shit."

"That's a goddam admiral. Or else we're at a costume party."

"Yeah, I don't think that's no admiral. Those guys wear costumes and stuff. Let's get the hell out of here."

"Wait a second." Hawk rubbed his straight, narrow nose. "They're walking up toward the mountain. Something must be up there."

"Well, there you go. That's all we need to know. Let's hit the trail, kemosabe."

"Shit. Shut the hell up. Let me think here." The voices drifted up the walls of the rift to the Americans. Unlike a European or other language, there was not a single word or intonation the observers could understand. The pair below appeared to be unarmed.

"We better go," said Joe. "If they're walking around naked, this place could be swarming with them. I tell you, I already heard something walking behind us back there."

"Nah, just wait. I think they're looking for a place to be alone. They don't want the others to catch them."

"Bullshit. How the hell would you know that? Japs do all kind of crazy shit. There ain't no telling what the hell they're doing. Did it ever occur to you that we're probably surrounded here?"

Hawk held his palm out. "Take it easy. Nobody can see us. You're gettin' all worked up. This could be important. This might be what we're here for. An admiral? Do you see any ships around? If an admiral got here, he didn't get out here the way we did, that's for damn sure. There could be an airfield or something on the other side of that mountain. Now, listen. You keep up with them, see? I'm going over on the other side of the draw. When you figure that I've about caught up with them, you yell something, like some Jap thing or something. I need a diversion. Got it?"

Joe batted his hand vigorously, indicating that he did *not* have it, and did not want it. "Look, Hawk, you're either gonna get us killed, or blow the cover on our whole mission. We're supposed to find Japs, not go fartin' around until *they* find *us*. You can't catch an admiral. How the hell could we get him out of here? It's crazy. He's got to have a body guard around here. Admirals got whole staffs and all kind of shit. Have you ever seen a Jap that wouldn't kill hisself before letting you capture him? He's got a staff."

"I don't think this one does. Not right now, anyway. Just do it. Don't be stupid."

Joe opened his mouth to make his next argument, but Hawk slid down into the rift, leaving Joe alone, with only an exhaled obscenity. He really hated it, too, because his next argument was a good one. He was going to suggest that looking at the other side of the mountain was more important than capturing an admiral—which, he still considered impossible.

Hawk slid down into the rift. Had the two Japanese turned around, they would have seen him. Had they not been talking, they would have heard him. He climbed up the other side of the canyon with the agility of a spider and disappeared in the shady jungle on the other side. Joe watched in horrified disgust. He was going to be a part of whatever maniacal thing happened next, and that was not a comforting thought. He moaned. He could see Hawk making his way behind them, a dark shadow, cutting rapidly through the lighter shadows, like a shark underwater.

"*Shit!* What did he say to do?" Joe got up. The Sergeant had told him something about catching up with the two Japanese. He swallowed and began following the admiral and his paramour. Since he had no intention of following the instructions at the time Hawk had been giving them, he had not been listening very closely. He saw Hawk stick his head out of the forest on the other side. All four of them were now abreast of one another.

Mercifully, Joe remembered *diversion*. It was a big word for Hawk, and so it stuck in Joe's memory. And with that prompting, he then remembered he was supposed to yell something in Japanese. *What the hell, I don't know any Japanese?* Joe didn't like the plan and he didn't like the idea. He aimed his rifle at the two men, as added insurance. Hawk winced when he saw this, having no idea what Joe might do next.

"Sayonara!" Joe screamed.

The admiral and the boy stopped walking. The admiral turned toward Joe and looked up. Joe's Japanese had a decidedly New York accent, but it was confusing enough. The embarrassed admiral thought for certain that he had been spied by a mocking Japanese peeping Tom. The admiral began shouting angrily up at Joe, who was still well concealed in the brush.

"Shit—on—this," Joe whispered, as he listened to the angry tirade. An ass chewing by an officer didn't sound much better in Japanese than it did in English. The boy looked up at the officer's angry red face with a docile expression. Joe's mouth opened as he saw Hawk sliding down the side of the rift toward the two of them. He had gained significant momentum and collided with the fuming admiral's back. The Sergeant's black-bladed jungle knife appeared on the front of the white uniform, in a clenched fist.

"What in *God's* name is he doing," Joe whined. It looked like Hawk was awkwardly holding the admiral, instead of putting the knife to the use for which it was intended.

Hawk found himself wrapped around a fairly strong, middle-aged man. *He's a big bastard,* the Marine thought, now that he had closed on him. His descent had been too rapid and now he was haphazardly tangled up with the man. He lashed frantically at the rib region, regretting that he had not targeted the kidneys. Nothing had gone as planned. He scrambled, trying to make anything happen. The blade hit bone, and folded back a slab of flesh and white fabric. Blood made the work slippery. He lunged higher for the heart. He realized that he was going to have to make up for his lack of finesse with savagery.

The Japanese officer fell screaming to the ground under the weight, his shiny white garment now stained with red. The point of the blade at last sank into the chest with depressing certainty. The strong muscles of his adversary relaxed, and Hawk jumped to his feet.

The boy now stood paralyzed in front of a giant and brutal American, clutching a grisly red knife. He began squealing, bowing, and then fell to his knees. *I gotta stop this shit.* Hawk brought the knife up under the small chin, fast and hard. He looked away from the mutilated and accusing face, and rammed the blade home twice more into the body. He looked both ways, up and down the rift. To the north, the canyon ran into the base of Delivalung. To the south it approached the swamp. As far as he could tell, it remained deserted.

Hawk looked up at Joe from the gruesome scene. "Cover me," he said in a normal voice, which barely reached the top of the ravine. He cut the epaulets off the uniform and stuffed them into his pockets. He looked at the lacerated blouse. It had more decorations than he had pockets, and they were even bigger and gaudier than the crap Americans wore.

"Shit," Hawk grumbled. The guy was probably showing off for the kid. More chopping ensued. He grabbed the admiral's collar and drug him toward the slope below Joe. He had to get the two of them out of sight. He dragged the admiral up the side of the ravine. "Go get the other one," Hawk told Joe.

"Why?"

"Do you want them to find him?"

"But he's naked."

"Are you shittin' me? Get the hell down there, and get the son of a bitch!"

"You lunatic. Why did you kill the little one?"

"What did you want me to do, send him home and tell him to write? Make him promise not to tell?"

Joe tightened his lips and climbed down the slope. He sucked air through his teeth when he saw the boy's face. But it was not the first dead Japanese that Joe Canlon had seen. He grabbed the arms and pulled the comparatively light weight up the bank. He was wheezing and sweating, and as he dragged the corpse into the concealing bushes, he was cursing Hawk. He stopped when he saw the scene in the shadows of the leaves before him. Hawk had removed the admiral's head.

"We gotta know who he is," Hawk shrugged. "I don't know what else to do. Make it look like that one committed *hara kiri*. Maybe they won't know who did it until we can get the hell out of here."

"They'll know somebody else did it. I don't know how to do it right. That's just crazy."

"You've seen the sons of bitches do it. It just looks like they pulled their guts out. They won't know the difference. Hurry it up."

Sweat poured off Joe's forehead. He shuddered. What if somebody found them doing this? Joe didn't so easily put the laws of civilization behind him.

"They aren't going to believe that. Look at his face. That ain't *hara kiri*. You already screwed that up," Joe said. "Japs don't stick knives through their own heads."

"Aw'ight. Shit. Don't do *anything*. I might as well be here by myself for all the good you are."

"We ought to dump them in the swamp," said Joe.

"Too damn far. They might not even find them here. This ain't exactly Main Street. They ain't gonna have Charlie Chan working on the case. Just a bunch of Jap shitheads." He angrily ripped the resisting coat off the headless torso. He spread it on the ground and kicked the head into the coat with his boot. He made a neat bundle of it, carrying it in one hand and the Thompson in the other.

"What if that ain't no admiral?" asked Joe. "Them guys like to play dress-up, you know."

"Then he picked the wrong damn thing to dress up like. He should have been a giraffe or something. Somebody else will have to figure out who he is." Hawk gestured, and began moving toward the volcano. "Let's see what we got up here."

"You gonna carry that shit around? What if they catch us up there?"

"Then they'll probably do the same thing to us, dumb ass. Hurry up. We're gonna have to shoot the shit some other time."

Hawk knew that the ravine would take him to Delivalung, but he did not know what he would find in between. In all likelihood, he would have to avoid coming back this way. He would have to carry the head with him. It weighed almost as much as the Thompson. Someone back at Sacred Blood, or somewhere, might be able to identify it. But Joe was right, the extra baggage made capture an impossible option. The Japanese would likely not see the clinical practicality of the decapitation in an understanding light.

The terrain changed on the way leading up toward the mountain. The jungle thinned, making travel in the open more hazardous. The earth consisted of spongy lava formations, streaked with blackness and natural glass. Joe stayed close to Hawk. Now he was more worried about something happening to Hawk, than to himself. If Joe was injured, Hawk would in some super-human way get him out. But if Hawk was injured, Joe did not know what the hell he would do; other than falling heir to Hawk's sins. Joe did not think that he could get himself out of this. He wasn't sure where they were in relation to the swamp. They halted on a low ridge, with a good view of the towering cauldron of hot mist. The outcroppings afforded a degree of conceal-ment. Hawk looked in several directions.

"See anything?" Joe asked. The air was humid and smelled hot.

"Not yet. Let's settle back a while. Them two gents didn't just come out of nowhere."

Dusk eased down on them. Being stuck here in the evil darkness did not seem to bother the Sergeant. He studied the star speckled southern skies. The fog lingered for miles, but through wisps of gray he could still see the black sky with millions of bright stars. The fog emanated from both the swamp and the volcano. Air reconnaissance would be difficult or impossible.

The sky turned navy blue, and the top of the crater glowed a red orange. A split in the rock on the moun-tain's western slope emitted this same glowing color. They could see red trees in the jungle behind Delival-ung. A sulfurous odor blew over them. A permanent river of flashing ooze slid slowly out of the split on the western side. The river of lava flowed down around the circumference of Delivalung's base. It protected the mountain's evil presence with a fiery moat. Perhaps, at some ancient date, it had created the rift below them.

Joe looked at the lump in the once white Naval uniform jacket. It rested comfortably between him and Hawk. He sighed and watched the mountain. It looked like hell itself. The weird vision added to Joe's uneasiness.

"You know, you're a mean son of a bitch," Joe commented. It was an unsolicited, uncalled for and isolated comment, considering the circumstances. Just about any other statement would have filled the time much better.

Hawk glanced at him. *Now what's eating the stupid ass?* "What the hell? Because I killed a Jap? What difference does it make? He was dead, wasn't he? Who are you, Sister Mary Canlon, now?"

"I ain't never done nothing like that."

"Well, so what? Is that supposed to be good? You ain't never done a *goddam* thing right, neither. This is serious business. Just knock off the stupid shit."

Joe looked at all of the creases and small lines in Hawk's face, highlighted by the strange red glow. Joe had never noticed all of that before. Hawk looked older, and satanic. He wished the other guys were here.

"You can't get away with that kind of stuff. You know, Lynwood was right about control. You got to control yourself. God will get you."

Hawk closed his eyes and hung his head between his shoulder blades. Now, it wasn't just Joe Canlon. There was God.

"I *was* controlled, shit ass. Do I do shit like that every day? I was controlled enough to do what had to be done on *this* day. Look, doctors do that stuff all the time, don't they? It's business. It had to be done."

Joe thought for a minute. *Why would a doctor chop off your head?*

"Why were you wrassling with the guy?" Joe asked. "I thought we were done for. You were rolling around with him like a stupid maniac. There was no need for that."

"Aw, shit. I fell into him. I was coming down that hill too fast. I got the knife stuck under his arm. Yeah, it didn't look so good there at first. You gotta expect that kind of shit." Hawk coughed, or laughed, Joe couldn't tell which. It was the sort of thing that would likely amuse him.

Joe nodded. "You know, when this is over, I think I *am* going to get religion. I'm gonna have discipline like Lynwood said, and be a decent guy. Being around guys like you has taught me a lot. Like, what not to be. When you're a kid, nobody teaches you about guys like you. You know?"

Hawk sighed. "Yeah? You goin' into the thing there, where you become a priest?"

"Maybe. I just might. Yeah."

"Aw shit, don't go nuts on me out here in the middle of nowhere. Stupid bastard. Now, he's goddam Bing Crosby."

"I ain't the one that's nuts. You are. What are you going to do when the war is over? Go around cutting people's heads off?"

"Well, I don't imagine there will be a whole lot of Jap admirals shooting at me back in Mississippi. That is, so long as we kill them all over here, and don't let them get over there. And, as long as we don't all become priests,

Bing. If I did stuff there like I do here, I would be in the penitentiary, you moron."

"But what if there weren't any penitentiaries?"

"Then I guess everybody would be here in the jungle chopping each other's head off." Hawk turned his fierce gaze toward Joe. "Instead of just me and you, buddy."

* * *

BAKER FIDGETED. "They ought to be back by now," he said. Lynwood and Luka nodded in agreement. They all looked anxiously at the blackness closing around them. Baker sniffed. "Luka, why don't you go out there and look around?"

Luka did not like that idea, but he nodded subserviently. He had decided that this would be his last involvement with the Americans. Determined to just get it over with, with as little controversy as possible, he stood, knowing that he would not find anything. Joe and Hawk were probably dead, in his estimation.

He walked along the bank of the swamp, going far enough that Baker could no longer hear his footsteps. Then he sat down. He would wait a decent interval before going back. He heard a noise in the jungle behind the swamp. It was an odd noise, like something sliding in the damp earth. He looked at the heavy verdure, dappled with unnerving, watery shadows, glimmering from the dull marsh surface. He stood slowly.

"Sergeant Hawk?" he called with relief. "We worry for you." The dark leaves shook, as if under their own mystical power. The sound of labored breathing came from behind them. Two searing red lights floated in the air toward Luka. "You scare me. Scary place." The red lights were narrow slits. Luka leaned forward. He realized that they were eyes. Two huge feet on hairy legs and haunches stepped from the concealment. Luka had come face-to-face with Gohoron. He saw a bare human chest on a two-legged animal.

Luka backed into the water out of sheer revulsion. He raised his rifle with nearly paralyzed hands. The beast swayed from side to side, closing in on him slowly. Luka was hypnotized by the sight of the fiery eyes, the horns, and the great furry head. Gohoron groaned, as if bored by the expected terror. He did not show his little teeth.

"Baker," Luka gasped. It was a soft, futile whine. Gohoron raised his long arm. There was a coughing sound and Luka dropped dead, in the heart of the *pantung* region.

He should have known better than to be there, for he had religion.

* * *

"HEY, CHECK THAT." Hawk pointed to the volcano. Joe sat up from a doze. Little dots of light were sprinkled above the lava moat. "Fires. They're in caves. They must have just come out. I *told* them that the sons of bitches were here," Hawk said with a low laugh. "They must sleep all day and come out at night."

"Yeah. I'll be damn." Joe strained his unfocused eyes. He could see outlines of pale and pointy fires. "How do we know they're Japs?"

"I'll bet my place in hell it is." Hawk slapped the

insects away from his eyes. "It ain't the Salvation Army. How many fires you reckon that is?"

"I don't know. Couple hundred. Maybe three or four. I ain't too good at figuring that shit. About that, though. Like, there's ten over here in that low spot, and at least twenty more that size scattered around." Joe sighed. "Might be natives. Whoever it is, they must know this thing ain't gonna blow up on 'em."

"Yeah. You put ten Japs to a fire, and we got a real mess here."

"Yeah. Let's call it one Jap to a fire."

They heard voices. "Look, down there." Hawk pointed down suddenly. "I swear to God, they're drillin'. Right under us there, see? Ain't it?"

Joe half stood. He saw dark shapes on the darker shadow of the ground. "I think it is."

The loud and distinct voice of a Japanese drill team leader barked from below.

Hawk smiled. "The stupid bastards are drillin' in the dark. I knew they would be here." Hawk looked at Joe and smiled broader. He nudged him. "Maybe you were right, too. Huh?"

"What do you mean?"

"Maybe Hitler's down there."

"Yeah. Okay. Well, that's all we need to know, why don't we get out of here?"

Hawk sat up with a weary sigh. It had been a busy day, followed by a busy night. He stretched. "Yeah, let's take our buddy and vamoose."

They followed the rift back in the deepening darkness, leaving its course after a while. Though Joe had just crossed this country, and though he had the same experience and training as Hawk, he did not know how the bastard could find his way in the dark. For the most part, a Marine did not travel in the dark. He stayed at his post until daylight. *Hawk is like a Jap, or some night animal*, Joe thought. Nonetheless, at the end of the black labyrinth, they unerringly reached the bank of the swamp. This gave Hawk pause.

"Here's that post we found," Hawk observed in a strange tone.

Joe nodded, looking down, and seeing nothing in the pitch-black night. "Yeah. So, which way now? This way?" Joe pointed in the proper direction. He assumed Hawk was using the post as a landmark. He did not know that it meant much more than that. Joe could at last see the ghastly shimmer of the swamp's murky surface.

Hawk looked out into the marsh, toward the point where he thought the solid ground lay. There was probably a sizable island out there. A crocodile bellowed a long vibrating call. Marsh gas glistened in disconnected little orbs, near where the phantom island must lie. An old village, or a temple, could be situated on the island, or under the mud between here and there. Way out here! The ethereal gas lights were caught by the thin drifting fog, to dance and play in the wisps of mist. *For seven hundred years!*

"This way?" Joe repeated, a little more demanding. *What the hell is the guy staring out there for?*

"There might be some buildings out there. Want to do a quick check? A little explorin'?"

Joe looked from Hawk out into the eerie marsh. "Oh, no. Shit, no! That's enough shit for one day. Don't you remember seeing about ten thousand crocs out there?" Joe stopped speaking suddenly and turned around quickly. "Listen, there's that noise again, it's something dragging. I bet it's one of those crocs. Let's get out of here."

"Okay, okay. Get going."

Hawk was quiet after that. Joe knew something was bothering him, but he didn't care. Hawk never knew when to quit. He was a stupid son of a bitch.

* * *

Mr. Arnold and Dr. Lepreaux sat at the table in the former's spacious hut. A kerosene lamp burned between them. Lepreaux was alert, but slouched, as though tired. Arnold looked strong and determined.

"That means, we know that Lieutenant Klemer is the cause," Lepreaux said. He had lost his French accent. It had been replaced by a New England brogue on this occasion.

"Yes, sir. Sergeant Gallagher and Lieutenant Cargill saw him put something in the canteen. The next day that was the very man that turned up sick."

"It's hard to believe, Colonel." Lepreaux shook his head. "The man would not hurt a fly. I know that man. Why did he do it? A decorated Marine veteran...it doesn't make sense."

"I don't know, sir. That's why we haven't let Klemer know that we're on to him. The obvious reason would be to disable our command. Sabotage. I'm checking his background now. He was born in Lithuania. That's a factor. I believe there is a large German population there, or at least sympathizers. We're checking the records of the FBI on the American Bund, the Nazi party at home."

"Hmm. Rather far-fetched, isn't it?" Lepreaux sighed. "Klemer, a Nazi?" He shook his head. "If so, he wouldn't be stupid enough to have joined the Bund. Just watch him, Colonel. Cut our losses wherever possible, but don't let on that we know that he has been contaminating the water. We have to know more about this. It is just too peculiar. What is his game? With everything that is going on here, he does this?"

"Yes, sir. But it will be hard to protect the men on the patrols. Klemer takes the canteens directly to them. He would be suspicious if we stopped him from doing it. I suppose we could let the men on patrol know about it," Arnold suggested. "Then they could dump the water and get their own after leaving."

"No, no," Lepreaux waved his hand. "Curry and Hawk are the only two affected. They can take care of themselves. No, it's not worth the risk. Just let it all ride and see what happens next. He has to make a move, and then we'll find out his objective."

Lepreaux stood, then Arnold. Lepreaux walked toward the door and Arnold saluted. Lepreaux returned the salute. A messenger met Lepreaux at the door with a shortwave message. The doctor read it and dismissed the runner.

"Well..." said Lepreaux, in a disappointed tone. "Klemer lived in Japan for three years in the 1930s." Arnold and the doctor looked at one another. "He worked in a hospital and went to a university to study physical therapy." Lepreaux had a painful frown. He could not believe it about Klemer. Everything about the man suggested caregiving and gentleness. Of course, he had been on Tarawa with the Marines. Nothing gentle there.

"Pick him up, sir?"

Lepreaux took a breath and stared into the lamp. "No. Not yet. Let it ride. Keep an eye out for a contact. Surely sabotage isn't his sole objective. Klemer and the Japanese?" The doctor shook his head. "He's privy to a lot of information. He can't be alone in this. Who does he talk to?"

"That woman. She's not an American, either. She was with the Japanese for years during the occupation, herself. *And*, she doesn't want to leave here. It all fits now."

"Oh, I don't know. The thing is, with Klemer, we have to be careful. He may know something about the jewels. We don't know how deeply he is involved. If he is in with the Japanese, does he know what the Japanese know? What have they told him?" Lepreaux asked.

* * *

HAWK WAS a day behind Biedeker's return to Sacred Blood, who had to move slowly with the injured man. Hawk had managed to move even slower, having run across another Japanese caravan, and needing to wait out its passage. But he moved more slowly for another reason.

During the entire return trip, he considered turning around and going back. He rested a lot. He finally gave up on the idea of searching for a lost temple in the marsh, after he had reached and passed the halfway point. Baker and Lynwood were the complicating, and deciding factors. He did not want to go back there with them. And that fool Luka ran off, right when he was needed, of course.

It was long after dark when they reached the outskirts of Sacred Blood. The Mission was under enemy attack. The patrol had heard the firing and explosions for miles. They could see the brutal flashes against the sky as they crossed the open plain. It had gone on all night. The Japanese machine guns knocked like old washing machines. The Marine machine guns answered, sharp, modern, and clipped. The Japanese rifles cracked, and the American M1's boomed. The sky shuddered with a little yellow light after each noise. Hawk and his party slogged on, toward it, at an unhurried pace. They found the fight to be over by the time they reached it. The battle had occurred mostly on the plains, east of the Mission proper.

The Japanese staggered across the plains in an apparent retreat. Hawk's patrol, almost running into them, sought refuge in the woods and watched them pass. The enemy looked defeated. Their clothes were dirty and torn. Half of them were bleeding, and half of those had to be carried. They had probably left a lot more dead behind. They always did. Lynwood counted about 500 Japanese still functional. In this wilderness, that was a daunting number. They were withdrawing in the general direction of Delivalung, but their precise destination remained unknown.

"Looks like...the Mission held," Hawk whispered. "Or the Japs wouldn't be here."

An hour later, they crossed the Marine perimeter with Hawk's slouching swagger in the lead. They passed the bodies, smoke, debris, scared faces, and torn humanity. All was as expected.

At the center of the American line was the biggest surprise, and an unexpected sight. A huge ball of flame whipped in the wind, dividing the trenches. The tail of a Japanese aircraft leaned out of it. It looked alien and bizarre in the dawn light.

"Kamikaze," an older gunnery sergeant told them.

"The Japs are serious about this, ain't they?" said Joe, his face lit by the reflection of the orange flames. "I was afraid of this kind of thing."

"Go find Biedeker for me. Tell him that I'm with Arnold, and will catch up with him later," Hawk told Joe.

Hawk found Arnold still distraught over the battle. His little hut was filled with officers, busily running around doing nothing in particular. Arnold cleared the room when Hawk walked in. He had been waiting anxiously for the patrol's report, until the greater anxiety of the attack interrupted his vigil. Hawk set his bundle calmly and unobtrusively on the floor. But Arnold noticed it.

"What do you have there?" The craggy, eagle face of Arnold didn't look so tough this morning. He had probably spent the night preparing his fingernails for some bamboo sticks in a Japanese POW camp.

Hawk threw open the blood drenched coat. "It's a Jap head. Looks like it might be a big shot." The head rolled about and faced up at Arnold. The damp climate had turned its formerly blue color green.

"Damn!" Arnold drew back from the decaying spectacle. "Get that out of here!"

Hawk dropped the admirals shoulder boards on the table. "Admiral!"

Arnold said, as if it were some sort of vision test. He let his eyes rest on the gentler view of the epaulets. "Wait a minute..."

"Yes, sir?" Hawk took out a cigar and lit it. He wasn't going anywhere. His features were stony as he sat down.

Arnold opened an oversized folder on the table, with a large spiral bound book in it. Hawk saw that it was filled with photographs, among other things. It resembled a mug shot album.

"Look at this." Arnold pointed to a photograph in the middle of the page, toward the beginning of the book. "That's Ishakawi. Isn't it? You saw him alive?"

Hawk stood and sauntered over to the right side of the book. He had never been good at reading upside down. He looked at the picture and grunted a noncommittal comment.

"Well, he looks like hell now," said Arnold. "But that is him, isn't it?"

"Could be, I reckon. Yeah, I think so. Do you know anything about him?"

"Hell, yes. He practically ran the Japanese government in 1939 and 1940. They say he helped plan Pearl Harbor."

Hawk saw a legend of campaign ribbons on the margin of the page. He looked at the filthy coat. "Did he serve in Singapore, China, New Guinea, and the Southwest Pacific?" Hawk coordinated the pictures with the ribbons.

"Yes, oh yes."

"He's got the ribbons for all of that. Must be him."

Arnold looked at the pictures of the ribbons and made the same calculations. "Look at this, Hawk. The file even has his fingerprints. He must've had a passport and gone to the United States, or lived there at some point. Maybe we can get the prints off the buttons of the uniform, or one of those medals."

"I was kind of thinking of something like that, sir. I didn't find no papers." Hawk brushed aside an overlapping ribbon holder, and unbuttoned the coat's breast pocket. He turned the coat over and shook it. A severed ring finger, complete with a ring, and a thumb, fell out on the table. The ring was tight around the bloated finger.

Arnold drew back. Now more accustomed to the horror of the forensic presentation, he looked at the ring. "A rising sun ruby. It's got to be him!"

"Can I have the ring, sir?" Hawk sniffed casually. He figured Jessica Pearson might like it. It might be worth a couple of bucks.

"Shit, no! Maybe later. Damn, Hawk, don't be so ghoulish!"

"Yes sir." Hawk figured Arnold was going to pocket the ring for himself. That wouldn't be nearly as ghoulish. That's how that shit worked. He should have just kept it and not mentioned it to the bastard.

Arnold pulled out a bottle and poured a drink. It evidently did not occur to him to offer his guest a drink. He noticed Hawk's sullen response to his answer about the ring.

"Maybe later," Arnold waved his hand dismissively. "I guarantee you first rights to it. We have to check it out. I'll get it if I can."

But he never did. The rising sun ruby disappeared into the history of World War II.

Hawk sat down again. His feet were tired, along with the rest of him.

This validates our entire mission, Sergeant." Arnold's eyes lit up with enthusiasm. The enthusiasm remained touched by revulsion. "I tell you, I was ready to give up tonight. I thought the Japs were after something else. But now we know, it's almost certain, they are moving their government down here."

"Yes sir. I'd say that's probably true. They're out at Delivalung."

"You saw them? How did you get him?" Arnold asked in amazement.

"We was just walking along and there he was, and I killed him, and we went on to the volcano, and seen the fires and come on back." Hawk recounted the entire horrible experience in a few bland words. With several details missing.

Immediately, Arnold noticed the lack of detail. "Nothing else? You didn't see any unusual activity?"

How did he know that? Hawk thought. "Depends on what you mean, sir. Just about all of it was unusual." Hawk wrestled with himself. "There is a lot of unusual stuff out there, sir. It's an unusual place." He decided to hedge his bets. "We saw some funny looking petrified wood..." Hawk looked up quickly and then back down at the table top. Arnold did not seem interested in that. It had been phrased vaguely enough.

Arnold still had an interest in the area north of Delivalung, where Curry had seen the Japanese searching.

"What kind of troop estimate did you make? Could two divisions take it?" Arnold asked.

"Two...divisions? Why, yes sir. I don't doubt that they could. That would be a lot. We saw a couple hundred campfires, and maybe a company or two drilling." Hawk shrugged. "Now, there's other sides to the mountain, a course. It probably gets too hot on that one side. I figured it was likely a lot less than a division, though. It's probably hard for them to get out there. That's a real hard to get to spot. But they been around here for years, you know. On the coast, for sure."

"We'll smash that mountain." Arnold pounded the table. "Maybe I should get another division. They're Army, you know. Do you think we could do it? Two Army divisions?"

Hawk shrugged. Hell, he didn't know. He had never run a campaign from the top, he had only been on the bottom. "Hawk, by next month a USO show will be playing at Delivalung."

"Yes, sir. That'd be...good," Hawk answered without emotion. Arnold's enthusiasm was not contagious.

"I can swing it. Two divisions." Arnold sat down, a suddenly deflated expression on his face. "That is...if they can get out here. Our logistics leave a lot to be desired. The Japs hit the riverboat, you know? It looks like they're going to sew up the Pageas. Our presence isn't exactly the surprise maneuver we planned. I only have a battalion here now, and I was supposed to have two. We are way off schedule."

"They hit the boat?"

"Yes. Sure did. Killed everyone."

"Killed? Who...? Like all that was on it?"

"Yes. It was all of the fever victims. Except Klemer. He's better, and wanted to stay. And, you know, the crew...those poor natives, and the old men. All gone."

"What about Jessica Pearson?"

"She was supposed to go but remained here. Fortunately, I did not let her leave."

"Excuse me, sir."

"What? Wait... Where are you going?"

But Hawk had already left. Arnold was alone with his admiral, and his thoughts.

Arnold cranked the telephone. "Dr. Lepreaux," he said into the receiver. He waited. "Yes, sir. Has Curry found anything, sir?" He waited. "Well, Hawk did. He hit the jackpot. He found a base at Delivalung. I suggest we take it. That will solve all the problems. You'd never guess what else I have here."

Hawk went to the commissary but Jessica was not there. At the hospital, a mortar round had torn through the roof, letting in the rising sunlight. The building had been evacuated. Now, she was the only one inside. She walked alone in the wreckage, holding a hand bag, and surveying the rubble. She wore a blue dress and a hat with a feather. A short necklace lay tight around her throat. She looked more like a beautiful lady of the world, than the girl he had last seen, and been remembering.

"Jessica."

She turned around. "James!" He took a couple of steps, and she walked the rest of the way. "You're back! Thank God, you're back. You're scratched to pieces!" She approached him in order to embrace him.

"Yeah. Bumped into a tree. Damn things are every-where. You might not want to get too close." He held her back and kissed her cheek. "You're decked out. Fit to... kill." He couldn't think of another way to finish the cliché.

"Yes, I was supposed to leave today. Did you hear about the boat?"

"Yeah. Goddam Japs."

"All of those poor men. I knew every one of them." He could see something of a change in her face. Her world was not as well organized as when he had left her. She had ventured a step or two into his world. The happy kaleidoscope in her eyes had been turned to a new setting.

"Don't worry. We can still get you out," he said. She clutched him in spite of his attempt to hold her back.

"I don't want out. If you're here, I don't want out. I've done nothing but think about you. It was the hand of God that kept me here. To be alive, and to be with you."

Hawk's eyebrows drew together. The emotion of the meeting had forced her words out a little sooner than she had intended. He was processing the conversation well, until God came into it. He wasn't quite sure about that. No one had ever, under any circumstances, associated him with God. It only emphasized the difference between the two of them; just as her standing there, clean and scrubbed, contrasted with his being covered in every known form of filth on earth.

"James, I believe that I am in love with you. Would that be so bad?" She turned her head and placed it against his bare chest. His arms closed around her narrow shoulders.

"No," he said. "It wouldn't. But, you know..." He stopped before he made some kind of mistake. How could he say anything? He had no vocabulary, other than a few obscenities and animal grunts. It always took a few seconds to translate those into English, and it made speaking a chore. He barely had any feelings. So, he just didn't say anything.

"Isn't it silly?" she said. He thought that she might be crying.

"No." But he felt a little silly.

She pushed back a few inches. "Is that blood all over your clothes?"

"I fell on a guy."

"How horrible!"

"What?"

"Falling on a dead person."

"Oh, yeah. Scared the heck outa me."

"How do you put up with it?"

"With...uh...well, I'm always stepping in something. How did you do in the attack?"

"It wasn't too bad in the Mission itself. They didn't get past the fortifications outside. The medics and Navy surgeons are taking care of the wounded. I should be. I didn't know if I was coming or going, literally. We had a few bomb scares." She squinted up at the sunlight pouring through the hole in the roof. "I was in the storage room. You can't imagine the noise. I've never heard such a thing. I could imagine them racing through the door and shooting me." She laughed. She did not mention to him how she had made several trips out to the perimeter, carrying medical supplies. She was quite brave.

"I don't think even a Jap would shoot you."

"They would shoot you."

Hawk raised his eyebrows. "Yes, ma'am!"

She laughed. "When can you leave here?"

"Me?" *Like, never,* he thought. "No time soon, that I know of."

"It's too dangerous here now. There will be thousands of Japanese..."

"Yeah, but, hell, it ain't no worse than anywhere else for me. In fact, they were talking about bringing in the Army, so it won't be too bad."

"I want to be with you."

"I'd like that. If things stayed like they were, and all. But like now, anything can happen in a deal like this."

The sun flowed in from above, putting the two of them in a circle, like a spotlight. They were young, healthy, and together, in this brief spotlight of time. That could certainly change.

She took his hand and they walked outside. Men were running around, some were shouting. Hawk steered her away from the officers. They would find something asinine for him to do.

"But, if I leave, when will I see you again?" she asked.

"Oh, that could be any time. You know. I might be going to Australia or New Zealand after this business cools down. That's what they been telling us for a couple years, anyway."

"I'll go there. I'll go home. I haven't been home in years. Will you be near Sydney?"

"Sydney? I don't know. I been close. Melbourne. Camp Balcombe, after Guadalcanal. But everybody talks about Brisbane now."

She twisted her mouth, as if the two were the same place. "Then, I'll go there," she said.

"But, I mean, I don't know when. You see? I never know what they're doing. The Marine Corps has a kind of a different outlook than other folks. They get a kick out of not telling you stuff."

"That's all right." Her eyes were happy again. "You won't be in that stupid thing forever." Her world had been turned right side up, it seemed. Everything out of place in her life fit once again. "Yes, I should go home. Father would be pleased. I could play the prodigal daughter for him. He would love that. I belong there. You are right. Just because you *can* do something, doesn't mean you have to do it. This—all of the disaster in this place—I know now...was a bit much. I shouldn't have come. But I never would have met you, if I hadn't come here. It's just fate. It's the hand of God."

"Yeah..." Hawk glanced up at the sky.

"And we can be together. It will be so much better in Australia."

"Yeah." Hawk liked optimism, and optimists. He didn't understand them, but it had a certain early childhood appeal to it. Optimists had lived a completely different life than his. His life consisted of one disaster after another, along with the necessity to crush the next disaster before it crushed him.

"Do you like the ballet?" she asked.

What the hell? he thought. "You mean...like dancin'?"

She smiled and suppressed a laugh at his expression. "Maybe that was too much all at once. Do you like to dance?"

"Sure," he said. He had never danced, and the sight of men dancing turned his stomach. Maybe she was afraid of his losing his legs. Why else would you ask something like that?

She pursued his discomfort, perhaps intentionally, but he failed to understand.

"And the opera? You like that, too?"

"Yeah. Maybe more than the ballet." He figured that was probably true. "The USO took us once in California."

"Oh, what did you see?"

"I forgot the name. The people were wearing..." He gestured and searched for the words.

"Clothes?"

"Yeah." He laughed uneasily. "And costumes." He thought of the dead admiral in his finery. It didn't take much of a discussion on any subject to cause him to have a grim flashback of something gruesome. "I think it was supposed to be a funny one. They had sailor suits on. It was hard to follow. They must have left part of it out, because it was almost all singing. The USO pulled a fast one on us that time. But in the military, you got all kinds of folks, so they try to appeal to everybody. Not everybody is ignorant, like me. It was real loud. The people in it were all a-bellerin'. I left at the half time."

She looked up at him. "I think we'll be really happy together, don't you?"

"Well, yeah. I would, I know."

"We can get to know one another better. We have our whole lives. We're young. It will be wonderful."

"Yeah."

They started walking again. He had lapsed into silence again, that wall that had intrigued her in the beginning. Now, however, it was becoming a challenge. She supposed she had overwhelmed him with the ballet. She put her hands behind her back and looked down as she walked.

In fact, he *was* thinking. He thought of the ballet, and the opera, or at least, what he knew of them. *"The finer things, lad. And you ain't one of 'em."*

"Sports, then? Baseball? I'll bet you have an interest in that? All Americans love sports," she said. "Babe Ruth?"

"Babe... Well, I'm kind of old for that sort of thing."

"Old? You're not old."

"Well, no. I meant, I'm a grown man. You know, sports is mainly for kids. Like, clowns and stuff. Maybe, boxing," he said, hoping that would please her. "If there

is a big match, with money on it. It can be kind of interestin' if you're drinkin' a lot."

"Actually, I never cared for sports much, either. Did
you play any type of ball as a child?"

"No, I didn't. There wasn't no kind of funny business
back where I come from. Even for kids. I guess kids up
north did that stuff. Or maybe in the cities. I had a
different sort of raising."

"Oh? What did you do as a child?"

"Picked cotton. Chopped cotton. Toted cotton. Lot of
cotton. I did other stuff, but the work always ran out.
You always ended up back with the cotton. Never run
out of that sh—stuff."

"So, what else do you like? You can't like cotton?"

"No, it wouldn't be cotton." He tried to think of a
good answer. Tobacco. Drinking. Fighting. Women. He
couldn't say any of those. He considered fishing. He
didn't have anything against that.

"You," he said.

She put an arm around his waist. She liked his
answer.

"You were gone a long time out there. I was worried.
Did you find what you were looking for?"

"Oh. I don't know. Sort of, I guess. Dependin' on
who you ask."

They talked for almost an hour, in a similar vein: her
asking things, and his not answering. She touched him
frequently, and each touch seemed to thaw out his
numbed brain. After listening to her plans, he could not
imagine a life without her—although, it was difficult to
see himself in the colorful pictures she painted. She had
so many hopes and dreams. He had only black and
white realities. He needed her hopes and dreams, as he

had none of his own. Maybe that was good, he thought. A lot of men and women go off on their own path, and it does not agree with the path of their mate. He had no path, so he figured he couldn't go very wrong.

He had forgotten about the U. S. Marine Corps, the pathfinders from hell.

* * *

LIEUTENANT OSASI ENTERED the cave of his immediate superior, Captain Sahumi. The Captain was working in the light at the mouth of the cave this morning. American air reconnaissance had almost entirely ceased. The view from the northern slope of Delivalung was invigorating. Basah was a beautiful place from up here, away from the more miserable aspects of the lowlands. Osasi handed the Captain his intelligence report.

Sahumi glanced through it quickly, and nodded. "You think we should turn our search efforts south of here?" the Captain asked.

"Yes, my Captain. The Americans are to the south already, and working. They appeared interested a week ago, and the night before last they arrived," the Lieutenant explained. "We know for certain now that they are aware of our location."

"I think not. That is a swampy region in the south. The records from China indicated that the site is located in a dry, flatland."

"Yes, honorable Captain. But much can happen in fifty years. Fifty or a hundred years ago, the swamp may have been dry. Findings in the north have not been encouraging."

"I suspect this was from Humuri. He gave you this

information, did he not? This colors the whole report." The Captain's voice had an accusatory tone.

Lieutenant Osasi hung his head slightly as he answered. "Yes, sir."

"You know what I think of Humuri's reports. They are not trustworthy. Why do you even bring them to me? And then you try to disguise them as something substantial? Factual? I do not wish to be harsh with you, Osasi, but I believe we have discussed this before."

"Yes, my Captain."

"Has anyone located Admiral Ishakawi?"

"No, sir."

Captain Sahumi shook his head. "The man simply disappeared from the earth. The cabinet ministers and the general have already departed. They believe that the Americans will continue to build local support along the Pageas. Somehow, once again, it appears that the Yankees have anticipated our efforts. I believe I can tell you in confidence, Osasi, that since our defeat at the Mission yesterday, they have decided not to relocate the government here. The absence of Ishakawi played a major part in the decision. He would not have permitted an abandonment of the plans so easily. I cannot understand what has happened to him. He is needed at home. How does a man with a staff that size, stationed in the middle of an army, just disappear? It's as if he wanted to. That would be the only way."

"With the change in plans, will we continue to stay here, honorable Captain?"

Captain Sahumi looked indignant. "Of course we will stay. We still have our primary mission. They are waiting on me, and I am waiting on you. Find the crystal site, Osasi, and we can all go home. If you *don't* find it,"

Sahumi shoved a paper across his makeshift desk, "we are to hold Delivalung to the last man. That is how important it is." The Captain began to pace. "Use your head, Osasi. And not Humuri's. You are a promising young officer. Humuri barely deserves his rank as a corporal. I know you have been close to him for many years, and he has many influential and sympathetic supporters, but we deal in cold hard facts here. Here is the fact you should remember: You and I will be part of a suicidal defense of this burnt rock if we fail to find the site. Time," Sahumi looked down and spoke softly, "time is against us."

"I will not fail, honorable Captain. I will find it."

11

ATTACK ON SACRED BLOOD

DR. LEPREAUX RETURNED FROM A TRAUMA EMERGENCY IN the perimeter. He asked Jessica to go to the commissary with him. Joe Canlon and Baker leaned on the hospital wall. Lynwood stood in front of them. For lack of any other entertainment at the moment, the three watched Hawk and Jessica part, as inconspicuously as possible.

"Touchin', ain't it?" said Baker.

"That is sure a beautiful girl," said Lynwood. The other two laughed at him. So much for control.

"You crack me up," said Joe. "Yeah, I don't know what that guy's got, but wherever he goes he's got the best looking chick around sprouting up out of nowhere. Of course, he don't have them for long, just till they find out what a bastard he is. You better stay out of his way then."

Lynwood didn't say anything. He didn't like being laughed at. He left.

"That old Lynwood is all right. I like that guy," said Joe, completely missing Lynwood's dislike of him.

"Yeah, he's all right. Got a little growing up to do."

Baker yawned. "Lot of kids in this outfit. Full of shit. Hey, here comes Hawk. Joke with him, so he don't send us out there to clean up that shit."

"*You* joke with him. He's kind of prickly."

Hawk walked by them, paying no attention.

"Hey, sailor!" Baker called out. "How about a date?"

Hawk stopped.

"Shit, what the hell did you do that for? He was going on by," said Joe.

Hawk walked up to them. "What are you two shit-bags doin'?"

"Lookin' lean and mean," said Baker. When he didn't wear his insane grin, Baker did look rather mean.

"He's looking mean. I'm looking hep," said Joe. "We're laying low till they clean up all that shit out there." Joe nodded toward the perimeter. "What'd the big guys say about the admiral?"

"They said, I thought he would be taller," said Baker.

Hawk ignored this. "He shit all over hisself. Says he's gonna call in the goddam Army."

"No shit!" Joe nudged Baker. Baker laughed for some reason. "The *Army!* The man behind the man behind the gun!" Joe did a little take off on a popular ditty from the First World War.

"That's what he says." Hawk nodded. His eyes wandered across the compound, to keep from looking at the two ugly faces in front of him. He saw an odd thing. It was so odd, that he could not quite believe it. He looked back at Joe. "Yeah, that's what he said." But then he turned away again.

He had been right the first time. He saw four uniformed Japanese soldiers strolling along in the shadow of the palisades. Three more walked in the other direction, along the fence. "What—in—the—hell?" He stepped toward the hospital door with his shoulders tensed.

"What's the matter?" Joe asked.

"Git inside." Hawk dove for the door. Baker and Joe didn't wait for any explanations. Their brains immediately reverted to the previous days out in the jungle. They were right beside him.

"What is it?" Joe asked again.

"Look out there. Damn Japs in the cantonment area." Baker looked out the door. Hawk raised his submachine gun. "What are they doin'?"

"They're...walkin' around," said Baker.

"Yeah. Son of a bitch!" said Joe.

"I wonder if I oughta tell the girl to stay out of sight," Hawk said. Joe looked at Baker behind Hawk's back. "I'm gonna check this other side. Y'all cut 'em down." He slipped to the other side of the unlit hospital.

Baker started the ambush, getting two of them easily. The Japanese reacted quickly to the sudden outburst. By the time Hawk returned, rifles were crackling all over the compound. Things had descended into chaos. It was difficult to tell how this had happened, or what the enemy was doing, or even where they were.

The main body of Marines lay east of the compound, outside the walls. The Japanese were inside the walls, with only a limited number of adversaries to contend with them. Hawk, Baker, and Canlon stayed near the floor in the hospital doorway, realizing that they had not missed the battle for Sacred Blood Mission after all.

For a while, at least, it looked like matters might be brought back under control. Sporadic firing could be heard outside the hospital, but it did not sound like an overpowering force. Perhaps some stragglers had come out of a hole somewhere. They had a habit of doing such things.

One or two ricochets hit the hospital wall, but the three Marines inside didn't see anyone training any direct fire on them. They decided to wait there, looking for targets of opportunity, expecting that eventually the Marines outside would re-enter the gates and mop up the outnumbered infiltrators. The sudden problem was unusual, and a little dangerous for individuals caught in the wrong place, but overall, it was somewhat contained.

The situation remained fairly tame by outward appearances, until the Marines outside the walls tried to enter the compound. Evidently, this was what the Japanese were awaiting. The gate stood opposite the hospital, so that the three men inside the building had a ring side seat for what was about to happen. The Marines did not charge the gate, but neither did they approach it cautiously. As they crowded through, a Japanese machine gun raked the opening, killing at least three of them right there.

"Where the hell did that come from?" Joe asked. It was loud and close. It sounded like it was in the building with them.

"Behind us," said Baker. The gun rattled again.

The main body of Marines took up positions just outside of the gate. Some were trying to climb over the wall, which caused the machine gun to fire again. The firing increased throughout the compound, as other Japanese joined in the defense of the gate from the inside. Spouts of dirt crossed and recrossed the open gateway, like a supersonic portcullis.

Hawk looked up. "That shit ain't behind us. The son of a bitch is on the roof."

The deadly jackhammer chugged again. They knew for certain that it was up there when the spent shell casings clinked down the sloping wood. The whole situation had changed. There could be no more "wait and see" for the men in the hospital. The location of the gun turned it into their responsibility. They pondered the rather unwelcome problem. Hawk looked at the hole the mortar round had punched through the ceiling.

"Shit, man! The Japs got the whole Mission!" said Joe. "Those guys outside are trying to take it back! We're on the wrong goddam side in here!"

"Yeah, well. That means the Japs forgot one thing. Us," said Hawk. "Watch the door," he told Joe. "Cover the windows. Don't get shot in the ass," he instructed Baker.

He slipped a grenade from the buttonhole on his herringbone twill utility jacket. He walked toward the middle of the building, picking his way through the rubble of overturned beds and tangled mosquito net racks. He saw shadows flicker across the hole in the roof. Men were moving about up there. Every time the machine gun fired, brighter flashes could be seen above, and they reflected on the dingy walls below. He squinted up and across the ceiling. In his judgment, the gun was situated toward the front of the building, probably right over the heads of Joe and Baker, at the front door. The mortar hole was in the middle of the building. It would be difficult to throw a live grenade up there: it was a long distance, at an odd angle, and would be like threading a needle.

Hawk stood a little behind the jagged hole, still looking upwards. The sunlight hit his eyes, blinding him for a moment. He straightened the grenade's cotter key on a nearby roof beam, in order to unleash the safety lever. He wrenched the ring pull free. The spoon sprang off. The striker snapped and the fuse hissed. The bomb spat angry smoke into Hawk's face, a little reminder of its impartiality as to whom it injured in the next five seconds.

Hawk reared back and heaved the grenade upward, barely clearing the edge of the hole, trying to make it arc high and fall straight down on the front portion of the hospital roof. It wasn't the sort of thing one routinely practiced. Like most of the rest of the life and death aspects of war, it would take a natural talent and a lot of luck.

"Grenade coming down," he shouted to Joe and Baker. There was no guarantee that it wouldn't knock part of the roof down on them.

The two men covered their heads and crouched against the wall. The explosion blacked out the sun. Hawk suspected that he might have held onto it too long, and that it may have fallen short. Debris rained down between him and the two men in the front of the building. Smoke drifted past the mortar hole. Dust, grass and particles of wood trickled down and swirled in the air. The three Marines slowly uncovered their faces and looked up. They no longer heard the machine gun in their ringing ears.

Joe looked cautiously out the front door. The Marines outside the gates were still firing at the inside of the compound. Joe stood and took a step outside. A forearm reached down from the roof above him, with a lightning, slapping motion. A stick grenade hit Joe full in the face, and bounced outside. Joe grabbed his eyes with both hands and fell to the ground inside the door. Baker lay on the other side of the opening, observing all of this.

Hawk crouched as the bomb exploded just outside the doorway. A half dozen lit spears of shrapnel in a semi-circular pattern radiated visibly across the room. Hawk was, by mere chance, located between the spokes of this deadly scythe. Clods of dirt, moving as fast as bullets, pelted him and angry dust shrouded the doorway. Both dazed and groggy from the concussion, Baker and Canlon crawled away from the door on their hands and knees. They finally managed to get up and run toward the rear of the building. Hawk met them there.

The enemy machine gun clattered again. Men screamed curses, and fired at it from out by the gate. A little tree growing by the gate, and leaning over it slightly, had suffered the ripping of its leaves by the steady fire. Now the persistent gun plucked and severed the smaller branches.

"That didn't get a lot done," said Hawk, shaking his head. He fixed his gaze on the hole in the roof again. The bridge of Joe's nose was bleeding. He couldn't hear well. Hawk finally looked down at him.

"How's the snout?" Hawk asked.

Joe looked cross-eyed. Blood poured from his nostrils. He tilted his head back. "Uh...okay, I think."

"Listen, if y'all boost me up through this hole in the overhead, I can get 'em," Hawk said.

"You'll get your head sawed off, too," said Baker.

Hawk considered the wisdom of this assessment. He moved toward a rear window. There had to be a better way up onto the roof from the outside. Those bastards with the machine gun had managed to get up there somehow.

He climbed out the window. Immediately, bullets splattered the outside wall, above, below, and beside him. They rang, whistled and spewed concrete dust. Baker ran to the window to help, and Joe staggered behind him. Hawk dropped under the window on the outside. The other two Americans thrust their rifles through opening, just over Hawk's head. They spotted the enemy soldiers who had targeted Hawk. Three of them were not under cover. Another one lay half concealed behind barrels near the log fence.

Hawk rolled up to a sitting position and hastily returned fire. He was sitting awkwardly, where he had fallen, with his legs tangled and his back braced against the hospital wall. He moved the jolting Thompson across the bodies of the three Japanese facing him, standing in the open. The legs were pushed from beneath the first one and he fell forward on his face. A knee on the second man blew out in a fountain of cartilage and blood. His leg bent in the wrong direction and he dropped violently. Hawk lifted the wild muzzle in mid-volley, managing to tear the stomach out of the third man, all of it done in a matter of perfectly coordinated movements.

The soldier struck in the knee crawled with a mad effort to retrieve his fallen rifle. Hawk raised up a bit on one leg, pushing against the wall with his back to help support himself, in an odd, half standing position. He held the heavy Thompson away from his body and pointed the muzzle down, steering a line of spewing rounds across the ground and over the head and shoulders of the Japanese. Once he was shot full of huge .45 caliber holes, the young man stopped moving.

The enemy soldier still hiding behind the barrels returned a bashful and wild shot. Rock dust flew into Baker's eyes after it hit the wall beside the window. He dropped his rifle, screamed and ducked below the opening.

Groggy, and with a numbed nose, Joe Canlon dropped his foresight and hindsight simultaneously onto a visible part of the hiding man's shoulder. He squeezed the trigger. The thirty-caliber explosion connected with flesh, spinning the Japanese from behind the barrel and into the open. Without using his sights, and aiming the muzzle, Joe pumped the rest of his clip into the wounded man. The stricken target fell back on folded legs, throwing his arms up spasmodically as each round landed.

"You all right?" Joe called out the window to Hawk. Baker knelt beside him, trying to clear his eyes.

"Yeah. Close one. Is Baker okay?" Hawk could be heard unfolding his tangled legs.

"I'm all right," Baker shouted in an angry voice. "We need a plan. They're all over the goddam place."

Hawk felt vulnerable, propped there against the wall in the open. He looked down the side of the hospital. A tall rain barrel sat against the wall, about halfway down its length. He imagined himself standing on it. If he did that, at least his head would be above the lower reach of the angled roof. It was hard to judge from where he was, but he decided that it was possible that he would be able to jump and muscle his way onto the roof from the rain barrel. It would not be easy, because of the downward slope of the roof. Gravity would be against him. If the Japanese with the machine gun had accessed the roof that way, he could do the same. There was no way to be sure. They might have used a ladder and pulled it up behind them.

"Okay," Hawk told the other two calmly. "I got the plan. We gotta knock out the machine gun so they can get into the gate. I see a way onto the roof." The other two did not argue. In any type of hazardous work, a point is reached in which you are on your own. They all knew the risks in what they were doing. Hawk had chosen his portion of the task.

Hawk ran to the barrel and leapt onto it. Standing, he could see up the angle of the roof. He could not see the machine gun on the other side of the roof's apex. The machine gun fired. It sounded louder, out here in the open. The spent casings could be heard rolling down to the ground below.

He pulled himself onto the ironwood shingles with great difficulty, having to dig his fingertips into their edges and tearing some free. He walked in a crouch up to the top of the roof, and quietly pulled in his breath as he looked over the top.

Three Imperial soldiers diligently maneuvered a 6.5 mm gun near the front edge of the hospital. A blue feather of flame leapt from the gun's conical flashguard. Men continued to shout and fire back at them from the gate, which seemed to be the gun's only target. It was the bottleneck preventing an American entrance into Sacred Blood Mission.

Hawk lifted his Thompson over the peak of the roof with a deliberate motion. He drew a bead on their unaware backs. He had maybe six rounds left. He would have to hit at least one of them accurately, and cripple the other two. This was well within the Thompson's capacity.

A prudent man, however, would have changed clips. Hawk did not want to waste the time, as he wanted this finished without any more surprises. Otherwise, they might turn around, or hear him fiddling with the magazine. Relying on his skills had become a habit, bordering on recklessness. He raised the butt plate of the weapon and lowered the muzzle toward the thin back of the man in the middle of the three. His teeth were clenched with great tension as he angled the Thompson. That was when he heard muffled feet pounding on the shingles behind him. It was the split, two-toed boots the Japanese wore, that made their feet look like hooves and made them hard to hear.

He flipped over on his back, fired by a burst of adrenaline. A bullet splintered the wood shingles where he had been lying. A soldier stood a dozen paces away, aiming a rifle down at him. The Japanese soldier held a bolt action Arisaka Type 99 rifle that had to be re-chambered. This gave Hawk time to thrust his submachine gun at the man and jerk the trigger. The soldier disappeared behind the lightning bolt flash. He bumped like a sack of potatoes down the sloping roof, leaving a wake of shining blood behind, and hurtling to the earth below.

The machine gunners immediately turned to find the source of these explosions. Frantically, Hawk rolled over on his stomach again, stretched his arms out on the wood and pulled the trigger again, this time in the direction of the gunner. A single round spat out, and it missed all of them. It was sufficient to cause the three Japanese to jump in panic, reach for their machine gun, and get in each other's way as they tried to turn it around to face this new threat. Their tramping feet were angled on the slope of the roof as they tried to maintain their balance. Hawk had perhaps a second or two as they attempted to complete the jerky maneuver. He thought of tossing a grenade, or of rolling backwards in a falling retreat.

He decided that the enemy preparations were progressing too rapidly for any of that. Bullets move faster than Mach one, and thought has to be faster than that when you're wrestling with them. Thinking is not usually as clear as is the trajectory of a bullet; but at least it was faster.

Hawk stood and ran along the ridge row protecting the roof's summit. He ran toward the front of the hospital, as quickly as he could, though occasionally having to slam a boot sideways to keep his balance on the curved surface. The Japanese managed to get the gun turned around in time, but their objective had moved. By the time one gunner pushed the other out of the way and seized the trigger, Hawk dove down onto them from the peak of the roof.

A vigorous push and the steepness of the angle of the roof launched him down into them like a missile. As his feet left the roof, and he flew over a dozen feet above its surface, he had an untethered sensation that left him believing that he was going to fly over the three of them, and onto the ground far below.

The gun erupted as he sailed over the slashing burst, with it barely missing him. He crashed across the bodies of all three of the gunners with the force of

Arnold began a lengthy dissertation about why it was *not* a poor risk. His basic theory was that they had no time limit on getting the Japanese out of their enclosures. It could be done. The speech contained a lot of rhetoric and little content. The officers nodded their heads gravely, agreeing completely with Arnold, and feeling only ashamed of Hawk's weak-kneed assessment. Such lack of insight.

They left convinced that they would be taking Delivalung. Hawk listened, preoccupied with the question as to why they would even want to take Delivalung. It seemed like an excellent place to leave just as many Japanese as wanted to stay there. He supposed that it was simply because they were there. That was the only reason he had been risking his life and limb on countless other islands scattered over half the world.

When it was over, Hawk got up to leave with the others. He saw Arnold moving toward him. Hawk tried to get lost in the crowd. He had no desire to defend the same argument again.

He bumped into Lieutenant Klemer. "This Arnold ain't a combat officer, is he?" Hawk asked Klemer.

Klemer looked pensive, more so than usual. "No," he answered, and walked off.

"Hawk," Arnold called, catching him before he could get out of the door. "Listen, we've got to get rid of those Japs." Perhaps Arnold was trying to make it simple, for the simple fellow.

"Yessir. I was only thinking that the place is as good as any to stow away as many of 'em as we can. They ain't hurting nobody out in the middle of nowhere. I mean, now that we know they ain't setting up a big headquarters hideout, or anything. Let 'em sit out there."

"Well, that's not the whole story. I want you to take five or six men and go back again. This time, check out all sides of the mountain. Circle it. I want to know what we're up against. I know you saw a strong presence on one side, but do we multiply that by four? Or is that it? You see, we are still in the dark. We can't be frightened away by something that may not be there. Sergeant Curry has not found what I am looking for, and so now my only alternative is to eliminate the Japanese. We are in a race with them to find some valuable raw materials. I need you to leave immediately and get back as soon as possible. Our native recruitment program is a failure, and I've got to move."

Hawk's steady gaze met Arnold's eyes. "Yessir." A glimmer of insight finally got through to the Sergeant.

Both Arnold and the Japanese were after this "something" near Delivalung, and Arnold could not get it with the enemy ensconced there. That was the unspoken other half of this story. Hawk knew what Curry was looking for. Or thought he was looking for. Should he tell Arnold that he knew what they were after? Should he tell him about the old column, and the likelihood of a temple in the swamp? A man had to trust the U. S. government, didn't he?

Hawk opened his mouth, but only, "Yessir," came out. Trust is hard to reach through reason, it requires some feeling. Arnold was not leveling with him, and he didn't like that. Especially since Arnold had levelled with Curry. Sort of. Granted, Curry had made a few implications on his own. Hawk wished he knew exactly what Arnold had told Curry. Had they been looking for an ammunition dump, or a submarine port, or anything consistent with the war effort, it would have been differ-

something from a catapult. The Japanese had no time to resist the collision. The four of them left the uneven surface of the roof and flailed out into space. There was not enough of the roof's surface left to fall upon, or to stop them.

The fall developed awkwardly, but it was not a fatal distance. Hawk believed that he had some control over it. He wanted only to be the one on top, and succeeded to a certain extent. One of the Japanese cushioned his fall. Hawk's head, however, proceeded to plow into the soft earth, bursting the straps of his helmet liner and numbing the top of his head. Before he could pull his face out of the dirt, the barrel of the machine gun, falling from the roof above, banged sharply across his back. The metallic blow forced him down on an elbow, but he managed to rise slowly to one knee. The Japanese he had fallen upon was unconscious, or dead. The other two bounded up from the ground in an instant, apparently with no injuries whatsoever. They turned their displeasure over the fall onto Hawk.

One of the Japanese kicked him in the chest. The Marine continued the slow rise to his feet, as if the kick had no effect. The other Japanese seized the American around the waist and tossed him over his hip. Hawk landed flat on his back, winded, in front of the hospital door.

Fifty rifles exploded from the gate, chopping down the two former machine gunners in a grim execution. Baker dragged Hawk through the door of the hospital by one arm. He sat him up and propped him against the wall.

"You need to practice your judo, Hawk. You just got

your ass whipped by a Jap." Baker held Hawk's face in his hands and grinned. Hawk's pupils looked all right.

"How is he?" Joe asked, watching the Marines pour unopposed through the front gate. The fight would end quickly now.

"Okay. Just fell on his ass." Baker laughed. "First time I ever saw judo work. The little fart threw him for a loop."

"Dumb bastard," said Joe. "What did you jump off the goddam roof for?" Joe pointed his rifle out the door, searching for fleeing infiltrators. "That's something a dumb bastard would do." Joe watched a Japanese soldier run out of the longhouse. About four grenades plopped and rolled under his feet. He skipped and twirled admirably for a bit, before they detonated. It was a clear case of overkill. That was the way it was done, until Sacred Blood had been retaken.

"Gimme a goddam drink," Hawk said.

* * *

"SERGEANT HAWK, I have been looking for you." Lieutenant Klemer stopped mid-step. Hawk and Jessica Pearson were talking in front of the hospital. They appeared to be old friends. Klemer thought a little less of Hawk. And her. "Mr. Arnold wants you at a meeting right away."

Jessica watched the two men walk away. She knew that she had to stay here a little longer. She wanted to tell James Hawk all about her life and hear more about his. She knew that he was not perfect. She knew that his bravery probably had certain moral, or rather immoral, compensations. That only made her want to know more, to understand, not to pass judgment. She did not especially want to change him, only to know more. And he had to know more about her. He had to know that she was not perfect, as well. She wanted to be, to be as caring and patient as she pretended. He would understand her.

Hawk felt the same way, about wanting to be with her. But not about wanting to be understood. As usual, he was involved in an interfering crisis. While she might not be "here" for long, at least he knew that she was there, in his life. She existed. That made it all worthwhile.

Going to Arnold's quarters didn't bother him. He had yet to realize how these interfering crises were not just a passing part of his life, they *were* his life.

Little information came out of the meeting. Hawk picked one interesting item out of the multi-syllable words and military jargon: the Japanese big shots were *not* going to Delivalung, contrary to his own eyewitness report, nor even to Basah itself, to create a headquarters for their new order. They had pulled up stakes and left for Japan. The latest theory was that their government and a weapons development program were moving to Korea, much closer to Japan, and easier to access. That left the purpose of Hawk's mission vague in his mind. Was Arnold after the treasure? Was that all that was left of this? Was the U. S. government still after it? Hawk trusted the U. S. government. If they wanted the treasure, that was fine with him. Arnold, however, was a different matter. Lost in all of these reports, and half-baked motives, was another loose end. What were the Japanese doing? If he knew what they were doing, he would know what he was doing.

He heard his name called out.

"Sergeant Hawk, in your assessment, do you think we can take Delivalung with what we have here?" Arnold's voice shot through his hazy thoughts. He looked up and saw the faces of all the officers turning toward him.

"Uh..." Hawk stammered. He had missed something. "Well, sir. If the Japs got what it takes to hit us here on our own ground, I'd say that would be a stretch. A big risk. I saw a pretty strong presence out there. Not just at the mountain, but between here and there." Hawk looked defiantly at the faces staring at him. "We won't be getting reinforcements?"

"I just said that we would not," Arnold returned abruptly. Some of the officers tittered. Enlisted men were so amusing, so quaintly ignorant. Arnold saw no amusement in it. The officers were only there for the theater of it. "I was just saying, Hawk, that we may get another battalion tomorrow. It might not get through. Transportation is an unknown without that riverboat. What do you think of two battalions?"

Hawk now had a better picture. "That would not be easy. I wouldn't try it." He had been in short changed operations before. Sometimes things worked out, and yet even when they did, a lot of things went wrong.

"Even with aerial bombardment and heavy artillery?"

"I wouldn't say it's impossible. It's a big mountain. I ain't seen but one side of it. Maybe, it can be done, but it's a risk. Getting the Japs out of all those holes is a big operation, sir. When they get in there like that, all that shelling doesn't do the trick. You gotta pry each one of 'em out."

Arnold began a lengthy dissertation about why it was *not* a poor risk. His basic theory was that they had no time limit on getting the Japanese out of their enclosures. It could be done. The speech contained a lot of rhetoric and little content. The officers nodded their heads gravely, agreeing completely with Arnold, and feeling only ashamed of Hawk's weak-kneed assessment. Such lack of insight.

They left convinced that they would be taking Delivalung. Hawk listened, preoccupied with the question as to why they would even want to take Delivalung. It seemed like an excellent place to leave just as many Japanese as wanted to stay there. He supposed that it was simply because they were there. That was the only reason he had been risking his life and limb on countless other islands scattered over half the world.

When it was over, Hawk got up to leave with the others. He saw Arnold moving toward him. Hawk tried to get lost in the crowd. He had no desire to defend the same argument again.

He bumped into Lieutenant Klemer. "This Arnold ain't a combat officer, is he?" Hawk asked Klemer.

Klemer looked pensive, more so than usual. "No," he answered, and walked off.

"Hawk," Arnold called, catching him before he could get out of the door. "Listen, we've got to get rid of those Japs." Perhaps Arnold was trying to make it simple, for the simple fellow.

"Yessir. I was only thinking that the place is as good as any to stow away as many of 'em as we can. They ain't hurting nobody out in the middle of nowhere. I mean, now that we know they ain't setting up a big headquarters hideout, or anything. Let 'em sit out there."

"Well, that's not the whole story. I want you to take five or six men and go back again. This time, check out all sides of the mountain. Circle it. I want to know what we're up against. I know you saw a strong presence on one side, but do we multiply that by four? Or is that it? You see, we are still in the dark. We can't be frightened away by something that may not be there. Sergeant Curry has not found what I am looking for, and so now my only alternative is to eliminate the Japanese. We are in a race with them to find some valuable raw materials. I need you to leave immediately and get back as soon as possible. Our native recruitment program is a failure, and I've got to move."

Hawk's steady gaze met Arnold's eyes. "Yessir." A glimmer of insight finally got through to the Sergeant.

Both Arnold and the Japanese were after this "something" near Delivalung, and Arnold could not get it with the enemy ensconced there. That was the unspoken other half of this story. Hawk knew what Curry was looking for. Or thought he was looking for. Should he tell Arnold that he knew what they were after? Should he tell him about the old column, and the likelihood of a temple in the swamp? A man had to trust the U. S. government, didn't he?

Hawk opened his mouth, but only, "Yessir," came out. Trust is hard to reach through reason, it requires some feeling. Arnold was not leveling with him, and he didn't like that. Especially since Arnold had levelled with Curry. Sort of. Granted, Curry had made a few implications on his own. Hawk wished he knew exactly what Arnold had told Curry. Had they been looking for an ammunition dump, or a submarine port, or anything consistent with the war effort, it would have been differ-

ent. This was off the patriotic spectrum. And, who the hell *was* this Arnold guy?

There was more than dollars and cents to all of this. Sergeant Hawk was not Clancy, or Curry, though both of them had mistakenly thought that he was. Hawk had not joined the Marine Corps to go on any treasure hunts. The countless men he had seen die, did not die looking to improve their financial bottom line. Their families were not waiting back home for a bag of gold, along with the telegram relaying the government's regrets. The families could not have Thanksgiving dinner this fall with a bag of gold. Or a telegram. Hawk did not kill men for a dollar a head. He did it for other reasons, mostly noble ones, but perhaps there were darker motives as well. Like revenge; for the memories of the men missing limbs and eyes, or the bodies lying under ponchos on the sides of roads: all looking at him, telling him that there was more to this. Very dark reasons. The dark reasons, that only a Marine rifleman would know. A burning desire to kill. But reasons that were not as dark, or as cheap, as a dollar bill. He was not the salvage boat operators at Guadalcanal, becoming millionaires off the tombs of dead sailors. There was more to this, a lot more. There was decency and duty, and there was just anger and the brotherhood. What would lead a man to do such low things for money? To become something like a salvager, or a Clifford Curry? Clancy had told him the answer.

"The finer things, lad. And you ain't one of 'em."

Maybe he wasn't.

* * *

HAWK SAW Jessica Pearson one more time before he left for Delivalung. They walked along the edge of the Mission's island, near the approach to the river. It was a secluded spot, less guarded than the perimeter facing the east. The shores had been spread with crushed rock, to make offloading the boats more convenient than the ass deep mud had been. They walked beyond the long pier and into the lazy shadows of the palm fronds. He was quiet. She was used to it now. Instead of talking to fill the void, she hummed *I'll be Seeing You*. He didn't recognize it. They stopped and she took his hand with both of hers.

"You have to promise that you will get a transfer to a base somewhere," she said, as she faced him. "I don't care where. How about that Camp Balcombe? Just so it isn't in a combat zone. Enough of this. I'm proud of what you do, and I know you are. But I think you have done enough, don't you?"

"Probably. But they'll be going into Japan. I figure I'll be in on that."

"You have to try to get out of that. They owe you that much. There must be something about how many times they can send you out on these things? You have to find out about that. Every organization has rules. You have to promise. If there is a way out, you will take it. You will not volunteer for anything. Promise?"

He felt odd about it. But not too odd, since there probably would not be a way out of it. "Yes," he said. "They go by points. You gotta have like ninety something points, but then it ain't for sure. You pick numbers. They gotta have replacements. It's a big deal. Just about everybody wants out. They can't just let everybody that's eligible go. But I'll check."

"Good." She smiled and slid deliciously against him. "Won't my father be surprised when I tell him about you?"

He nodded. "You're probably right about that."

"He'll say, 'that sounds like you, Jessica. Always rushing into things without any thought of the consequences. I could have predicted this.' He always says that, especially if I don't present things in the best light. I guess he has a right to feel that way. I have gone off on a few...adventures."

"Maybe," he said slowly, "you oughta listen to him."

"Well..." She shrugged. "My mother taught me to always look at things in the best possible light." She laughed. "He should have straightened her out before she corrupted me. You are lucky you didn't have parents."

"Yeah."

"Oh, I'm sorry. That was such a stupid thing to say. I let my tongue run away with me sometimes. I guess I was feeling a little too giddy."

He smiled and shook his head, as if the comment meant nothing to him. And, it probably didn't. It's hard to regret things that never were.

Her eyes narrowed. "Do you like children?"

Once again, her quick transitions caught him off guard. They were two young people, looking desperately for answers, quickly, before something happened. It sounded like a yes or no question, and he had just enough social skills to know the acceptable answer. Who was going to say: shit, no, I don't like kids?

"Yeah. I like kids. But I mean, it's not like I've ever been around any." He couldn't think of any reason for someone to say that they didn't like kids. You could tell a kid to go away, if you didn't like him. What could a kid do?

"That's wonderful! I just love them. So fresh and new and growing. Such fun to interact with, such imaginations, such a delight to entertain!"

"Sure enough."

"And the little ones, the babies!" She held her hands a foot apart. "A little person this big. It's such a miracle! But, not a lot of children, mind you," she said with mock seriousness.

"No. I expect not."

"With their little hands and little feet, like little dolls!" She laughed, then frowned suddenly.

Hawk looked at her, conscious of every shade of expression in her gentle face. He caught the moment, on the backdrop of his memory, as if in a photograph. "What's the matter?" he asked. He would wish that he hadn't.

"Oh, I don't know. It's sad, sometimes. To see these men here and to know that they were children, and babies. To know that someone loved their little hands, their sweet little heads...and they came here to this awful place and left their mothers, worried at home."

Sweet little heads.

Hawk smiled at the innocence of it all, for only a moment. He had inadvertently stumbled too far into her female mind. It was as alien and dangerous a place as any of the others he had stumbled into.

He had a rather strong flashback, as if he were there, in that different and tense place; it was something akin to a physical pain. His smile faded as he managed to control a shudder. He saw, and felt, Admiral Ishakawi's neck beneath the blade of his knife.

He cleared his throat. "Let's sit down some place," he said. A man can get too relaxed, he thought. The slack only provoked the recurrence of nerve tautness felt in other emotional states. One particular state remained vividly before his mind's eye.

"Very well," she laughed. She had no business being near something like him.

He sat against a palm tree. She pulled her dress under herself and sat close beside him. He removed his helmet and breathed deeply. His hand reached for the chewing tobacco in his shirt pocket. No, couldn't do that.

"Kind of hot today," he rasped. "Damn place."

"Well, it *is* on the equator." She smiled and looked at the ugly gray water creeping out from under the vegetation at the swamp's edge. "It's a shame women don't run the world, isn't it? Things would not be in such a mess. Mothers do so well, until their children grow up. There is nothing more orderly than a neighborhood with young mothers and young children. And then they leave and go into the bigger world." She laughed. She was happy.

He wasn't laughing.

"Damn sure hot, ain't it?" he said.

"Wouldn't you rather have women in charge of the world?"

Her words seemed to echo in his head. "Couldn't do no worse, I guess. As long as the other side is run by women, too."

He tried to imagine Japanese women. He remembered their unsmiling photographs from the pockets of dead enemy soldiers, with accusing expressions. And

Japanese children. He had all sorts of fun memories, for all occasions.

"Well, that's the point, isn't it? Maybe there wouldn't be another side. Childhood is such a happy time. Isn't it?"

Having had no childhood, Hawk was on thin ice again, and not feeling up to the mental challenge. "Yeah, nothin' bothers kids." He took a deep breath. "And old people get pretty tough. I guess it's in between that's the problem." For some reason, he thought of Clancy. The old bastard.

She eased her arm around his back. "Oh, I don't know. *You* are pretty tough," she said in a low voice. She looked up quickly at him. She could tell he didn't feel well. She hoped that it wasn't the fever. "Aren't you?"

Hawk nodded slowly. "I'm afraid so," he answered, in an almost apologetic tone.

12

THE FALL OF MAN

HAWK SELECTED JOE CANLON, BAKER, DUPUY, LYNWOOD and a scout to go with him on the last of the patrols to Delivalung. Joe took a little convincing, but he was an adventurer, and he liked the company. The new scout was a relative of Luka's, named Gepu. They walked past the erstwhile battlefield, then past an area of the *ladang* method of farming, which resembled a battlefield, and from there into the forest.

Hawk would try a more direct route this time. He had recorded a number of bearings in the course of his journeys. It took a while to get the lay of the land in this living haystack. He knew a lot more about it now. He set a leisurely pace. He knew all about the disadvantages of arriving exhausted at the mountain destination.

They spent the night with some Murut tribesmen, friendly to the Allies. The natives were on their way to the coast, blissfully unaware of all of the trouble in the area.

A Penan man accompanied them. He had a bowl haircut and a pigtail. His distended ears swung to his shoulders with brass ornaments. He serenaded the group around their campfire with a pipe instrument, consisting of a gourd bowl and vibrating reeds. Hawk thought of Jessica and *I'll be Seeing You* as he listened. But no one would be seeing him in this old familiar place. He had already forgotten the tune. The Penan explained his blowgun, and the poison for the darts, made from the bark of the ipoh tree. Their firelight created an orange island in the vast black sea of the night. Joe found the evening entertaining, relatively speaking, until he noticed something out of the ordinary.

He saw two weirdly glowing red lights, almost like eyes, in the dark jungle behind the heads of the others. He thought that he could discern a frightening silhouette above the eyes, resembling widely spaced horns. As the unearthly vision floated closer, he was brought out of his dreamy reverie, and it scared the hell out of him.

"Look at that!" he said, setting up a general alarm. Following the direction indicated, the others began searching the underbrush as Joe continued to describe, rather unimaginatively, what he had seen. Finding nothing, the Americans branded Joe an ass. It was discovered, however, that the natives took advantage of the searching process to execute a nighttime exit from the presence of their hosts. Even the wandering country folk had heard of Gohoron.

Joe found it difficult to sleep after that. Every time he closed his eyes, he could see the leering vision. Gepu, who had not seen the unwelcome specter, had to use his imagination to disturb his own sleep, and it served well enough.

The next day began with Gepu regaling the men

with tales of the victims of Gohoron, including the suspicion that his kinsman, Luka, had been one of them. Hawk found all of this extraordinarily irritating, especially with Joe's addition to the legend. Now, American nonsense could be added to the local foolishness, only increasing its credibility. Hawk felt worse today. Tales of the supernatural did not mix well with his gory flashbacks. His stomach cramped and he always felt overheated. A fever was just what he *did not* need, in the middle of all of this. He took a drink from his canteen. It tasted like crap.

HAWK FOUND THE RIFT EASILY. He and Joe both thought of the slain admiral. Hawk looked over his shoulder frequently now. The ghosts were closing in on him. It was kind of hard to breathe. And, *damn it was hot! Either I've got the fever, or I'm going nuts.* He opened his canteen and took a longer than usual drink. He took a salt tablet. He saw Joe looking at him.

"What the goddam hell are you looking at?"

"You're sweating like a pig," Joe answered. Hawk almost never sweated.

"Is that right? I wonder why?" Hawk replaced the canteen in its holder and closed the flaps. "I guess you ain't sweatin'?"

"Yeah. Yeah, I'm sweatin' all right." *I bet the son of a bitch's sick. He won't quit though,* Joe thought. He had never seen Hawk sick.

Hawk calculated the distance to the swamp. Everything was going faster, and much smoother. The night's rest had made a big difference. He knew it was a crazy idea, but he felt that last drink of water made his stomach hurt even more. It was almost like it had this weird, inside-your-bowels taste that never went away. Well, that was just too bad. His stomach had hurt before. That swamp was close. He would be a fool not to check it this time. What if any part of the stories of the Chinese Emperors were true? He may have actually located the legendary Emperor's horde.

Boiling steam filtered through the foliage, bouncing angrily up from the earth. The black hulk of the summit of Delivalung peered sneakily, here and there, just above the treetops. *Damn, we've covered some ground,* Hawk thought.

Hawk's boots pounded the sand steadily. The loose, soft surface made the walking more strenuous. His shirt, black with perspiration, was open, and his sleeves were rolled up over heavily veined arms. The sand reminded him of Ishakawi—and the other victim. *Sweet little heads.* Right around here is where that had happened. He felt a chill. *Now what?* He had been able to explain away the other sensations, but this was not good. This was a real medical symptom of...some damn thing. A chill was not logical in this place.

For a moment, he wanted out of here. He wanted to be with Jessica Pearson. To turn over a new leaf in his life. He thought of her angelic face, and the cool, watery shade along the old pier. Her eyes, that said everything was all right, and that leaving all of this behind was the right thing to do. *All right if you bring home the bacon, mate.* Then he could hear Clancy's voice. His *dead* voice. And the moment passed. He did not want out of here, after all. He was James Hawk again. It was time to do the job or die trying. And make damn sure somebody else died along the way. He stopped.

"What's up?" Joe asked.

"Nothin'." He moved leaves out of his way and looked at Delivalung. "Here's the plan. We'll spend the day circling this bastard to get troop estimates, then we'll meet back here. I'll take Joe and Baker. Dupuy, you take Lynwood and Gepu. Everybody stay out of trouble. Hide and seek. It's important to come back. It won't matter what you see if you're dead."

Joe had been developing a plan. He had decided that if they split up, he did not want to be in Hawk's group. The chances for survival were better that way. Hawk did reckless things that the others would not do without even considering that they were dangerous. He didn't even *know* they were dangerous.

"Listen, Hawk," said Joe. "Why don't you take Dupuy and let me take the other two guys, since I've been here before and all."

Hawk looked at Joe. He batted the sweat out of his eyes. Joe's face seemed a little hazy. "If that's what you want, go ahead," the Sergeant finally said. He didn't understand the request, or try to.

Joe nodded, feeling uneasy. Did Hawk represent safety...or danger? Hawk didn't look so good, from several different perspectives. "Yeah, let's do it that way," Joe said.

"Okay, then. That's it. Get going," Hawk ordered, throwing up a pointing hand.

Joe and the other two dashed across the rift. As Hawk watched Joe's familiar scrambling limbs, it occurred to him that Joe was the only other person who knew about that stone column buried in the mud.

A lot of what happened next could be explained by the unusual mixture of personalities that remained there, when Joe and Lynwood left. In most military units there is camaraderie and friendship; a key factor in holding the unit together and enabling it to fight. Hawk, however, was a loner. It was difficult to be his friend. He was protective of the new men, but Baker and Dupuy were not new. Baker was a little off, and therefore, was generally avoided by the others as somewhat strange and unpredictable. Dupuy was neither crazy, nor a loner, but was a distinctly unlikeable fellow. He was arrogant, opinionated, crude, outspoken, and stubborn. These three personalities were not going to be doing any joking, back slapping, or misty-eyed talking about old times.

The Sergeant unsnapped his canteen again. He watched the torrid vapor rising from the sand. He knew that he was drinking too much, but he was thirsty. He opened the little metal bottle. He poured some in his hand and splashed it onto his face. *Damn, that felt good,* he thought. That was almost better than drinking it. He poured out another handful of water, looking down at it in anticipation. It was brown. He smelled it, and there was no odor, or especially different taste. He threw it down and dried his hand. His hand must have been dirty. He looked at the calloused hand. Rough, scratched, tough, but all things considered, pretty clean. There was not enough dirt on it to float the mud puddle he had seen. He poured another handful of water. It was brown. He poured some into a little depression in a rock near his feet. It lay brown in there as well.

"Somebody shit in my water," Hawk muttered. His head wavered. He felt his body drying out around his skeleton. He had to have a drink. "Dupuy, give me your canteen," he ordered and stuck out a shaky hand.

"You ain't getting my water," said Dupuy. "It's a hundred and ten in the shade out here." Dupuy drew back.

Hawk turned away from him. "It's all shade, shitball. It'll be cooler on the northern slope. There'll be hills and streams over there. We gotta double up on the water. Hand it over."

"Go to hell, Hawk. There ain't no clean water for miles. You should have been watching it, like I did. Drink your own canteen." The burly Dupuy was adamant, and apparently not budging on the subject.

Hawk turned half around and studied Dupuy through foggy eyes. He didn't like what he saw. Someone had put something in his water. He thought of the illnesses at Sacred Blood Mission, the men crying out for water in the hospital. Dupuy was acting funny. He had always been a big, nasty bastard, but this was different. What was so special about *his* water?

"Here," Baker said, thrusting his canteen at Hawk. As crazy as he was, the grizzled Baker sensed a tense situation in need of defusing. These two were not the sorts to settle disagreements in a gentlemanly fashion. They were not even the sorts to let U. S. Marine Corps ranks bother them very much.

"No," said Hawk with clenched teeth. "I want *his*."

"You ain't *gittin'* mine!" Dupuy insisted. "What's the matter, Hawk? Afraid you ain't gonna make it back to that little Aussie whore? You should have stuck with the natives like I had to. Clawing my eyes out and screaming every time you grab hold of..." Dupuy appeared quite angry, with some sort of smoldering grievance that had unexpectedly leapt to a full flame.

"*What?* What did you say?" Hawk snapped his head around to face Dupuy full on. He leaned over and grabbed Dupuy's canteen. Dupuy pulled back, knocking the grip free. "Give me that goddam water, you son of a bitch." Hawk pawed at it again, and Dupuy backed farther away.

Hawk took a step forward. Apparently, with some forethought, as he did it smoothly, Dupuy drew his Ka-bar knife quickly from its scabbard. They had all been trained in fighting with knives. But it was Hawk's untrained fist that settled the matter. He leaned almost his entire body forward in rage, with only his toes still on the ground, reaching over the blade and blasting the point of Dupuy's chin with all of his weight. Dupuy slumped over like a dropped paving stone. He didn't get up, twitch, or move. Baker grinned. Dupuy had been large, strong, and powerful. But that wasn't enough. Hawk's arms were pipes bound in cables and powered by a dynamo. They had been abused since his childhood with repetitive use of saws, axes, hoes, shovels, plows, and anything else heavy and dirty. His fist was a spring-loaded block of cement. Worse than any of this, however, was his frustration with the nagging occult illness, his bursting anger and rage with every aspect of being a lonely killer at war.

They couldn't turn Dupuy's head around. They left it turned to the side and buried him there.

It started to rain. The heavy drops pressed down on them, soaking their clothing. Hawk shook his head as he looked at the wet mound of earth. *Well, there's your new leaf, all turned over,* he thought. Now, you're not just killing Japanese, you're killing everybody.

He spoke for the first time since the incident. "Check your canteen, Baker." They checked, and the water in it was clear. Dupuy's contained clear water. "I didn't mean to kill him," said Hawk, "he must have had a glass jaw or something."

Baker grinned. "I know. I saw. You barely tapped him." He said this with some conviction, even though he had never seen one human being hit another so hard in his life. Hawk's body had been almost horizontal with the earth, and in total disregard of the seven inches of sharp steel aimed at him, when the fist connected with Dupuy. "I seen the whole thing. He was being an asshole. And then he pulls the knife, outa nowhere. I don't know what he was thinking. I wouldn't worry about it."

"All I did was ask him for some water."

"Yeah. I seen that. And he went nuts," said Baker. *Or somebody did.*

The rain poured from the brim of Hawk's helmet. There was plenty of water now, and it was cool. It smelled like the South China Sea, like salt and dead sea life. Baker slapped him on the back. Hawk glanced at him. He felt certain that Baker would not tell anyone of the incident. Baker was no good, just like Hawk. He would always be on the wrong side of everything. A loser, of the lowest class; a word or a step away from life in an iron cage. It was good that Joe Canlon had chosen to go elsewhere. He might not have been as accepting of all of this.

Hawk took a drink of Dupuy's water. He could see the head turned to the side under the dirt. In a way,

Dupuy's mother had entrusted her son to Sergeant Hawk and the U. S. Marine Corps. And, there he was.

Hawk brushed a hand at the blasting rain angling into his eyes. "That son of a bitch." He took another drink. He imagined that the clean water, and the cool rain, made him feel better. "Come on. Let's get this stupid shit over with."

* * *

JOE CANLON and Lynwood burst through the jungled highlands on the northern slope of Delivalung. The rain had stopped there. The scene, however, was not as placid as the one on the southern side. At least two thousand sharply outfitted Japanese troopers bustled before them. Some were moving heavy equipment, some were drilling, and all were moving. Men were coming in and out of caves near the top. It looked like they were expecting an attack on this side of the volcano. Over here, it looked less like a volcano and more like any other mountain. Artillery jutted from some of the caves, and at times, rolled backwards, becoming completely concealed. Joe had not seen this degree of armament on the southern side of the mountain, where he and Hawk had first noted the Japanese presence. This would not be the side to attack, in Joe's estimation.

He and Lynwood retreated into the jungle and maneuvered eastward, having the general purpose of returning to the southern rendezvous point.

Joe called for a rest after about an hour. They sat in the shade discussing what they had seen.

"That's gonna be trouble, all them Jap bastards.

We're gonna end up in the big middle of all that shit, you wait and see. I'm telling you," Joe said.

"Maybe. You never know what they're doing, to tell you the truth," said Lynwood. "I don't understand the Japanese. Or, our command, for that matter."

"*Shee-it.* You know it ain't gonna be good for us. You know that much. They'll throw us at that mountain. You know, sometimes I wonder why God allows so much shit to go wrong. I mean, *shit.*" Joe seemed more upset than informed by his discoveries. "Does every goddam thing in this world have to turn to shit?"

"Well," said Lynwood, in a serious tone, "that's in the Bible."

Joe faced him with a disgusted expression. "Come on. *Everything's* in the Bible. People always say that kind of goddam crap, but where the hell is it? They just give you a bunch of mumbo jumbo. In the Bible—my ass."

"It's all through it, I guess. But mostly, in the beginning. Man was protected by God on a good earth, but man chose to go his own way. To live by his own reason. He didn't want to be told what to do—like when kids grow up and leave home. And so now, man is subject to the laws of Nature, by choice. Which can be pretty... random. We have to rely on our own faulty reason to deal with it. You see, God isn't random. Things always go right for Him."

Joe stared at Lynwood. "Aw, shit. Let's get goin'."

* * *

HAWK AND BAKER reached the western slope, and saw much the same assembly of strength as did Joe Canlon, but from a different perspective. As they laid on their stomachs, Hawk studied the throbbing glow in the split of Delivalung's western side. The lava moat flowed slowly, all around the base, but was intersected by infusions of swamp water at various intervals. Clouds of foul steam rose along the course.

"Yeah, that's a couple thousand for sure. Maybe that many more inside. That's too much for what we have. You can't attack a bigger force up on a mountain like that with a little one. I told them that." Hawk rolled onto his back and looked up at the sky.

"If you told them that, what are we doing here?" Baker asked.

"I don't know. When you see a pattern to things, some folks stop and ask why. But some just keep buttin' their heads up against it. Especially, if they can get somebody else to do the buttin' for them."

Baker supposed that this was his answer. He didn't really expect one anyway.

They turned south to meet with Joe Canlon and Lynwood. Halfway back, Baker slipped and he felt his leg being swallowed by the soft earth. His weight and the hole pulled him down rapidly. He cried out.

For a moment, he feared that Hawk would not aid him. After all, he had been a witness to the Dupuy killing.

The thought crossed Hawk's mind as well.

Hawk grabbed Baker's flailing arm and leaned back, pulling him from the deep hole. They looked down into it. It was too deep to see a bottom, but the peculiar thing was, that it was wide, and still widening.

"That's a tunnel," said Hawk. "Damn top of the thing's caving in." He lay on the ground to get a better look, but the ground loosened even more, and he had to leap to his feet and jump back to avoid tumbling inside. "It's an escape hatch from the mountain, I expect. Damn Japs is like a bunch of gophers."

"Yeah," said Baker, rubbing his scraped leg. Baker was growing fearful of Hawk, even after his rescue. While Baker was crazy, he knew that Hawk was not crazy—he was entirely, rationally, evil. There was no craziness about the Sergeant, only villainy. He watched Hawk's face and wondered how long it would be before they reunited with Canlon again. The Sergeant took out his map, and he drew a line through the middle of the volcano, to the point where they now stood.

The enemy could use the tunnel to escape or mount a rear attack. Or do just about anything else they wanted to do with it. Hawk looked in surprise at the black valley below Delivalung's southern slope. It was no longer black. It had turned a watery gray. A foot of water covered the valley floor.

He craned his neck and stepped closer to the ledge along the rift. The water was rising. "Look, the damn place is flooding."

Baker scratched his head. "We better get out of here."

"Nah. It won't get up here."

"That ought to take care of the Japs."

Hawk rocked his helmet back. He did not see anyone moving around on the southern slope. "No, they're kinda high over on that north side. This is important, though. We can't get at them from the south. This must be a flash flood from another river. It will damn sure flood that southern valley."

He looked at the far side of the valley. Water gushed down over a straight edged cliff from dozens of rivulets.

The rivulets widened as they fell, until it looked as if they would join into one massive waterfall. Great boulders washed away. The jungle above the valley itself lay under a few inches of water. A shiny gray surface swirled about the green legs of the plants rooted there. A cloud of disturbed flying insects darted for another few feet above the water, looking like a mist.

"Hell, that might even be from the ocean," Hawk said as the volume of water increased. "I mean, where is all that water coming from?"

* * *

JOE CANLON WAS FINDING out a little more about the practical aspects of the flood from the other side of the valley. It was not academic for him. His trip to the rendezvous point was through the rushing water tearing at his legs. All manner of dislodged creatures washed by him before being catapulted into the valley below. His least favorite of these were the snakes. He knew that there were a lot out there, but he had no plan to meet each one personally. The snake's held no interest in the men, however, as they floundered across the current and dealt with their own difficulties.

Joe inhaled the sickly tasting insects.

Gepu urged them on with terrified warnings. He entertained them with the superstitious prediction that the water would rise over the summit of the volcano. They did not need a lot of motivation. It seemed entirely possible. Joe kept his eyes on the trees, ready for a quick climb should the prediction approach reality.

Ultimately, the water never rose much higher than their knees. It took a psychological toll, however, and they reached the rift in a state of panic. Only a slightly elevated natural levee along the brink of the gorge separated the floodwater from the rift's water running before them. The rift boiled with white, braided bolts of floodwater. Joe looked at it in horror. They were trapped on the wrong side of the rift from Hawk and Baker.

Hawk reached the rendezvous point with a contrasting lack of concern. His side was high and dry. He knew that Joe was a good swimmer, but Joe had another outlook. He had no intention of swimming the deathtrap.

Hawk spotted Joe's party, climbed down the side of the rift for a few feet, and waved them across. He thought they were lost. Joe shouted a few obscenities back at him. Hawk realized that the comments had something to do with the depth of the water and began to take the rising flood more seriously. A large tree teetered over the edge on Joe's side and splashed into the gorge. It shot along the course of the ravine, toward Delivalung. It never once came close to Hawk's bank of the rift.

Hawk signaled to them, pointing south. The rift did not run all the way to the swamp. Perhaps they could get around it. The ground lying to the south was higher, before it descended into the marshlands. Joe, ready to try anything, successfully waded through the furious cataract on the edge of the rift. Gepu and Lynwood followed him. Their legs were tired of fighting the current. They finally took heart because the water rose no higher.

After an hour, they reached the end of the rift on a rocky plateau. For the first time, Joe stepped out of the flood waters. He and Hawk met at the source of the raging rift and looked across the flooded valley at the eerie spectacle of Delivalung's black hull.

"Check that, would you." Hawk shook his head. An ocean lay between them and the mountain. This morning it had been dry land. The volcano's red crown rose out of the ocean like an island. "The Japs damn sure knew which side was the safe one. I think they're a little more on the ball here than we are."

"Yeah," said the breathless Joe. "Wish I had known."

"Ah, a little runoff can't hurt you."

"Run off? We figured that the tide done come in and got us. Hell, yeah, it was runoff from where you was standing." Joe's eye caught Baker. Baker, characteristically, was grinning. "Hey, where is Dupuy?"

Hawk sniffed the vapory air. "Fell. Fell and bumped his head," he said.

"Yeah. And drowned," Baker added.

Joe turned his head from Hawk to Baker and back. "Oh, yeah?" He did not want to know anymore. He already didn't like it.

"Told him to be careful," said Hawk, lighting a soggy cigar. The cool air from the flooded lake invigorated him.

"Yeah," Baker said thoughtfully. "He bumped his head on a limb and drowned." Baker looked down mournfully. "Wasn't being careful. Gotta be careful. Goddamnit." His voice trailed off.

"I thought he fell," Joe said quickly. He didn't want to know anything, but he wanted them to get their story straight.

"Shit, yeah, he fell," Hawk said impatiently. "Told you that. Wouldn't you fall if you bumped your goddam head? Come on. We'll hook it back to that swamp. We got a lot to report here. Did you see all of them Japs?"

"Yeah." Joe nodded solemnly. He decided that this was probably not his line of work. These guys were rough. Rough, and getting rougher. No telling what had happened to Dupuy. Obviously, questions were going to stir up anger. They started walking. If Lynwood had figured out what was going on, he did not show it. He had sense enough to know that you did not mess with Hawk and Baker when you were two days from civilization. Dupuy must have forgotten about that.

After a while, Hawk told Joe, "Give me your canteen."

Baker looked at Joe's surprised face and grinned.

Joe handed it over without hesitation. Hawk poured the water into his hand. It was brown, a darker brown than even his had been. "You had two canteens, didn't you? Did the first canteen have shit in it, like this one?"

Joe frowned. "No, I don't think so. Why does that one have shit in it?"

"Feel all right?"

"Yeah. I feel just dandy. Shirley Temple ain't got nothing on me."

"Got any fever?"

"Fever? No."

Hawk nodded. "Save this canteen. Just don't drink it."

"Carry around a damn jug of water and don't drink it?"

"Just do it, goddamnit."

A cold, damp darkness, lonely and threatening, closed around them. Joe's heart pounded as he followed Baker through the unfriendly vines. Joe was sure of one thing, and that was that he was not getting into this kind of shit again. He would do his fighting from the front lines. That's all a man should have to do. Going out into the wilds behind enemy lines with crazy men was for other people. People like Baker could do this horse shit: the damn maniac.

Joe wondered which of the two of them had killed Dupuy. If they had any sense, they would have said the Japs did it. Their story was a dead giveaway. Two idiots. Probably, Baker did it. He was a certified maniac. Hawk was certainly capable of it, but what reason would he have? He had that temper, but Dupuy knew that, and he would not have crossed Hawk out here. No, it was Baker, all right. He probably killed the guy just for the hell of it. But...any way you looked at it, there were *two* maniacs: because Hawk knew what had happened and was covering for Baker.

Hawk stopped. He crouched over his map. They were a few hundred yards from the swamp. He sighed and rubbed his straight narrow nose. *The finer things.* Hawk was so isolated from the finer things, he had only a dim concept of what they were. But women knew. Hawk did not know much about women, either. From where he was standing, women were about as real as the planet Saturn.

He looked into the darkness ahead of him. Insects sang. A night bird rustled above them. A man would be a fool not to try, they were this close to it. He was here to do reconnaissance, wasn't he? Arnold said to be on the lookout. Arnold said they had to find—something. He would not lose any time, just a little sleep. He did not need sleep. He could easily keep up with the others, even when he was dead tired. City boys. City people. *The finer things.* He felt strong.

"Yeah..." Hawk exhaled slowly. "We'll bed down here."

The others surveyed the clutching stomach wall of the jungle that they were lying on the bottom of. The greenish black vise moved in and out on them.

"Here?" Lynwood asked, his voice an octave higher than it should be. It did not feel safe here. Of all of them, Lynwood was the most normal. He would not make excuses for Hawk, the way Joe would. He would not let "little things" slide like Baker did. He could feel his difference from the other three men. It felt as if they were alien beings from some far-off race of creatures, akin to the Neanderthal. He was just a guy from middle America, who had volunteered to defend his country. These were some pretty bad guys, here to do bad things. And perfectly comfortable with it.

"Yeah," Hawk replied, as if the hellish spot were the most obvious place on earth for an overnight stay. "Tell you what. I might even just go on up ahead and eyeball the swamp some. It might take a while. Y'all take it easy a while." Hawk bit off a plug of tobacco. He chewed quietly and didn't get up. Maybe he should take a man with him. A man alone can get his ass in a crack. Sometimes, all it takes is another hand to pull him out. Like what happened to Baker, falling in the hole. Hawk, who had never wanted to be bothered with another living soul, convinced himself that he needed a buddy on this one. He didn't consciously think of needing someone to share the blame with him. Would he take Joe, or Baker? They represented two different things.

Hawk spat. "Joe...you're going, too."

"Me?" Joe looked up in alarm. "Take this goddam Baker. You two are buddies."

Hawk hesitated, chewed some more, spat, and snapped, "I said you. We ain't takin' no votes."

"All right, all right." Joe slung his rifle. He would show him. He would pull his sullen act. That always worked. He would make Hawk feel like shit, and then next time Hawk would leave him alone. This one probably would not be too bad anyway. What could they do in the dark? The next crazy plan might be worse. Passive resistance was the best way to handle Hawk. Any other kind of resistance was met with a bulldozer.

They slipped through the caressing creepers and jerked their limbs through the biting briars, coming out of the forest at the very spot where the decaying column lay, almost as if Hawk knew where it was. The war moon, evil and in perfect tune with James Hawk, burst from behind a cloud and lit the post's porous surface.

"Here we are," Hawk said. He spat and looked at Joe with a half-smile. Joe stuck his lower lip out a little farther. He figured Hawk had not received the message yet. His pouting had to become more intense. Hawk was too stupid to catch on to anything subtle.

"What's eatin' you, shit ass?"

"Nothing. Here we are. So, what?"

"How would you like a kick in your fat ass?"

"I wouldn't. Are we going back now? It's dark as hell out here."

13

THE ABOMINATION IN THE TEMPLE

AN ANGRY GOHORON THRUST HIS GROTESQUE HEAD OUT in front of each labored step. A steady growl came from his chest. He ceased moving when he heard voices, his volcanic eyes burning. He saw the four Americans and Gepu, cowering in his jungle. Two of them left and three stayed behind. He plotted how best to destroy all of them. The two would be the first eliminated, as it would be easier that way. He brushed through the heavy moss, the moonlight striking his massive head. He followed at a sound-muffling distance behind Joe Canlon's shadowy helmet.

"You hear something?" Baker asked Lynwood.

"Guilty conscience?" Lynwood asked.

* * *

HAWK SPAT. Joe's mood had finally succeeded in irritating him. "Now, listen. Here, sit down, stupid. I want to tell you something."

"About Dupuy?"

"About...what? No, listen. I said...you don't always have to be saying something stupid, do you? You and me is buddies, right? We go way back."

"What's the matter, getting lonely?"

Hawk spat and nodded. "Now, Joe, you're getting on my nerves." Hawk raised his voice impatiently. Joe stared silently at the swamp. His attitude was working. "Now..." Hawk gestured at the air, "I want to ask you a question. What if you had a chance to make some money, big money." Hawk stopped and lost his thought. Persuasion was not his strong point. "What would you say about a man who had a chance like that?"

"I'd say that's a guy that *ain't* you and me."

"That's the point. It *is* you and me." Hawk nodded, pointing to Joe and himself. "They say that there's a Chinese treasure buried out there. It's got to be here by these old buildings. Right where we're sitting. See? It can't be nowhere else on earth."

Joe looked down. He saw an old column—if that's what it even was. Probably just a stupid rock. He did not see any buildings or treasure. His eyes opened wide and he looked out into the swamp. The stinking miasma rising over it became lit by the moon, and by other nameless gaseous discharges.

"Oh, no!" Joe shook his head. "I might have known this!" Joe stood. "If you want to go swimming with the crocs, go right ahead. I'll stay here and notify your next of kin."

"Sit down, sit down. Shit. I ain't got no next of kin." Hawk's tone was dramatic. He knew that he could outwit Joe. But it was taking longer than he had planned. The night was deepening.

"Hawk, that's against the law," Joe said, sitting down.

He had to abandon his attitude for the time being. Hawk was closing in on him too quickly. Passive resistance was not going to be enough in the path of the bulldozer.

"What the hell? I ain't done nothing. What law?"

"There ain't nothing that you *ain't* done, except this. When you're discharged, they might let you keep a pistol or a hula doll or something, but you can't go on no gold hunt and bring back a treasure chest. They go through your shit like crazy when you get to the States. You gotta have written clearance on every item. You're misusing your authority or some kind of shit like that."

Hawk hung his head. "I ain't *got* no authority. Look at this." Hawk waved his arm at the wilderness surrounding them. "Let's just check it out. That guy Arnold is after something and I think this is it. He's sent me and Curry out to find something, and we don't even know what it is. Maybe Arnold don't even know what it is. I don't think he's on the level. So, we just...see...what's there. Maybe after the war we come back, for old time's sake. If we put a couple of souvenirs in our pocket ahead of time, so what? Do you know that bastard kept that goddam admiral's ring? This right here, what we're doing, is part of our job according to him. It ain't no big deal. A couple of souvenirs and were fixed."

"Yeah, fixed for Portsmouth." Joe tightened his lips. "It's that babe, ain't it? You never gave a shit about money in your life. That time we found the Jap payroll in the islands, you couldn't care less. You ain't thinking right Hawk, you ain't yourself."

"Okay. Fine. You want to talk crazy talk? Where is the woman I was mixed up with in those islands? She hit the road. Listen, you only get so many shots."

"I knew it. You ain't thinking right. You're always doing some crazy shit for some woman, and it always goes bad. What's wrong with you? Don't you know nothing about women? They're just people, not some gods you gotta kill yourself for."

"What in the *hell* are you talking about? This is what we were sent here to do. This is what they want. This is our mission. Calm down, you're gonna shit your pants. Ain't nobody talking about women, or prison, or whatever in the hell you're screaming about."

"They wanted troop estimates on the volcano. That was the mission. That ain't what this is. This is just...crazy."

"I'm telling you, they want *this* as much as the troop estimates. Maybe more. The Japs want it, too. This is why they're way the hell out here. Curry saw them lookin' for it. That's probably what this whole thing is about. I mean, look at this place. Does this crap look like something two armies would fight over?"

"Curry is so full of shit he's going to float away." Joe took a deep breath. However, somewhere in the middle of the argument, he had accidentally started listening. *Right where we're sitting.* So, what if they waded out there ten feet, and maybe they found something? It would be kind of dumb to pass that up. Go ten feet, bend over, pick it up. He took another deep breath. "Well, I guess it ain't such a big deal."

"Naw. Probably nothing to it. In a couple of days this place will be crawling with Marines. Maybe the damn Army. How would you like a couple of draftees sittin' out here laughing about what a couple of suckers we were, with their pockets full of gold?" Joe slid the handle of his bayonet down onto his M1's standard until the nub on the guard also slipped into the rifle's boss. The Army pissed Joe off.

"Maybe I can stick them crocs with this," Joe said, "but I'm warning you, I will shoot if I have to. I might do anything when I see them. I ain't gonna be no crocodile's K-ration."

Hawk slapped him on the back. "It won't matter what you do. You ain't gonna see 'em. They come up under the water and grab ya in the ass." Hawk snapped his hand shut. He stood and stretched.

Joe rubbed his bayonet. "So, if they see us, there's nothing we can do?"

"Probably not. They eat at night. We're the trespassers."

"Then why don't we do this in the daytime? It'll be dark as hell out there. You can't see shit right here. If this is all legal and holy and all, why can't we have the other guys with us? It's the mission, right? Remember all that shit?"

"Because...right now it's nighttime, and we're here." Hawk pulled up his pants leg and exposed a thick oily rag tied around his leg. He untied it and stuck it under his helmet. He took another one off the other leg and handed it to Joe. "Torches," he said. "I'll go first. I believe there's an island out there. We'll only be in the water a couple of minutes. The gators won't have much of a shot at us. Nothing to it. People been doing it since the dawn of time. Lotta people live in swamps."

Joe stared at the slimy, black liquid bubbling near his feet. His eyes swiveled up at Hawk without any movement of his head. "I would never even think of going out into that shit on my own in a million years. It's just nuts. Okay. Go ahead." Though he was late to the party, Joe may have been catching his first glimmer of gold fever.

Hawk stepped into the water. The mud rolled thick under his legs. Silt gathered tightly around his body. He moved with a quick caution, breaking the unwholesome film that covered the surface. The cold water warned Joe's warm flesh that he was somewhere he did not belong. Hawk pulled his boot out of the mud and struggled on. The water gurgled with each step.

"Smells like shit," Hawk whispered roughly.

"Croc shit," Joe answered. As he said it, a reverberating groan shivered through the swamp. A bull crocodile was hungry. Or listening. Or something. The men froze for a moment. The noise echoed as it would in a large empty building. Joe started moving again. He did not want to wait for company. They walked beside each other, instead of with Hawk in the lead. The bottom fell gradually. They held their weapons overhead, swaying from side to side. Hawk noticed the pagoda roof he had seen from the shore. He took a few steps off course and waded toward it. The hook shaped object rose about a foot above the surface. He reached for it. An oozing, soft, parasitic sludge slid off the pagoda and into his hand. He dipped his hand under the water to wash the residue off. He felt the object again, and it was solid. It had to be a roof.

Another two-legged creature slipped into the water behind the two men. It moved silently, its fierce crimson eyes ablaze. But the two did not look behind them, even as the creature closed the distance. Had they but glanced over their shoulders, it would have been easily seen. They had no reason to do so. What could be way out here?

Joe did not stop, as Hawk momentarily touched the rooftop and paused there. The bottom of the marsh felt harder under Joe's feet. He moved faster now, without the clinging, diluted mud. Hawk saw the moon hit the dome of Joe's helmet. He left the roof behind, and began following him. He peered into the swamp ahead, lit by this new light. Dripping moss and upturned, pleading dead limbs writhed forever in the forgotten eternity surrounding them. He saw the island clearly now. It stood out, with a riot of living trees, festooned with vines and shrubs. It looked dry, being much higher than the level of the swamp that they were wading across.

Hawk, too, felt the more secure earth beneath his boondockers. Rock, he thought. Maybe a street—or another rooftop.

The danger was utterly meaningless to him as the fantastic legend creeped closer to his side of murky reality. Could it be any less real than this awful unreal place?

Joe reached the island first. He slipped and splashed as he climbed out of the water. "Slick," he called back. "Goddam thing ain't nothing but a hunk of mud." Joe cursed. Hawk climbed beside him, faintly smiling at Joe's ungainly moves. Joe muttered obscenities.

The monster behind them paused upon seeing this. It would be difficult for the beast to climb this slippery obstacle. It did not have the agility of a James Hawk, or even that of a Joe Canlon. It slowed, waited, and watched its prey.

"Look out for quicksand," Hawk said. "This is some nasty shit here." He saw his arms had turned oily black in the wet slime.

They clambered up the island's steep bank, and

stood on the high ground. A cold, damp wind had blown off the mountain and across the island.

Joe shivered. "Why is it so cold?" he whispered. It had been warm on the other side of the swamp.

Hawk shook his head and spat. His teeth shined in the somber light. "Don't you know nothing? It's haunted, I reckon. The hoodoo is flying around."

"Knock that shit off," Joe growled. "If them natives won't come within twenty miles of here, they must know something. If you want to be an ass about it, you can just do it yourself. Natives won't come here and we come barging in the middle of the night like a couple of damn..." Joe went on interminably. Hawk found the noise amusing in the grim silence, until it continued for too long.

"Shit...take it easy," Hawk urged as he stepped forward into the gruesome shadows. "We're onto it, I tell you."

The heavy trees grew close together in the island's limited space. The undergrowth became sparse in spite of the trees. The earth lay solid under them. Another gust of wind pushed with a spirit-like urgency at their backs. A cool wind on the equator can feel frigid.

Hawk turned his head half around; not far enough around to see his follower. "Must be a blue norther," he said into the rushing wind. "Probably a storm at sea. Probably had something to do with that flood." The wind whipped, and spat contemptuously at him.

Joe glanced over at the whites of Hawk's eyes. They looked inhuman. "Yeah."

The two men walked through the tall colonnade of tree trunks. The ground became sandy. It was an ashy, dark sand. The trees thinned in the useless soil and

Hawk entered a clearing. The black sand glistened under fuzzy beams of moonlight, that reached through leafy awnings hanging at various heights. Stones scintillated on the plush, dark earth.

"Look!" Joe gasped. A groove moved along the sand in front of them, as if it were being tilled by an invisible plow. The fine grains tumbled into the rivulet as the groove crossed the clearing in front of them. Joe crouched tensely and lifted his rifle.

"It's the wind," Hawk muttered calmly. His hands tightened on the Thompson that he still carried. He knew it was not the wind. The wind then blew only tiny wisps of the ash, as if to protest its innocence to him. The groove was deep and animated, like a living thing.

"That's your ass, too," Joe whispered. "No. That ain't no wind. That's like a ghost, Hawk. It's a ghost walking. Look, there it goes again." The depression in the sand crossed their path and disappeared into the trees.

"For crap sakes," Hawk snarled. He raised his eyebrows over the bridge of his nose and spat. It did have earmarks of the supernatural. But Hawk was neither ignorant enough nor educated enough to believe in such nonsense. And, what if it was? Still, he hesitated to step over it. He had no fear of spirits, it was just instinct. There was something peculiar about the groove, and the groove was very real. Reality can be a lot harsher than spirits.

Joe turned his head in all directions. His pursuer drew quickly back under cover. "Let's call this off. Something's here. Something is watching us," Joe said with conviction.

Hawk spat. "What if it is? You gonna let a hole in the sand stop you?"

"I've been thinking about that. If we're only going to put a couple of souvenirs in our pocket, how is that going to keep the draftees from getting the rest of this whole load of gold?"

"Because Arnold will rope the place off. The government will get it all."

"What government? Don't this belong to England or something? God save the King, and all that shit?"

"Why don't you shut up? You're asking more questions than my crystal ball can answer." Hawk looked up. "And it belongs to Holland. Dumb ass," he half whispered.

"I tell you, there's something here. There's something walking out there."

"I hope there is."

"Don't say that."

Hawk walked toward the groove. *I'll be as full of shit as he is if I listen to any more of this. The guy has been shot at for three years and runs away from a hole in the dirt?* Hawk stepped over the line in the sand. Joe followed slowly. They passed into the trees again. The shade overhead blocked the moon. Hawk stopped at an irregular bump in the ground. The earth again felt muddy. He went to one knee.

"This is something," he said in a low voice. The cold wind hit his open mouth. He would not have been surprised to see air make vapor of his words. He ran his hand along the earthen hillock. "There is something under here, I tell you."

"All right, all right, I ain't arguing. There's something under there," Joe replied. He huddled next to Hawk, holding his bayoneted rifle in front of himself. "Would one of them crocs come up here?"

"Nah." Hawk lied convincingly. The reptiles went wherever they wanted to go. "Keep a lookout for snakes. Them cobra things will kill you quicker than shit." Hawk slid his knife out and jammed it into the hillock. The point stopped two inches into the dirt. The blade hissed a gritty sound. "Rock." Hawk smiled.

"Yeah, yeah. There's a rock under there," Joe stammered. "There's rocks back in Buffalo, too." Joe watched the heavier underbrush. "And no cobras."

Hawk scraped at the dirt while Joe searched the ill-defined shadows. The Sergeant cleared a foot square area. The dirt fell off in clumps. A carved figure appeared beneath the sticky earth. A bizarre little demon with strange eyes gave Hawk a menacing stare. Hawk smiled.

"Look at this guy!" he whispered.

Joe looked over Hawk's shoulder at the exposed figure. "What?" Joe asked. "You gonna take that piece of shit to the bank, Hawk? My uncle's got one of them things in his flower bed." Joe glanced at the dark shadows again. He knew that he heard that same dragging sound. Was that sound always in the jungle? Was it the tree limbs blowing against one another? *What the hell was that damned sound?*

Hawk stood and walked around the mound. It had a roughly rectangular shape. Half of it was sinking into the ground, giving it the impression of being a natural formation. It was, in fact, a huge block of stone. Hawk went to the side highest above the ground and began chipping at it again. The knife occasionally struck stone.

Joe's pulse slowed. He became calm and interested. He studied Hawk's determined features. Perhaps there were advantages to hanging around with a maniac. It dawned on Joe that this was the first time Hawk had ever demonstrated any human characteristics. He was showing an interest in something besides an animal drive to eat, drink, or kill. Joe leaned closer, his ghosts forgotten for the moment.

The mound resembled an Egyptian mastaba. More mud fell away and more stone appeared. Hawk had uncovered an apparent entranceway that led under the earth, sealed with a heavy, well-hewn stone. Joe helped Hawk claw at it.

Joe breathed heavily and screamed to himself, *We've got it!* The seal would not budge. They did not have it.

Hawk stood and walked away. He looked around the nearby forest for other structures. In the intricately tangled foliage he found another half column. Around it, and facing him stood an arc of little statues: white, glowing, and half buried. He breathed through his mouth. He heard something else breathing.

"Hawk!" Joe yelled. His voice broke the angry silence of the island. Hawk ran back to him. "Look!" Joe pointed to the side of the mound. A dislocated column lay beside it. The moon shone helpfully upon it. Behind the column, a deep crack in the mastaba mound yawned. Hawk swallowed, knelt on the column, and put his eyes to the clammy opening. It was dark as hell inside.

"We gotta see this. Get a stick," Hawk ordered, pulling the grimy rag from under his helmet. His hair smelled of gasoline and drain oil. They wrapped the rag around an old straight limb and lit it. The flame shot high into the air, bathing the dead old atmosphere in a newly living orange light. A hundred red eyes glared at them from the jungle. Joe gasped and pointed. Hawk squinted and walked toward the eyes with the torch. Joe craned his neck and saw the eyes dart away into the forest. They looked like the faces of elves.

"Just some goddam rats," Hawk said. They were actually little tarsiers, native to the island, with eyes almost as big as their heads.

Joe sighed and Hawk walked back to the mound. He held the fire down to the fissure. "I think I can squeeze through that thing," he choked.

"You could get stuck in that son of a bitch, too. That thing could fall to pieces on you. And there's snakes everywhere. You get snake bit out here, we're screwed. You said we were going into old buildings, not old holes in the ground."

"Ah, shit." Hawk wriggled through the narrow gap, holding the torch in the hand he left outside. Once inside, he pulled the flame into the tomb-like hole. It whooshed in the cramped niche below.

Joe shuddered. It would be their luck to light some sort of underground natural gas.

"Anything?" Joe bent over and looked into the opening. Hawk stood fully upright inside, glowing in a hellish, orange-lit pit. Joe saw only blank gray walls around him. It looked old, empty, wet, and frightening. And not particularly solid.

"Nah. It goes down," Hawk's voice echoed from the sepulcher. He put his face to the opening and looked up at Joe. "It's got steps. I think we're onto something, though."

"Yeah, maybe so," Joe agreed. "You goin' down? Does it look safe?"

"Safe? Shit, no. What do you think? Look at this shit. I'm going to see where it goes." Hawk turned around and held his torch higher. He saw nothing but moldy steps. They looked green in the leaping false light. The narrow dungeon smelled like an abandoned ice box, an enclosure unused to air. Hawk clenched his teeth. *The finer things.* "You coming?"

"I'll...you know...stand guard. Better to have...uh..."

"Aw'ight. Gotcha."

After a minute, Joe could no longer hear Hawk's descending footsteps scraping the stone. The light appeared as nothing more than an ochre-colored smudge in the earth. Joe looked over his shoulder. Where before the moonlight had felt like sufficient illumination, without the torch the surroundings now loomed about as if in utter darkness. Joe felt the full impact of being alone in this place. Without Hawk's enthusiasm, he felt unenthused. He missed Lynwood and the real world, and people who thought normal thoughts. And—there was that sliding noise again. Was it circling him?

"Hawk...?" he called in a shaky voice. "Hawk, hey, I think I'm coming down." Joe decided that maybe it was better to stick together. They might not be able to get along, but they were stuck together out here. He thrust a leg inside. He envisioned the discovery of a pile of golden objects, with strange foreign and ancient names that he had heard of and forgotten. *Scarabs and scimitars.* "I'm coming!" He took the steps one at a time, putting both feet on each one, the way a novice might climb a ladder. He saw the glimmer of flame below. "I'm coming!"

"I heard you, goddamnit. Come on, the son of a bitch has gotta stop somewhere." Hawk's pace was cautious, but quicker than Joe's.

"Why?" Joe whispered. "Why does it have to stop?"

"Everything stops," said Hawk. "You stupid son of a..."

The steps finally ended in a cold, airy room, far below the surface of the island. Hawk raised the torch. It played mindlessly across the walls, which were beautifully carved with ugly dragons and demons. The swaying torch played across shadows of horrid noses and lips, and long nailed claws, making them seem to slither back and forth. Joe stood in open mouthed wonder at the nightmarish spectacle. Every wall of the large square room was covered with lifelike, raised artwork. A few post-sized slabs with carved faces ringed the room. Each presumably represented some deity in an unknown religion.

"That's Chinese," Hawk said in a steady voice. "You know what that means."

"Yeah. But I don't see no jewels or nothing." The floor was bare, thick with an oily congealed dust and spiderwebs.

"No. But it means those stories are true. It took a hell of a lot of Chinese people doing a hell of a lot of *something* to put all this here. They didn't come way out here in the woods to draw pictures."

"Think so? Yeah. But like, where is the, you know, stuff?" A huge spider ambled around the corner and onto the wall of the stairway. Joe stepped away from it. It crawled up the wall like a giant disembodied brown hand with a mind of its own. "Check the legs on that mama," Joe whispered. He crushed the massive creature with his rifle butt. The spider shut its legs like the fingers of a clenched fist and plopped on the ground. "Son of a bitch could bite your leg off." Joe cursed as he stomped the hapless wayfarer.

"It's here," Hawk nodded. "I can smell it."

"I smell croc shit."

"That, too."

They stepped onto the floor, leaving perfect foot-prints in the undisturbed dust, perhaps the first in several centuries. On a side wall, a doorway shimmered in the flame's light. Hawk glanced around the empty room and entered the door.

"Watch for holes. And snakes," Joe cautioned. Hawk raised his torch.

"Snakes?" The new room contained no less than fifty black snakes, lying motionless along the four bare walls. They looked like inanimate decoration, so many discarded fire hoses.

Joe lost his boyish interest in exploration. "I think I'm getting out of here."

"Wait," Hawk insisted. Another door opened from the far wall. "There's a door over there on the other side."

"Damned, if it ain't. Good luck, old buddy."

"Shitball." Hawk stepped between two of the sleeping snakes. The light reflected in their shiny, nugget eyes. He passed through the door and the light went with him. Joe saw two of the arm-thick reptiles moving toward him at a snail's pace as the light faded.

Joe stood in absolute darkness. This was unlike the surface, with its minimal moonlight and starlight. He heard the grit slurping beneath the sliding reptiles. "Crap!" he whispered. "Hey! Bring the light back, you stupid bastard!" Joe's voice echoed in the subterranean chamber. It sounded like the underground halls stretched into eternity. His lips trembled. "Hey!" he shouted again.

The light appeared in the door. "Shit. Can you hold that down? Your voice carries for forty miles in this thing."

Joe ran across the room, through the snakes, to the other door where the light waited.

"Don't worry. They're hibernatin' or something," Hawk told him. "See how dopey they are?"

"Yeah. They're gettin' *undopey*." The light had upset the snakes. They began moving in hideous coils.

"I don't think they're poisonous. Come look, in here." Joe walked gingerly into the next room, becoming more interested when he saw that the next floor was free of snakes. "See this?" Hawk held the torch over a small circular well in the floor of the round chamber. "We can go down some more."

A wooden ladder peeked out of the dark well.

"Hell, that's wood. It's rotten. We can't go down that thing."

"Nah, it's teak or something, that won't rot in a thousand years."

"Shit—it's probably been there two thousand years."

"Well, then listen. Stay there. But don't start screaming like a shitball as soon as I get out of sight. Reckon you can do that much?"

"Why the hell didn't you bring two sticks? You try standing around in the dark." Joe looked up at the torch. "The damn thing's gonna go out. You're gonna get us trapped down here without a light."

"Nah. Good for hours." Hawk put a hand on his shoulder. "See, I brought one stick on account of I came in here by myself. Remember? One guy don't need two sticks. I need a light, because I'm the one looking. You don't need a light, because you're the one standing around sayin' stupid shit. What the hell is the matter with you? You're getting on my nerves."

"We're gonna get trapped in this snake hole without a light."

"I got matches. You got another torch. We gotta stick. Now, shut up." Hawk winked and shook him again. "Sayonara." He put a boot down into the well. The ladder rung crunched in agony. Heedless of the noise, he let his full weight rest on it. It crunched a little less. He put the other foot on the ladder. It held.

"That don't sound so good," said Joe.

"No, it don't sound good. But it's holding up. It'll be okay, I think. The wood is okay, I don't know about this shit that it's tied together with, though." Hawk look skeptically at the dried-out vines binding the rungs.

An eldritch and prolonged cry blew mournfully through the whole of the underground chambers. It permeated the rock walls, gurgling, echoing, and lingering for almost a minute. The two men stood perfectly still until the cry stopped, each studying it in his own way. Joe had ceased breathing. Hawk looked up into his wide eyes, lit by the torch.

"Baby Jesus!" Joe whispered. He turned his rifle to the door. "Get out of that hole! Let's make a run for it."

Hawk remained on the ladder. "It wasn't nothing," he said. "Something settling."

"Wasn't nothing?" Joe tensely aimed his rifle at the door to the room full of snakes. "Don't tell me that was the wind. There ain't no wind forty feet under the ground. It had to be something. Something's in here. Come on, let's go!"

"Awright. What was it?" Hawk demanded. Joe shook

his head. "What was it?" Joe shook his head again. "A ghost?" Hawk snarled.

"I don't know what it was. I didn't do it. You didn't do it. It sounded like a person's voice to me. Somebody knows we're here. Somebody is in here, and they probably ain't alone."

"What if it is? Who's gonna stop us? Are you gonna let somebody get in your way?"

"Damn right I am. That didn't sound human."

Hawk snorted. "Okay. First, it's human, then it ain't human. Probably some crazy ass animal. Maybe a native or something. They been living here forever; they've bound to have found this place. Are you scared of spears?"

"Damn right, I am. They got them blow guns with the poison darts. Them wild bastards, that live way out in the woods." Joe swallowed. "They chop you up and stuff. Shrink your head. We're trapped like rats in here this way. Let's go outside for a while and take a breath. Scout around. It's only good tactics. We can come back."

"Ah, don't make an ass of yourself. That noise came from way off. Sounded like a goddam crocodile to me. I think that was just a girl crocodile."

"Now you know the difference between girl and men crocodiles?"

The chilling wail glided briefly over their helmets again, the echoes distorting it. Hawk could not tell what the hell the sound was. He tried to come up with an answer, if only for Joe. He did not want to say what he really thought—that it sounded almost like a human, Japanese accented voice; a woman, or a child. Which, of course, was impossible.

"Be still and see if you hear anything moving," Hawk

said. "It would have to get a hell of lot closer to do anything to us." Joe aimed his rifle at the door. "Anyway, if it's people, they gotta bring a light. You see any light? When you do, we blow their ass to kingdom come."

Hawk crunched a rung lower on the ladder. The weak ties on the rungs seemed a more pressing threat to him. Joe turned to see the torch diminishing in size as it descended deeper into the well. The well was deep and the ladder shook and bounced gently against the wall with each downward step. Air brushed Joe's face as he looked down. The wind. He craned his neck over the edge. Hawk was way the hell down there now, and still going.

"They could smoke us out, you know?" Joe called down. He smelled the oily smoke from the torch. There was no answer. Just scraping, and the moving of the torch. Always down.

"Hey!" Hawk's voice finally came from the bowels of the shaft. "Hey...come hold the light. I found a tunnel down here."

"Aw, shit!" Joe complained. *So, what? Another tunnel?* He paced nervously around the edge of the hole. He looked at the door. Maybe the noise had been the wind. There was wind coming from the shaft, and wind coming from the door. Wind could fashion some odd noises in the myriad of channels. But the presence of the wind was far from bad, because at least they would not smother in here.

"Hey!" Hawk's voice came up again, not to be denied. "Hurry up!" Muffled obscenities followed.

"Aw, shit!" Joe slung his rifle and swung down onto the ladder. "Okay, okay." The ladder gave and swayed even more for Joe than it had for Hawk. "I knew better than to get out in some damn shittin' place with you, Hawk. You ain't got one brain cell in your whole skull!"

"Yeah, yeah. Hurry up," Hawk said disinterestedly. Maybe he *should* have brought Baker. Baker might have had the same misgivings, but he would have kept them to himself. "Shitbag," he mumbled.

"I hope this old bastard will hold two of us," said Joe.

Hawk looked into the narrow intersecting shaft. The heat and smoke from the torch rose toward Joe. Hawk had a feeling that this might be it. The breakthrough, the find. He looked up the ladder. It was shaking and bouncing like hell.

"What the hell is taking so long? Are you climbing down headfirst or something?" Hawk shouted, his voice echoing in the tunnel. He knew that the noise they had heard came from this newly found tunnel, but he couldn't tell Joe that. Something was in this tunnel with them. "A goddam one legged baboon could have gotten here by now," Hawk called.

Joe gingerly took a step at a time. It was a long way. "Would you kiss my ass? Would you do that, Hawk?" came Joe's unsteady voice. He clutched at the dried, dusty, age-splintered wood. He felt the swimming eternity under him. His hands welded to the rungs. "Climbing up this thing will be a bitch," he mumbled. He remembered the time the fire department had to get him off the downtown water tower. No fire department here. Just his own sixteen-inch biceps.

He reached Hawk more quickly than he expected. He looked up and saw the pale circle of the opening at the top of the shaft. "Shit! Look how deep! Shit!"

"Here," Hawk handed him the torch and climbed into a tunnel opening off into the shaft's wall.

"Aw, that hole ain't nothing. Ain't no sense going in every rat hole you see. The light's going out, I tell you."

"Would you shut up for five minutes?" Hawk grunted as he forced himself into the mouth of the small intersecting shaft. It was a tight fit. He did not like tight places. His limbs moved slower, restrained, without their accustomed agility. His knees thumped the unyielding sides of the tunnel. There was no slack. He gasped for breath. Blood rushed to his head. *The finer things.* The curved walls were pressing in on his very eyeballs.

He dragged himself up the gullet of this unknown beast. It seemed to gradually slope upward, making it more difficult to move. *I ain't stopping*, he insisted. The light flickered behind him. Ahead was nothing. Cold wind swirled around him. He drank the fresh air greedily. It had to be coming from somewhere. His hands touched mud. He could see into another chamber. But how? In the dark? Then he noticed that the base of the far wall of the chamber lay exposed to the outside world. An inch at a time, he had crawled that far up.

The earth had washed from beneath the wall. He saw moon glow on the swamp water beyond the wall. Mud stalactites hung from the base. He saw something else: ponderous bodies on short, fat little legs. The room was a crocodile lair, the washed-out wall their front door.

The blood drained from Hawk's extremities. He tried to back out. He was stuck. His gullet constricted. He relaxed and slid backwards. He was in too far; it would take too long to back all the way out. He was stuck.

He held his breath. He talked to himself. *Relax. You*

ain't stuck. You got in here, didn't you? He slid back again. No, it was too far, and too long, and yes, he was stuck. He stopped. There was only one option left.

He crawled forward into the mud floored room with the lounging crocodiles. His legs bumped on their steel-hard, sharp pointed bodies. He turned around and headed face first up the imprisoning culvert. The torch and Joe's distant and shadowy face led the way. Here, from the source of it all, he recognized the odor that permeated the lost tombs. Joe had been right. Wet crocodile excrement.

He thrust his head into the well where Joe waited. Without pausing, he eagerly latched onto the ladder and pulled himself out of the confining shaft.

"I told you, Joe. That noise was crocs. The damn tunnel is like a bullhorn. Feel that wind?" Hawk gasped and feigned nonchalance. *That* had been a close one. "Nothing down there?" Joe asked.

"Nope. Crocs and a hole in the wall to the outside." Hawk stared blankly into the shaft. Joe noticed that his voice had weakened. The orange light made Hawk's jaw muscles, chin and the space over his mouth look like angular building blocks. But there was a new weakness in the dauntless eyes. Joe was not sorry to see it, he felt it was a good thing: *maybe the bastard has gotten some sense.*

The petroleum smelling smoke flapped across Hawk's face. He did not seem to notice it. "Let's go back to that first room. We must've missed something."

"You got it," said Joe. "Looks like there's nothing in here. Right?"

"There's got to be something, somewhere," Hawk said, without his old brainless conviction. "I mean, what is all this crazy shit doing here?"

He climbed.

"No, it don't have to be here. There's buildings everywhere, all over the world. A lot of 'em are empty. Why does anything have to be here? If it was a treasure, it could be under the swamp. If, it's here at all. Like you said, people have lived here forever. You don't think they had sense enough to look for it?"

They climbed up and walked back to the first room.

"It's got to be here." Hawk shook his head. He held the torch high. Joe saw an unnerving site. It looked like defeat on the face of James Hawk.

"No, it don't, Hawk. We're just starting out here. This thing could go for miles," Joe looked up quickly. "I don't see no end to it."

He heard a hissing sound. Dust fell from the roof. No, it wasn't dust, it was sand. A curtain of dark sand rained into the room from a weakened line across the sagging ceiling. Hawk pointed to the sand.

"That's what caused that rut in the sand up there," Hawk said with depressed amusement, "the sand is caving in on that crack. Our weight made it fall in through the overhead. 'It's ghosts walking', says Joe Canlon. Damn fool."

Joe smiled in embarrassment and watched the fine particles glisten in the torches dying flame. "Yeah, you're right. That's what it was." Joe's smile faded. "Except... who is walking on it now?"

Hawk held the torch higher. His square bicep fell out of his torn shirt. "Uh...nobody," he said. "Probably just falling. The thing is weak, you know. The whole damn place is falling to pieces."

He strained his eyes at the area near the ceiling. Between a couple of cartouche displays, he saw a large hole in the wall. The position of the hole lay higher up, and he could see where a ladder once led up to it. Only shreds of wood, blending with the cobwebs, remained.

"See that? Another tunnel. Give me a boost." He propped the torch against the wall.

Joe locked his fingers. Hawk stepped on them, grabbed the bottom of the opening, and chinned himself up into it. Joe handed him the torch.

"Another tunnel," Hawk reported. "It's a long one, bigger though. Shored up like a mine shaft. This one has mud walls. You could walk in this one."

"You going in?" Joe asked. He was getting used to the place. Perhaps he even feared that Hawk was giving up. Maybe he did not want to give up. And yet, how many of these tunnels were they going to follow?

"Yeah." Hawk sighed. "Are you coming? Give me your arm." Hawk pulled him up. "Here's something interesting." He pointed with the torch to a skull lying in the mud at his feet.

"An old one," Joe said, glancing away from the chalky head. Most of the skeletons Joe had seen were only weeks old, at most. Not counting the ones that some of the guys had boiled for souvenirs. "Real old."

"So, somebody has done been here before us," Hawk said. "Maybe that means something. We'll check this last one out and go back and get some sleep."

"Hawk, you ain't gonna tell Baker about this, are you?" Joe asked as they filed down the narrow mine shaft of a tunnel.

"Why not? Like I ever tell that son of a bitch anything, anyway. Ain't nothing here."

"There might be."

"I ain't too hot on telling anybody I made an ass of

myself. What difference does it make? Four million-aires, five, six, who cares, as long as you're one of them."

This conflicted with Joe's more absolute concept of greed. He sensed that Hawk's animal psyche was returning. The noble beast had sensed failure in its effort to evolve into a human being, and resurfaced. Hawk no longer had any fleeting human desires.

Joe had to contend with the animal carefully.

"Yeah, but Hawk, when we go after the volcano, this place will be crawling with troops, remember? We can still come back and hunt this place for the rest of our lives, if we want. If, nobody knew about it, that is. See, we could get in with some Seabees, you know, cut them in for a little share, drain the swamp, dig the shit out of this place. The Seabees can turn this place into a park in a day's time. We can do it, I tell you. A bunch of guys with lights and plenty of time could find something."

"Yeah. We'll see." Hawk stopped and looked down the endless shaft. They had already walked quite a distance. "You know, this is heading north. I bet we're under that swamp by now, maybe even past it."

"Yeah, we oughta pop out of the ground and scare Baker." Joe laughed.

Hawk thought of Dupuy. "Yeah, and get an ass full of lead." He continued walking. "I wonder if this goes all the way to Delivalung. I bet we're under that valley by now."

A wet, mud smell closed in heavily around them.

Joe thought of the flood. "Hope this son of a bitch don't leak."

"Yeah, we could be under the water, for sure."

They came at last to an end. It was an unnatural end. The shaft was walled by blockage, timbers, mud, and debris. Only glowing sparks remained of the torch now, in the total darkness.

"Well, that's that," Hawk said. There was no echo. The words died in the solid walls of close mud. He turned around. He felt worse than foolish here at the end of the failed adventure. He felt degraded. What the hell was he doing down here? He could easily still die in here. This was against everything he believed in. He was here to fight Japanese. He had as much as betrayed all of the selfless men who had died fighting them on this island.

Anger replaced the shame. He felt his way along the side of the rounded wall.

Joe did not say anything. He was thinking—and not about the Japanese. They stopped when Hawk saw a silver dot in the wall. His hand had accidentally knocked the dirt from something.

"What's that?" Joe stepped quickly next to him. "What in the hell *is* that?"

"Quiet."

It was a hole. Light shined through it from somewhere.

Hawk looked through it. "Look at this shit."

Joe put his head against the mud. There lay a tunnel, walled in plywood, on the other side of their mine shaft's wall. An electric light hung from its uppermost surface.

"It's a curve in a Jap tunnel. A curve in the Jap tunnel nearly ran right into this shaft. They don't even know this bastard is here, probably," Hawk said. He scraped at the mud wall and felt the back of the plywood wall. He rubbed the globs of mud off his hands and looked through the hole again. "I don't see no Japs." As he leaned against it, the plywood rose freely from the bottom. "Look at this! We can get in!" Hawk said, with what Joe thought was too much delight.

"Yeah, ain't that nice? Just what we want, to get in a hole with four thousand Japs. Let's get the hell out of here." Joe suddenly felt even less comfortable than before. Having a half inch of plywood between him and the entire Japanese Army was chilling.

"You know, this is pretty good," Hawk said. "We can spy on them twenty-four hours a day from here. Maybe even sneak some explosives up their ass."

"Shit, yeah, if you want everybody from MacArthur on down to know about this place."

"Shit, man, this is important," Hawk growled. "This could save lives, you know?"

Joe groaned. That was it. The old Hawk was back. There wasn't a trace of the human one anymore.

"Hell, they probably don't use that tunnel," Joe said. "What would they be doing way down here?"

"Treasure hunting? They're burning that light bulb for some goddam reason. They're tight for fuel for their generators. They're doing something down here. Something that they think is important." Hawk nodded. He tilted the panel up again. "Stay put. I'll be right back. I need to get an idea of what this is."

He ducked into the comparatively blazing light before Joe could even so much as think of how insane it was. It was totally unexpected.

* * *

AFTER THE PERSISTENT tracking of his prey, Gohoron climbed into the same mineshaft as his two victims, breathing heavily. There was no one here to help him. As is common for monsters, he was on his own, as he had always been. He had to push the slab-like statues beneath the high opening, and clamber up alone. His misshapen legs were not made for the task. His twisted soul, however, was made for the other tasks ahead of it.

He sensed that he had the two noisy Americans trapped in the dark, narrow tunnel. He could see quite well in the darkness, an advantage that they did not have. The irregular mud walls and floor swam a light green before his eyes. He dragged his heavy feet slowly. His breathing grew louder with both his exertion and anticipation. He never slowed to catch his breath. There was no need for stealth this time. They were effectively trapped. He wheezed a prideful crescendo of angry noise. Side to side, his body swayed with each step, and with each step he thrust his horned head determinedly forward. He held his longer arm with his shorter arm.

* * *

IN THE TOTAL silence and total loneliness in which he stood waiting, Joe thought that he heard that same unidentifiable thing he had heard so many times before. But now, he wasn't in the jungle, where there could be a dozen explanations. Now, he was under yards of silent earth. He could hear breathing, or perhaps something being dragged. Was it in his head? *Was it in here?* Joe looked through the knot hole in the plywood.

"Where is that goddam bastard?" Joe grumbled to himself. The breathing became louder. He could see nothing in the well-kept, well-lit Japanese tunnel on the other side of the wall. The noise had to be coming from farther down the enemy's tunnel. Perhaps it was machinery. But it didn't sound like it. It actually sounded more like it was emanating from the dirty, crumbling mineshaft in which he himself stood.

Joe rubbed his thick neck and squinted down the course of the narrow old mine. He couldn't see anything but the low, irregular overhead, the timber braces and the rocky floor. He would swear that the sound was getting louder. He decided that he better light the other torch. The effort would provide something to occupy his imagination. He took the rag from under his helmet and wrapped it around the burnt rag already on the first torch's shaft.

"That son of a bitch has the matches," Joe breathed in disgust, after finishing the wrapping. Hawk was the source of all his problems.

Shit, you know, that's getting louder, Joe thought, looking up again. *It's in here with me.* He had heard the sound many times, in many places, but never with such clarity. It couldn't be a generator or anything from the other side of the plywood. *It's in here.*

"Where is that damn Hawk?" Joe demanded of the mud walls. He smashed his eye against the hole in the wood again. At least there was light over there. "Come on, you stupid mother..."

The sound became increasingly distinct. It was moving down the mineshaft toward Joe at a slow and steady pace. An inevitable pace, like that of time and death itself.

Ah, huff. Ah, huff. Ah, huff. The sound was like that of a patient with a terminal respiratory ailment. Along with it, was the sound of movement. Scrape. Pause. Scrape. Pause.

"Son of a...!" Joe whispered. *It's coming.* He rubbed his big broken nose roughly. It must be some kind of an animal. Maybe it was some big ass tiger. *Didn't they say they had tigers here? There was something about bears. Those bastards are all big.*

He looked behind him at the debris blocking the shaft in the faint light coming from the knot hole. He couldn't move all that stuff. There was no way out. He was completely cut off by whatever it was, coming in his direction.

There was no place to run, unless he went into the Japanese tunnel where Hawk had gone, or ran directly into whatever was coming toward him. Hawk could very well be a Japanese prisoner by now.

Joe was not going into that damned lit-up thing, that was just stupid. Fighting whatever this was would be better than being a Japanese prisoner. There were horrors and there were *horrors*, and he chose the unknown over the Japanese.

He went to one knee and raised his rifle. Would the shot alert the Japanese? Would it collapse this entire ancient structure on top of him? Would it be enough to stop whatever was coming?

Then down the straight shaft, he saw the red eyes. He remembered them from that dark night in the jungle, when they had all sat around the camp fire, and the natives ran away. The red things were two narrow slits of searing light, swaying back and forth across the entire width of the tunnel. They looked alive and floating of their own power in the absolute darkness. Whatever sort of creature it was, it was as tall as Joe.

It moved slowly, shrieking its breath out with each step. Sweat flowed from Joe's pores. The reason remaining to him abdicated all authority to his ready reflexes. But then, his trigger finger reflexes abdicated all authority to chaos.

"God Almighty!" Joe jumped to his feet and flattened against the blind end of the shaft. He had no idea what the thing was, but he was fairly convinced that it was something supernatural. He no longer aimed his rifle. It hung loosely in one hand and the torch hung in the other.

"Hawk!" he shouted this time, caring little who might hear. He tried to tear at the beams and mud blocking the shaft behind him. He turned again to face the thing. The red eyes loomed closer, as if swinging on the top of a metronome. "God!"

Scrape. Pause. Scrape. The thing advanced unhurriedly.

Joe raised his rifle again. He was far from defenseless. At least, whatever it was, it would have to get past a .30 caliber barrier to get to Joe.

The bottom of the exposed plywood paneling flapped upward suddenly in a flash of light and Hawk ducked into the shaft.

"Goddam, it's hot down here, ain't it?" Hawk complained in a blissfully casual tone. "Did I hear you yell? It's a damn good thing there ain't nobody over in that tunnel. You gotta be the stupidest son of a..."

"Look! Look!" Joe hissed. "The match! Gimme the match! Light the goddam thing!"

Hawk strained his eyes into the darkness. He had been in the brighter electric lighting. He couldn't see well, but he saw the approaching red slits and heard the breathing.

"What in the hell is that?" Hawk asked, reaching for

the matches in his shirt pocket. He struck one with his thumbnail and stepped toward the torch.

"I don't know! *I don't know!*" Joe cried out. The torch lit poorly. It produced half as much illumination as the first one. Joe saw no terror in Hawk's face as the latter took the flaming stick in hand and raised it overhead. What became visible in the flame may have changed that, but Joe was too focused on the monster to notice.

Joe sucked in his breath as the light played across the shadowy specter. The eyes, the animal legs, the human chest and the great horned head forced him to whisper: "The Devil! It's the Devil!"

Hawk scowled. It seemed like a pretty good description to him. What the hell *was* that thing? It was still some distance away. Without thinking, Hawk raised the Thompson, pointing it at the unnatural sight. He knew that he couldn't shoot, with a Japanese Army waiting a half inch behind him. Maybe he would have to. Maybe shooting wouldn't do any good.

His brain required some sort of logical conclusion, and so he decided that it had to be a kind of animal. Animals' eyes often glowed in the forest at night, when struck by a light.

His finger relaxed on the trigger. Animals were afraid of fire. He aggressively thrust the torch in its direction. Gohoron's little teeth shined in the light of the flame. Animal teeth should be larger.

"He's after *you*," Joe gasped. "I ain't done nothing." Joe set the rifle down and clawed at the bottom of the plywood panel to raise it up.

Hawk looked over his shoulder. "Hold up there. Don't mess with that," he said distractedly. Had the guy gone completely nuts?

Gohoron raised his longer arm. Hawk squinted, with a perplexed expression on his face. He didn't like the look of the raised arm. It seemed almost as if a weapon were being trained on him.

For a moment, he didn't know what to do, then he dropped the Thompson and drew his knife from its scabbard. Without any further hesitation, he charged at the demon.

He heard a pneumatic coughing sound, and something whirred past his head and smacked into the mud wall. By then, his raised arm was within striking distance of he knew not what. His teeth clenched and every muscle tensed to meet with something supernatural, or at best, a powerful animal, he brought the knife down toward the human looking chest. The beast's long arm raised and the knife glanced off it. It was knocked from the Hawk's hand, and he was unarmed.

The red eyes looked like two panes of glass. Logic dictated that Hawk flee, but there was no retreat in him. He knew that he should have shot the thing when he had the chance. Now he likely faced a buzz saw of claws and teeth, with nothing but his hands for defense.

He closed with it, running into it with great force. He expected to either bounce off it or be seized by superhuman muscles and ripped by fangs, or gored by horns. Instead, the creature collapsed under him, falling over like a rickety platform.

Hawk folded his upper lip against his teeth and narrowed his eyes until they were almost closed. He clawed his way up the abhorrent body, seeking a throat hidden in the matted hair. He tensed himself for a death-dealing blow from the metal-hard arm that had deflected the knife. But no blow followed. The monster's arms did not move.

Hawk's powerful fingers found the throat in the mass of hair. The neck, however, was thin and child-like. His thumbs snapped onto it, smashing it flat like a paper milk carton. Mercifully, the excessive hair kept the blood from spurting onto him. The creature was unable to even wheeze again. It lay motionless.

Hawk got to his feet in utter amazement. He had steeled himself for a hand-to-hand fight with a powerful creature, and instead met virtually no resistance. He pulled quickly away from the dead thing. He backed away, either in disgust, or some subconscious instinct that it might be feigning death. Perhaps it was something supernatural, and would rise and turn him into a pillar of salt. But nothing happened. It behaved like any other dead being.

Hawk caught his breath. "Hey, bring that goddam torch over here," he gestured at Joe.

Joe approached in a crouch, holding out the torch at arm's length. He, too, expected the supernatural thing to rise up. "I don't think it's dead," said Joe. "It's the Devil."

"You're so fulla shit. Hand the son of a bitch here," Hawk choked. "What in the hell is this?" He held the torch near Gohoron's hairy face. The fire could only provide factual evidence of the repulsive sight.

"There might be more of them," said Joe, looking down into the quietly threatening darkness of the shaft.

Hawk went to one knee. He pulled a pair of goggles off the hairy face.

"It's a...it's a Jap," said Hawk, looking closer. "His skin is kinda pale. You know, this is one of them Ainu fellas. Look at all the hair. They're like Jap Indians or something."

Joe stepped forward. "Bullshit. What is that? Goggles? Why is he wearing that in the dark?"

"Yeah." Hawk held up the goggles. "I think he could see in the dark with it." A case was attached to the eyewear, with a wire covered in a rubber tube. The case was strapped to the body of the dead man. "This is a battery pack for it, some kind of infrared rig. Ain't that the shits?"

He held up the lens and looked through it, seeing a green Joe Canlon swimming before his eyes. "I saw this on a scope one time. It gives you a jump on somebody, if you can see them in the dark."

"It looks like some kind of animal. Look at its arms!" The upper arms were about the length of those of an average man's. The forearms were thin, short and shriveled. The hands were long and claw-like. A rifle with a pistol grip in place of a stock was wired to the little right arm.

"Yeah? Does an animal carry a carbine? That's a DeLisle silent carbine. See that thick barrel with the little hole in the end? That's a silencer. It's an English rifle. I think the Australians use them. .45 calibers. It can put a damn good-sized hole in you. He could barely hold it with them little arms. He's deformed or something. I wonder where he got all this shit."

Joe's eyebrows came together and he bent down. His fear ebbed as his curiosity took over. "Wait. He ain't human. Look at those legs. He's like a goat."

Hawk held the torch over the legs. "Naw, he ain't no goat. He's wearing chaps, like them singing cowboys."

Hawk slid his knife out and looked for a tie on the

hairy chaps. He cut it and pulled the leggings off. He came closer to proving Joe's assertion, however, for under the leg wear, were two legs shaped more like a goat's than those of a man. They were thin, hairless legs, looking human, except for their shape. The knees were inverted. Two large triangular boards were strapped to the shriveled feet.

Joe drew back. "God! What *is* that?"

Hawk rocked his helmet back. He shook his head. He did not know exactly what it was, but he knew that this had to be an explicable anomaly in the human condition. "Deformed, I reckon." Hawk almost felt sorry for the person that had just tried to viciously kill him. "Look here, he's wearing these homemade snowshoe things to help him walk. Something wasn't right with the guy. Crippled up."

"But he's all hairy, and look on his head." Joe reached down for the horns.

"Yeah, he's decked out to scare them natives, see? This is that werewolf thing that they were always bellerin' about." Hawk smiled. "And not just them, some other shitbags, too. *'The Devil,'* says Joe 'shitbag' Canlon."

Joe pulled on one of the horns. It did not come off. It was firmly attached to the oversized head. Joe pulled his hand back quickly and backed away. "Shit. Those horns are *real*. That ain't human."

"Aw, horseshit. They're just glued on or something." Hawk spread the thick hair aside and put his face close to the creature. He saw the base of the horns growing quite naturally from the head. He took his hand away slowly. He didn't comment this time, and stood.

"What's wrong?"

"The sons of bitches *are* real."

"Oh my God! He's got horns like a goat, Hawk!"

Hawk rubbed his nose. "Well...yeah." Hawk took out his plug of tobacco. He chewed for a minute and spat. "So, what?" They stared for another minute at the formerly terrible Gohoron. "That's a good rifle." Hawk snapped. "See if he's got any clips in the pants. I wonder where he got all this stuff. You know, this could be the something unusual, like they been talking about. This is some odd gear. Them snooper scopes are the latest thing. The Japs are behind this. Which ain't good. This guy knew we were in here. Which means the Japs probably know. It's getting late. This is enough of this shit. We've got to go. If, we can."

Joe did not move. Hawk had to find the DeLisle clips himself. He searched the chaps and found two. "How'd you know what kind of rifle that is? I never seen one like that."

"I don't know. I seen one, one time. And, there's a DeLisle, Mississippi, so I remembered the name," Hawk answered from one knee.

"I don't know, I don't like this, Hawk."

"Why? You scared we done killed the devil? Don't worry, nobody will know the difference. He's got lots of buddies to take up the slack." Hawk stood. "Hell's full of 'em. I just hope this tunnel ain't."

"I ain't never seen nothing like it," said Joe, still staring.

"Yeah? I guess they ain't got carnivals in New York, like they got in Mississippi. Probably spent all your time in them peep shows."

Hawk slung the carbine across his Thompson and started walking. He looked over his shoulder at the mesmerized Joe. "Come on, stupid. What the hell? It's dead, ain't it?"

Joe remained there. Hawk walked back. They both stared at the corpse. With something approaching a sad expression, for him at any rate, Hawk spat down onto the horned head.

14

WAR NIGHTS

THE TRIP BACK TO FIND BAKER AND LYNWOOD WAS SHORT
and solemn. There was no conversation. Joe slumped to
the ground as if dead, and fell asleep. Hawk offered to
take the next watch. He claimed that he was not tired.
He probably believed it. He had seldom been as physically, mentally, and emotionally exhausted all at the
same time. He almost immediately fell asleep with his
eyes open, his hands wrapped around the submachine
gun.

Only his will remained. It refused to let his deadly
blue eyes close. The rest of his body could not be
denied. He was sound asleep. Due to the peculiar
circumstance, he experienced yet one more trying
phenomenon: He entered the world of mixed nightmare
and reality. His sleeping mind spun into bizarre dreams,
while his eyes registered on the real jungle around
them. The wind blew at the hair under his helmet. In
the misty dampness, he heard rustling. He clicked off
his safety. Something creeped ever so cautiously toward
him. He leveled the Thompson. He wanted to warn the

others, but his mouth would not open. Defiantly, and alone, he awaited the stealthy approach until it became no longer stealthy. He didn't need help. He didn't need anyone or anything. He never had.

Three hulking shapes surged out of the phantasmagoria of vegetation. They were quiet and determined. Ten yards before him, the moon struck them and he could see them clearly: a headless admiral, a Marine with his head turned sideways in *rigor mortis*, and a misshapen human with horns. At once, they all reached for him. His basic character could not be changed by sleep or hallucination. He fired into them stubbornly. But they did not stop. Bullets meant nothing to them.

Hawk shook his head. The ghastly blood-demons disappeared into the pareidolia of the jungle. He had not fired at all. The safety had never been taken off. But his finger was tightly jammed against the immobile trigger. The jungle was still there, only the ghosts had left. It felt strangely real. If the backdrop was real, could not the ghosts have been real?

He rubbed his clenched fist back and forth across his lips. His steady fingers reached for his tobacco. Sweat covered his face, but he was cold. His soul was shaken, but his vicious, hard nervous system was calm as ever. He could not comprehend the stark realism he had experienced. But there were many things he did not comprehend, and it made little difference to him. His primitive mind operated like a child's, simply accepting what it did not understand, and moving on. Reason slowly warmed his body. He wished it was daylight. When daylight came, the hell behind his forehead became no better. Only the backdrop had changed. Now it was a cold, wet, and gray jungle, instead of a black one. The uneasiness reached deep into him this morning. It seemed to control his very movement. It had finally reached the point where it could take away his free will. He sat quietly struggling with this strangeness as the others awakened and made preparations to leave. He could not define the uneasiness as guilt, or fear, or anything in particular. He had gone beyond all of that. Whatever it was, it had him, it had a life of its own. It was an angry, squirming thing, twisting his brain.

Losing control, he thought. It would be a horrible thing to lose control of your own mind. He had to move. He had to walk. If he sat still any longer, he might scream. Something in hell was moving his limbs like a puppeteer. He stood, as calmly as ever.

"Awright," he said casually, "get off your asses and get moving. Long day ahead of us." He betrayed none of his feelings, showing only his usual surliness.

After the arduous trek began, he felt better. He was tired, totally drained, with only a spark of meanness pushing him, but he felt better. He had beaten the hell back into some unused guest chamber in his head. It fought to escape the unlocked door, but he held it in there. He knew that it would get out again, some night. Perhaps every night. He would defeat it, as he did everything else.

He thought of Jessica Pearson. He had failed to find what he went after. He had failed to find what he wanted for her. Instead, he had found more horror. How would she like these nights that he had to face? To face them with him, for how long? Forever? How would she like to share in these pleasant evenings that the U. S. Marine Corps, the U. S. government, and the Empire of Japan had bestowed upon him?

Just tired, he assured himself. His will drove his spent body onward. It forgot why it was driving. It was too strong to stop. Reason, health, insanity, were gone, only the great physical strength remained. *Maybe it was that damn water.*

Joe walked beside him. "We were looking at a fortune back there, Hawk. It's still there. We had to be close. I say we don't tell nobody nothing."

"Oh, I don't know. A man was meant to work for a living," Hawk rumbled drunkenly. "Money'll turn you into a weakling. You gotta work with your hands for what you get, or you ain't worth shit. You wanta be one of them guys that races cars and flies planes because you don't know what the hell else to do with your stupid ass? We was born men, and that's the way it is."

"Uh...yeah, I *can* be one of them guys, and do just fine without the cars and planes. Hell, no, I *don't* want to work for a living, with my hands or anything else. You wasn't saying none of this crazy shit last night. What about that woman in Sacred Blood? Is she gonna be working with *her* hands? What if you had a family to think about?"

"I don't."

"You will. You gotta think with that thick skull of yours. We're talking about plain old security. I ain't talking about living on the Riviera." Joe laughed nervously, and grabbed Hawk's arm. "Maybe you're right, you know, a man ought to do this...and that. All that shit. But you get older and all, and things change. You ain't just a man anymore. You got a family. You don't know nothing about that kind of shit, Hawk. That's scary shit. You need money. You need security. You got people counting on you. They ain't gonna like living in a tent and eatin' acorns. And then it's too late, you're all old and stupid. Old guys can't run around turning flips like monkeys like we do now. Remember that old guy on the boat? Still trying to work like a young guy? That's the kind of crap we're headed for."

"Nobody never gave me nothing. I got by."

Joe could see that sentiment and hearth fires were not going to work. You couldn't appeal to Mom and apple pie to a guy who had never had either.

"Listen, everybody ain't like you and me. Some people got to have four walls around them and a blanket. Some people can't live like we have. They think they need a buncha shit just to get by, like cars and shit. And, that costs money." Joe stood in front of him. The others were looking on curiously now, causing Joe to speak in a lower voice. They wondered what the hell was going on with the two of them. "You just don't understand. Those guys back home ain't been doing without nothing. The more they got, the more they think they need. They spend half an hour picking out the right color shirt to buy. They eat something different every day. The Depression is over. For them, there ain't no war. It's a new world over there. They've got three years on us, while we been donating our time to Uncle Sam. They got three years of time and a half overtime, while we got twenty goddam bucks a week, and a kick in the ass."

"We tried, didn't we? What the hell? We didn't find nothing. Forget it."

Hawk stepped around him. Joe nodded and fell behind the others. "The guy's nuts," he said to himself. "Nuts. He's just gonna throw it all away."

And, of course, he did. They reached Sacred Blood Mission the next day and Hawk made a full report to

Arnold, holding back nothing of any great significance. He was a *little* circumspect. He reported Gohoron as an ordinary Japanese soldier in disguise. He felt to do otherwise might jeopardize the veracity of the whole exercise, and he wanted Arnold to understand that there was a strong enemy presence at the volcano.

"And Lance Corporal Dupuy fell and bumped his head and drowned, sir," Hawk said.

"Terrible. Too bad."

"Yeah. We took it pretty hard. Something else, funny, sir. My canteen had something in it. Somebody put something in Canlon's water, too."

Arnold smiled shyly. "Oh, I can explain that. We've had a break on the issue of the illnesses here. Lieutenant Klemer had been putting dead organisms in the water. We picked him up. He's locked in one of the huts. I still can't explain why he did it, other than the fact that he lived in Japan for a while. Incredible, isn't it? Such a nice fellow. I think he must have emotional problems. The germs shouldn't cause much harm. In fact, you probably will be immune to all sorts of diseases now. I'm surprised you didn't get sick, Hawk. You've been with Klemer for a long time. You probably got the heaviest dose of that stuff, more than anyone. You must have an iron stomach. Have you felt any nausea or cramping? Dysentery?"

Hawk stared intensely at Arnold. "Naw."

"No hallucinations, trouble sleeping, fatigue, dehydration?"

"Nah."

"I didn't think so. You have an iron head, too." Arnold laughed. "You look fit as a fiddle."

Hawk did not laugh. "Clean living," he said evenly.

Arnold felt a little uncomfortable. "So…" he said, glancing away from Hawk's wild eyes, "this is very important information. I agree with you, the Japs are pretty strong out there. But they're sitting on a strategic location."

Hawk studied Arnold skeptically. Delivalung was about as strategic, and as easy as get to, as the North Pole.

"They are becoming too strong. Keep this under your hat. I've received word that the Japs may even conduct an aerial bombardment of Sacred Blood. You know what that would be like?"

Yes, as a matter of fact, Hawk knew exactly what that would be like. *Let me loose. If I were your sister, you would let me loose!* He knew what a lot of things were like.

"We have to get their yellow asses out of there. I'll have almost two battalions tomorrow. We're going in with what we have. We've got to neutralize their strength at the very least. Perhaps these tunnels you found can turn the tide. That and a few rafts on the flooded south side will surprise the hell out of them. I'm going to order continuous bombardment, twenty-four hours a day, from now until our assault. It looks like the Army might even make it. I think we will be all right. Don't you?"

Hawk rocked his helmet back. "It depends on who and how many you're referring to when you say 'we', sir."

* * *

CURRY ROAMED THE FOREST, ranging south, out of his assigned territory. He wasn't going to let that bastard

Hawk find the treasure. It had to be around Delivalung, or the Japanese would not be devoting so much time and effort there. Everyone's attention had shifted to the volcano, and Curry was nothing if not adaptable. Four Muruts, reliable and dedicated men, accompanied him. As darkness came to the forest, Curry made preparations for the night. He felt somewhat depressed. He was becoming afraid that he would never find it. This was a big place, not the location he had expected when he first heard that he would be going to an island. This island was more like a continent. Hope springs eternal, however, for he received a radio transmission from Arnold.

"I've had a little falling out with Sergeant Hawk," Arnold told him. "It's all up to you now, Sergeant Curry. I believe Hawk may have found the location. There is an island in the swamp five kilometers to the south of your present position. I won't ask what you are doing there. On this island, you will find an underground structure of some sort. Find the crystals there, Curry, and you will save a lot of lives. If you don't, I have to attack Delivalung with an inadequate force. Hawk is angry about that, but there isn't much he can do about it. The Japs cannot get those crystals, Curry...is that clear?"

"Yes, sir."

His depression gone, Curry smiled for almost an hour before he set out for the swamp. Crystals. That's what we're calling them nowadays. Dumb old Hawk had done him yet another favor. Two favors actually: First, he found the place, and then he was too stupid to look for the treasure. Who else would, or could, do that? All of that saved Curry from having to haggle for his fifty percent. Now, Hawk would be the one haggling.

Curry laughed as he crossed the swamp in the moonlight. With the bearings given him by Arnold, he was at the location in no time. He had no trouble with any fear of the eerie location. His highly developed sense of greed dwarfed that of even poor Joe Canlon. He found the entrance to the temple and fairly raced down the mineshaft with his four men in tow.

His accompanying scouts, however, did not share his greed. When they saw the dead remains of Gohoron strewn about, they immediately beat a cautious retreat back down the shaft. This only served to further amuse Curry. Now he would not have to go to the trouble of killing them. Killing four armed men would have been troublesome.

Ignoring the reports of the proximity of a Japanese tunnel, Curry set a small charge in the blockage at the end of the shaft, where beams and debris barred further passage. He had more of the natural instincts of the burglar, sneak thief, and pickpocket than Hawk. The barrier had the look of having been put there to cover up something. A thief knew that something had to be beyond it. Consumed with passion, he thought it only logical that the blast would not expose the enemy tunnel. And, purely by accident, it didn't. It opened a small enough space for a snake-like man to crawl through. Curry slithered into the smoky darkness. Amidst all this great good luck, he was still astounded by what he found. He was so astounded, that he did not notice water leaking from the top of the newly damaged shaft, until it was ankle-deep. Passionate, but far from suicidal, he slithered quickly back through the hole. He was a man of property now, he had to be careful.

Curry looked up and saw the cascade of water

gushing through a crack in the earth. The blast had opened the weakened floor of the flooded valley. He still had a little time, he thought. He cursed and crawled back into the hole. He brought out all that he could carry. He looked up in tears at the water coming down. It splashed halfway to his knees now.

"Got to get out of here," he whispered. Reluctantly, he turned down the shaft, passed the now floating Gohoron, and began wading back toward the mastaba at the surface. As he walked, he realized that all was not lost after all. In fact, the leak might just be another stroke of luck in his endless series of lucky breaks. No one would ever find the treasure now. It would be securely buried. He could even tell Arnold where it was and the son of a bitch could not get to it. Of course, he would not go that far. He would simply deny having found anything.

The water rushed past his knees. He had to swim to the stairs in the mastaba's main room. But he managed to get out. He spent most of the next morning making an excellent map. He was pretty good at that.

* * *

HAWK WAS NOT PLEASED. Arnold had not been impressed with the report of the large Japanese presence at the volcano. He was still considering an attack. Hawk stopped at the hut where Klemer was being held prisoner. He wanted some answers. A young guard stood dutifully before the padlocked door. He had orders to let no one see Klemer, for fear that the Lieutenant had another contact at the garrison, aiding in the sabotage. Klemer had not been forthcoming. He almost certainly had another colleague still here.

Hawk walked up to the guard. "Give me the key," he said.

"Sorry, Sergeant. I don't have the key. Do you have orders from Lieutenant Biedeker? Or Captain Terhune?"

"Yeah." Hawk snatched the guard's M1 from his hand and brought its butt plate down on the padlock. Like everything else, the cheap lock had to surrender to the fury of James Hawk. Hasp and all fell to the ground. Hawk shoved the rifle back into the guard's hands. He kicked the door open. The guard touched his shoulder lightly.

"Sorry, Sergeant. You have to have orders," the boy said.

Before he knew it, the guard saw a thick forearm jutting from his body. A fist had driven his diaphragm into his backbone. Winded, he dropped gasping to the ground.

"I told you I did, didn't I? Goddamit." Hawk stepped inside. Klemer, dressed in an undershirt and dungarees pressed against the hut's back wall.

"Sergeant Hawk! What are you...? Don't hurt me! Don't hurt me!"

Hawk closed the distance between them in two steps. "I ain't gonna hurt you, I'm gonna kill you, Klemer. You ain't gonna feel a goddam thing."

"No!" Klemer wailed. His attacker was unarmed, but Klemer knew that his fleshy little body was defenseless against Hawk's hard, peasant muscle. Hawk pushed him roughly and he bounced off the wall. *"No!"*

"Unless you start talkin', I'm gonna loosen up your

jaws for you. And every other bone in your body. You believe that, Klemer?"

"Yes. Yes!" He did.

"Why did you put shit in my water, you little son of a bitch!"

"I can explain. Please, don't hurt me."

Hawk drew in his breath and stepped away. Klemer had never been a bad fellow. Hawk felt a little like a bully. "Awright," he said, in a more controlled tone. "Awright." Hawk held up his hands. "That's all I want."

"Promise you won't tell anyone else?"

"Don't give me no shit, Klemer!" Hawk's rage quickly returned with the placing of conditions on the confession. "Don't try to stall till somebody comes to save you. I only need to hit you once, and I can hit awful fast."

"Very well. Very well. I didn't mean to be impertinent. I'm sure you will understand when I explain, but the others will not and I—"

Hawk slapped him forcefully. He bounced off the wall and sat on the floor with a bleeding nose. Hawk grabbed the entire front of the undershirt in his hand and pulled him to his feet.

"You don't listen so good, do you! I don't wanta hear nothing about your goddam feelings."

"No...No...I'm sorry. I did it for Humuri. I didn't hurt anyone. I just didn't want anyone to hurt him." Klemer held his nose.

"Who in the hell is that? Some kind of Jap?"

"Yes. Yes. May I sit? Please, please you sit, too."

"Be my guest." Hawk sat, staring expectantly.

"I worked with the physically handicapped in a hospital in Yokohama. There I met a poor Ainu man. The Ainu are the original inhabitants of the Japanese islands. They are treated poorly by the Japanese. Have you heard about them?"

"Yeah. I know who they are. Guys liked to cut their heads off on account of their beards."

"Yes," Klemer admitted sadly. "A poor and proud people. This man was horribly disfigured by a birth defect, *genu recurvatum*. He worked in carnivals mostly. He was known as the human goat. My heart went out to him immediately. His legs were misshapen and he had a rudimentary tail and horns. Although it was forbidden by law, he married a young girl, a Japanese girl, who must've pitied him. The man asked nothing for himself. He was proud of his livelihood. Unfortunately..." Klemer looked at Hawk with tears in his eyes. "He had a son. And the son..." Klemer shook his head, "was even more horribly disfigured. He was losing the ability to walk. His horns were more pronounced. The man asked only that I teach the boy to walk. That he not be an invalid. I agreed, and to my surprise the man died soon after. He had a limited lifespan and I suppose he knew his time was short."

Hawk relaxed. He recognized the Gohoron in Klemer's description.

"I worked steadily with the boy. I made special shoes for him. I loved him like a son. I suppose I loved his mother, too. I decided it was best that I leave Japan. I did not know it, but his mother followed me. She is in a relocation camp near the West Coast now. She never found me, but she contacted my mother recently. Through her, I found that Humuri had come to the Dutch East Indies. He felt it was his duty to be a soldier, to fight for his country. He was bitter about the treatment his mother received in America. I could not conceive of how this would be possible, or where he could be. Then, from nowhere, I hear of a way to be sent here. We were briefed on the trouble with local tribal recruitment. I knew immediately that the stories about Gohoron were true, and that Humuri was Gohoron. He was only a poor, tortured, misguided boy. I did not want him hurt."

"You wanted a lot of other men hurt, though."

"I did what I was morally bound to do. I am a good American. I have fought for my country against the people I love. I am not sorry for what I did. I know you won't understand, Sergeant Hawk. You are a man with one nation...a nation that is everything to you. You do not have a feeling for the human race, as I do. I am a vagabond, a citizen of nowhere and everywhere. But people are important to me."

Hawk stood. He felt a little sorry for the slobbering Klemer, though he did not show it. He felt a little sorry for Humuri, too, even though he had killed him in self-defense. He wasn't *real* sorry, when he remembered the .45 slug from the DeLisle carbine trimming his hair. Once again, he felt like the only devil in the jungle. Everyone was pure of soul and divine in motive—except for him.

"You're right, Klemer," Hawk said in a low voice. "The American people are all I care about." Hawk turned and stood in the door with his back to Klemer. "That kid was out there bumping guys off every night with a snooper scope silencer."

Klemer sat crying, perhaps for himself, perhaps for Humuri. Or, maybe for the men he had killed.

"I'll make you a deal, Klemer. You're an officer. You knew what was going on here. You tell me what Arnold was after, and I won't tell anybody about this Gohoron."

Klemer looked up in surprise. "You would do that? Why, all I know, is that Arnold was after some green jewels, or crystals they called them. That's all that I've ever heard."

Hawk nodded. "That's kind of what I figured. Thanks. I'll keep my end of the bargain." Hawk stepped out the door.

Klemer heard the Sergeant shout at the man posted outside the cell as he left. "Get on your goddam feet! You're supposed to be on guard duty, Private! Anybody could walk right in there!" Klemer felt fortunate to be alive.

The next day, they heard the American airstrike begin on Delivalung. An ominous thunder rumbled from the mysterious eastern jungles. Marine and Naval planes based in the Celebes Sea dared the low, clinging fog and steam to pound the mountain. It made the men who did not have to climb the volcano wonder how anything could survive such destruction. The men who *did* have to climb it, however, were not as awed by the American airpower. They had been to mountains, and islands, that had been bombed before, with little result.

The tough Marines waited anxiously for what was ahead of them. The exact time of the assault was kept from them. Company sized reinforcements arrived at Sacred Blood in frequent increments now. The Pageas River had been forced open again. Naval PT Boats cruised it. Major Bearn arrived. All of these developments inspired confidence in Mr. Arnold and Dr. Lepreaux. Bearn had never been defeated in battle, and was not bashful about taking casualties. The rifle companies knew Bearn wasn't there for idle garrison duty. They were going in.

Hawk trusted Bearn, as did the other Marines. But for once, Hawk was doing a very unsoldierly thing: he was thinking. He did not see this operation as advisable. It's only purpose, he thought, was to get some nondescript jewels, or to prevent the enemy from getting them. Bearn, Biedeker, and Terhune were one thing; they were the Marine Corps. He knew that kind of business. Arnold, however, was something else.

Hawk had other problems. Terhune was asking questions about the attack on Klemer's guard. Hawk felt sure that if an assault were not imminent, he would end up in the brig. That didn't bother him a great deal, as that was just another minor legal entanglement that the morally bankrupt have to put up with in a world full of people who are better at hiding their moral bankruptcy. It wasn't going to be a major problem, because the assault *was* imminent. It was not going to be that easy to get out of this one, or the assault and battery rate would suddenly soar.

When word came out that the attack was to begin at dawn, two days hence, Hawk had a bigger problem: Jessica Pearson. No one else there had a problem like that. She announced that she was not leaving. She shared Arnold's conviction that a great victory was coming, and that the area was secure. Hawk knew that Arnold based his conviction upon what he was going to get out of all of this, and the assurance that he would not be the one getting his ass shot off on Delivalung. Jessica Pearson had to be basing her conviction upon trust in Arnold. That didn't seem like a good bet to the Sergeant.

Hawk began looking for her as soon as the time of the attack came down. He waited for her to come out of the commissary. He did not go inside. He stood outside thinking. He was thinking clearly now. Attacks had that effect upon him. As the waiting time grew longer, he resolved to go inside. He took a deep breath.

"Hey, Hawk, hear about the attack?" Joe Canlon stopped him in midstep.

"Yeah. Hey, listen, I forgot to tell you, don't tell nobody nothing about that fella we found with the horns and all. Got it?"

"Why not? I thought you done told them all of that." Joe was argumentative by nature.

"Why not? If some guy told you some crazy thing like that, what would you think of that guy?"

Joe laughed stupidly. "I'd think he was nuts."

"That's right." Hawk pushed Joe's chest. "See, you ain't so damn stupid after all, are you?"

"What do you think of the big assault. Big show, huh?"

Hawk did not look enthused. "We might not come out of this one."

Joe's face fell. He had never heard Hawk say such a thing. "Why?" Joe asked in a serious tone.

"I don't know. Uphill. Outnumbered. A crazy ass place with a bunch of smoke. Caves. But the worst thing is, why would you even try such a thing? Don't make sense."

"So, it's that bad?"

"I don't know. I ain't no general. But it ain't good. Because they don't know, either, and they ain't too interested."

As Joe pondered the possibilities, Jessica Pearson

walked out of the commissary. "Disappear," Hawk snapped in a low voice. Joe glanced at the girl, nodded, and walked away. This meeting looked like it might be something worth avoiding.

A lot of things about a person belong to a certain time and a place. But two people together, as a unit, can belong to a completely different time and place. James Hawk and Jessica Pearson no longer belonged to America, or to Australia. They belonged only in this magical time and place.

The island had waited until today to look its most beautiful. A cool breeze rolled over the top of the jungle, from the ocean far away. The wind swooped down from there, low over the ground, to stop and touch everyone. For a young man and woman in love, the setting could not have been more romantic. Except for the war; and even that supplied a kind of adventurous newness to the rhythm and the energy of the air swirling around them. Excited and fearful voices in the distance called—the lovers cared not what. It was as if God was on their side, and holding them harmless in this random roulette of danger. Being there together, and yet apart, was tantalizing, but to be together forever was their destiny. Because they had been together for such a short time, God, or the better part of the universe, owed them additional time.

Hawk wanted to lift her, to swing her around, to carry her off until he couldn't go any farther. She looked perfect today, irresistible, and he felt so good about her. She was afraid for him, and longing to hold him, and to be held by him. They could barely restrain themselves as they felt their youth, their differences, their sameness, and their attraction draw them together. Brightly colored birds, with long tails, flew by them, calling softly, encouraging them. Insisting, on a just love. He wanted to fall on his knees, to put his arms around her waist, to tell her he would never leave her. He would say that he might never be rich, but that he would give her everything he ever had for the rest of his life. That no harm would ever come to her. That he would study war no more, and only study her. To say, that she may not ever have many material things, but she would own his soul, and he loved her with all of it.

But--he didn't do any of that.

Hawk walked her toward the loading dock. The Navy had turned it from a rickety pier into a solid dock. Heavy artillery was coming in. Rumor had it that even tanks would magically appear in the next two days.

"I know," she said, "that you will be careful? I mean, I realize that you have to go, but in some of these situations a person can take precautions, you know what I mean?" She stared uncomfortably into his cold eyes. Hawk had not shaved in a while. He looked hard and mean, even to her. "If you stay...inconspicuous and let someone else tend to the questionable details. There are ways to lessen the odds of a mishap. There will be a lot of other men there. Do you understand what I am saying?"

He understood all right. She did not. Whatever it was that she was talking about, it was not James Hawk.

"You're worried about it, aren't you? I can tell. Oh, I don't blame you." She stopped and put her arms around him. "You've done your share already. I think you could get out of it. You have the points. We can go to your commanding officer and tell him that we are going to be married. My God, you would be the only man here who is getting married. That alone would be worth some-thing. We could even ask him to perform the ceremony. He can, can't he? And then, when we fill out the immi-gration papers, we will be married and a step ahead of all those who just have a fiancé. I think it just might work. They couldn't send..."

"I ain't worried," he interrupted her. The thought of asking Terhune for anything disgusted him. It was time to be truthful. "No, I ain't got a lot of friends here. All I want is for you to get on one of them boats and get out of here. Leave today. This is a mess here. They don't really know what they're doing. This is the kind of thing where a lot of bad stuff happens. There might be Jap planes soon. It's dangerous. You go today."

"Well, I couldn't possibly. With you here...like this? What if you're hurt? What if something... What if you needed me?"

She wasn't listening. He had to get her out of here. "I won't, see? I don't ever need nobody. That's just the way it is. I don't need you." She pulled back from him. His tone was odd, different. In this instant, she was looking at the same James Hawk that the rest of the world saw. "Yeah, I got this wife in Texas. I was meaning to tell you about that, but it never came up. Hell, I got to go back to her and all, you know? I mean, like if I didn't get killed?"

"A wife?" Pain choked her vocal cords. "You said you had no family."

"Well, family—I meant like blood relatives. But, the wife, you know is different, and we got seven little ones. She's kinda on the heavy side, but cooks a lot. I always liked that kind of food. She's from a whole different culture. I...uh...don't know any other way...now, and all."

"Seven children?"

"Yeah."

"But how long have you been married?"

"Oh, hell. A long time, now. Probably five years before I came overseas."

"Seven children in five years?"

Hawk calculated quickly. He hadn't planned on a quiz in mathematics. And women knew all that shit about having kids.

"Well, you know, with twins. James and Jose." He thought quickly. "Jose is the younger one. And one died."

"I see."

"Yeah, the damn malaria in Texas is bad."

"Why are you making up such a ridiculous story? I'll go, if you want me on the boat that badly. You don't have to try to hurt me. It's much easier to do than all that."

Hawk exhaled slowly. "I don't know." He shook his head. "I guess you and me are just going in two different directions. You're a really decent, normal kid. I'm just not the one for you. I've been around the block a few too many times, I guess. I'm like a guy that—I can't even tell you... I don't know even know what I am. The war is making new kinds of guys."

"You can tell me anything. It wouldn't change anything. It would seem that I should be the one to decide what you are," she said. A tear was on her cheek. He didn't look at her. "Don't you think?"

Hawk cleared his throat. He wasn't one to back away from anything. Not even this. "No. The thing is," he said, "you ain't no good for me, either." He said it quickly. "I belong here. I'm part of this, see? This stuff. This is me, this is what I do."

"Oh!" she gasped. Her body flinched. "I see." She nodded her head and looked at him. He really was a mean looking bastard, when you got right down to it. "Well, all right then. I won't ask why I'm so bad for you." She tilted her head back and gave him a look that a decent person is able to give the world. He couldn't look at her. "In that case, I should leave today. They have been waiting on me, in fact." She turned. He took her arm and turned her back around.

He kissed her with all of the love that they would never share. Regret and pain surged through her and she held back the tears. She would never realize how fortunate she was to be able to walk away. She had the stamina and the character to argue no more with him. For some reason, though God had turned his back on everyone else there, he still watched out for her.

Hawk stood there for a minute, until she was a safe distance away, then he followed the same route, back to the compound. She went into Arnold's hut and was there for a minute. He saw her next go to her billet. He went and stood by the hospital door. Men bustled around him. He watched all the activity without interest. She soon came out, dressed, carrying a handbag and a single suitcase. He didn't see the Victrola. He turned his back to the sight of her walking toward the dock. He could still see the glow of her yellow hair and pale white skin on his retinas. It was only a ghost. Because she was gone. Injured men were moaning in the hospital. It was up and running again. Hawk rested his chin on his chest.

He hadn't said the right things, he supposed. There was a better way to have handled it. He ran the knuckle of his thumb up and down his stomach.

"Well, you never do anything right, so what'd you expect?" he mumbled. *God, that was stupid. The whole thing.*

Dr. Lepreaux stepped into the doorway. "Are you all right, Sergeant Hawk?"

"Oh. Oh, yeah." He glanced quickly over his shoulder. "Yeah, I think I got indigestion or something." He ran his knuckle deeper into his hard, flat stomach. "Got anything for that?"

"Sure. All you need is a little bicarbonate of soda. Come on in."

"Yeah. That oughta do it." Hawk let go of the door jamb and stepped heavily after the doctor.

"It's that chewing tobacco." Lepreaux shook his head. "The stomach is a delicate organ. You should leave that alone."

"Sure enough," the Sergeant answered.

* * *

NIGHT CAME. Hawk regretted what he had done. Like all of the rest of the horrible and wrong things he did, there was no undoing it. He sat with Joe Canlon and Baker around a low fire. His brain no longer churned with complications. Everything was simple again. He was just numb. Joe spooned some C-rations into his mouth. He smacked and chewed until Baker finally looked over at the commotion.

"Good, Canlon?" Baker asked.

"Kiss my ass. Hey, Hawk, didn't I see that girl leave today?" Joe asked.

"How do I know what the hell you saw?"

Baker looked up quickly at Hawk. Something about

the tone reminded him of the last conversation Hawk had with Dupuy.

"Did you ever...you know?" Joe smacked louder.

Baker stood suddenly. "Well, see you guys around." He took his ration can with him.

"You're all class, Joe," Hawk said in a dead voice.

"Yeah, I had an uncle once, said I'd make a good butler."

"If you put your mind to it."

"What's wrong, did she dump you? Coulda toldja that." Joe smacked. "What'd you do? Finally grabbed her ass? We go through this every time. You oughta be catching on."

"Maybe your uncle was wrong. Maybe you shoulda been a chaplain," Hawk said.

"Don't worry, you'll find another one. You always do, don'tcha? Women like you. We just gotta polish you up a little. You're just too...I don't know, crumby, to put up with. Most guys got the opposite problem. They're nice guys, but the women don't like how they look. Women go for bastards like you, at first. See, you can change. I mean, you're a no good asshole, but you could change just enough. Like no grabbing "em and no slapping "em around, to start with. All that—cussin' and spittin'. Maybe not act so...Mississippi. You know? Women like a little class."

"You're so full of shit. Your uncle must've run a charm school, too, huh?"

"Nah, he was a runner on this garbage truck. Another thing is, you take all this shit too serious. You're exactly the kind of dumb jerk that ends up gettin' married. You gotta wise up. When it's over, it's over. You gotta understand women. They ain't no better than we are. You know how all that shit got started? With your mother. Guys think women are like their mothers."

"I ain't got no mother. You can shut up whenever you want, since neither one of us knows what the hell you're talking about."

"You gotta go into it knowing the ropes, not like a sucker." Joe threw his tin down. "And another thing. You stick with that Sir Cornpone act, you'll end up married. They ain't giving you any breaks because you're a dumb ass. Messin' with women is a tough racket. I'm gonna give you some lessons when we get back from this deal."

"Lessons on being a moron? I told you, we ain't coming back."

"Well." Joe laughed nervously. The light hearted banter had turned sour. "Maybe not. But that's bad luck. Don't say shit like that. What's wrong with you? You better snap out of it. Them Japs don't need any help."

"Shit on them sons of bitches. I might not come back, but ain't *none* of them sons of bitches coming back. I don't know. I guess I don't see any point to anything. Including taking that shitass mountain."

"Why, that's crazy talk." Joe nodded his head as he silently thought. He had an insight, and finally figured it out. Hawk was going to fake a psycho case so he could go away with the woman. "You know, I could back you on that angle, if you claimed a section eight? You been acting like a crackpot, and they'll need witnesses. Maybe we can both get out of this. I might have to go somewhere to testify. I'm good at shit like that. I got kind of a legal vocabulary."

"That you do. Thanks, Joe, you're a real buddy."

"Huh?"

"I said, thanks, you're a real buddy."

"Huh?"

"Goddam! Are you deaf *and* stupid?" Hawk stood. He figured Joe Canlon could get on a man's nerves just about as well as anything. Hawk walked away.

"Just remember. I'll back ya," Joe called.

* * *

CLIFFORD CURRY regretfully reported that he could not locate what Mr. Arnold sought. His report triggered the final decision: Arnold had to take the mountain and get rid of the enemy, before the Japanese found the crystals. The Marines would move out.

Hawk, no longer a privileged character, crossed the plain with his platoon, on the way to Delivalung. It was time for the forces of good to meet the forces of evil in a final showdown. It would have been difficult for those who knew James Hawk best, people like Baker, Joe Canlon, Klemer, or Jessica Pearson, to say in which camp Hawk belonged.

The terrain seemed relatively harmless to the advancing columns. It held none of the mystery it had held only days before when the first small patrols had crossed it. Hawk thought of the lost Chinese city. It would soon be a tourist attraction, added to the travel routes of the wealthy; first stop out of Angkor Wat, get your tickets now. Joe Canlon, not giving up as easily, still insisted that he was going to get some properly equipped Seabees to dredge the swamp. If he survived.

"Give my share to the orphans in Poland," Hawk told him.

"I'll give your share to me," Joe answered, with perhaps more honesty than a Clifford Curry.

The battalion bivouacked halfway to Delivalung. The Americans proved unable to master the local water buffaloes quickly enough, and mules were brought in to haul the equipment. The first night, back out there in the boondocks, was among Hawk's worst.

He felt the guilt more on this night. He felt guilty about the men he had lost. Perhaps he felt some guilt about those he had killed. But the origin of it all was the guilt he felt about Jessica Pearson. That was the new guilt. He saw himself in an entirely new light. Even he knew that he really was no good. He felt bad about wanting a treasure for her in the first place, and then felt bad about losing her.

Oddly enough, his worst night was followed by his best morning in many days. Maybe the effects of Klemer's diet supplements were finally wearing off. When the columns moved out again, Hawk felt strong. Unlike the others, he looked forward to the battle, to the challenge, to the opportunities. He even stopped to help Joe Canlon get a mule off its butt, which was a little like moving a mountain.

The mule aimed its big nostrils at Joe and sneered. Joe screamed every obscenity his adolescent mind could imagine. At Baker's suggestion, Joe gathered some firewood and stacked it around the animal. Fire was a known antidote to mulishness.

Hawk walked up to them and took the bridle. "Come on, Sugar," he said. The mule's big ass rose from the ground. Gun parts jostled on its back. "You just gotta have more sense than the mule," Hawk advised.

"You gotta be a jackass yourself," Joe responded. "Always handy to have a mule jockey around. Lookit the ass on that thing."

"You get a little smarter, maybe you can be a mule," Hawk said. The mule showed its teeth and snorted at Joe.

"Big stupid walkin' pile of shit," Joe told the animal.

The following dusk found the troops with Hawk and Joe digging in on Delivalung's northern foothills. The tunnel and raft operations, courtesy of Hawk's reconnaissance, were already under way on the southern side. The very place where Baker had stepped through a tunnel roof was used as an infiltration point. In the half-light, it was difficult to tell the effects of the aerial bombardment. There didn't appear to be much to destroy on the moonscape of the mountain side. All of the bad stuff lay hidden inside.

At about 2100, American artillery opened up on the slope. They played the enemy's game with a night war. Biedeker climbed down into Hawk's foxhole. The enemy did not remain unresponsive to the nocturnal attack. Hard, leaping muzzle flashes returned from the caves above. The flashes only served to provide the American artillery with more definite targets. Within half an hour, the Japanese saw the error of their ways and stopped firing, rolling their hardware back into the safety of the interior of the mountain to await the coming assault.

Engineers rapidly assembled angle iron and pipe bridges, with plumbing fixtures and welding. The rough bridges were constructed for the purpose of crossing the lava moat surrounding the base of the mountain. Porous channels of water ran under and beside the lava, as well as directly into it, cooling it enough to convince the engineers that the barrier could be crossed. In a dozen spots, the oozing fire was no wider than twenty feet, and in most of those, much less. Still, it could not be walked upon or run across. Touching a boot to it caused flames to leap up one's leg, like a spark to kindling. But it could be bridged. The moat would be impossible to cross elsewhere along its fiery breadth, other than the chosen spots, because of the heat and noxious gasses. Flame retardant wood was attached to the bottoms of the bridges. The lava was not the only barrier to consider, as twenty feet could be a long way to run, with enemy guns trained in advance on the clearly visible spans; and so, the bridges had to be even longer, to allow for access and exiting.

"They'll cut us down on those bridges," Biedeker complained to Hawk. "This is worse than the photographs showed." The Lieutenant's ears stuck out until they nearly touched the edges of his helmet. "We would be better off trying to jump that stuff. At least they wouldn't know where we would be crossing ahead of time. This is like putting a spotlight on us." An occasional Japanese shell passed overhead, and the officer ducked appropriately, as if that was all that was necessary to avoid being vaporized. "They can see from their elevation to where the lava flow is narrowest. They'll have their guns trained on the places before we can even roll the bridges there."

Hawk listened to all of this and glanced up at the split in Delivalung's western slope. He didn't really need anyone to tell him the disadvantages of climbing Delivalung. One look could tell you all about that. The American bombardment was colorful and vigorous. A red fire fall spilled from the western tear in the rock, and down into the protective moat. The sulfurous odor was overwhelming, and the heat was palpable. *What a hell of a mess*, Hawk thought. He had no change in expression as he listened to Biedeker's "pep" talk. The Lieutenant's tone did not improve.

"I think the bombing has made that hole the lava is coming out of bigger. I hope they've allowed for that. We don't need any more lava pouring down on us. It will widen the flow at the crossings. A dozen machine guns trained on the bridges can stop us cold, if they're set up right," said the Lieutenant.

"They will be," Hawk said. He leaned back in the hole and sighed. He figured they would get across. He didn't know how, or how many. He had made landings and he had climbed mountains. They had all looked impossible. Someone always made it.

As the Japanese shelling decreased in volume, Biedeker wished them all well, and leapt from the hole.

"Hey, where's the Army, Hawk?" Joe asked, more than a little edgy. "You said the Army would be here."

"I didn't say nothing about nothing," Hawk answered. The Sergeant continued to get the impression that this looked even worse than he had expected. He saw no silver linings.

"This really pisses me off. I mean, it's always the same guys in on every one of these dirty deals. I bet you could get a list of five thousand names of the guys that have fought every damn battle. Millions of guys on this side of the world, and it's always the same guys," said Joe. "Mainly, me."

"Yeah, but we got leadership," said Hawk, tightening his lips. "The Japs ain't got that. We can think for ourselves. They go all to hell without their leaders."

"You got rocks in your head. If we can think for ourselves, what do we need leaders for? All we got is leaders telling us to go up there through all that shit and wrassle with them dirty lunatics."

"Well, shit, you wanted to be rich, and race cars and fly planes. You wanted to parachute and climb mountains and do all that fancy guy shit. Here you go. This beats the shit out of any of that. A thrill a minute. Here's your challenge. The rich asses couldn't buy a ticket to this show anywhere."

"Challenge, my ass! A ball of fire dropping out of the sky onto you! Some goddam challenge."

Just then enormous explosions jittered across the face of Delivalung, almost completely covering it in flashes and smoke.

"Damn!" said Hawk. "Things could be worse. You could be sitting under that right now. Better to be on our side. Even if the bastards killed every one of us, that ain't gonna stop that artillery from hittin' 'em."

"Bull shit, those bastards are about fifty feet underground right now, laughing their asses off. Waiting for us to come up there to them."

The artillery throbbed against the mountain all night. Some of the hits exploded in orange and yellow flowers with red streamers arcing outward. Others struck with a more solid intensity, looking like the hard blast of a huge flash bulb. Alongside this display, the lava glowed a steady, supernatural red, brought up from the eternal, infernal underworld. The shadow of the flickering furnace lit tomorrow's battlefield, and gave tomorrow's participants plenty to think about. Nothing about the harsh scene looked friendly to a human organism.

At dawn, the order was given to attack. The command was no surprise, but walking into Delivalung would nevertheless be a startling experience for everyone involved. Men pushed the scaled down Bailey bridges on cylindrical pipes, with logs serving as supplemental rollers, where there were insufficient pipes. A dozen of the structures went into motion at once. Seabees had jury rigged another half dozen draw bridges to be dropped across the moat, should an opportunity for another crossing arise in the ever-changing channel of molten rock.

The first of these proved impractical upon trial, the span melting and bowing it in the middle as soon as it touched the fiery lava, and the wreckage being carried away by the flow, only to strike one of the more stable Bailey bridges suspended above the fire. The warped steel remains lay beside the good bridge, threatening to dislodge it. It seemed likely that the wreckage would eventually carry away the other bridge, and when that happened, the resulting debris could only threaten every other bridge in its path along the course of the red and black braids of lava flow. Then again, no one knew exactly what would happen. The wreckage could just melt.

Hawk and Joe focused on this disaster with great interest.

"We're supposed to cross that shit?" Joe asked, as the ruined metal drawbridge clanged, hissed and crumpled, with smoking spirals blowing back over their heads. "Who thinks of this stuff?"

"This is some real stupid shit," Hawk admitted. "You couldn't give them sons of bitches a better target."

Major Bearn took note of the structural failures. He ordered more bridges be constructed. Meanwhile, he had to attack. The order to jump off was given. He didn't like it, but he would do it.

Hawk wondered about Arnold and the treasure, as he saw the first few men scream and fall before even reaching the bridges. Now, however, treasure and trickery were no longer his problem. He had a whole new set of difficulties. Machine gun fire had already been trained on the access to the bridges. Eluding the endless swinging blades of gunfire was going to require a great deal of focus.

* * *

"The attack is under way," Major Bearn told Mr. Arnold. He lowered his field glasses. He didn't sound very happy about it.

"Any indications of progress? You expect trouble?" Dr. Lepreaux asked.

"Yes, sir, I do. I think it is ill advised," the Major answered.

"How can you say that, Major Bearn?" Arnold asked with displeasure. "Curry was unable to find the crystals, but Hawk located a tunnel right on top of them. We have to neutralize this position. We don't have to win. We just have to keep the Japanese away from that fuel."

"That's not my kind of war, Colonel," Bearn said. "I don't know who is going to neutralize whom here. Curry told you that he flooded the tunnel. It seems to me that should have been sufficient."

"Well, it isn't," Arnold snapped. "As long as there is a viable Jap force on Delivalung there is a problem. They have a chance of retrieving it. A mere company of them could find it and get it out of the country."

"I think the whole thing is overblown. Hypothetical nonsense. Preposterous," said Bearn. "Casualties will be heavy."

"You don't realize all of the implications, Major." Dr. Lepreaux took up for Arnold.

"They will be carrying the implications down that mountain this morning, General. My name will be the one on the death warrants. And in the records," said the testy Bearn.

* * *

THE JAPANESE OFFICERS met with Colonel Iwataki, the man in charge, and currently in possession of Delivalung. Lieutenant Osasi and Captain Sahumi were in attendance. Osasi was worried about Corporal Humuri. He had not returned from his patrol to locate the crystals. Osasi feared the worst. He had been sure that Corporal Humuri was on the proper trail. The lost Chinese temple under the swamp had to be the location of the legendary treasure. Osasi knew that the Americans were also close to finding it. Otherwise, they would not have attacked the mountain. Knowing all of this did Osasi, or anyone, little good. Everyone looked up as Colonel Iwataki spoke. Osasi had tears in his eyes.

"Honorable soldiers of the Emperor, I come to you in grave circumstances. As you have seen, the American Marines are now in the process of attacking our position. Many of you will be unfamiliar with this type of adversary. They will be unlike any you have faced. They are without any honor or mercy. Soon you will see this for yourselves. I will not dwell on it. You who are veterans of the war with the British and the Chinese must steel yourselves. We have no time for shock.

"As most of you already know, our highest hopes for the position on this mountain have not been realized. It will not become the second Tokyo, as was planned when I took this assignment. This does not mean we have no purpose here. Many of you do not know of the strategic importance this mountain still represents. That is why I have chosen to speak to you at this critical hour. It is why we have waited until the last possible moment for this meeting. Our defense must be unyielding. I only regret that each man here can only give his life but once. You must assure me today, this hour, that each of you will give his life, to the last man, if necessary. Our intelligence demonstrates that the Americans have a force equal to our own in strength. But we are the defenders. We should in all military probability succeed here. Our defensive positions double, or even triple the value of our strength. An American force has never overwhelmed a Japanese force that was its equal in strength."

Colonel Iwataki looked fiercely around the cave. Solemn, unquestioning eyes met his. The Colonel was already assured of a fanatical defense, but he went on.

"Many will die today," he began with a consoling tone. "I know that. I am a man who believes that men should know why they die. Security forbids disclosing every reason for our being here to our honorable soldiers. To die for their Emperor is sufficient glory for them. But you, I will tell, and the example of your dedication will inspire every one of the soldiers out there.

"There are two highly classified scientific programs being conducted in Japan at this very minute," said

Iwataki. "Project A and Project B. These are key to our successful conclusion of the war with America. Project A involves a uranium bomb of such power that a single bomb can destroy an entire city. We and our allies in Germany have made considerable progress on developing this bomb, whereas the Americans have not. It would take years for them to develop it. Project B is of equal importance. It involves another secret weapon, the death ray. It will stop the American aircraft from ravaging the homeland. We have made considerable progress on this weapon as well, and in fact have perfected a test model with limited capabilities.

"You, honorable colleagues, are privileged to be informed of these matters. And I tell you today that our presence here is vital to both of these projects. There is a chemical element common to both of these projects, an element that will greatly speed their development. Finding it will render all previous research to an antiquated status. We can have these projects completed within two years. No matter how powerful the American war machine becomes, it cannot crush Japan in two years. So it is that plans to relocate our government here have ceased. Our work is not ended, however." Iwataki swallowed.

"The element we seek here is actinium, a heavy metal. It is excellent for what our scientists call nuclear fission. I confess to having no advanced knowledge of these procedures. Actinium is contained in pitchblende. Pitchblende often occurs in green crystals known as uraninite. A rare and high grade of these crystals, resembling emeralds, occurred in nature. The only location ever known of these high-grade crystals was in northern China. The stones, mistaken by the ancient

Chinese for precious stones, have appeared on the Emperor of China's personal collection of objects d'art. These are the only known examples of the crystals in the world. We have experimented with some of them and the results are astounding. Unfortunately, our supply was limited to only that: experimentation.

"We have found records, however, that even larger amounts of the stones were used on Chinese artifacts exported to this very region. They are, we believe, buried by the thousands near Delivalung. Reinforced with this knowledge, I am sure that you realize the importance of our position. We are fighting for sacred ground. For the future of Japan."

Colonel Iwataki stepped back for dramatic effect. "I do not ask that you survive the coming battle, my dear friends, but that you let none of the mad dogs climbing our mountain survive. We are very close to success here. The American interference has surprised us. Treachery is suspected in their ability to follow our every move. I assure you that a stronger force will come in our wake, maybe before this battle has ended. But we alone, today, must hold."

Iwataki bowed and walked from the cave.

15

THE BATTLE FOR DELIVALUNG

"I THINK MAJOR BEARN MUST BELIEVE WE ARE AFTER THE Chinese treasure," Dr. Lepreaux laughed. "Is that old legend in the Encyclopedia Britannica or something? Everyone seems to know of it."

"Hell," said Arnold. "It doesn't matter what he thinks. We aren't the ones that need the crystals, from what I've been told. It's the Japs that need them, to catch up with our research. All we have to do is keep them from getting them." Arnold snorted indignantly. "You can't worry about what every stupid ass thinks. Does he think that the United States government would go on a treasure hunt in the middle of a world war?"

* * *

THE JAPANESE GUNNERS had been waiting tensely all night. Their guns had been well placed at their leisure over the course of the last several weeks. Their pent-up emotions drained down into their trigger fingers. As the bridges rolled across the fiery moat, chains of raging bullets danced the lengths of the spans. The fire stacked up bodies on the approaches to the bridges before the Marines could set foot on them.

The American plan had been neatly laid out. Perhaps a little too neatly, and too predictably. The bridges were numbered one through twelve. The sector in front of each bridge carried the same number as its fronting bridge: sectors B-1 through B-12. The men assigned to these sectors were to cross and push to the summit. All of the neatness vanished as soon as the assault began. Companies and platoons fell apart, and intermingled with other units, and with other sections of their own components. The very core unit, the squad, had difficulty staying together. Officers were lost in the shuffle. Most wore no insignia, to avoid being selected as targets. The attackers had been assembled from all over the Pacific, and many did not know the individuals in their own units well, much less their officers. As the mass of sweating humanity collided at the narrow points of access to the bridges, the only viable order that still existed was to get to the other side alive.

Sergeant Hawk's mood was murderous, and he found himself in a situation appropriate to the mood. He had convinced himself, through his lack of faith in humanity, that he was fighting for the financial benefit of Arnold and Lepreaux, and by some not too difficult mental gymnastics, also for the greed of Clifford Curry. He had lost all trust in authority, now that Major Bearn was going along with this madness. Had the Major sold out, too? Would it be a surprise? Didn't Hawk himself almost sell out? Before he finally let go of the treasure, and Jessica Pearson, and everything else? Nevertheless, the Sergeant and Joe Canlon were there, racing blindly for Bridge 6, in the center of the lead-blown front line. He had half hoped that the enemy would knock out the bridges with their artillery and prevent the whole operation. By the time he reached the bridge, they had not done so. In fact, the Japanese had no intention of doing so. They preferred having the attackers arranged in tidy little chutes like livestock.

American artillery opened up on the now identifiable enemy machine gun locations. Weapons platoons halted in the advance and trained mortars on the Japanese, while still on the safer and more stable side of the moat. Platoon automatic weapons scattered, and could do little damage. An early and fortuitous artillery shell landed on a pair of Japanese machine guns, leaving one American bridge poorly covered from above. Men were able to rush across that bridge and dig into the ashy rock beyond. They fired blindly up at the defenders, knowing only that they were up there somewhere.

Hawk and Joe Canlon had been assigned a bad bridge. Unlike most of the other men dumped into this chaotic scene, they did not abandon their assigned number and look for the easiest point of access. Through either a lack of imagination or flexibility they persisted in reaching their assigned goal. Their bridge turned out to be the one with the molten wreckage of the drawbridge pressing against it. It groaned and vibrated and threatened to slide away, whether it be in a position parallel to the lava flow or across it. Adding to the general confusion was the steam that set up a foggy mist enshrouding large portions of the span. Smoke from the gunfire blended into the swirling hell, and high velocity lead rained down and through the unwelcome cloud. Men fell in front of Hawk and Joe, and men fell behind them. Few screamed, as it seemed that they were too horrified to even do that much, as they died. A wounded man rolled off the bridge, flamed up like lit gasoline, and hissed onto the lava. Too light to be sucked under by the melting rock, he was incinerated there on the surface. The helmet burned and floated for a while, before being swallowed as if by a living thing.

Hawk ducked futilely at unidentified sounds. He jumped and dodged the dead as he sprinted gamely for the far side of the bridge. Reaching the other side of this contrived hell was his sole purpose in life, his sole purpose on this false and deceitful earth. His determination was shattered when he saw the white vapors of a line of machine gun fire speeding down the bridge straight for him. He stopped to avoid colliding with the bullets. The enemy gunner then began to wag the machine gun back and forth. The bullets struck on alternating sides of the walkway. Each struck with a different sound as it lashed upon different types of material. The lead shrieked off the angle iron with a shrillness that stopped the heart, and it hit the pipe with hollow metallic sounds. It whistled as it skimmed between the two and whirred in a loud whisper when it hit nothing. The odd and constant sizzle had to have been the hundreds of bullets striking the lava below. Hawk crouched, listening to this symphony and hanging onto the sides of the rails as the slugs passed him. He waited for the shock of one hitting him, for it all to be over. Any instant, it could happen.

I got to move faster than this, he realized. This was no place to be hypnotized by the strangeness of it all. He was obviously being targeted. Joe never stopped. As the fire concentrated on Hawk, Joe took advantage, running along the right portion of the bridge, looking hungrily at the dark soil on the other side. There wasn't much cover there, but it had to be better than here. He dove for it and buried his face in the volcanic ash, holding his helmet down with both hands. He heard men crashing to the ground beside him, some for the last time. He heard the litany of anvil sounds behind him as the shells struck the bridge. There were too many sounds for any one of them to register. Though the machine guns were far away, their voices were of particular importance, and their crazed and steady belching of fire rose above all the other noise. He considered what would happen if the Japanese artillery caught them there; if it rolled out of those caves. But, no matter what, he had crossed the lava field, and was off the deadly bridge.

Behind Joe, continuing to be pinned and stalled, Hawk was able to see the entire bridge in his peripheral vision. He realized that he was no more targeted than anyone else on the span. It was paved with bodies. Helmets lay everywhere, including the flaming ones, floating on top of the lava. Blood did not pool because of the spaces between the metal planking, but red stripes crisscrossed the gray metal, and streamed into the molten rock below. Men had fallen half way across, three fourths of the way across, or almost all of the way across the bridge. Hawk found himself blocked by the corpses from having a clear path off the horrible thing. The guns concentrated on movement, and moving people. Still, boots pounded on the metal and some would make it. The bridge groaned as the wreckage of the failed drawbridge pushed at it. Hawk noticed a tremor this time. The bridge slid about a foot under the irresistible weight. Trapped like a rat, he suddenly understood the major flaw that the designers of this maze had missed. The bridges were too long for the narrow tendrils of lava that they crossed. In an overly cautious effort to ensure safety from the lava, the planners had only increased the danger from enemy fire. Yet these were the cards that Hawk had been dealt. There would be no trial and error here, with an improvement in tactics for the next time. This was no game, it was a once in a lifetime occurrence; if not a once in human history occurrence.

A Marine crossing the bridge, who had stopped next to Hawk, leapt madly off the bridge, for no discernible reason other than the excessive fire the bridge was taking. He landed on the wreckage abutting Bridge 6. The former drawbridge was a tangle of iron and pipe jutting from the angry red river. Hawk noted that somehow he had not been incinerated. Something insulated the drawbridge from the incredible heat. The metal of his own Bridge 6 grew hot beneath Hawk as it descended toward the lava, threatening contact. If Bridge 6 were pushed any farther downstream, it would reach a wide spot in the lava, touch it, and melt. He could not get to the other side and yet he could not stay here. His choice was similar to that of a person in a burning high rise: catch fire or jump. He leapt for the wreckage behind the other man already there. A single shot hit his companion, slapping into his back as if a fist had hit him. He fell limply, hanging upside down with one foot wedged between two cross beams. His dog tags hung down from his neck. Hawk reached out and wrenched them free, sticking them in his pocket. Before the moving glacier of watery and bubbling scarlet could carry Hawk off, the triangles of wrecked metal miraculously swirled into a jutting rock, giving him a slim chance at jumping to the other side of the moat. He carried a ten pound Thompson, ammunition, a four-pound helmet, and grenades; a dragging foot would be burned off. He jumped, and missed the leap by inches, but a momentarily floating corpse saved his leg, as his boot pushed off it. He crawled higher up the bank, toward Joe and the others who had success-fully made the crossing.

"Hey, where you been? I thought they got you," Joe shouted over the bullets striking the rock and ash. His face was tense and streaked with tarry dirt.

"Got hung up," Hawk answered breathlessly.

"Yeah, we ain't going nowhere here. Pinned down. You might as well rest a while," said Joe.

"Everybody is pinned somewhere," said Hawk. "We got to break out. They'll target this place pretty soon."

"Just hang on. Something will give." Joe looked from beneath his helmet at the top of the volcano. "The men are still coming across." Behind them, Bridge 6 had been swept into a wider place in the lava flow, causing the span to come into direct contact with it, and the metal was aflame. A mortar round hit it for good measure, folding it like a jack knife and tossing body parts skyward. Two clichés joined into an alarming reality for the men who had crossed the moat: there was nowhere to go but up, and they had burned their bridge behind them.

"What a set up!" Hawk gasped in the stifling chem-ical air.

Joe cringed under a vicious spewing of ricochets. "The Marine Corps gives you one way out," he said.

"Not me," said a voice on the other side of Joe. "I'm staying right here until I get hungry, or the Japs run out of bullets," Baker shouted. He sounded different... Normal.

"You jokers will do something when they start bowlin' grenades down on us," said Hawk, rolling over on his back. "This ain't no place for nappin'." He examined his submachine gun. The clip had been dented in one of his desperate leaps. He ejected it and began fishing the shells out of it. A dent could stop the flow of firepower. Since firepower was the only negotiating chip he would have with the Japanese henceforth, it was worth a few seconds to tend to it. As each brassy little blunt round rolled into his hand, he could only hope that it would do its duty and kill someone. There was no concern for the hopes and dreams of the men they would kill. No sweet little heads were up there waiting for him; there were only packs of no-good bastards that needed killing, and killing quick. For better or worse, James Hawk was back in his own chosen world.

He put the new clip in and snapped it against the trigger guard. Bullets: a peculiar way to decide who was right and who was wrong. A step beyond fists, clubs, knives and spears. Fast moving lead, I'm right and you're dead. Simplicity for the simple minded, right there in the palm of his hand. Brute stupidity, and he didn't even have to be a brute to use them. But he was.

A runner crawled behind them. He had scrambled all the way from Captain Terhune's position in front of Bridge 3. It had been a long nasty trip and he was covered in ash. "The attack is at 0745. The Captain says attack." That was it. Then he crawled on.

"What the hell?" Hawk muttered. "Seven forty-five?" he shouted after the man.

"Yes! Is your watch synchronized?"

"Yeah, yeah." Hawk waved him on. The runner crawled away. Bullets hit in flashes of dust and rock behind him. He never changed his pace. He knew his business.

Hawk looked at his wrist. There was nothing there but a little red gash in the flesh. The watch had been torn off or shot off—somewhere. "What the hell time is it?"

"Watch stopped," said Baker. He had probably never set it, much less wound it.

"Hey!" Hawk screamed at the runner. Hawk's bellow was made for battlefields. "Attack what?" The runner turned around when he heard the wild, animal sound.

"The Japs!" The man turned and crawled a few more feet before having to stop and duck a line of fire. The dozen rounds hit the earth in a little over a second, and yet the brain could still discern a space of time between them. The runner had been targeted throughout his trip. It wouldn't stop him. He kept going, and after a courteous pause, the line of persistent bullets dutifully followed after him.

Joe shook his head and hugged the spot of earth God had graciously granted him. He turned his head sideways and squinted at Hawk. "I figure it's 0730 already. Why don't we wait here? If we jump up and run now, we're dead."

Hawk peered over an ashy rock with a thoughtful

expression. "Maybe. The son of a bitch didn't give us anything to attack. Do you have a watch? What's it say?"

"It says keep your ass right here," said Joe. He closed his eyes and let his head drop.

"If this ain't some shit. I guess we'll see what happens. See if somebody goes somewhere, or something." Hawk growled. They were stuck in a mass of incomprehensible chaos.

"You know, I haven't seen any artillery coming down," said Baker.

"No, I damn sure saw one of their mortars hit a bridge, though," answered Hawk.

"Maybe our guys in the tunnels knocked some of their heavy stuff out," said Baker. Hawk looked up. Mortars, from his side of the bridges, were pummeling the middle of the slope. Some of the mortar crews had made it across intact. The higher reaches of Delivalung looked uninhabitable under the heavy American artillery concentration.

"You know, I think the goddam machine guns are slowing down," said Hawk. He was beginning to think an attack was feasible.

"It looks like we're knocking the shit out of them," came a voice from Hawk's other side. He looked over to see Lynwood. He had that feeling of satisfaction that comes from having your comrades with you, even as the bottom of the world collapses.

"Hey wake up, Joe." Hawk nudged Joe, lying there with his eyes closed. That kind of gave the Sergeant an uncomfortable cold chill. He didn't like it.

"Knock it off, Hawk. How's it look?"

"Better than it did. Better, I'm telling you. It's better."

"We'll know when everybody starts climbing," said

Lynwood. And a few minutes later, that's what happened.

The men in front of Bridges 1, 2, and 3 raced quickly upward. Higher up, lumps that had looked like rocks, turned into men and charged up. Sector B-4 had stalled, and B-5 had no contingent at all. The men assigned there had wisely gone elsewhere. Hawk and about twenty men were all that was left of the B-6 assault group. Bridge 6 had been hit heavily by machine gun fire, and Bridge 7 had been hit by a mortar round, leaving less than a platoon to get across there. Sectors B-8 through B-12 were the strongest positions, located on the western flank. Men were still crossing those bridges with comparative ease. Occasional mortar rounds hit the lava near them, creating spectacular red shooting fountains, with yellow underbellies along each spray. Waves of molten red sloshed up and fell down, dripping across the lip-like base of Delivalung. The 6.5 mm and 7.7mm machine gun ricochets whined over every vacant square foot of ground. It was difficult to tell now whether they were trained on anything, as they were just everywhere.

"Looks like a hole in the middle of our line," Hawk said. He saw men fall as the machine guns tagged them in the wavering American line. "Right the hell where we're supposed to be. Let's get ready. If them sons of bitches come out of those caves, they'll tear right through our lines." Joe looked at Baker who looked at Lynwood. They were a little taken aback by Hawk's apparent interest in the overall look of the battlefield.

"Let's go," Hawk barked. No one moved. They continued to look at him. He jumped to his feet. Still, they lagged. They expected him to collapse with a dozen bullets riddling him. When he didn't, they had to follow him. That wasn't just Marine Corps policy, that was *their* policy.

Joe got a good look at Delivalung as he slunk up the steep grade. A mushroom shaped Tetsubo helmet darted into view here and there, and then disappeared; all of it, too close for comfort. Maybe, the enemy was pulling back. The Marines were getting too close to them, and it looked like the advance was going to degenerate into hand-to-hand combat. And that was never good. Stacks of logs that were probably pill boxes spat puffs of smoke from mid-slope. Above that barrier lay the caves. As a safety measure, American artillery had ceased firing before the Marines approached the enemy lines. Joe tried to run faster, seeing only gray ground and white smoke. The men remaining in sector B-7 began to charge up, after seeing the B-6 contingent gaining some ground.

The right and left flanks surged up the mountain. The sparse and timider middle of the line sagged. Being sparse in numbers finally proved to have some advantage. As if on cue, a line of enormous field pieces peeped down from the caves like enraged dragons. Their pre-set trajectories aimed low. Until now, they had been withheld in the interior of Delivalung. The smooth and sudden movement indicated they were not only on wheels, but likely on rails. More concerned with closer objects, Hawk had not noticed their sudden appearance as they leapt from the dark cave mouths. He had no warning.

The Japanese artillery barrage closed the base of Delivalung under a solid blanket of shuddering black-ness. From his vantage point on the civilized side of the lava moat, Arnold thought for certain that the entire American force had been devoured by the cannon fire. Hawk might have thought the same, had he been able to think. The ground jolted at him, the way a hand tries to dislodge a stinging mosquito. Black pellets slammed across his face like raindrops in a hurricane. His eyes closed and would not open. His brain huddled deep within his skull and waited for the unending concussion to end. He rolled backwards, and consciously tried to somersault to his feet. He only succeeded in rolling down farther. Finally, he stopped, lying on his back. Groggily he rolled over. The earth shook from side to side and up and down. He had a suspended sensation of having left the realm of gravity and grabbed his helmet to keep the concussion from lifting it away. The shells were not as many here, but they spared no sector. They sounded like hurtling Eiffel Towers, rather than mere foot long projectiles.

The great flambeaux of the seventy and thirty-seven millimeter Japanese guns speared straight down into the black clouds of the target area in bluish white sheets. The bright and elongated spears lit the lower regions of the dark clouds, nearest the ground, giving the tops of the clouds a magnificent translucent glow. The play of the lighting had its own horrifying fascination, outlining men and faces.

Under all of this, the right and left flanks stopped cold. A few of the bravest climbed on. These received the full attention of the enemy riflemen. A ring of ululating cries stretched across the northern slope. The pitch of the panic in the voices varied, but the cry was almost always the same: "Corpsman!"

Arnold and Dr. Lepreaux congratulated themselves

on the progress they had made. But there was still a long way to go, and a lot of hardware to be dealt with.

Hawk climbed in a crawl, seeing no cause for celebration. From his perspective, the only goal was to kill the enemy before they killed him, or his men. It was as if an alligator were chewing its way up his leg: he knew the leg was gone, but the alligator had to be killed before it chewed any farther. And it was chewing fast. Hawk buried his face in the ash as a Howitzer round exploded in front of him. His hearing descended deep into his head.

The dirt trickled down. He stood and ran into the swirling smoke. He saw no one around him. On he climbed, fired by animal rage. He had to get some of them, but he had to reach them first. The rage had to be satisfied or he would explode.

He stepped over his first Japanese body. The head had been torn off, the legs stretched to full length with the feet pointing away from one another. Another body squished under his boot, an arm blasted off leaving only a blood black hole in the torso. On he climbed, against the current of bullets coming through the opaque smoke. They sounded insignificant beside the artillery, the mind-deafening artillery. He stepped over another bloated body, probably lying there since the aerial bombardment. It lay stiff and clutching like a statue. None of these had been his victims. These were not enough. All of the defenders above had to be destroyed. Black, white, and gray smoke blossomed from the rock and blended into the stinking fog. Flesh, wood, rock and chemicals burned in a familiar odor. It was a smell that he understood. He moved on with the false conviction of invincibility provided by bloodlust.

Through the smoke, a log pillbox burst with arresting suddenness upon his vision. He squinted, kept his teeth clenched, and his Thompson in front of him. Labored breath squeezed out of his body through barely parted lips. The wind blew into his open shirt. His hairy chest and face were black with filth, and his sleeves were rolled in a knot over his veined biceps. He fired a burst into the bunker. It became clear now that rather than a viewport, the little fort had a low front wall and no roof, leaving a larger space for the occupants to fire from. A more prudent man would have thrown a grenade into it. Hawk walked up to it and inspected it as though he were a curious pedestrian at a traffic accident.

Bodies littered the floor of the emplacement. They were unmarked by wounds. Deep craters surrounded the bunker, edged out of the solid rock by incredible power. Concussion had killed the inhabitants. Light trickles of blood led from ears, mouths, noses, and eyes. Flies and gnats were already on the scene. A busy caravan of ants crisscrossed the sandy black floor. Hawk looked around. He remained alone in this forbidden world. Above him, the American artillery pounded the caves again. He saw the shield on the front of a Howitzer duck back into a cave opening directly above him. The barrel was short and small bored.

Geysers of rock dust spewed to twice his height and played along the ground behind him. Tracers hit the solid surface, slapping out little flames in a line. A log on the front of the pillbox took a hit from the volley and snapped in two. Hawk dove inside with the corpses. He hugged the wall as more of the massive shells poured inside. A log gave way and sagged on the back wall.

Those rounds must be big, he thought, in order to chop a log in two: around 50 calibers. American fire. Someone below was shooting at him. He was too far ahead of the others. They thought that he was Japanese. Hawk had been on the receiving end of American fire-power before. Its intensity was several times that of the Japanese. He did not want that. He put his helmet on an Arisaka rifle and waved it. The firing finally stopped. He sat quietly for a minute.

He rubbed the stubble on his jaw. He looked at the dead faces around him. He was the one out of place here, the insomniac in the sleeping ward. Hawk felt no horror, revulsion, or alienation. To him, they were the fanatics who sought this for themselves. This is what they wanted. They were only a few of the murderers he had to eliminate. There was no room for fear within his consuming hatred.

He waved the helmet again. He peered out. Marines advanced up the slope. He climbed out and joined them as they reached his position. He didn't know any of them. They were Americans, and that was all that mattered. The skirmish line refused to straighten, despite the cries of "Dress it up," coming from some-where. There was no conversation, only the unspoken grim determination that all could feel. *End this. Quickly, brutally, but just end it.* Some men lagged behind. Some did not. They were halfway up the slope and trudging on.

The advancing line hit three or four rifle pits. The Japanese were grossly outnumbered in this specific locale. The line did not stop. Few men ducked when the enemy soldiers bobbed up for a shot or two at them. The Marines riddled the trenches with semi-automatic fire. Hawk jumped into an enemy rifle pit, and like a madman, blasted a long burst from the Thompson at the wounded Japanese lying there. At about that time, a Banzai counter charge hit the right flank.

Being in the middle of the line, Hawk received none of the impact of the charge. The men that were there on the right reported that the attackers had been drunk. The Japanese poured from the caves in startling numbers, swinging swords and bayonets and howling like banshees. They had probably lost their officer and didn't know what else to do. The right flank had been the strongest part of the American position before the launching of this counterattack. Grenades took a heavy toll of the Americans. The Marines dug in and absorbed the down rushing pressure. They held, but their own advance had been stopped.

The middle of the line met a different sort of resistance. The machine guns had returned. Howitzers popped in and out of the caves like jack-in-the-boxes and spouted downward at Hawk. He climbed on, under the crisscrossing lines of machine gun fire that danced between the heavy artillery explosions. The huge black fountains increased in number. Hawk fell to crawling. He saw others doing the same. They crawled slowly until they met a string of barbed wire. One man fell onto the coils, as he had been trained to do, that the others might climb over him. The ground beneath the wire was mined. The man shot skyward in about five large pieces and several smaller ones.

A new chapter would have to be added to the training manual.

Hawk struggled through a loop of barbed wire. Bullets shook the shivering coils. He got through it, but with a loop clinging to his leg. It tightened around him and cut. He dragged several dozen feet of wire with him. Within a few yards, he met with another line of wire. Spouts of dust peppered his face. He crawled back a few inches behind a negligible defilade. Turning, he severed the wire hanging into his calf with a short burst of the Thompson. A nearby Marine shouted at him, thinking he was being fired upon. Hawk lay there stoically, still with a spiny anklet.

The Marines traded shots with the enemy and tried unsuccessfully to get past the second line of barbed wire. This went on till noon. A man died every 15 minutes or so, a greatly accelerated rate than the deaths one would hear of in peaceful civilian life. It was worse because these people were doing the same job—a job still unfinished.

A runner brought Hawk a handheld radio. Bearn himself ordered Hawk to dig in and hold the ground that he had. By that time, the right flank was in the midst of their third Banzai charge. Crazed attackers with satchel charges strapped to their waists leapt from the high ground and into the Marine positions. The odds were now less than even on the Marines holding the flank. If they could not hold, Delivalung was lost. Bearn promised flamethrowers and bazookas to the poorly manned middle line. Were the Japanese to exert the same pressure in Hawk's sector that they were exhibiting on the right, the line would crumble quickly.

That was how the day ended. The Marines had half the slope, with the enemy pressure indicating that the initiative lay with the Japanese. Hawk tired of listening to the bad news on the radio. He turned it over to Lynwood. Hawk had managed to find most of the men assigned to him that were still effective. Battle fatigue, the nerve cases, ran unusually high. The Sergeant took up night positions in a line of former Japanese trenches.

Hawk studied the layout. The darkness brought a clearer understanding of the situation. Muzzle flashes belched from caves with stark clarity. Bazooka rockets streaked into the caves all night. Action and reaction, the chaotic battle almost made sense now. As a sizzling ball of rocket streamers splashed out of a stricken cave, enemy fire would blaze from another. Later, the stricken cave somehow would return to life and have to be hit all over again.

Joe sat quietly in the trench, saving his ammunition. Red flashes pulsed across the jet black sky overhead. Cruel, unrelenting noise assaulted his frayed nerves. There were screams, wails, pleas, and the answering explosions.

"What do you think will happen next?" Joe asked Hawk. Hawk spat chewing tobacco and rubbed his eyes. "I expect we'll take the top," he answered. He truly expected the Japanese to eventually collapse. But that was the big picture. The big picture was meaningless to someone hanging onto the middle of the north side of Delivalung. The losers would get plenty of the winners before it was finally decided who was whom. Then you get buried, somewhere, and maybe a kind word on the 4th of July. That was about it. It might make the newspapers, it might not.

"We'll be clearing those caves tomorrow," Hawk said. "That ain't gonna be easy, climbing straight up there."

"Yeah? No tanks or nothing. That could take forever," said Joe. A badly wounded man screamed in the dark.

Flamethrowers arrived on a dolly at midnight. Two were designated to be assigned to each platoon. Instead of platoons, there were only strings and knots of terrified human beings in holes. Six flamethrowers were on the hand truck.

"I'll take care of them for you," Hawk told the supply sergeant. "Leave 'em here." Red and white flecks of burning steel drifted down around him like snowflakes.

"Oh...I don't know..." the man protested. Three platoons' worth of flamethrowers were involved. The man did not even see one platoon in the vicinity. He wasn't sure what was here, other than a few dark empty holes. A mortar round scooped a crane load of rock twenty-five yards below them. Everyone flattened. Arisaka rifles cracked to the left, sounding like a torched firecracker stand.

"It's kind of dangerous up here," Hawk advised the supply man. "Better get back down while you can." The same wounded man continued to scream.

"Uh...yeah, but do you have six men checked out on these things? And back-ups?" The wounded man screamed; evidently, he was pinned in an inaccessible place.

"Well, shit, yeah. Does it look like we're crazy?" Hawk asked. The man had no answer for that. "Just tell 'em Sergeant Clifford Curry took the whole load. They'll understand. They won't say shit to you." Hawk slapped the man's shoulder. Battle was his accustomed environment. It's a rare environment, even in a war. Struggles like this one were the real thing. You did what you could to survive it. He wanted those flamethrowers.

"Well, okay," the man said, looking at the tortured, twisted and somewhat mystical faces of Hawk, Canlon and Lynwood. Then he ran for the safety of the lower regions of the mountain, with the cries of the wounded man still in his ears.

Hawk winked at Joe. "Fried Japs in the morning."

"I ain't been checked out on them goddam things. Them things are dangerous," said Joe.

"Dangerous?" Hawk held his hands out and turned about, indicating their surroundings. "Are you shittin' me?"

Biedeker sent a signal at 0200. Hawk was ordered to move up fifty yards. The men climbed under sporadic fire. It became rough during the last ten yards, when four men were hit. Hawk let the Japanese have the last ten yards, and dug in. Unfortunately, the enemy were not satisfied with the bargain. Hawk had drawn attention to himself. The defenders began shifting men to sector B-6. By 0230, a machine gun had opened up on the Marine position.

"We pissed 'em off," said Baker, huddling behind a pile of smoldering debris that might have been wooden. A stick grenade whirled end over end out of the vermillion sky. Men scrambled. One was killed and two were injured.

"Corpsman!"

Two more grenades flew down from the caves. They both exploded short. The Americans were a little too far away for grenades, but the first one had nevertheless been successful.

"We're too goddam close," said Hawk. "This ain't no place for sittin' around." As if to confirm his suspicions, he almost immediately had to duck a burst of automatic fire.

"Holy, shit!" Joe gasped. "They're coming out of the caves!" He raised his rifle and fired up the slope. Dozens of pale uniforms glowed in the satanic light. The Japanese swarmed from unseen sources, first into clusters and then into a teeming horde. They dashed about quickly, at a pace that could not be followed by the eye. There were angry silhouettes of arms, legs, and torsos. Furious cries erupted from their throats. Joe never heard the word "Banzai," but he heard a lot of other things.

"Hold 'em," Hawk screamed. "Fix bayonets!" He had no time to look back at his own frightened men, and he figured it was better that way.

"They are *really* pissed off," Baker hissed through his gnashing teeth.

Grenades came vaulting from the middle of the horde at a rate faster than the Marines could cope with. A wall of metal tornadoes obscured the view of the ghastly demons descending from above. The Marines hugged the rock, to let the concussions pass over them, and prepared to come up shooting. One or two arms went back and slapped grenades into the black smoke in reply.

A hoarse shriek of united madness burst down on the Americans from the smoke and darkness. It sent knife blades of panic into the throats of the stalled American assault troops waiting to receive the charge. Hawk strained his eyes at the dissipating dust from the grenades. He lifted his Thompson and squeezed a burst into the concealing fumes. The breechblock shuddered back and forth with a feverish clanking and the spent shell casings rang hollow on the rocky ground. The roar of the counter attackers drowned out even the exploding .45s. Distorted and devilish faces fell out of the black cloud of doom. The jagged muzzle flash crackled from Hawk's Thompson and into the cursing faces, like a blue electric current exploding from post to post. An incalculable number of them fell and rolled into him, lying against him on the edge of the hole. He stood and a body rolled into the hole with him. He climbed out, stepping over more of the fallen bodies, walking up and into the stampede.

He fired until the firing pin clicked on an empty chamber. He found that the charge had taken a path of least resistance, going around him, and leaving him to the right of the general attack. With eyes narrowed and mouth open, Hawk's hand searched like a paralyzed claw for another magazine. He had trouble moving his fingers. They had been clenched so tightly they no longer wanted to function.

The thrashing conglomeration of humanity fell into the few Americans left. They struck like so many boulders, aided in their descent by rage and gravity. The hurtling Japanese launched themselves without hesitation onto upturned bayonets. The flying weight tore the rifles from the Marines' hands, allowing more of the attackers behind them to grapple with the unarmed men. Rifles became clubs, and knives were teeth in a mad prehistoric battle to stay alive.

Hawk tried to slip in another clip. A Japanese officer, himself thrown to the right of the main conflict, bore down on the American sergeant, swinging a heavy samurai sword back and forth. Hawk fumbled and dropped the clip, backing away. He turned his submachine gun around, pointing the butt of it at the scythe closing in on him. The razor-sharp blade collided with the wood, brushing it aside, and taking a chunk out of it. The officer snarled like a panther, advancing rapidly. The sword struck the Thompson again. The officer aimed lower, striking at Hawk's hands. But the American backed away and again the sword hit only the blocking weapon. Hawk slung the Thompson at him as hard as he could with both hands. It struck the Japanese in the chest, producing a hollow and sickening bark. The officer fell and Hawk kicked him in the face. He brought the heel of his boot down sharply, again and again, into the man's head, until it broke through the bone and pounded only a mashed pulp on the solid stone. He picked up his submachine gun and rammed the stubborn clip into it.

Breathless, he tried to understand his location. He was completely isolated from the heart of the battle by now. He was behind and to the right of the chaotic enemy assault, which was moving down the slope. He opened fire on the backs of the Japanese. Some turned to retreat, instead running headlong into their attacker. He swung the muzzle back and forth, firing without missing, but knowing that there were too many. But to his amazement, they ran around him, retreating as madly as they had come, toward the caves above. He ripped a grenade from his webbing, tore out the pin, and without counting, threw it underhanded up the slope. The retreating men ran directly into the obliterating flash.

Hawk's lungs hurt from the exertion, feeling burned. He picked up a dead man's MI and began walking along the point that had once been the American lines. There, enemy soldiers still grappled energetically with their foes. The Sergeant visited each struggle. Hawk laid the M1's heavy barrel against the head of the proper opponent methodically, ending the hand-to-hand contests one by one. He had to pick up extra clips and eject them. At the end of the line, he found two reluctant Japanese soldiers huddled in a hole. They held up their hands to surrender and he emptied his last clip into them.

Within three to five minutes of the beginning of the charge, it was over. Hawk realized that it was nothing less than a miracle that he was still alive; but the miracles were as abundant as the catastrophes tonight. His lust for battle had cooled. His automatic fire had been a major factor in breaking the attack. Joe Canlon, Baker and Lynwood had survived due primarily to their proximity to his redeeming automatic fire.

Another dazed young man, named Osage, had survived through his own great luck. The rest of the platoon were dead or wounded. Hawk was numbed by the entire experience. He should have expected it, but he hadn't. He found it all incredible: he was alive, in this flaming, screaming madness.

Voices from above intruded on his numbness. They were gathering again, and it sounded like even more of them this time. Defiantly, he faced upward. Choking smoke billowed down and over him. Lynwood jammed the radio into his hand. He slumped down against a stone with it.

"Uh...heavy casualties." He pressed the transmitter. "Need reinforcements. Corpsmen. About wiped out. Need automatic weapons," he petitioned the little box of metal and bakelite, while breathing heavily.

"Identify. Identify. Over," the little box hissed back disinterestedly at him.

"First Platoon, B-6, about sector 11. Sergeant Hawk. We need men. Getting counter attacks. They're coming outa the caves. Need grenades. Three men left." Hawk swallowed. His head fell against the unyielding stone. "Get artillery on B-6-12."

"Identify. Identify. Unclear. Say again, over."

"Shit, you goddam... I said artillery on B-6-12, Baker 6-12."

"Negative. Our positions are on B-6-11. Endanger friendly position. Negative. Over."

"That's *us*. We're on B-6-11. *I'm B-6-11*. I'm there now. They're breakin' the line. They're in our laps. B-6-12, now. Put it between 13 and 12 if you want to, goddam it, just do it!"

"Roger that. A high B-6-12. Confirm B-6-12?"

"Yes. Yes."

"Verify B-6-12? Verify B-6-12? Over."

"Yes! Yes! B-6-12!"

"On the way."

The Japanese massed above them. They looked at one another, and began screaming back and forth to each other. They crouched, and sprang about in furious postures. Hawk dropped the radio and rammed a new clip into the submachine gun. An unexpected wind blew the smoke aside. He saw horror unfolding. The enemy pounced at the air and shrieked, straining every muscle in their faces and necks. In unison, they turned furious eyes down the slope.

An unseen light source illuminated the demonic eyes, seemingly from within. Hawk could see only a strip of a reddish gray sky far above and behind them, because of the blocking height of the mountain.

"Joe! You all right, Joe?" Hawk turned quickly, feeling alone.

"Yeah," Joe answered. He had a knot on his head and was mercifully groggy.

"They're coming back. Get your grenades ready." Hawk set the Thompson barrel on the berm of the hole, and the grenades beside it. He knew that he would be their prime target this time. They had to get rid of that Thompson. It was hell against a crowd of them at close range.

Joe crawled up to face the onslaught. He drug his rifle slowly up his body. Half of the stock had been broken off. His fingers hung loosely over a cold grenade that lay on the edge of the hole.

The Japanese throats exploded. They fell en masse on the position. Hawk slapped a grenade at them. Baker slung another. Lynwood clumsily shoved a third at the human avalanche. By then, Hawk had slammed his second at them. A heavy artillery shell sliced overhead, sounding like it was taking the skin off Hawk's back in the process.

An echo that sounded like a locomotive in a culvert split the sky. The knots of approaching Japanese erupted in one enormous wedge of a blast. The center of the blast was a hard red, the bulk of the flash was orange, with a lighter orange on the fringes. The top of the giant explosion simmered a hot white.

At the end of the cataclysm, the enemy were gone. The concussion lifted Lynwood out of his hole, and he caught a piece of shrapnel in the chest. He was alive.

Hawk grabbed the radio and called the strike off. He

did not want to risk another one of those bastards hitting nearby. He crawled down the slope, leading the others. They carried Lynwood. Men screamed in agony on all sides. Lynwood was their only responsibility now. He was their own.

Hawk stopped the others with a raised hand. "Son of a bitch, look, there's Japs under us now."

"There's more of them in the caves, too," said Baker, looking back and up.

"We're surrounded," said Joe, in a whisper. They heard things all around them. Furtive sounds crept in the dark rock and sand. It was 0315.

"Hey, y'all. Here's some holes. Get in these holes." Hawk's voice was steady in the deadly half-quiet. The Sergeant dragged Lynwood into a hole with him. Joe followed. Baker and Osage slithered rapidly into another. Baker found a bazooka in the hole. He had never fired one. He remembered standing around in the back of a gathering once, engaging in horseplay, when they were showing them how to use it. He now applied his full memory and intellect to learning the task.

"I gotta crawl down there and get a flamethrower," said Hawk. "We're almost out of ammunition, and I don't think them sons of bitches are coming up here with any more." His eyes narrowed painfully as he looked down the slope. There was no telling what he would encounter. It was a fifty-fifty proposition.

"Don't leave us here," Joe whispered. "I hear 'em."

Lynwood's hand reached up like a claw and grabbed Joe's utility shirt, scaring the hell out of him.

"I didn't want to kill anybody," said Lynwood, choking on tears. Blood leaked from his bare chest. "Shut up!" Baker called urgently from the next hole.

"It was our job. It was a game. I didn't want to kill anybody." Lynwood's voice cracked in his split chest. "I wanted them to get up."

Joe nodded and lifted Lynwood's head. "Yeah, I know. Listen, Lynwood, you gotta hold it down. They're all around out there. Can you...can you do that? We're gonna get you to the aid station in just a second." When Joe looked over at Hawk, he was already crawling back into the hole with the flamethrower, scratching and clanking on the rocky soil. Joe never knew that he had left. Hawk's face looked like it always did: all business.

"Could only find one," Hawk snapped. "Hope them Jap bastards didn't get the rest." Hawk's voice sounded like it always did: cut and dried.

"You had to have *all* of them," Joe hissed. "I ain't got no ammo, Hawk. I ain't got nothin' to fight with."

Hawk turned the valve on the back of the tanks. "Awright. Get a hold of—"

A grenade interrupted him.

The night flashed up all around him and his ears buckled under the tremendous noise. He could see shapes in the dusty cloud outside the hole. He had no idea whether he was alive or dead, injured or dazed. His reflexes pointed the nozzle up and squirted the rod of jellied liquid at the approaching forms. He triggered the igniter. An orange dragon curled and swirled down the rod of jelly and exploded in front of him. Enraged flames leapt to the height of a house at the speed of lightning. Screams filtered into his auditory nerves, only half registering there.

A black stickman, still afire, lunged out of the flames and fell in front of the hole, his chest vibrating with agonizing shrieks. He continued to crawl at Hawk and the nozzle. His face had melted from the blackened bone and still he crawled forward. Joe raised his bayonet, but could only watch.

Hawk put a leg up on the edge of the hole and waved the fiery broom at the hidden attackers. "Banzai!" he bellowed at his tormentors.

A Japanese raced from behind the flames. Hawk steered the torch toward him. The soldier flanked Hawk, jumping from a low cliff in an effort to escape farther down the slope. But engulfing flames wrapped around his back in midair. He hung in the air for a moment, a nightmarish specter, writhing horribly above the earth. The tanks ran out of fuel. Hawk tossed the heavy weapon down. He picked up his Thompson. He had about half a magazine left.

They heard the lapping flames and thrashing men on all sides. "Well, we're lit up good now," Hawk gasped in the petroleum fumes. The hellish fire and squirming demons dwarfed them, refusing to die down. The new sound of scraping rocks could be heard. Men were moving, and there were a lot of them.

Joe and Hawk looked on all sides for them. At the last moment, they saw them, coming from above. Hawk opened fire at point blank range. The crackling lightning speared into the enemy. Two bodies fell into the hole and the rest disappeared. Hawk looked down at the dead faces. They were still angry.

Baker was out of ammunition. A Japanese, evidently in the same predicament, charged him with a bayonet. Both attacker and defender were silent. Baker raised the bazooka, and fired at a range of ten feet. The rocket hit the man in a whirlpool of shooting sparks without exploding, having burned completely through him. It could burn through heavy tank armor. The body was cut into parts and the parts were cauterized by the intense heat, without bleeding. Baker never saw any of that, because the rocket propelled the remains a hundred feet down the slope.

"Hawk! Lynwood's hit again! Do something!" Joe shouted. Hawk turned and saw Lynwood's entire chest opened up. He could see organs moving in the leaping orange firelight. "He's bad! He's bad!" The open chest made a reptilian sound. Hawk ripped off his filthy, torn shirt.

"How did that happen?" he asked Joe.

"I don't know! I don't know! Do something!" Joe got to his knees, forgetting his surroundings.

Hawk stuffed the shirt into Lynwood's gaping chest. It was immediately saturated. Hawk shook his head negatively as he tucked the shirt in the edges of the wound.

Joe closed his eyes and threw back his head. "Oh, my God!" He grabbed his kneeling legs and bowed his head. His helmet plopped onto the ground. He threw up his arms.

"Okay. He's dead," said Hawk. He spun quickly and looked outside the hole. "He's gone, Joe."

Joe fell against the side of the hole, sobbing. "Shut the hell up!" Baker shouted at Joe. Tears cut a path through the dirt on Joe's face and his body shook in despair and horror.

Hawk's eyes were wide as they aimed out into the darkness. "You hear 'em? They're coming, Joe," he said. The Sergeant could hear shuffling on the stone. The attack appeared to involve a more careful approach this time. The edge of the hole was higher than the ground around it. Hawk pulled his head down, reached over and grabbed Joe by the arm. He pulled the sobbing man up to his knees, and dumped the helmet back onto Joe's head, backwards. He shook him.

"Hey, they're comin'. Understand?" Hawk rasped, and shook him again.

"Don't you feel nothin'?" Joe whined. The pitch made Hawk's skin crawl.

"I ain't gonna be feelin' nothin' pretty goddam soon if you don't straighten up. You givin' up?" *Shuffle. Shuffle. Shuffle.* Hawk held up Joe's arm. "This is all there is between you and them!" Joe hung his head. Hawk let him fall against the side of the hole. "Aw'ight then, buddy. Take it easy." Hawk aimed motionless eyes at the berm of the hole. He stood in a crouch and took out his knife, ramming it into the earth on the side of the crater.

He looked for a better weapon, but there weren't any. He returned to the knife, pulled it out, and held it as a drowning man holds onto a life preserver.

Like a resurrected spirit, a closely cropped head loomed out of the rock right before Hawk's eyes. The eyes narrowed with hate and murder, meeting those of Hawk for a split second. Two strangers from different sides of the world came together, with every intention and fiber of their being bent on killing one another, as if they were lifelong enemies.

"No!" Joe grunted, when he saw the shirtless Japanese jump and strike the shirtless Hawk full in the chest with his flailing body. Hawk saw a knife. His own arm went back. They hit the ground and Hawk felt his wrist in a strong grip. He squirmed to free it. The arm of his attacker rose high over him with its glinting orange blade. Joe looped his own arm around the soldier's knife arm and slung the man off Hawk. Hawk rose half to his knees and drove his knife forcefully into the hairless stomach.

The man screamed a loud and eerie death cry, unreal and foreign, like the last moments before death are. Hawk jumped up to await another attacker, scooping up and replacing his helmet in the same motion.

He looked to the right and left, to the front and back. He repeated the exercise, a dozen times. Where would the next one come from? His ferocious blue eyes were more white than blue, more trapped than murderous. He could feel his rapid, shallow breathing as he clung passionately to his grim life. His neck ached from all of the unusual motion.

Another ghostly forehead rose from the rock beside him. The head was nearly shaved and the hair looked like black paint on it. Again, the encounter was a surprise for both antagonists. The powerful little man dove at the Marine. Hawk stiff-armed his neck with the knife point. The attacker's inertia and Hawk's raging emotion carried the knife edge down from the neck until it stopped at the breast bone. Hawk shook and pulled the knife free, ramming it again at the twisting, bleeding thing on the ground.

How many times could he do this and survive? They were so close, he could smell them. All around him. All over. Out there.

It was 0400.

Hawk stood poised and continued his vigil. Right, left, front and back.

"Marine! Marine!" a snake-like voice sliced icily through the darkness. It was within the range of a grenade toss. "You die soon! Die soon!" The voice laughed. "See you, Joe. See you."

Hawk exhaled harshly, only to suck his breath in again. He put his dry tongue on his teeth. Joe moaned. The enemy called all Americans "Joe," but that was of little consolation.

"See you, Bak-uh. See you, Hok. See you, Joe." And then the unearthly laugh.

Son of a bitch, they really do know our names, Hawk thought.

"You forgot me!" Osage screamed. Osage was nine-teen years old and foolish.

Time passed. The adversaries kept their meager distance. Hawk was afraid that he would stop breathing and be unable to keep the vigil, afraid some internal organ would just lack the stamina to keep this up, in spite of his will. Right, left, front and back. There was a thud and thrashing in Baker's hole. A Japanese voice screamed. Hawk's head pivoted, the helmet straps swaying and creaking. It was too much. He would have to stop eventually—and just wait.

"Can you watch the front?" he whispered to Joe. Joe stood weakly. "Stay down!" Hawk cautioned. Two bodies flew down on them from the night, front and back. Hawk hacked wildly at the one that struck him, as it knocked him down. The body felt limp as he pushed it off himself from the bottom of the hole. He bounced to his feet without his knife. It was buried deep in the infiltrator. He saw the other Japanese in the half light, feinting at Joe with a knife. Joe was unarmed and dodging madly.

Hawk took off his helmet and brought it down with both hands on the back of the unsuspecting round head. The almost naked attacker slumped to the floor of the hole, emptying his bowels as he dropped. Hawk recovered his knife.

It was 0500.

Right. Left. Back. Front. Hawk's eyes blurred from the repetitive motion. He felt dizzy, nauseous. Still, his head kept moving.

"Anybody up there?" an American voice came from below. "This is Captain Morrison, United States Army. Anybody up there?"

Hawk fell to his knees. Exhaustion swamped his body. Everything was gone, even his will. His helmet butted the rock as he bowed his head. His fingers tried to open on the knife handle, but they had been shut so tensely that he had to remove the knife from them with the other hand. His nails had dug bleeding holes into the heel of his knife hand. Blood shined on the blade and the handle of the knife lying in the dirt. The short length of sharpened steel had been the only thing between him and death for...ever?

"Yeah, we're up here," Baker answered.

"Don't shoot, we're coming up."

Hawk raised his head. "Don't shoot?" he gasped to Joe. How long had it been since they *could* shoot? How long had they been fighting in the stone age?

Three American soldiers advanced on the hole. In the pile of bodies, they didn't see a wounded Japanese soldier holding his own knife. As they pulled Hawk out by the arms, the dying man thrust at Hawk. If the Americans had pulled any slower, the knife would have hit Hawk's heart. As it was, it hit his leg. Hawk kicked the man in the face and jerked the knife out of his calf. He felt nothing.

"Shit," he said. "Did you see that?" The soldiers looked at it, without speaking, and then at Joe. They pulled Joe out more carefully. Another soldier shot the knife wielding and wounded Japanese in the head. Hawk pulled a colorful *hachimaki* headband with inspirational writing on it off a dead attacker, and wrapped it around his leg. He stood.

"You'll need help getting to the aid station," said Captain Morrison. "We've got some stretchers coming."

"Nah, I don't need nuthin'," Hawk said. "I'll walk down." He noticed the charge of adrenaline still trembling through him.

"Appreciate it, though, Captain."

* * *

HAWK LIMPED down with his three surviving companions. They passed Marines filing up the hill. Men look silently, and curiously at them. After a while, Hawk stopped to rest. The pounding of the descent on his wound was making it start to hurt. The others stopped to rest with him. They watched the new troopers climb. An Army platoon filed by.

"Well, you ain't gotta ask about the Army no more," said Hawk, draping an arm on Joe's shoulder.

"Yeah," Joe managed to say. He had been unable to say much. Perhaps he was in shock. He stared at the ground.

"Say, Canlon. Your head's on backwards," said Baker, in reference to Joe's helmet. Baker was feeling pretty good about being alive, and walking in the opposite direction from the fighting. He grinned.

"He's been watching his ass too much," said Osage.

"Hey, look at that guy," Hawk said suddenly. Joe looked up. He saw several hundred guys, and none of them looked very distinctive. Hawk shouted at somebody. "Hey, buddy! Hey, Marine! Come, here!"

A young man stepped out of the line and walked toward Hawk. A shiny yellow object was tied to the back of his web belt.

"Hey, where'd you get that thing?" Hawk roared.

As the man came closer, Joe saw the object of interest. A golden effigy beaker in the mold of an Asian head swung from the man's back. Red and green jewels were mounted around the top of it to form a crown.

The man stared at the four blood-stained creatures seated before him. He kept his distance, as one might from a street person. They stared at the exotic cup. The sight of it brought even Joe Canlon out of his daze.

"Where did you get that?" Joe asked quietly. It was not the sort of thing one would be carrying into battle.

"A guy from Fox gave it to me for my BAR." The man held up an M1 carbine. "I guess he wanted to get rid of this pretty bad. I think he was going into those tunnels. I'd rather have this, myself, if I was going into those things."

"Yeah," said Hawk. "If."

The man smiled and pulled the cup around without untying it. "This has gotta be worth fifty bucks," he said.

"Yeah," said Hawk. "But if some son of a bitch offers you a thousand, don't take it." Hawk rocked his head back. His neck hurt even worse. "That thing is a genuine art-ee-fact. Did you catch that fella's name? The bastard that got your BAR?"

"Yes. Curry. I think he's an officer. He had the run of the place down there."

"Thanks, podnuh," said Hawk, waving his hand.

The man gave them a puzzled expression. He had expected them to try to buy—or more likely—*take* the cup. He didn't know what they were thanking him for. He turned and rejoined the advancing troops.

Hawk and Joe looked at one another.

"I'll have a word with Officer Curry," Hawk told Joe. He stood on his leg and winced. "I imagine I'll find him somewhere in the rear. As far back as the rear goes."

"You better do something with that leg," Osage told him.

"No, shit," said Hawk, limping away. "Goddam Japs."

Hawk had been in a continuous state of rage and horror for several hours. It had not been a pent-up stress, it had been lived out loud, channeled into endless fury. He had matched his bloodlust against that of his vicious opponents. He killed wantonly and with a vengeance, all sanctioned and encouraged from on high, with emotion not easily turned off.

It was in this frame of mind that he sought Clifford Curry. He sought everything that was still wrong with the world, the war, the U. S. Marine Corps, and even with himself—Clifford Curry.

He didn't find Curry in the rear. He learned that Curry had been impressed into the final assault on the summit. Doggedly, Hawk reclimbed Delivalung. The pain in his leg kept his mind off his paralyzing exhaustion. He might lose a leg, but he was going to find Clifford Curry.

He found him, too. Another Marine directed him to the spot. Curry sat alone, in front of a bombed-out cave on the eastern slope. It was a safe, isolated spot, one that might appear in a newspaper photo, with a caption of how it was taken on the frontlines.

Curry took a long drink from a half pint of whisky as he watched Hawk limp up the slope toward him. Curry could always get possession of such things. His long hair was greased back with his favorite hair tonic as well.

Hawk didn't look so good, he decided. Pale, dirty, shirtless and bloody, he hobbled endlessly, until he stopped in front of Curry. How had the bastard found him?

Curry was no psychiatrist, or any sort of student of human nature. He saw only a broken, dirty man. He didn't see the soul. He was no priest, and worst of all, he was no penitent. Success had not prepared him for the most important conversation of his life.

Hawk raised his boot and the leg with the maroon stained headband, resting it on a stone in front of Curry's face. He leaned his arms across it. They stared at each other.

Curry took another drink, and said, "You look like shit. How's it going?"

"Pretty good. Pretty good." Hawk spat chewing tobacco between Curry and himself. "Cut myself shaving my legs this morning."

Curry nodded and shrugged. "Gotta be careful." He belched and smiled. "Looks like you lost your shirt in the deal, too."

"Yeah. Gave it to a fella that needed it more than me. That's in the Bible, you know." Hawk's eyes burned into those of the seated man during the odd pause.

It was a perplexing, and rather chilling thing to hear scripture from the lips of James Hawk. His gaze was as level and steady as a tabletop. Curry shifted uneasily. He tried a casual laugh and searched his pockets for a cigarette. Hawk noticed that Curry kept the corner of his eye on him.

"What's on your mind?" Curry had been feeling good, with the alcohol just hitting home. He wished Hawk would go away. He didn't want to talk, and especially not to him. He wasn't giving Hawk his fifty percent, and he wasn't negotiating.

"You."

Curry nodded and looked down. He wasn't getting into a staring match with the sorry bastard, either. "My favorite subject."

"Yeah, I figured. Been thinking a lot about you. Where is it?"

Curry smiled. "What?" He pointed toward the summit with his bottle. "The flag?"

Hawk looked up. "Oh, yeah," he said, lost in thought for a second, as if he had forgotten what brought him here.

"Pretty, huh? Makes you proud," said Curry.

"Yeah. It does." He watched the flag for a second. It looked good to him. "Start talkin'."

"Me? I got nothing to say. I'm the strong, silent type. You know me, Hawk."

"You got that right. And you know me, I hope," Hawk spat. "I hear you done got generous in your old age. Tradin' for automatic rifles. Now, did you get religion, or could it be that you found something else out by that old swamp down there?"

"Hallelujah, brother." Curry laughed. "You know, you could have been the one that found it. You had to be a shitass and they got rid of you. You just ain't never been smart, Hawk. You think that stupid act will get you by." Curry's eyes shifted nervously back and forth, watching the men far below, around the base of Delivalung. "If it'll make you feel better, I'll tell you something."

"Yeah? Why don't you make me feel better?"

"You never could have found it without explosives. You gotta have the proper tools. A whittling stick and a chaw won't do it any more, in this modern world. And now, ain't nobody gonna find it. I am the only man in the world that knows where it is." Curry took out his black crackle cigarette lighter. Hawk watched the thin hands closely. He didn't miss much. Curry bit a cigarette out of a package with the corner of his mouth. He lit the cigarette, and Hawk noticed that he now had a folded-up piece of paper in his hand. Curry lit the paper and dropped it. "The only man."

"Except, that I know that you know where it is. You ain't getting away with it."

"What the hell you mean? I'm not getting away with anything. And who's gonna listen to a crumb like you?"

"Somebody put you up to this, didn't they? Somebody big? You don't have sense enough to find your ass with both hands."

"Sure. Big. And stupid," Curry said. "But he ain't gonna get it. Nobody can get it. See, I heard about this treasure up in Canada one time. It's way down under the ground. Been there for centuries. Big corporations can't get it out. The ground keeps shifting around, every time they dig. The treasure moves around down there with it. Suckers that don't know where it is, they dig and move it around some more, hiding it even better." Curry laughed. He wished that Hawk would go away. He might as well get to the point, and clear the air. "You know, I work alone, Hawk. Now, there was a time I was willing to deal, but you didn't want that.

"I tried to get along with you. Cut you in. You were too high and mighty. Squiring the Queen of England around the Mission. You ever hear the story about your girlfriend back there? She and Klemer were just there to take care of some crippled Jap. They were old Red Cross sob sisters. That was her only interest in you. To keep tabs on where that Jap was. And she kept Arnold posted on everything you did, too. To make sure *he* got the treasure, and not you. She had a good two hour sit down with him right before she left. You gotta watch your friends, Hawk. See, that's why I work alone. They had a few laughs about you. She got the hell away from you as fast as she could, in case you were wondering why she left so sudden. I saw your stupid face dragging around. She got what she wanted out of you and scooted."

"You're just full of a lot of interestin' shit. They might just put you on that *Quiz Kids* radio program."

"Don't believe me? Believe whatever you want. That's what that flag up there stands for. That's what the U. S. Marine Corps fought for here. It's a free country. A man can be as ignorant as he wants to be. And you're going for some kind of record."

"You're a pretty smart guy, Curry, but there's one angle you didn't figure out. It's a bad mistake, too."

"What's that?"

"There's some folks…you gotta be careful how you talk to." Hawk smiled slightly, with his teeth and only dead eyes, as might a contemplative panther. He looked up at the flag. "You know, Curry…probably four or five hundred decent men died taking this rock. Decent men. That was their temple you stole from."

"It was worth it, believe me."

"Near as I can figure, they died for nothing. That don't mean much to you, does it?"

"Don't mean shit. What's it mean to you? You gonna tell me you're cryin' in your beer tonight? If you had found it, you would be sitting here, and I'd be standing there with my screwed up leg, like a dumb ass, saying stupid shit. They pay guys overtime in the States to make bullets for us. They don't pay us shit to use them, though. Some guys like campaign ribbons, some like cash." Curry took a drag on his cigarette. "I'll get the same campaign ribbon you get. Kind of makes me special, don't it? I didn't tell nobody to come out here. Some guys like to put the marbles on the table, and some guys like to pick them up. See?"

Hawk saw. He vaguely remembered something similar that Clancy had said. He nodded, spat, and looked around. He nodded again.

Curry leaned forward in a comradely sort of way. "Come by and see me. Listen. I am a man of property now. I'm like the guy that owned that saw mill you used to work in for a dollar a week. I'll need a lot of crumbs to work for me. I'll pay you what I can afford to throw away. You'll get a pretty good job out of the deal. Don't worry. I don't forget my old war buddies. I'm serious. Best job your ass'll ever get, compadre."

Hawk closed an eye and looked up at him.

"What're you looking at me for?" Curry said. "I didn't do nothing. You act like I'm a crook or something."

"Naw. You ain't got the guts to be a crook. You're just a two-bit chiseler."

"Not two-bit," Curry laughed. "You ain't payin' attention." He reached into his pocket and flipped a gold coin to Hawk. The reflexes of Hawk's hand, unaffected by the last few murderous hours, snapped it in midair. He looked at it. It had a square hole in the middle. "Something to remember me by."

Dusk was coming on. The jungle below turned a beautiful purple, with the higher dancing leaves turning a sort of a fluffy, whitish green. The swamp, in the distance, however, was as black and forbidding as ever. Curry wished that Hawk would go away. If Hawk would not leave, he would. Hawk was part of a past that was already forgotten.

He stood. "See you, Hawk."

"Reckon?" Hawk looked to the right and left. No one was around. There was the dusk, Curry, and a cave.

* * *

HAWK YAWNED and lay against the side of the foxhole. He and Joe lounged near the base of Delivalung. The night glowed with the natural fire of the volcano. It didn't look as horrible tonight. It was sort of warm and welcoming. Like a hearth. Occasionally, a lonely shot could be heard in the distance, as yet another unfortunate defender was discovered in the caves.

Hawk stretched out his newly dressed leg, and waved his boot back and forth.

"Did you ever find that guy? That crazy guy?" Joe asked.

"Yeah. Yeah, sure did." Hawk spat and rubbed his eyes. He nodded affirmatively. "I found him."

"Did he say anything?"

"Yeah. Quite a bit. He found that stuff. We figured that." Hawk threw the golden Chinese coin in the dirt.

"That son of a *bitch*. I say we get our share," said Joe, picking it up. "I say we keep looking. He's got no more right to it than we do. Or anybody else, for that matter. Hell, who owns this goddam island, or whatever it is, anyway? The King of England? He ain't no pirate that can just do what he wants with stuff. He's got a long ass way to go before he gets that shit out of here."

"Nah. He ain't got too far to go. He said he buried the whole thing with a charge, and flooded that temple, and everything else. Says nobody will ever dig that shit out now. He had a map, but I seen him burn it."

"Flooded it? Hey, that's a clue. I bet it was right there where we killed that wild man. I bet we were right on top of it," said Joe. Joe looked up, and realized that maybe Hawk had already come to the same conclusion. His eyes narrowed. "Sounds like this guy had quite a bit to say?"

"Yeah. Yeah, he got to talkin' up a storm right there before it was over," Hawk admitted.

Joe eyed Hawk's face. The cruel mouth had a strange, tired twist to it. "What do you mean, before it was over? Before *what* was over? What happened?"

"Aw," Hawk sighed, as if weary of lies and long stories. "You know how that goes."

IF YOU LIKE THIS, YOU MAY ALSO ENJOY BLAZER: GHOSTS OF WAR

A COP THRILLER BY G.C. HARMON

GO BACK IN TIME WITH BLAZER AS THIS HEART-STOPPING ACTION TAKES A CLEVER LOOK AT HISTORY.

Before Steve Blazer was given command of SFPD's Special Forces—before he was a crack Homicide Inspector—he was an elite up and comer on the Vice Squad.

During an Asian drug smuggler bust, two Vice cops are murdered. The killer leaves a signature—one that means something to Blazer's mentor, Captain John Stanson—leading him to believe the smuggler gang is tied to a wealthy Vietnamese businessman who rules San Francisco's Little Saigon district with an iron fist. As Blazer dives deeper into the investigation, he clashes with the Federal Agency providing his protection, and when the Vietnamese businessman is murdered, the feds put Blazer on the top of their suspect list.

While the Vice squad pursues a drug ring from the Golden Triangle and a cop killer, Stanson goes on a perilous journey of his own, reliving parts of his violent pas where he was taken as a prisoner of the Vietnam War. Blazer takes notice and sets out to prevent Stanson from crossing a line he can't come back from.

But will Blazer get to him in time? Will the mysterious killer connected to Stanson's perilous past be brought to justice once and for all?

AVAILABLE NOW

ABOUT THE AUTHOR

Patrick Clay was born a fifth generation Texan, in Galena Park, Texas, and went to a Catholic elementary school there. He attended St. Thomas High School and graduated fifth in his class. Patrick also received a scholarship to the University of St. Thomas and graduated cum laude from there. He then graduated magna cum laude from South Texas College of Law, where he was fourth in his class and a member of the law journal. While attending law school at night, Patrick operated his own locksmith shop. During the time he waited for the bar results, he began writing fiction. He began his second novel, *Sgt. Hawk*, in February 1977, and finished it in six weeks. Patrick had a well-known agent, who tried to sell it to major publishers and television. It was finally sold to Leisure Books in 1978, and by that time, Patrick had finished *The Return of Sgt. Hawk*, which was published in 1980. *Sgt. Hawk Under Attack* and *Sgt. Hawk Tiger Island* followed in 1981 and 1982, respectively. The titles of the latter two books were selected by the publisher, Leisure Books, as they originally had different names. *Sgt. Hawk and The Firebolt* was written in 1982 when Leisure Books went bankrupt, returned the rights, and never fulfilled distribution. Patrick had by then begun a solo law practice and gave up writing. He worked in a poor neighborhood, with plenty of wonderful clients, but not much compensation. So,

Patrick became a captain in the Civil Air Patrol and was Houston chess player in 1990, more for his tournament directing ability than playing skills. After fourteen years, he gave up the private law practice, and worked as an attorney for the federal government for the next thirty years. The podcast, *Paperback Warrior*, rekindled his interest in *Sgt. Hawk*.

Patrick met his beautiful wife at Astroworld in Houston, the first year that the amusement park opened. When he began writing in 1977, he had no children, and by the time he stopped writing in 1983, he had three daughters; he now has nine grandchildren. His father, a disabled veteran, and six uncles served in the South Pacific during World War II. Patrick was named after one of them, Patrick Clay, who was on a U.S. Navy ship with four battle stars. Another one of Patrick's uncles was at Pearl Harbor when it was attacked.